The Sea Prince

The Coral Throne, Volume 1

Elizabeth Schechter

Published by Elizabeth Schechter, 2025.

Published by Raven's Wing Books

Editor: Michael Schechter

Sensitivity Reader: Kendra Herber

Cover design by GetCovers

Raven's Wing Books

ravens-wing-books.com

Table of Contents

Author Note

APPROXIMATELY A MILLION years ago (okay, it was 2009,) I woke up one morning with an idea for this world and the main character. I fleshed out some of the details on a drive to IKEA (long car drives do wonders for worldbuilding!) and when I got home, I shared my notes with a writer friend. We'd written together in what was the start of both of our writer journeys – a play-by-email role playing game called *The Night Court,* based on Jacqueline Carey's **Kushiel's Dart** series, and we'd collaborated on the first two novels in a series that sadly never sold. When I came to them with this idea, they loved it, and we dove right in. We worked on it together, filling out the details, and there are parts of the first couple of chapters that neither of us can say anymore which of us wrote in the initial draft – we had very similar writing voices and writing styles.

Then the story broke, and neither of us had the time to triage it. So the project was shelved. I picked it up and poked at it a few times over the years, but didn't really figure out what was wrong and where it needed to be fixed until 2023. That was when I reached out to them and said "Hey! I know what went wrong! Let's finish this!"

It was at that point that we discovered that our writing voices no longer matched, and our writing styles no longer converged. They'd published their own work, and I'd published mine. We tried to get back in sync, trying for a few months to find the flow that we'd once had. It didn't work, and when they bowed out to work on their own projects, I promised to credit them when the book finally came to print.

This is that credit: **The Sea Prince** is dedicated to, is inspired by, and in some ways, is entirely the fault of Austin Daniel. We may not have finished the journey together, but you were there at the start. You helped set some of the guiding lights in the worldbuilding, and you've been the biggest cheerleader for this entire journey.

Love you bunches, and maybe one of these years we might actually meet in person!

Chapter One
Battle

"Where is that gun?"

The question roared across the decks of the *Wave Runner*, piercing the sounds of the battle as another wave of Imperial troops in dark uniforms swarmed the ship like rats. The wire-wrapped hilt of Tarjiaan's cutlass was wet, and it slipped under his gloved fingers as the blade sheared sparks along the edge of his attacker's saber. Blood? Sweat? He had no idea. It didn't matter — there was no time to clean his hands. As soon as one attacker fell, another charged him. Tarjiaan shoved the nearest assailant back, shooting him with the force-pistol in his other hand; the Imp tumbled back over the rails and Tarjiaan raised his raspy voice again, "Ishantar! Where is that gun?"

From the forecastle deck, a woman with skin the color of polished mahogany stuck her head out from beneath an armored and heavily-guarded construct. "Ten minutes, Captain!" she bellowed.

"Five minutes, Ishantar! Get that thing working!" Tarjiaan heard the whine of a force-pistol charging — too close! — and turned, firing before dodging into the shadow of the foremast. He took advantage of the cover and an unusual moment of quiet to rest his back against the mast and breathe. Great Mothers, he was tired. His lungs burned with effort. The salt mist of the sea mixed with his sweat and stung his eyes.

His crew's weapons were better, their armor stronger than that of the Imperial forces, but what good was that when the enemy refused to stop coming? They must have been crammed to bursting in their ships; it seemed as if one fell and another five appeared! And damn them to the depths, they had finally learned that while they couldn't match Meradonese tech, magic-less Meradon couldn't counter an arcane attack. There was a mage on one of the Imperial ships, and they were holding the *Wave Runner* dead in the water. If the rail-cannon had been functional, the battle would have been over hours ago, but the cursed cannon had malfunctioned. Again. A good Mancer would have — Tarjiaan dispelled that thought. Only the best served on the flagship of the Meradonese fleet. It wasn't Ishantar's fault that the rail-cannon technology was temperamental at the best of times. Which these were not.

None of this made any sense. If the Imperials just wanted the ship, they could have already taken her. Had already taken her, as much as that galled Tarjiaan to admit. But they were still alive, still fighting, and the Imps kept coming, which meant that their goal wasn't the ship.

As if to confirm the thought, Tarjiaan heard a shout: "Death to the Butcher of Meradon! Immortality to the man who takes the Butcher's head!"

Tarjiaan snorted at the old epithet as he checked the charge on his pistol. Immortality? He had to give the Emperor credit for coming up with new incentives. And it wasn't as if there would be a complaint when it turned out that the promised immortality was just another lie.

The battle cry reignited the ferocity of the Imperials and more swarmed onto the deck. Tarjiaan's crew rallied to him in answer, surrounding him and standing with him in the heart of the battle. It was, Tarjiaan knew, the reason the Imps never seemed to see him, even though he towered over his men and his rank was clear on his armor. Imperial captains would never be in the heart of the battle. They'd be hiding somewhere behind wards and shields and whatever else their mages could conjure, sending other men to do their dirty work. Tarjiaan would never be like them. He was as much a soldier of Meradon as any of his men. They were his as much as he was theirs and they fought together as one, building a wedge together and attempting to drive the land-fighters back. There was only attack and defense, charge and parry, shots fired, sweat on his brow, blood on his armor. A scream split the cacophony just behind him, and Tarjiaan felt one of his men fall against his back and slump to the deck. They had to end this. Now. They had to board that bloody mage-ship and—

Tarjiaan suddenly heard Ishantar's high voice through the comms: "*Got it!*"

"Fire!" Tarjiaan shouted into the comms. In response, he heard the high-pitched whine of the rail-cannon's generator, slowly increasing in volume until it rattled his teeth. He prayed to the Great Mothers that this worked...

The rumble and roar as the rail-cannon fired was near-deafening, followed almost immediately by an explosion from the closest of the Imperial ships. Then a second explosion that Tarjiaan didn't understand. What else had gone up? Aboard the *Wave Runner*, the fighting stopped abruptly as both Imperial and Meradonese troops turned to stare at the burning wreckage. The warship fell in on itself, burning embers of its ruined hull sizzling as they fell into the ocean. As the ship sank, the full extent of the damage from the rail-cannon became obvious. Just beyond the first vessel, a second ship listed drunkenly to one side, clearly the source of the second explosion. Something else on board that ship exploded, and through the smoke, Tarjiaan saw men scrambling across the burning decks and jumping into the water to escape the quickly-spreading flames.

"Great Mothers," he cursed, activating his communicator, "Marikaar!"

"*Sir!*" His first mate's voice crackled in his ear. "*What was that?*"

"The battle is over. Get a rescue party in the water immediately," Tarjiaan ordered. He turned, seeing his own men surrounding the shocked and silent Imperial troops, taking weapons from limp hands as they gathered the stunned prisoners. He holstered his pistol and raised his faceplate, and as he turned, he almost knocked down a thin, hollow-eyed man who stepped into his path. Tarjiaan took a step back, noticing the gold braid and collar pins on the man's uniform tunic. An Imperial officer, actually in the fight? A junior officer, but still. This was a first.

"Captain?" The man began, not meeting Tarjiaan's gaze. His voice cracked a little on the word and he bowed his head, clearing his throat before starting again, "Captain, as I... as I am now the ranking officer of this attack force..." He stopped again, his breath catching, and Tarjiaan realized just how young this boy was. If *he* was the highest-ranking officer remaining of the Imperial force, that meant...

"Which was your ship?" Tarjiaan asked softly. He turned to see the first of the Meradon rescue launches heading towards the burning, sinking hulks.

"The closest one, Captain. The *Sea Witch* was the command ship."

Tarjiaan glanced towards the wreckage again. "My men will save all of yours that they can."

"I thank you for that," the officer said hesitantly. "I had not expected mercy."

"You shouldn't believe everything you hear," Tarjiaan told him as he turned his full attention to the officer. "What's your name?"

"Girantivar, Captain." He looked flustered, but he held steady. "Commander Girantivar," he answered. He paused for another moment, then unclipped his saber from his belt to offer it solemnly. "Captain, will you accept my surrender?"

There were rules to defeat. There were laws that governed every battle on the waves. Tarjiaan's father had written most of them. Tarjiaan nodded gravely, taking the sheathed blade. "Don't worry, Commander. Despite what you may have heard, we're not monsters here in Meradon. Your people will be seen to properly." He hailed one of his lieutenants – a sharp-featured refugee from Lastalt who bore Tyracan slave tattoos down the side of his neck. "Ferrica, take the Commander below-decks and see him settled. Bring his men to the hold. Are the physicians ready for the wounded?"

"The physicians were ready before the first boom," Marikaar answered as he jogged up to them, "What in the name of the Great Mothers happened?"

"I intend to find out," Tarjiaan answered, turning towards the quarterdeck. "Mancer Ishantar!" Barely contained fury colored his rough voice as it rang through earpieces. "Day cabin, now!"

Two hours later, Tarjiaan had bathed and changed into a fresh green and gold uniform, and was at his desk in the day cabin, trying to focus on reports. The need for sleep prodded him while he read, making it hard to focus on the details – damage to the *Wave Runner*, the number of survivors from the Imperial vessels, recovery efforts for the dead, and the casualties on both sides. Better than he'd expected on damage to his ship, but they'd lost three of the crew. The survivors from the Imperial forces were confined to one of the *Wave Runner*'s holds, where they were being fed and tended to by Tarjiaan's physicians. After his next duty, Tarjiaan would meet with them, see that they were comfortable, and give them the choice. But for now...

The knock on the cabin door sent it swinging wide; Marikaar waited just outside, a roughly barrel-shaped silhouette against the late afternoon sun. He stepped into the cabin, and Tarjiaan could see one dark eyebrow raised in a silent question.

"The lock was shot off," Tarjiaan answered. "A stray shot, I assume, since nothing in here was disturbed. It's on the list to be mended; I'm surprised you didn't know."

"I haven't yet seen the list, and no one reported it to me." Marikaar's green eyes narrowed and Tarjiaan wondered who was going to get their head handed to them for not keeping the First Mate informed. "I'll get it taken care of before sunset. I've brought the Commander as you requested, Prince-Captain."

"Bring him in." Marikaar came the rest of the way into the room, followed by a confused-looking Girantivar. Tarjiaan stood to face the young Imperial officer. "Commander Girantivar, thank you for joining me. Do you prefer that I use your full name or your given name?"

"Thank you, Captain. Prince-Captain," Girantivar amended swiftly. He bowed from the waist, the only sign of his nervousness a slight tremble in his voice when he spoke. "My given name is fine. It's Antivar, but I'm guessing you know our naming conventions, to ask that question. You've been very kind. My men appreciate your concern for their well-being."

Tarjiaan gestured to the long ward-table and walked around to his own place. He noticed Antivar studying the armor that Tarjiaan still wore below the waist. He didn't ask, though. They never did. Tarjiaan sat down in his heavy chair at the head of the table and gestured to the chair at his right. "It was never my intention to sink your ships. Do you drink wine?" He lifted the decanter, pouring a glass when the young man nodded, then filled his own glass with water.

"So you said, Prince-Captain. Your crew seemed as surprised as we were," Antivar admitted as he sat down and took the offered wine glass. "May I ask what happened?"

Tarjiaan grimaced. "Our Mancer seems to have discovered a new setting on our primary weapon. If she had discovered it during testing, it would have been a valuable addition to our arsenal. To discover it during battle... it was an inexcusable loss of life that I deeply regret."

"You regret..." Antivar blurted. "You actually mean that?"

"I do." Tarjiaan sipped his water. "I don't want to fight your people. The only reason I fight is to protect my people and defend my ship." He paused. Every battle. Every capture. There was always some variation of this talk. "I know some of what you've been told about the Butcher of Meradon. None of it is true. It's what your Emperor wants you to think of me." Tarjiaan shook his head, then looked up as his aide came into the room, pushing a rolling cart before him. "Ah, right on time, Logiri. Thank you. Antivar, would you dine with me?"

"I... thank you, Captain." Antivar turned and looked over his shoulder at olive-skinned Logiri, and his eyes widened. "You... you're Tyracan!"

Logiri placed a covered platter on the table and spoke without so much as a glance in his direction, "I was born in Tyraca."

"You've been with me... what is it now, Logiri?" Tarjiaan asked, fighting the urge to grin. Every time he hosted an Imperial officer, there was also a variation of this conversation, something he found much more amusing. "Ten years?"

Logiri placed the smaller platters and serving bowls on the table. "Eleven at the turn of the year, Highness."

"Of course." Tarjiaan gestured as Logiri reached for a plate. "You can go, Logiri. I am capable of serving a meal."

Logiri sniffed, making clear his opinion of Tarjiaan's ability to do anything of the kind, then bowed slightly and left. He hadn't so much as graced Antivar with a kind glance.

"Is he your slave?" Antivar bit his lip as his face turned dusky. The young officer was more than a little rough around the edges, and Tarjiaan wondered if that lack of polish was the reason he'd led the boarding party. Clearly, his discretion was in need of polish. Either he'd offended a superior officer, and had been sent to die, or he'd been sent as a test — if he survived the encounter, then he would be considered worth further time and attention.

"We don't keep slaves in Meradon," Tarjiaan said. "Is that something they tell you?"

"Among other things," Antivar mumbled.

"Logiri is my aide, and my friend." Tarjiaan lifted one of the covers off a platter. "May I offer you some Sualimani spiced rice?" When the younger man nodded, Tarjiaan served the food, sliding a plate laden with rice, vegetables and stewed fish across the table. They ate in silence, and Tarjiaan was equal parts amused and disturbed by the enthusiasm with which Antivar attacked his food. He studied the younger man for a moment, the hollow face and too-prominent high cheekbones. The Imperial ship's log he'd read had said these men had been at sea for only a few weeks, but from the state of their provisions, it could have been twice that. Were the rumors of famine they'd heard actually true? Tarjiaan made certain that the plate stayed filled until Antivar finally slowed, sighed and set his fork aside.

The Imperial looked at Tarjiaan and his cheeks darkened as he said, "Captain, thank you. This was the best meal I've had in quite some time."

"You're welcome," Tarjiaan answered. "You're... what? Twenty?"

Antivar turned darker still. "Nineteen, Captain."

When Tarjiaan had been nineteen.... "I remember being your age. I never could eat enough to fill the chasm." Tarjiaan stood, waiting for Antivar to rise before asking, "Would you do me the honor of introducing me to your men?"

Antivar went ashen. "My... my men? Captain?" He drew himself up to his full height, but still had to tip his head back to look Tarjiaan in the eyes. "Captain, leave my men be. Let them live. If you must take a victim, then I insist it be me."

"Victim?" Startled, Tarjiaan fought to keep his expression calm. He could hear a hint of panic in Antivar's voice, but saw a hint of officer's steel in the way he fought past his fear for the sake of his crew. By the Mothers, this boy had so much *promise*. "What are you talking about?"

"You... you're the Butcher of Meradon," Antivar stammered. "You take the heads of your victims and use their skulls for drinking bowls. Your men braid the entrails of your captives into the rigging and drink blood in their rum and... are you *laughing* at me?"

As tired as he was, Tarjiaan couldn't help it. He'd known they told stories about him, but this? The sheer absurdity was too much! Tarjiaan wiped tears of mirth from his eyes. "I apologize. Truly, I do. It's just... I've been called the Butcher of Meradon for over ten years now, but no one has ever been willing to explain just what it is that I'm supposed to have *done* to earn that name." He picked up his glass. "Does this look like a skull to you?" He shook his head. "Have I treated you or your men in any way to indicate that I am the monster you were led to believe that I was?"

"No, but..." Antivar frowned deeply, as if he were searching for some evidence to disprove reality. "We're told that ships captured by your people are plundered and put to the torch. That our sailors are tortured and killed for your pleasure. I've never actually met anyone who survived an encounter with you, and I thought... seeing what happened to the *Witch*... but now you've been so kind and..." He scrubbed a hand through his hair. "I don't know what to believe!"

Tarjiaan sipped his water and set down his glass. "Allow me to address at least a portion of your concern. The reason that I want to meet your men is because I intend to ask them one question."

"And that question is?"

"Do they want to leave the Empire and live as free men in Meradon? I ask this question to every Imperial officer and sailor who crosses my path, and have done so for nearly eleven years." Antivar's face went gray, and he swayed on his feet. Tarjiaan crossed the distance between them in two heavy strides and steadied the young man. "Deep breath, Antivar. Sit down."

"Is that why ships don't come back?" Antivar murmured. "Whole *ships* defect to Meradon?"

"Exactly why," Tarjiaan agreed. "Logiri was the first of nearly..." He paused for a moment, thinking. "About two thousand. I forget the exact number. There are twenty-seven on this ship alone. You can speak with them, if you like."

"And you welcome us?" Antivar asked weakly.

Tarjiaan didn't answer at first, pouring another glass of wine and pressing it into the young man's hand. Then he rested his hand on Antivar's shoulder. "Completely. Oh, there are limitations, at first. You would start your life with us in the fleet below, then you would earn your way back above the waves, if that was your desire. The men who serve above the waves have been in Meradon for five years or more. Many of them have married or otherwise made a life for themselves under the waves."

"And what happens to those who refuse your offer, who want to go home?" Antivar asked.

Tarjiaan took a moment to refill his own glass of water. "We send them on their way. I don't know what happens to them when they leave us. I don't like that you say you've never met someone who survived an encounter with me, because that's not the case." He paused, then added, "Antivar, I can see that you have the potential to be a fine officer. You'd be a credit to Meradon if you stayed."

Antivar gazed down at his hands, looking distant and lost. Tarjiaan waited quietly, until the young man shook his head and answered, "I can't. If I run... the Emperor keeps hostages for his officers. And... I understand now why he insists on it." Antivar took a deep breath and met Tarjiaan's eyes. "There are people watching my mother...." He shook his head again. "I've said too much. I can't. I do appreciate the offer, Captain."

"The offer stands, Commander. My word on it – you'll be safe if you can find a way to bring yourself and your mother back to Meradonese waters." Tarjiaan set his glass down. "Now, it's time to meet your men."

Antivar seemed unsurprised to see the guards waiting for them, accepting without question their escort down into the hold that had been hastily converted into barracks. Tarjiaan trailed behind Antivar, meeting the sailors, listening to them and asking questions, pretending not to notice that there was one young man in particular who they never allowed to come to the front and be introduced, who he never got a clear glimpse of among the others. The sailors all seemed surprised by the attentions of physicians and by the lavish meal that had been provided, and one brave man asked Tarjiaan if he intended to fatten up the survivors to feed to his men.

"No one is being fattened up. No one is being fed to anyone," Tarjiaan told the man, pitching his voice so that it carried. "The stories that you have heard of me and of my crew are false. Trust your eyes. Any of you who wishes to leave will be returned to your remaining ship and allowed to leave our waters. Any among you who wishes to stay in Meradon is welcome."

"Beggin' yer pardon, Captain," the same brave fellow called, "but do you know what we are?"

Antivar cleared his throat. "A good majority of these men are conscripts, Captain. This is a penal battalion. I should have said, but... given everything, I'm surprised I remember my own name!"

"Criminals?" Tarjiaan looked back at the brave one. "What crimes? What did you do?"

The man lifted his face, tightening his jaw as he said, "I spoke out against the Mage-Tyrant."

Tarjiaan asked, "How many other political prisoners are there?" He watched as hands were raised. "And what other crimes?"

"Theft, sir," another man answered. "I stole food to feed my family. Like as not, they're dead now because of it."

Tarjiaan considered their gaunt faces and baggy uniforms. "Then what we've heard of the famine is true?"

"Yes, sir," the man answered, ignoring Antivar's hiss. "The poor go hungry while the Emperor's favorites feast."

Tarjiaan turned and looked at Antivar. "Are there any violent crimes in your battalion?"

"No, Captain," Antivar answered immediately. "Violent criminals are sent to the salt mines or executed outright."

It was possible he was lying, though Antivar seemed like he'd be bad at it if he tried. Tarjiaan stood straighter and looked out over the men, seeing the hope on their faces. "Those of you who would stay, give your names to my men, and tell them exactly what crime you committed that put you out to sea."

"And then what?" someone called out. "What happens if we stay?"

Patiently, Tarjiaan repeated what he'd told Antivar, before calling in Marikaar and his assistants, who would interview the men and separate those who were staying from the rest. Then he excused himself, and somehow managed to keep from yawning until the hold door closed behind him.

"How many this time, Highness?" Logiri asked as Tarjiaan entered the great cabin.

"Total or staying?" Tarjiaan settled into his chair and accepted a steaming cup from Logiri. "Six hundred and fifteen survivors total. Staying? I won't know until Marikaar is finished." He drank the tea and sighed, tipping his head back against the chair. "By the Mothers, I'm tired."

"You can take a nap. I'll rig a lock on the door," Logiri offered.

Tarjiaan smiled and shook his head. "If I lay down, I'll sleep for days. Just keep plying me with tea so I stay awake to see them off."

It was nearing sunset when Tarjiaan stood on the deck of the *Wave Runner* with Antivar at his side. The sun gleamed wide and orange, dipping gently past the horizon as the launch ship returned for the last group of Imperial sailors who would be returning home. The sea was smooth as glass, dimming with the sky above her.

"I want to thank you again for your courtesy," Antivar said. "My men appreciate the supplies and the attention of your healers." He straightened and looked out towards the Imperial ship waiting for him. "I should go."

Tarjiaan stopped him with a gesture, then held his hand out to Logiri, who passed Tarjiaan a sheathed saber; Tarjiaan offered it to Antivar. "You'll need this... Captain."

Antivar caught his breath, taking the saber from Tarjiaan and holding it in both hands. "Thank you, Captain." He bowed deeply. Then he hesitated, and for a moment, Tarjiaan wondered if he was going to change his mind. But he followed the guards to the launch, and he didn't look back.

Once it was gone, Tarjiaan yawned against his fist. "I am going to sleep," he announced. "Where's Marikaar?"

"Here, Prince-Captain." Marikaar appeared out of the crowd. "I'm afraid that your rest will have to wait."

Tarjiaan growled under his breath, then noticed the worried look on Marikaar's face. "What is it?"

"The royal pod is signaling. They're below us. You've been summoned."

Chapter Two
Summons

TRAPPED... HE WAS TRAPPED... pinned... couldn't move... couldn't breathe...

Tarjiaan woke with a jerk, shaking his head to clear away the seafoam left from the nightmare. At his best, he could maybe stay a few days before enclosed spaces started to smother him, before the nightmares began in earnest. As tired as he was...? He should have insisted on at least a few hours' sleep before coming below the waves. Grimacing, Tarjiaan rubbed his eyes and turned to look out the porthole of the submersible. He could do this. He had to do this. But Mothers grant that he'd only need to stay a day or two onboard the *Chimaera*. He'd be fine once he was back on the *Wave Runner*, out under the open sky.

Someday, King Ikaanaji told his people, the people of Meradon would retake their ancestral home overlooking the sea, but for now, the people of Meradon would stay safe under the waves in the shadow of the Great Mothers. It made perfect sense – the royal family and the civilian population were safer there.

Tarjiaan couldn't live like that anymore.

Whatever the reason for the summons, it had to be important, he reminded himself as he peered through dark water to try and catch a glimpse of the *Chimaera*. His uncle had thus far been understanding where Tarjiaan was concerned; he knew what happened when Tarjiaan was too long under the waves. For Ikaanaji

17

to call Tarjiaan below with no warning and with no time to prepare...
there must be something seriously wrong.

Unless Ikaanaji hadn't been the one who called. Tarjiaan
drummed his fingers against the dull metal armor on his right thigh
and frowned. He'd heard that his sister was back on the royal
below-ship. It would be very much like her to abuse her authority
like this. She claimed it was the duty of an older sister to take care of
her younger brother. But Tarjiaan had long since stopped believing
that she had his best interests at heart, and her idea of care had led to
her being exiled to one of the other below-ships, a punishment that
had only recently been lifted. It had been years since he'd last seen
her, which meant that she had no idea of the extent of the damage he
lived with, or her role in making it worse. He also had no intention
of letting her know, and thereby handing her a weapon she could use
against him.

"Highness, we're coming up on the *Chimaera*," the pilot called.

"Thank you, Commander," Tarjiaan said absently. He dragged
one finger over the porthole, watching the gleam of dull metal
growing brighter in the outer lights of the submersible. If he hadn't
been called below, the *Wave Runner* would be headed to the floating
dockyards for some much-needed repairs. And perhaps a reunion.

No one had ever been willing to tell him what had happened
to his battle-companion after that last battle. Daanir's latent power
had awakened in his attempts to save Tarjiaan's life, and he'd gone
to formally train as a Mancer. That much Tarjiaan knew. But in the
fifteen years since, Tarjiaan hadn't had a single word from the man
who'd once guarded his back. Who'd once held his heart. Who he'd
gotten his father's blessing to marry. And who had since vanished
without a trace. After that disastrous last battle, it was as if any
mention of his existence had been scrubbed from the official rolls.
Until a snippet of trivia from the floating dockyards had caught
Tarjiaan's attention and set his course. Hopefully, this duty would be

done soon so that he might finally be able to ask the question he'd been holding close to his heart for fifteen years.

He heard the solid thump as the submersible came to rest in the docking bay, and the machine whirr and hiss as connections were made.

"All clear, Highness," the pilot announced. "You're free to go aboard."

"Thank you, Commander," Tarjiaan said. He took a deep breath, got to his feet, and walked out into the last place he wanted to be.

The first person Tarjiaan saw as he came out into the *Chimaera's* entry bay was Ilaris, his uncle's Lord Chamberlain — a tall, skeletal-thin man with thinning gray hair. He bowed deeply. "Welcome home, your Highness."

This isn't my home. Tarjiaan bit down on the retort and nodded in acknowledgment. "Thank you, Ilaris. Is everything well? I'm not usually sent for with no warning."

"Your uncle requires your presence. However—" Ilaris paused as the entry bay's metal door opened to reveal the very last person Tarjiaan expected to see on the royal below-ship.

Daanir.

For a moment, all Tarjiaan could do was stare. There was no mistaking him, for all that fifteen years had changed him. He'd finally grown into his hands and feet, standing only an inch or two shorter than Tarjiaan's shoulder in his armor, and the top of his head brushed the low lintel of the door as he came into the bay. He'd grown in the shoulders and chest, too. His white-blond hair was cropped short and spiked with streaks of oil, evidence of a hurried attempt at being presentable without the aid of a mirror. He must have been shaving without a mirror, too – there was a scar long his jawline on the left. That had never been there before. His eyes were still the same bright, gleaming blue above the same mischievously crooked grin. Amazing, how such an uncomplicated expression could leave Tarjiaan feeling so very confused.

"I'll take him from here, Lord Ilaris," Daanir announced. "If you'd rather get on with your various and sundry other important duties."

"I am aware of my duties, Mancer," Ilaris retorted. "Highness, as I was about to say, His Majesty requires your presence, but as he did not know when you would be arriving, your audience has been moved to tomorrow morning. Your cabin has been prepared. Is there anything you require at the moment?"

Tarjiaan looked past him at the blond man, still trying to shake off the shock. Years of searching ships' rolls and rosters, crew lists and reports, wondering if perhaps Daanir had died and they'd hidden it from him. And Daanir had been *here*? Since when? And why had no one told him? Ilaris had known about Tarjiaan's search, and so had the Physician Royal. "No," he said, dragging his attention back to Ilaris. "There's nothing I require except sleep."

And answers.

"Very good, Your Highness." Ilaris stepped back as a serving girl hurried inside, pushing a rolling chair. She looked up, saw Tarjiaan looking at her, and averted her eyes, her cheeks flaring red. "Your chair, Your Highness."

Tarjiaan sighed. There was no way to delay the inevitable anymore — he could go no further into the ship wearing his armor. He walked over to brackets and vertical rails set into the wall, his steps echoing in the small space. With meticulous care, he locked the armor into place, then pointed to a spot next to him. "Put it there. Make sure that the lock is set."

The girl's hands trembled on the handles of the chair as she pushed it to him and fumbled with the latch.

"I got it." Daanir slipped to her side and brushed his hand over the arm of the chair; the locking mechanism flickered red. "You're good to go." He glanced at the serving girl with a wink, "And so are you."

Tarjiaan waited until the girl was gone and the others had turned their backs, then triggered the hidden release mechanism on his armor; the armor hissed slightly as it cracked open, padding deflating as the shell around each leg parted slowly, revealing what remained of Tarjiaan's legs — his right cut off mid-thigh, and his left, gone at the knee. Slowly, he maneuvered himself into the chair, touching the control that closed the carapace and activated the mechanism, feeling the itchy tingle as the receptors built into the chair started analyzing his nervous system and syncing with his body. At last, a light on the control panel under his left hand glowed green. With a thought, he set the chair rolling, heading out of the entry bay and into the corridors of the ship. Behind him, he heard the sound of footsteps following him down the corridor.

"You didn't hurt my ship, did you?"

"She's my ship," Tarjiaan said without turning.

"I might have designed her for you, but she's still mine." Daanir squinted. "You didn't hurt her, did you? Does she need repairs? How bad is it?"

Tarjiaan swallowed around the iceberg lodged in his throat. Once, his welfare would have been first on Daanir's mind. And ships? Daanir was designing whole ships? Since when? "I'm fine. Thanks for asking," he said in a low voice. It didn't shake. Much.

Daanir didn't seem to notice. "Well, you don't look like you're bleeding out. I assumed—"

"What are you doing here?" Tarjiaan interrupted, hearing the ragged edge to his voice and hating himself for it. Slipping. He was slipping. He couldn't... not now. He steadied himself. "I had no idea. None. No one would tell me where you were, what happened to you. I couldn't find you, no matter how hard I searched. I finally heard you were stationed at the floating dockyards. I... I thought I'd finally found you." He swallowed and forced himself to look up. "We were heading there."

"I haven't been at the dockyards in a year. You didn't get my letters? I sent...." A long pause. "Wait. You didn't know where I was?" He paused. "You didn't know that I designed the *Wave Runner* as a gift to you?"

Tarjiaan stopped, startled by the tone in the other man's voice. Stunned? Shocked? Horrified? Tarjiaan wasn't sure. He turned, and for the first time, he saw past the memories and the too-familiar and really looked at Daanir — his black trousers pooled at the knees above a pair of thick leather boots. His dark green tunic was equally over-large, hanging halfway to Daanir's knees. Heavily embroidered cuffs had been rolled up to his oil-marked elbows. "I... no. I didn't know any of that," Tarjiaan stammered. "I think we need to talk."

Daanir bit his lower lip, ducking his head, and flicked a quick, unsure glance up through pale lashes. "Right. I think we do."

A swell of nerves made the chair start to roll out of control. Tarjiaan stopped it, then looked up and down the corridor; seeing no one, he raked his fingers through his hair and finally let himself relax enough that his shoulders slumped. "While I'm still coherent. I'm tired to my bones. I haven't slept since..." He stopped and frowned. "The day before yesterday, I think."

Daanir whistled under his breath. "Yeah, of course. Follow me."

"I know the way to my room, Daan."

"Not anymore. Your uncle had you moved to the heir's suite." Daanir nodded to the left down a branching corridor. "Don't worry. When I found out it was happening, I oversaw it myself. Everything is right where you'd want it."

Tarjiaan looked up at him. "You put my things away?" he asked. Without thinking, he sighed, making it as overly dramatic as possible. "I'm never going to find anything again, am I?" he drawled, then snorted, surprised at himself. Old habits – they'd always bantered like this. But there was no answering gibe; Daanir rested his hand against the wall, apparently preoccupied by the grain of the metal. "Daan?"

The Mancer turned back. "Hm? Oh, I'll show you," he offered. "And I think Kaapi took notes."

"Kaapi?"

"My assistant. Ilaris insisted I have one. The lab gets into what he calls 'a state of disrepair.' Which isn't fair. Just because he doesn't know where to find anything doesn't mean it's out of order."

"So you're designing ships, making decisions for me, and you rate an assistant now. What rank are you these days?" Tarjiaan turned, and caught sight of the emblem peeking out of a fold of Daanir's over-sized coat – the royal Kraken's eight tentacles clasping a crest of crossed lightning bolts in a silver grip – the badge of the Mancer Royal. "Daan!"

Daanir looked down at his baggy uniform, touching the crest with one hand. "When Riguaarin took ill last year, he picked me from the Mancer rolls, and His Majesty called me in. I apprenticed here until — well. Riguaarin passed three and a half weeks ago."

Tarjiaan felt a momentary pang at the news — Riguaarin had been a good man. "I hadn't heard. I'll have to pass my condolences on to his family."

"You just did." Daanir scratched the back of his neck, wearing a grim expression that Tarjiaan had never seen outside of battle. "Right. You wouldn't know that either. He adopted me; it only took thirty-three years, but I'm a Meranas now."

Tarjiaan took a moment to absorb the news, then nodded. "Congratulations. If anyone deserves the honor of being a royal fosterling, you do. So you were sworn in as the Mancer Royal? If I'd known, I would have been here."

"Would you have?" Daanir's smile flickered on again like an afterthought. "I keep thinking I'm going to wake up back at the dockyards, or at my first station."

Tarjiaan looked Daanir up and down. "Daan..."

"I know the uniform doesn't fit." He shrugged. "I only wear it when I have to."

Tarjiaan sighed, shaking his head. Some things about Daanir, at least, would never change. The fact was somehow comforting. "Where are we going?"

"This way." Daanir gestured. He looked distant. "You aren't injured, are you?"

Tarjiaan licked his lips. "No, I'm not injured."

"And my ship?" Daanir asked quietly. "I designed her just for you, from the kelson up. She's a special lady."

"She is that. She's still sailing. Scratched up, but she'll survive."

Daanir exhaled a quick relieved sigh. "So... what happened? Can you tell me? It's just..." He hesitated, falling in on Tarjiaan's left as someone came down the corridor, bowing as she approached them. As she passed them, Daanir cleared his throat. "Kaapi's a good kid. Crèche -born, like me. She's smart. Smarter than I was." He flexed his hand again, then dropped it on Tarjiaan's shoulder. Just for a moment. Then a door they were approaching slid open; Daanir moved ahead of them and stepped inside. "And here you are."

Tarjiaan entered the room and looked around. It was far more opulent than his former quarters, with heavy, polished wood furniture appointed in the royal greens, browns, and golds, and doors that led to other, inner rooms. "All this? This is... impressive. I'd no idea the heir's suite was this lavish."

"There was a carpet thick enough to lose your feet, too," Daanir said as the door closed behind them. "I had them take that out. Bare floor is better for your wheels."

"Thank you," Tarjiaan answered absently. "Which is the bedroom?" he asked, pointing at the two inner doors.

"The left. The right is the consort's suite." Daanir abruptly gestured at the bookcases. "I alphabetized your books and grouped them by subject."

"I'll never find the one I want, will I?" Tarjiaan rubbed his temple tiredly. "Not that it matters. I don't come down here often enough to need these." He looked up at Daanir and risked a smile. "But... maybe I'll come more often now that I have a reason to come below."

There was no answering smile. Daanir looked down, then said, "So... Imperial ships?"

"Yes," Tarjiaan answered. Something wasn't right. No. No, it had to be how tired he was.

"At least you can always count on the Imps to cause trouble, right?" Daanir cocked his head to the side, waiting. "Is this when I'm supposed to stop asking questions?"

Tarjiaan closed his eyes and tried to focus through the fatigue. "There's nothing you can't know. The Empire is getting desperate. The rumors we've heard of famine are true. This lot were all half-starved, and most were conscripts sent to sea for stealing to keep their families fed. So... three Imperial ships. New designs on the ships, and they're smaller and faster than the ones we've seen before. I'm sure the cameras got footage for the reports, so you'll be able to see what I mean. I can't be certain, but from the way the battle went, I'd say they sent more than a hundred guns after us."

Daanir shuddered. "So many?"

Tarjiaan nodded, unfastening his collar and unbuttoning his coat. "Looked like it from where I was. Not that I stopped and counted, mind. I didn't have time. But they still haven't made a gun powerful enough to pierce a Meradonese hull." He yawned and ran his finger under his loosened collar. "I'm not even sure how many men they packed onto those ships. Only one mage, and he held us dead in the water."

"Don't you have a rail-cannon? I thought I ordered that for you when it was available."

"Is that why we got it? I thought my uncle... Never mind. The temperamental thing fried itself."

"It isn't temperamental. It's sensitive."

"Is that what we're calling it? It took hours for Ishantar to get it working. Once she did, the battle was over in ten minutes. We blew two of the ships out of the water."

Daanir looked shocked, "Jiaan!"

"I was only planning on sinking one, and only if we had to. But Ishantar's failures are even more spectacular than yours. And more explosive," Tarjiaan said. "We saved as many as we could, then I met with the surviving senior officer. They're getting younger, Daan. This one was nineteen. A commander at nineteen. The Empire is sending boys...." He stopped, remembering when he'd been nineteen.

"We were at war when we were nineteen," Daanir said quietly, mirroring Tarjiaan's own thoughts. "We've been at war since we before we were born."

Tarjiaan nodded. "Regardless, we have a hundred and thirty-six refugees that will need to be rehomed. Marikaar is seeing to them."

Daanir squinted thoughtfully. "Marikaar? The last time I got a look at a report, your first mate was Quentas."

"So I'm not the only one missing information?" Tarjiaan said. "Marikaar has been on the *Wave Runner* just over a year now. He's a good man. Solid. Built like a barrel. Quentas returned to the crèche -ship where his family lives. He's tired." He grimaced. "I'm exhausted. How big is the bed?"

"Massive." Daanir squeezed Tarjiaan's shoulder. "Come and see?"

Tarjiaan whistled when Daanir led him into the bedroom. Even with the enormous bed and the other furnishings, there was still enough space in the room for his chair to move freely. "You weren't exaggerating. That bed alone is bigger than our cabin was on the *Marauder*."

"To be fair, we had a really small cabin." Daanir grinned. "There are some perks to being the Sea Prince, eh? I still have a pallet on the floor."

"Why does the Mancer Royal have a pallet on the floor?" Tarjiaan asked. Then realized the answer and found himself grinning. "Daan, you went and sent your bed away again, didn't you?" He laughed when Daanir looked innocently at the ceiling. "You are such a crèche -boy!"

"Be that as it may, it wasn't ever as big as this one. Or as comfortable." Daanir bit his lip and looked away. "You should rest. Ikaanaji's going to be in a mood tomorrow."

"Why?" Tarjiaan asked. "I didn't go looking for trouble. It found me. As usual. This time, they came looking for me specifically. Apparently, the Mage-Emperor wants my head on a platter."

"Your head looks better on your shoulders. How did they manage to find the *Wave Runner* specifically, out of all the other ships of Meradon? If — they'd have to have some way of listening to our tracking channels." Daanir fidgeted as he thought. "They shouldn't be able to do that. Not without Meradonese tech, and that's all accounted for. And I rechecked our frequencies only a few days ago and they were in the clear."

"I've no idea. The raiding party didn't find anything unusual on the surviving ship. It might be something to do with their mages. I don't know." Tarjiaan shrugged and yawned, then looked at Daanir, suddenly curious. "How do you know the bed is comfortable?"

"Look at it." Daanir waved his arm at the bed. "Can you see me resisting jumping on something that squishy looking?"

Tarjiaan looked at the bed, then back at Daanir. Fifteen years. He didn't want to know, but he had to ask. "So... who'd you try it out with? That assistant of yours?"

Daanir snorted. "Your exhaustion has clearly gone to your brain."

"That's not a no."

"It's also not a yes. She's fourteen, Jiaan. And officially? She's not just my assistant. She's my daughter. It's been... five months now? Yeah, five."

Tarjiaan blinked. "Now those are words I never thought to hear from you. I apologize, Daan."

"You didn't know. And honestly, me? Family and kids? Why would you expect that? I mean, I had you. Why would I want anyone else?" He coughed, his face flaring red. "I... I should go." He turned toward the door. "I..."

The words registered, and carefully crafted walls shattered like glass; Tarjiaan reached out and grabbed his hand. "Daan. Stay. Please." He swallowed. "I...I've missed you." He tugged Daanir closer, closed his eyes and forced the words out. "I... I don't remember much of those days, right after... everything. All I remember is waking up the first time and you were there. Then you were gone and all that they would tell me was that you'd been sent for training. Then..." He stopped, his throat closing. No, he wasn't going to talk about that. Not now. "I never could find you." He looked up again. "I never stopped trying. Every dispatch, every crew list, anything I could think of. I was starting to think you were dead. That I'd dreamed you were there when I woke. That they'd lied to me about you'd going off for training. That no one was brave enough to tell me you'd died with Father and Ranji!" Tarjiaan's voice cracked, and he stopped to catch his breath, looking down at his clenched fists struggling to get himself back under control.

"I'm here. And I'll stay." Daanir exhaled a shaky breath, Then he cupped Tarjiaan's face in his hands and kissed him. Tarjiaan remembered every one of his kisses. He could have cataloged them – the quick, the soft, the oh-so-fervent, and the ones filled with laughter. This time, those distantly familiar lips were charged with sparks, and Tarjiaan's chair rumbled like it was purring. Daanir drew back and brushed one hand gently over the arm of the chair. The light on the console blinked yellow, then the carapace whirred, releasing Tarjiaan. Daanir kissed him again, this time more gently. "Shall I take you to your royal bed, your Highness?"

"Only if you're going to be there with me." Tarjiaan closed his eyes and, for a moment, let himself hope that things hadn't changed over the years. That the answer would be yes. He laughed softly, taking Daanir's face in his hands. "I never stopped missing you," he said. Then he kissed him, running his hands down Daanir's chest. He had started unfastening the buttons of the over-sized coat when he heard the chime that signaled the outer door opening, followed by a woman's voice, "Tarjiaan?"

Tarjiaan flinched. Then he groaned and tipped his head back. "Not her. Not now."

Daanir straightened. "I could go get rid of her—"

"No! Just... stay here. Stay quiet." Daanir mimed clamping his mouth shut, but his eyes were hard above the playful gesture. Tarjiaan wondered how much Daan knew. If he knew any of it. But that didn't matter right now. He dragged his fingers through his hair, took a deep breath, and forced himself back behind barriers of pure will. "I won't be long." He closed the carapace of his chair and directed it towards the door.

Chapter Three
Audience

IN THE MIDDLE OF THE sitting room was a tall woman with gray-shot dark hair. She was dressed in the green-and-gold royal uniform, and her features were a mirror of Tarjiaan's own. She scowled at him and coldly said, "No greetings for your sister, Tarjiaan?"

"I would have seen you in the morning, Aanaji." Tarjiaan yawned, mostly for effect. "Is this important? My bed is calling."

"And is someone waiting for you in there?" she asked, nodding towards the closed door. She lowered her voice, narrowing her eyes mockingly, "Of course there is. Tarjiaan, really. A doxy? How disrespectful!"

Tarjiaan bit down on the inside of his cheek. "You honestly think I'd take a doxy to my bed? Under Uncle's very nose? You know how he feels about that."

"Well, who else would want to be in your bed?" Aanaji asked, her voice sickly sweet. She gestured toward Tarjiaan. "Look at you. You can't honestly think anyone—"

"Tell me what you want or go away," Tarjiaan snapped, his voice cracking. She smirked at him, and he almost heard her mentally tally the point she knew she'd won.

"It's about time you had the heir's suite." Aanaji looked around the room approvingly, then moved over to the couch and sat down.

"This is as it should be. You belong here. Being above, shouting orders, that can't be doing your voice any favors—"

"You didn't do my voice any favors, and yet here you are. I belong with my ship. Now what do you want?" Tarjiaan repeated, trying to keep a rein on his temper. Meetings with Aanaji never ended well, and this one looked like it was going to degenerate faster than usual.

She smiled slightly. "Poor dear. You spend all your days with commoners, and you forget all your manners."

"Father was a commoner," Tarjiaan said. "I shouldn't need to remind you of that."

She scowled at him, and he tallied his own mental point as she answered his question, "Very well. I came to discuss Naajir."

Tarjiaan rolled his eyes. "I'd prefer to actually see him, but then you'd have to tell me where he is, because he's not where he's supposed to be. He was assigned to the *Wave Runner*."

"I am aware." The look that she leveled at him wouldn't be out of place if she'd smelled bad clams. "He's too young."

"He is fourteen, he needs training, and he is old enough to stand duty above the waves. He'll be king someday–"

"The king doesn't leave the royal ship," Aanaji interrupted him briskly. "The heir shouldn't leave, either. And my sweet Naajir is the only heir left. He needs to be protected."

"You know what I think of what you call protecting," Tarjiaan snapped. "And the king needs to lead the fleet. How can he do that if he doesn't know how to command a ship? You know as well as I do that Ranji was serving as Father's first mate before he was eighteen. Cousin Ilijiaan was Uncle's heir, and he served as mate on the *Vagabond* for five years—"

"Yes, and look how that ended. With our brother and all of our cousins dead!" Aanaji snapped. She stopped, visibly composing herself. "He's a sensitive boy," she continued in a milder tone. "You of all people should understand that, Tarjiaan. You were a poet, a musician—"

"I was the sixth prince! I had the luxury of an older brother and four older cousins. And you see how fragile a line that was!" Tarjiaan fought to control his temper and took a long breath. In a calmer tone, he added, "I understand that you want your son safe. I want him safe as well. But the kingdom must come first. Naajir must stand duty above the waves. He will be the Sea Prince when the time comes, and he needs that training. I promise you – I will keep him safe." Tarjiaan sighed, rubbing his forehead. "I don't want to fight with you, but your son is my heir. And he must learn to be a king."

"Jiaan..."

"Do not call me that," Tarjiaan growled. "I am serious. I will take it up with Uncle if I have to. Is there anything else?"

Aanaji glared at him, then swept out of the room without another word. Once she was gone, Tarjiaan sat in the empty room for a moment, listening to the slight, off-tune whistle of the air returns before silently rolling the chair back into the bedroom. "Where were we?" he asked.

Daanir was sitting on the bed, his back against the headboard, his knees drawn up to his chest. He looked absolutely perfect — he'd taken off the bulky uniform and Tarjiaan could see him finally, lanky and lean, his arms covered with smudges of oil. His eyes were closed, fingers fiddling with something Tarjiaan couldn't see; they stilled when Tarjiaan spoke. "I'd rather be where we are. Wouldn't you?"

"From where I am, the view is wonderful," Tarjiaan laughed softly, then added, "I just wish I wasn't tired to the bone."

Daanir glanced at him. "Do you want help?"

Tarjiaan almost refused the offer. He didn't need the help, even as tired as he was. But... it was an excuse for Daan to touch him again.

Pride fell before the need to have Daanir's hands on him once more. He nodded. "Please?"

Daanir pushed Tarjiaan's chair close to the bed, locking the brakes and opening the carapace. He smoothed his hands down the front of Tarjiaan's chest, parting the unbuttoned cloth and brushing his fingertips down bare skin, then slid his hands back up to hook beneath Tarjiaan's arms. "Ready?"

Tarjiaan gripped Daanir's shoulders. "Ready."

With a grunt, Daanir lifted Tarjiaan up to the bed and fell back, gasping as he landed with Tarjiaan on top of him. "I don't remember you weighing this much," he teased. "Either I've gone weak or you've been overeating your topside rations."

"My aide keeps complaining about having to order new shirts for me. I keep putting on inches across the shoulders." Tarjiaan grinned down at Daanir, spreading his fingers over the other man's collarbones. "I remember you liked my shoulders."

"I still like them," Daanir assured him. "I'm just out of shape."

Tarjiaan shifted to lie next to Daanir and ran one hand down his side. "I didn't used to be able to count your ribs, and you were thin as a rail the last I saw you. I might have to steal you from my uncle for your own good."

"You can't," Daanir said quickly, then flushed. "I eat when I remember, or when Kaapi makes me," he continued quickly. "You don't have to worry about me."

Tarjiaan raised himself up on his elbow to study him.

"What?"

"I haven't forgotten your tells, Daan. You're hiding something." Tarjiaan studied him for a moment, then grimaced. "To quote you: is this where I'm supposed to stop asking questions?"

"I'd appreciate it," Daanir murmured. "There are things I'm not allowed to say."

"Not allowed?" Tarjiaan rolled away from Daanir, pushing himself up so that he could sit against the headboard of the bed. "Daanir..." He trailed off. No... he wouldn't ask. He didn't go seeking trouble above the waves; he wouldn't do it below them. Especially not questions that might lead to Daanir leaving. It had been too long, and there was still an uncharted sea between them that wouldn't be crossed in one night, or a single conversation. "Come here, then. Tell me, you said that you wrote me?"

Daanir drew back and met his gaze: wide eyes the color of calm afternoon seas and filled with unabashed affection. "I sent at least one letter with every dispatch ship. I wasn't supposed to. I was supposed to focus exclusively on my training. I had to bribe the couriers. Maybe my bribes weren't good enough, if you never got them." He stopped, then shook his head. "It's not important now." Daanir rolled over and plucked at Tarjiaan's belt, meeting his gaze. "You're here. I'm here. Want some help getting rid of these extra layers?"

Tarjiaan smiled. "Please?"

Daanir helped to peel the jacket and the shirt free, dropping them off the side of the bed. He knelt over Tarjiaan for a moment, studying him in almost reverent silence, then he leaned down and gently pressed a kiss to the small, round scar on Tarjiaan's collarbone. "I've missed you. So much."

Tarjiaan took a long breath, running his fingers over Daanir's arms, up his shoulders and down his chest. "I've missed you, too. Before... before anything, we should lock that damn door."

"No one else should bother us," Daanir said absently. "I told Kaapi that I might not come in tonight, and that she should go to Wilaanger if she needs anything. And we've been on a skeleton crew for the last month."

Tarjiaan stared at him, suddenly realizing that the empty corridors had been *too* empty. Even this late in the ship's day, there should have been some activity, but there had been only a scattering of crew, and he'd been too tired to think twice about it. "This... this is part of what you can't tell me, isn't it?"

Daanir's cheeks darkened again as he lifted his eyes. "I'm not good at this, Jiaan. Can you leave it be?"

Tarjiaan stroked Daanir's cheek with his fingers. "You weren't made for the court. You're too good for them."

"I'm not," Daanir disagreed, wrinkling his nose. "And, court or not, this is where I need to be." He glanced back over his shoulder. "Do you want me to go check the doors?"

"I don't want you to leave me. Now come here. I'm going to make you do all the work."

"I like it that way." Daanir kissed Tarjiaan's shoulder, tracing the line of muscle with his tongue, and then kissed down his arm. Tarjiaan closed his eyes, reveling in the sensation. How long had it been since he'd last been touched like this?

An easy answer. Fifteen years.

"If you're not careful, I'll fall asleep," he warned.

"If I'm doing the work, I get to decide what the work is," Daanir mumbled against Tarjiaan's skin. "And when. I want you to enjoy yourself. So... rest. Be with me, for now."

Tarjiaan stared at the ceiling. For now. It used to be for always. He closed his eyes and whispered, "I've missed you, Daan."

"I missed you, too, Jiaan. More than you know."

Tarjiaan woke up in near darkness, unable to move. It took him a moment to realize that he was buried under rubble, and the knowledge that someone would come for him, that Daan was probably looking for a way to free him at that moment was all that kept him from panicking. He forced himself calm and took stock of his injuries. Pain, but not enough to make him think he'd broken anything. His right arm was

stretched out behind him at an odd angle that made his shoulder ache, and his left was pinned underneath him. There was something under his back, stabbing him through his armor, but there was nothing on his chest. In fact, there was clearance over his torso of several inches. His hips were twisted and pinned, but he could move his legs a little. It wasn't the most comfortable position he'd ever been in, but he'd survive. The worst part was the odd smell; there was something acrid in the air, and it was getting stronger. He couldn't see much because of his visor, but he could have sworn there was a glow.

As his eyes became accustomed to the faint light, he could see that what was pinning him down were the remains of the construct that had attacked the Marauder. *The hole that he'd punched in the armor was visible just above his chest. There was a faint blue glow coming from inside, and he could see a pale, glowing droplet of something hanging from a jagged piece of metal just before it dropped onto his chest.*

He couldn't hear anything. Could anyone hear him? He raised his voice and shouted, "Ranji! Daan!" He couldn't hear anything other than his own breathing, so he took another breath and shouted again, "Daan! Father! I'm here!"

No answer. Maybe he could move, try and make some more noise. He shifted his legs slightly, kicking the rubble to give the people who had to be looking for him a way to find him. His right boot hit something, and the rubble over his legs shifted. He heard something snap, and then a wave of boiling liquid washed over his legs, drenching his right leg from mid-thigh down, and his left below the knee. He cried out in pain as the liquid scalded him, then bit down on the pain and waited for it to subside.

It didn't. It grew, the burning increasing until Tarjiaan was screaming, thrashing, unable to move, unable to do anything but scream until finally, mercifully, he passed back into darkness.

Tarjiaan woke with a start, biting back a scream, feeling the scalding pain in legs that were no longer there, that hadn't been there for fifteen years. There was a weight on his chest, holding him down. He was trapped, pinned...

Then the weight on his chest shifted, and Daanir pushed up onto his elbow, blinking blearily down at him, the worried look on his face just barely visible in the sleeping-dim lights. "Jiaan?"

Tarjiaan took a long breath and nodded. "I'm all right."

"Nightmares?" Daanir ran his hand down Tarjiaan's chest.

"I'm all right," Tarjiaan repeated. It was a lie and he knew it. He'd been below for less than a day, and the memories already had their hooks in him.

Daanir pulled Tarjiaan into his arms, shifting until Tarjiaan's back rested against his chest. "You're safe. I'm here, and you're safe." He ran one hand over Tarjiaan's hip, kissed his shoulder. "I've got you, my Prince."

Tarjiaan took a deep breath, feeling himself starting to relax as Daanir's hand moved slowly up and down his side. He let himself be moved onto his stomach, and felt Daanir kneeling over him. His hands were warm and strong as they started kneading the muscles in his shoulders. Tarjiaan groaned as Daanir found a knot and started working at it. "You haven't lost your touch."

"That's good to hear. I haven't been practicing." He slowly worked his way down Tarjiaan's back. Tarjiaan was starting to drift back to sleep when Daanir's lips brushed the back of his neck. "I feel as though I need to learn you all over again."

Tarjiaan looked over his shoulder, suddenly as nervous as he'd been their first time. "It's been a long time, Daan."

"You don't have to remind me." His hands traced long rivers down Tarjiaan's back, then stilled. He shook his head. "I'm sorry. I shouldn't. You need to rest. I... I should... tomorrow."

Tarjiaan shivered, anticipation and frustration raging in equal measure. He made himself nod. Made himself face Daanir. Made himself smile. "I... tomorrow. We'll both be rested, and I'll have this meeting behind me." Tarjiaan tightened his arms around Daanir, hearing the other man catch his breath when he squeezed too tightly. If he held on tight enough, maybe he wouldn't have to let go. "Just let me hold you, Daan. Just hold me."

For one night, let me believe you're still mine.

A gentle tapping on his nose pulled Tarjiaan from a thankfully-dreamless sleep; he opened his eyes as Daanir held a mug down and blew the fragrant steam towards Tarjiaan's face. "I brought you breakfast."

Tarjiaan blinked up at him sleepily, remembering countless mornings that they'd woken like this on the *Marauder*. The old response was automatic. "Hmmm... come here, breakfast."

Daanir laughed and shook his head. Tarjiaan saw that he was once more dressed in the ridiculously large uniform. "There's no time. Ilaris was here. His Majesty will see you as soon as you're dressed and ready. You want the tea or not?"

Tarjiaan made a face. "I suppose I'll settle for it." He pushed himself up into a sitting position and took the mug from Daanir, glancing towards the door when he heard a clattering outside the bedroom. "Who's out there?"

"Logiri. Ilaris sent for him."

Tarjiaan looked at Daanir. "Why did Ilaris send for my aide?"

Daanir shrugged, looking almost-but-not-quite guilty. "I asked him to?"

Tarjiaan arched an eyebrow. "Keep going."

"You said that you keep having to have new shirts made. And Ilaris told me that it's been four years since you were last onboard for any length of time. You need your court uniform to see your uncle this morning, and I didn't think the court uniform you left here would fit, so I asked Ilaris to have Logiri bring something for you to wear," Daanir finished all in one breath, then bit his lip. "You mind?"

Tarjiaan laughed, and spoke without thinking. "Daan, if you keep on insisting on ordering my life like this, I'm going to tell my uncle that I'm finally getting married."

Daanir stared at him. "What?"

For a moment, Tarjiaan was more terrified than he could remember ever being. He hadn't meant to say anything. Not yet. Not so soon. But he never could hold his tongue around Daanir. He looked down at his tea. "The morning of the attack. I spoke to my father. He approved; I was going to ask you, but I never had the chance. Then I woke up and you were gone and I...I never changed my course, Daan. I still love you." Tarjiaan looked up and held out one hand. "I was going to ask you at the dockyards. If you still loved me. If you'd have me, even after... even after so long. Daan –"

"Don't." Daanir shook his head, swearing under his breath and shutting his eyes. One sharp breath, then another. "You can't ask me and I can't. I... I can't. Just... toast." He thrust a plate into Tarjiaan's outstretched hand. "I had them bring that preserve that you like. I... do you still like it?"

Tarjiaan stared at him for a long moment, taking the words apart and putting them back together, feeling his world shifting around him. This wasn't how this conversation was supposed to go. "I... yes, I do," he stammered. "What do you mean I can't ask you?"

"You can't. You can't say anything about this." Daanir scowled towards the closed door and muttered, "I like being alive."

"What in the Deep is that supposed to mean? I haven't known for certain if you were alive or dead for fifteen years. Who's making you think..." Tarjiaan paused. "Not Aanaji?"

Daanir scrubbed a hand through his hair. "Aanaji has been a menace ever since she came on board, but that's nothing to do with this."

"It's something, if you're making comments about wanting to stay alive." Tarjiaan frowned, considering the over-sized, outlandish uniform. Daan wouldn't have made a fuss about wearing Riguaarin's old uniform, but someone in the court should have cared how the Mancer Royal looked. Unless they wanted him to look like a fool. It was the kind of snub Aanaji liked. "What's her game this time?"

"She's not important," Daan insisted. He set one of his shoulder-boards askew with a jerk of his shoulders. As Tarjiaan reached to straighten it, Daanir caught his hand and said, "Jiaan, can you promise me one thing?"

"Anything."

"Don't hate me after this morning." He looked down, staring hard at their clasped hands. "Or at least try not to?"

"Don't—?" Tarjiaan stopped, then set the mug down on the bedside table. He raised his voice, "Logiri! I need to get ready!"

"I should go."

Tarjiaan caught Daanir's wrist as he drew away. "I promised you a long time ago that I would never, ever hate you." He focused on Daanir as Logiri hurried in. "The idea that you think that whatever is about to happen will change my mind about you scares me more than anything you've been trying so hard not to tell me."

"Don't let it." Daanir laughed and the sound was strained; he looked down at his wrist in Tarjiaan's hand and turned his hand to clasp the other man's forearm. "I... Jiaan, I just wanted to — I swore an oath I wouldn't say, but—"

"Mancer Royal!"

Daanir jerked like a fish on the line, turning to face the door as Ilaris came into view. "Good morning, Lord Ilaris, I was just telling—"

"You're needed in the audience chamber. Make your way there."

Daanir met Tarjiaan's eyes and squeezed his hand. "Nothing to be scared of. Don't worry. It's—"

"Lord Meranas," Ilaris spoke in a low voice. "Now."

"I don't like—"

"Daanir." Ilaris' voice took on a sharp edge.

Daanir looked at him and nodded. "I'm going, I'm going." He met Tarjiaan's eyes nervously. "You promised."

"I promised," Tarjiaan echoed. He watched as Daanir and Ilaris left, then surrendered to Logiri's ministrations. Before too long, he was trying not to fidget like a child as Logiri set the last few details straight on his formal uniform and settled Tarjiaan's rarely-worn circlet of rank on his brow. The two silver studs he wore in his right ear were polished, while the two gold studs he wore in his left ear were replaced by a pair of drops — one gold, the other pearl.

"There. Now you're presentable," Logiri said as he nodded to himself, a satisfied look on his face.

"Thank you, Logiri," Tarjiaan said absently. He set the chair into motion, hearing Logiri's footsteps behind him as they made their way through the too-quiet corridors to the audience chamber. The doors were closed, and there was no one waiting. Tarjiaan frowned slightly, drumming his fingers on the console of his chair, the wheels shifting ever-so-slightly as he did.

"My lord," Logiri cleared his throat. "Your chair is twitching."

Tarjiaan grimaced and took a deep breath, forcing himself to focus until the chair stilled. Then he looked at the closed doors to the audience chamber and murmured, "What is keeping them?" As if in answer, the door slid open slightly, and Daanir slipped through. Tarjiaan sat up straighter.

"He's ready for you." Daanir inhaled deeply and then let the heavy doors open to allow Tarjiaan a full view of the throne room. For a moment, Tarjiaan couldn't speak. Couldn't think. He looked up at Daanir, then back into the room.

"Logiri, you're dismissed," Tarjiaan said without turning around. He rolled into the room, then stopped in confusion as he tried to take in the number of machines surrounding the Coral Throne. Overwhelmed, he looked back at Daanir.

"How long?" he whispered.

"Longer than I've been here. I picked up where Riguaarin left off. I'd have told you—"

"That's enough, Mancer." Ilaris bowed to Tarjiaan and then rested a hand on Daanir's shoulder. "We'll leave you to your private audience."

"I'll tell you whatever you want to know. After." Daanir's gaze shifted to the floor as he headed out into the hall.

Before Ilaris could turn to follow Daanir, Tarjiaan cleared his throat, "Ilaris?"

"Highness?"

Tarjiaan nodded the way that Daanir had gone. "Do something about that ridiculous uniform. Unless there is someone who intends for the Mancer Royal to look so...disrespectful of the court and his office?" He looked up and caught the hint of embarrassment in Ilaris' face. Tarjiaan cleared his throat and continued, "Because if that's the case, I will take great exception to such a petty display. And to all those who cater to it." He turned back to the frail-looking figure who looked as if he was asleep on the throne, then looked back at the Lord Chamberlain. "I have spoken, Ilaris."

Ilaris inclined his head sharply, bowing as he backed out of the room.

Tarjiaan approached the throne slowly. This Coral Throne wasn't the true throne – that one had been left behind by necessity when Meradon had fled beneath the waves. Tarjiaan had been told that the true throne was massive, carved from a single piece of fossilized coral that had been discovered when they'd dug the foundations of the Palace Over The Sea. The throne aboard the *Chimaera* was a smaller scale copy: every whorl and wrinkle and pattern meticulously recreated in driftwood, signifying the promise that someday, the people of Meradon would return to their Palace and the true Coral Throne.

He stopped a measured distance from the Coral Throne, and for a strange, dreamlike moment he thought that no one was there, that the figure seated there was another carving out of driftwood that had been seated on the throne. Then the figure moved, his gnarled hands the same rough, stiff white of dead coral. His nails were too long, thick and curled, and his eyes were the color of night seas when they were covered by restless foam. Ikaanaji, the great Sea King, the man who had saved Meradon by leading his people from their beset nation to their sanctuary beneath the waves. For Tarjiaan's entire life, this man had been the center of Meradon, strong and just, adored by his people. To see him now...

The man who'd made that promise was as much a shadow of former glory as the copy of his throne.

Chapter Four
Surfacing

IKAANAJI OPENED HIS eyes, and it clearly took a moment before he noticed Tarjiaan in front of him. "Taarik?" He looked puzzled for a moment, then his brow smoothed. "Tarjiaan. It took you long enough," he chided, the laughter in his voice softening the rebuke.

Tarjiaan bowed from the waist, crossing his right arm over his chest in the royal salute. "I apologize, Sire," he said. "I was detained."

Ikaanaji's laugh deepened until he broke off in a cough. Once the cough quieted, he asked, "And just how many ships detained you this time, nephew?"

"Three, Uncle," Tarjiaan answered. "New ones. I've never seen their like before."

"Interesting. How did they get close enough to engage? Are you losing your edge, my nephew?" Ikaanaji shifted in his seat, gesturing, and the lights in the room brightened. Now Tarjiaan could clearly see the series of grand interconnected machines that rose like sentinels behind the throne; Tarjiaan noted how each of the king's smallest movements made the machines flex and flutter, lights flickering like a school of small fish in sunlight.

"They were flying Sualimani trade flags. They appear to know about our alliance...."

"Or they guessed."

Tarjiaan nodded. "Or they guessed. If that's the case, they have confirmation now."

Ikaanaji frowned. "Tell me the whole of it, nephew," he commanded.

Tarjiaan closed his eyes for a moment, ordering his thoughts. Then he began, "We had set course for the floating dockyards. My crew is tired, and my ship needs some repairs that the shipboard mancer and her team can't handle. There's a problem with the hydroponics—" Tarjiaan made himself stop and focus. The hydroponic problems had no bearing on this report. "Three days ago, we spied three ships moving to intercept. We changed course, they followed. We shortened sail to see if they would sail on or engage, and that was when we saw the Sualimani markings and the trade flag. There were a type of ship we'd never seen before. Smaller and faster than Imperial ships, and different lines. We had no idea they were actually Imperial until they attacked."

Ikaanaji was glowering before Tarjiaan finished his report. "How badly damaged is your ship? How many casualties?"

"The ship was not badly damaged. Mancer Ishantar says that she can put things to rights in a day or so, but she still needs a drydock," Tarjiaan answered. "Four men hurt, three dead. That was why I was delayed."

"You sent the men to the Deep?"

"Yes, Sire," Tarjiaan said. "And saw the wounded off to the crèche -ship."

"The crèche -ship of the royal pod, I am told," Ikaanaji added. "Where is your pod, Tarjiaan?"

"With the *Dauntless*. As I said, we were en route to the dockyards." Tarjiaan sat up a little straighter in his chair. "It is standard that when an above-ship goes to the dockyards, their support pod is reassigned, Sire."

Ikaanaji leaned back in his chair and closed his eyes again. "I understand why you fought, but this could not have come at a worse time."

"They came after me!" Tarjiaan protested. "All I did was defend my people!"

"Did I say that there was fault involved?" Ikaanaji snapped, his face growing red. There was a warning beep from one of the machines behind him, and he scowled and settled back into his chair. "Tarjiaan, I am dying." Tarjiaan shook his head, opening his mouth to protest and closing it again when Ikaanaji held his hand up. "Listen to me and do not interrupt. I've known for some time. I kept my illness secret so as not to alarm the people. But I cannot hide it any more. Now it is time, Tarjiaan, for you to fully take up your duties as my heir. I've given you what freedom I could, what leeway I could. I understand the... difficulty you have being below the waves. So I have made... arrangements. Before this year is out, you will take your place on the true Coral Throne in the Palace over the Sea."

"Uncle?" Tarjiaan couldn't have heard him right. "I'm sorry, but... how?"

The king looked at the viewing ports, then said, "Over the body of my uncle, your grandfather, I swore that the people of Meradon would again walk free under the sky. I will see this happen before I go to the Deep, and I will need your help and your cooperation."

Tarjiaan didn't hesitate. "Anything."

Ikaanaji smiled. "My loyal Prince-Captain, will you marry as I bid you?"

Marriage? Tarjiaan had always known that marriage for alliance was a possibility – his father had made it very clear that even the sixth prince was a prize in the marriage market. But after so many years, he'd stopped thinking about it. Especially since he had his own marriage plans.

But Daanir had refused to hear him. Told him to not speak of it.

He knew.

"Of course, Sire." Tarjiaan bowed to his King as he tried to steady himself. "I will marry as you bid me. But I don't understand. How will my marriage accomplish...." He stopped as a thought occurred to him. "Sire, you're not marrying me off to a Sualimani chieftess, are you?"

Ikaanaji laughed hard enough to set off the sensors on one of the machines. "No, Tarjiaan," he gasped as the bells and chimes softened. "No wild Sualimani chieftess will put a marital collar around your stubborn neck."

Tarjiaan felt his shoulders creep down from his ears. "That's a relief. Who, then?"

"She will be arriving shortly." Ikaanaji coughed roughly and the machines behind him began to flex and grind until he breathed normally again. "The *Chimaera* will rise to meet her."

Tarjiaan stared for a moment. "You're ordering the *Chimaera* to surface; Sire, is that wise?"

"There is no other choice."

Tarjiaan frowned. It was unheard of for the royal below-ship to rise above the waves for any reason. And arriving? Arriving from where? A Meradonese noble would arrive via submersible, not by above-ship. A cold chill ran down his spine. "Sire, what aren't you saying?"

Ikaanaji was quiet, leaving the only sound the hum-and-ping of the machinery. After a long, nerve-wracking silence, Ikaanaji spoke, and calmly shattered Tarjiaan's world.

"Jiaan?"

Tarjiaan didn't turn at the sound of Daanir's voice; he stared out the viewing portal at the dark water beyond, watching the Mancer's reflection in the glass. He had no idea how long it had been since he'd left the throne room and his uncle behind. He'd been grasping at shards, trying desperately to shore up the barriers that kept him from falling apart ever since Ikaanaji had told him of the plans and the treaty, and informed Tarjiaan of his new duties as heir to the Coral Throne. At first, Tarjiaan had argued, making his protest loudly known, but Ikaanaji had refused to be swayed. There was nothing to be done. The King's word was law. Before the sun set on the waves that night, Tarjiaan would be married for the good of Meradon.

Daanir stepped behind him, clearly waiting for Tarjiaan to say something. Tarjiaan tried to ignore him, but found that he couldn't. Finally, he forced himself to ask, "What else haven't you told me?"

In the reflection of the port window, he saw Daanir shift, looking down.

"I understand orders, Mancer Royal. You told me about your oath. I understand that you couldn't tell me." Tarjiaan gripped the console of his chair hard enough that his knuckles were white, trying not to lash out at Daanir. None of this was his fault. "Now I know. So I want to know what you know."

Daanir rubbed his hands together. "He's been ill for some time now. Wilaanger can't find a cause. It's a problem with the heart and lungs. Mostly the lungs. Riguaarin made the first breathing mechanism. I improved upon it. It seemed for a while like he might recover, or at least be able to live with continued assistance. Then he got worse, and Wilaanger says that the illness has gone too far." He stared at his oil-stained fingers, red-faced to his roots.

"And the rest?" Tarjiaan shook his head. "I've been thinking. Putting things together. You knew before I even got here that I wasn't going to be leaving the *Chimaera*. And you knew I was to be married."

"I knew that much," Daanir confirmed. "They wouldn't tell me the details – sensitive negotiations, they said; I wasn't supposed to know about it at all, but his Majesty let it slip while I was working on his support mechanisms. I thought... when you said you were going to be married, I thought I'd given it away. I wouldn't have kept it from you, Jiaan, but it was a direct order and...."

"That was why you took such care of my things, and why you stumbled over telling me about the consort's suite in my rooms. And why you told me not to speak of marriage."

Daanir grimaced, fiddling with the embroidery at his cuffs. "I'm sorry," he whispered.

"I understand." Tarjiaan looked away. "They're taking the royal ship above the waves. She's here, apparently."

"Oh." Daanir shifted awkwardly. "That was quicker than I expected."

"Apparently," Tarjiaan growled, "they didn't want to leave anything to chance. So they boxed me in – they have my armor, they have my ship, and I promised my uncle." Tarjiaan could hear the sharp edge in his voice and took a deep breath before meeting Daanir's eyes. "Congratulate me, Daanir. I'm to marry an Imperial princess."

Daanir choked on air, horrified. "What?"

Tarjiaan looked bleakly at Daanir. "The Tyracan Emperor's granddaughter. Or... or grandniece? Something. I forget the relationship. But my uncle sold me to the Emperor in exchange for a chance to walk on land before he dies."

"No, he couldn't!" Daanir sputtered.

Tarjiaan turned back towards the viewing portal, focusing not on the water outside, but on Daanir's reflection. "It was never his goal for Meradon to remain below the waves. He brought us here to save us from the Empire..."

"And now he's handing us all right over to the Emperor?" Daanir blurted out. "He... wait, he's actually making you *stay*? Permanently? You're not going back above?"

Tarjiaan looked back over his shoulder. "You didn't know about that?"

"No!" Daanir snapped. "I thought a few weeks at most."

Tarjiaan looked back out at the water. It was getting brighter. Changing color as they rose toward the light. "Uncle wishes for me to conduct the final treaty negotiations with the Tyracan ambassador. The talks will happen aboard the *Chimaera*. I tried to reason with him, but he won't change his mind. He did say that after the talks were over, I'd have more flexibility. But the talks are too important. I can't leave until they're done."

"That could take months," Daanir murmured. "Years. There's so much anger. So much blood muddying the waters. They just tried to kill you, Jiaan."

"Don't remind me. I'm trying very hard not to think about it." Tarjiaan looked at the reflection in the viewing port, seeing Daanir standing just behind his chair. His breath caught, and he studied his own reflection for a long moment before he covered his face with one hand.

"What is it?" Daanir asked, crouching down next to Tarjiaan's elbow.

"It's too big. My armor," Tarjiaan said, his voice strangled, feeling the panic rising. "It's too big to wear below. I can't... not here. Not below. I can't stand. I can't fight. Daan, I'm helpless down here."

"You're never helpless." Daanir turned quickly towards the door at the sound of voices in the corridor. He rested his hand on Tarjiaan's shoulder. "Let's get out of here, back to your rooms until you have to..." His voice trailed off. "I don't know about you, but I think I could really use a drink."

Tarjiaan nodded. He never drank anymore, except for one solemn occasion, but for this, he'd make an exception. It might steady him enough to actually go through with the wedding without screaming. But he also hadn't eaten anything except for a bite of toast, so he would have to limit himself to one drink. It was bad enough that he would have to meet his prospective bride while chair-bound. To meet her while drunk would shame the entire nation. He followed Daanir out of the room, both of them silent, and Tarjiaan was intensely aware of the different sounds of the royal ship around him. They would reach the surface soon. Then? His mind shied away from what would happen after. An Imperial princess. A woman of the people who had murdered his father and brother. The people who were responsible for putting him in this chair.

"You're quiet," Daanir said softly.

"Thinking," Tarjiaan answered. He looked up at Daanir, then saw a look of sheer panic cross the Mancer's face; Tarjiaan looked back down the corridor to see his sister coming towards them, her anger fairly scorching the air around her. Tarjiaan didn't even have to ask why — he stopped, pointed at her and snarled, "Not in the corridor!"

She froze, clearly caught off-guard by his reaction, then turned on her heel and stalked towards the door to Tarjiaan's suite.

"Mother Deep, the look on her face — do that again!" Daanir murmured. Tarjiaan fought the urge to laugh, setting his chair in motion and following Aanaji into his suite. The door slid closed behind him, and Tarjiaan glanced back to see Daanir standing ready at his left shoulder. His posture was familiar, his hands still but ready at his sides.

Battle stance. Daanir had fallen back into the patterns ingrained into him during the years that he'd fought as Tarjiaan's battle companion. The Mancer was expecting an attack, and was ready to defend Tarjiaan from any threat. That he was reacting to Aanaji as a serious physical threat disturbed Tarjiaan to the bone, but he shook it off and turned back to his sister, who looked as if she were about to burst into flames from sheer fury.

"You've heard," he said flatly.

"Of course I heard!" Aanaji shrilled. "How could you?"

"What makes you think I have any say in this at all?" Tarjiaan snapped back.

Aanaji folded her arms over her chest, "You're the heir. Of course you have a say!"

"I promise you, Aanaji, I don't," Tarjiaan said slowly. "All I knew was that Uncle asked me to wed as he bid me. He didn't even tell me who I was to wed until I'd agreed to do it."

"You should have refused!" Aanaji insisted. "You still can! Go to Uncle and tell him you won't! These people murdered our father, Tarjiaan! They murdered our brother! You can't possibly—"

"Use your head," Tarjiaan growled, frustrated to his core. To have spent years making a place for himself above the waves, building the image of the Sea Prince for his people so they'd see him as a worthy heir, only to be trapped in this way? And then for Aanaji, of all people, to accuse him of just... meekly submitting to this? Of giving up without a fight? Did she honestly think that if there had been a way out of it, he wouldn't have already pounced on it? "Our uncle wants to die on land. He made his bargain months ago and it's too late now. She's here. The *Chimaera* is rising to meet her ship. If I refuse, if I don't marry this woman, someone will have to take my place. And the only other candidate is Naajir..."

"No!" Aanaji gasped, rearing back as if Tarjiaan had stabbed her through the heart. "No, I forbid it! My son will not marry an Imperial whore! And neither will my brother!" She started towards the door. As she came close to Tarjiaan's chair, he reached out and grabbed her arm.

"No, Aanaji."

She tried to pull free from his grip. "You cannot do this, Tarjiaan. I won't have it. What would Father say, if he knew?"

"He'd say that no matter what, we must do our duty," Tarjiaan answered firmly.

Aanaji tugged once more against Tarjiaan's grip. He let her go, watching as she rubbed her wrist. "It's an insult," she snapped. "An abomination. To think you'd mingle your blood with that of an Imperial whore—"

"She's the Emperor's own kin, Aanaji. Either his granddaughter or grandniece. Which means her blood is every bit as good as yours—"

"How dare you!" Somehow, Tarjiaan never saw the blow incoming. It was hard enough to snap his head to the side; he gasped at the unexpected shock, then heard Aanaji squeal. He looked up in surprise to see Daanir in front of him, his big hands enveloping Aanaji's wrists, pushing her back and away from Tarjiaan.

Daanir said over his shoulder, "Wasn't fast enough. Are you hurt?"

"I'm fine," Tarjiaan answered, rubbing his jaw gingerly. "Aanaji, I think you should return to your quarters and stay there for the foreseeable future. Consider that an order from the heir. I was going to ask if you would come and see me wed, but now I think that would be a very bad idea."

Aanaji glared at him, trying to shove past Daanir, but he held her at bay until she backed towards the door.

Daanir grimaced. "Should I escort her ladyship to her quarters, Prince-Captain?"

"I don't think that will be necessary, Daan. She can find her own way. You stay."

"Oh, by all means, yes, stay, Mancer," Aanaji repeated, her voice cold and mocking. "You'll probably do more damage to this marriage than ever I could, just by breathing." She sniffed, glaring once at Tarjiaan before turning towards the door. "You realize that they probably plumbed the dregs of the Imperial blood to find someone willing to marry the Cripple of Meradon. Do you think they told her? Do you think she knows her future husband...."

"Enough!" Tarjiaan barked.

She smirked at him, her long skirts hissing as she swept from the room. Daanir closed the door in her wake and locked it. "I'm sorry," he said after a moment. "I should have–" He shook his head, abruptly launching himself away from the door as if he'd been fired from a rail-cannon. "I should pour those drinks."

"What?" Tarjiaan asked, watching Daanir's flight across the room, waiting until the Mancer turned, a glass in each hand.

"Here," he said as he passed one to Tarjiaan. "Jiaan, you remember how people would talk to me?"

Tarjiaan nodded. "Yes. They still do?"

Daanir nodded. He looked down at the glass in his hand, and Tarjiaan stared in shock as the Mancer drained the glass in a single swallow.

"Who taught you to drink like that?" Tarjiaan demanded. "You never could. You got sick."

Daanir looked at the empty glass. "I learned. It was... something to do." He coughed, then met Tarjiaan's eyes. "Riguaarin talked to me. And he drank. Maybe too much. But he told me what she'd been doing. Your sister has petitioned to have you removed as heir, Tarjiaan. The petitions arrive like clockwork, every year since... since the *Marauder*."

"She what?" Tarjiaan gasped. "She wouldn't!"

"She did," Daanir said quietly. "I heard whispers of it from one of her maids, and got the rest from Riguaarin while he was in his cups. I don't know why — she can't hold the Throne. Her son is already your heir, and she wouldn't be Regent. There's no reason."

"I wish I could say I was surprised." Tarjiaan studied his drink for a moment. He shouldn't. It would be all too easy to start again, and so much harder to stop. He shouldn't, but... he closed his eyes and drained half of the glass into his courage. "It flows along the same currents as... as how she treated me..." He bit his lip before he said anything else. He could feel the sharp edges of panic, cutting the surface like sharks, slicing through his defenses. He drained the rest of his glass, looked up and saw Daanir staring at him.

"She was banished. I knew that. But I didn't know why," he said quietly. "Jiaan, what did she do?"

Tarjiaan shook his head. "Not now, Daan. Not..."

Daanir looked stunned. "It was that bad?"

Tarjiaan shook his head. There was too much on the line in the present moment to go diving into the past. "It's too deep of a tale and I don't have the time." Silently, he added, *If I tell you now, I'm not leaving this room or that bottle.* He coughed and changed the subject. "Tell me, how did my uncle take these demands?"

Daanir scowled into his empty glass. "Riguaarin said that the last time, she was barred from ever making a petition again, and nearly banned from the royal presence again," Daanir answered. "That was maybe four months ago."

"That recent? The plans and his treaty were already underway. I'm surprised she doesn't time it to the anniversary. That's her level of drama." Tarjiaan ran one finger around the rim of his empty glass. Another drink would be good. And bad. He set the glass down firmly on the closest table. "Let me guess what happened after Uncle banned her from his presence. She started to take it out on her servants. On anyone she could get away with tormenting. On you."

Daanir shrugged, taking a deep breath. "She's not kind, that's for sure. But she never was." He held his arms wide. "This ridiculous rig doesn't matter. It makes it easier for her to deal with the fact that I wear it in the first place. And she knows now that if she abuses any more of her servants, I'll find out and it won't go well."

Tarjiaan blinked, then started laughing. "You didn't! You threatened my sister?"

"No." He looked sidelong at Tarjiaan. "I just reminded her that she doesn't know how anything works. Including the oxygen gauge."

"Daanir, you are insane!"

"You just now realized that?" Daanir asked wryly.

Tarjiaan leaned back, studying the panels on the ceiling as Daanir went to make himself another drink.

"I should have been there for you," Daanir said quietly. When Tarjiaan looked, Daanir was facing away from him. "Today. And before. I was supposed to protect you. I couldn't get back to you, and I had no idea if you even wanted me to, or if you were alive. I couldn't get any information. When I was reassigned to the dockyards. I could crack the systems to get some information, but I didn't have the right permissions, so I had to be careful. But that's when I found out you were above the waves, and that's when I started working on the designs for the *Wave Runner*. When I got here, I lost all my access. Anything to do with you is for the King's eyes only. I..." He paused, then sighed. "I would have said yes. I thought we would have time." He swore under his breath. "I always think we'll have more time."

Before Tarjiaan could ask what Daanir meant, he heard a hiss and click, then the air coming through the vents took on a salt tang that he knew all too well.

The *Chimaera* had surfaced.

Chapter Five
Meeting

A FEW MINUTES AFTER the *Chimaera* surfaced, there was a knock on Tarjiaan's door, and Logiri entered. "Prince-Captain, you are wanted in the audience chamber," he began, then looked closely at Tarjiaan. "What happened?" he demanded, his voice cold. He glanced at Daanir, and Tarjiaan saw the murder in his eyes.

"Easy, Logiri," Tarjiaan murmured. "It wasn't him. Ilaris didn't properly introduce you, did he?" He gestured to Daanir. "Daanir was my battle companion before he became a Mancer. Daan, Logiri's been with me for ten years now. He hasn't killed me yet."

Logiri snickered at the old joke as his temper faded away. "Ah. Yes. You have told me about him. A man to be trusted in all things." He bowed. "I'm honored to properly meet the Mancer Royal."

Daanir gestured for him to rise, looking uncomfortable. "I appreciate you taking care of him, Logiri," he said. "And not killing him. How soon do you need him in the audience chamber?"

"Soon." Logiri turned his attention back to Tarjiaan.

"To answer your next question," Tarjiaan said, "this was courtesy of my sister. Is it that obvious?" Tarjiaan asked, looking over at Daanir. "How bad is it?"

Daanir cocked his head to one side, looking at Tarjiaan with such frank regard that Tarjiaan had to force himself not to look away. Daanir finally answered, "Looks like you got slapped by someone wearing a ring. It'll fade."

"It would hardly do for you to go to your wedding looking as if you'd been in a brawl," Logiri said. "Let me make you presentable."

Tarjiaan sat still as Logiri fussed around him, then cleared his throat, "Logiri, tell me about Tyracan wedding practices. What should I expect?"

Logiri hummed softly, then asked, "How old is the girl?"

"I don't know," Tarjiaan admitted. "Daan, have you heard anything?"

"That information never sailed past me." Daanir shook his head. "All I knew was that there was a marriage for alliance. No one told me any details."

Logiri nodded, his nimble fingers brushing over the braid on Tarjiaan's shoulder. "If she's anything older than fifteen, Captain, her very presence here is an insult."

"Fifteen?" Tarjiaan's stomach dropped. "Logiri, I can't marry a child!"

"If she is that young, I'm certain your uncle would not allow the match," Logiri answered. "But if she is older, she would be considered too old for a royal bride in the Empire. Shall we?"

Tarjiaan nodded once and set his chair rolling, Daanir and Logiri falling in behind him. A hand settled on his left shoulder, and Tarjiaan looked up to see Daanir staring fixedly ahead. He reached up and covered Daanir's hand with his own; a weary smile crossed the Mancer's face.

"Ah, there you are, Mancer Royal." Ilaris appeared in the corridor ahead of them; Daanir's hand immediately fell from Tarjiaan's shoulder, and the Lord Chamberlain made no sign of noticing. "His Majesty wishes you to be a presentable member of the welcoming party. Come with me."

"Ah..." Daanir looked down. "Of course. Prince-Captain?"

"Go ahead." Tarjiaan watched Daanir follow Ilaris out of sight, then entered the audience chamber. Ikaanaji was being attended by the Physician Royal, a rotund man whom Tarjiaan had known practically forever, and who had once been the Sea King's own battle companion; Wilaanger glanced at him as he brought his chair to a stop, nodded once, then went back to examining a small machine sitting on a table next to the Coral Throne.

"And this will do everything that your larger apparatus does?" Wilaanger asked, sounding doubtful.

"So claims the Mancer Royal," Ikaanaji answered. "Where is he, by the way? Ilaris!" He frowned at Tarjiaan. "Fighting again, my nephew?"

"A disagreement, Uncle. With my sister," Tarjiaan answered.

"That will never do. Wil, see to him?" Ikaanaji waved towards Tarjiaan.

"Thank you. To answer your question, Ilaris took the Mancer Royal off somewhere, Uncle," Tarjiaan said.

Ikaanaji gestured to a servant. "Tell them to hurry," he said, tipping his head back against the Throne as the young man hurried out of the throne room.

Wilaanger shook his head and gestured to a small table near the wall. Tarjiaan followed him. "And they're where?" Wilaanger asked.

"A new uniform for the Mancer Royal, I think," Tarjiaan answered.

Wilaanger nodded. "Your doing?"

"I might have said something." Tarjiaan glanced toward the throne. "My uncle didn't notice?"

"We've tried to keep the worst of your sister's tantrums from him," Wilaanger murmured softly, touching Tarjiaan's cheek. "She provokes him, and her disrespect angers him to the point that his illness grows worse. After the last time, the Mancer Royal and I have been trying to keep her in line."

"That ridiculous rig is in line?"

Wilaanger snorted. "It was a minor tantrum, and not worth the fight, according to Lord Meranas. I think he actually convinced the King that he prefers it. She broke the skin here," he added, tilting Tarjiaan's face toward the light. "It won't need much, but let me clean it, just to be safe." He took out a bottle and a cloth pad from his medical bag. "I wish I could be there to see you wed, Jiaan. You know I look at you like you were my own. Taarik would be so proud."

Tarjiaan smiled, letting the shelter of Wilaanger's unwavering support and affection settle into wounds that still had yet to heal. If he had no one else, he had Wilaanger, and it helped. "Thank you, Wil," he murmured, feeling his cheek growing warmer, then slowly cooling as Wilaanger gently dabbed astringent on the cut. "I wish you could be there, too. What do you know about this girl I'm to marry? Logiri says that marrying age in the Empire is—"

"Obscenely young?" Wilaanger offered. "Yes, it is. We specified that any candidates be no younger than seventeen. The young lady is, I believe, only a few weeks short of being eighteen."

"I'm twice her age, almost." Tarjiaan grimaced. "Wilaanger–"

"That is an insult to our Prince," Logiri insisted. "She's sure to no longer be a maid, at that age."

"It's been sworn in writing that if she is not, that the marriage will be deemed non-binding and the treaty will still be enforced," Ikaanaji said, raising his voice. Tarjiaan blinked in surprise, and heard his uncle laugh. "I may be dying, but there is nothing wrong with my ears, nephew. A mistake your sister makes often. Wil, you haven't kept anything from me. In truth, it's been amusing watching you and the Mancer Royal try. I am fully aware of the insubordination in my court. Now, where in the Deep is my Mancer? We cannot leave the emissary waiting."

"Here, Your Majesty," Daanir called out, hurrying into the room. As he passed by, Tarjiaan could see that Daanir was still buttoning his coat. The new uniform fit him perfectly, the dark green coat dramatically accentuating his pale hair and skin. There had been a time when a new suit on his battle companion would have been cause for a stolen hour or two of thorough private inspection. But those days were gone, and Tarjiaan forced himself away from those memories as Daanir picked up the small machine and whispered something to the inner workings. The machines all fell still, and the silence of the throne room was deafening. Daanir finally nodded and looked to the Coral Throne. "She's prepared. Are you ready, Your Majesty?"

"And you are certain this will work?" Wilaanger asked.

"It will work," Daanir said firmly. "Every test has gone perfectly. We'll have three, maybe four hours away from the main support systems, and no one will be able to tell that His Majesty is wearing it."

"Let's begin," Ikaanaji said, shifting forward in the throne. Wilaanger left Tarjiaan's side, and Tarjiaan watched as the Physician and the Mancer released his uncle from the machines that kept him alive, and applied the smaller machine, hiding it neatly beneath Ikaanaji's cloak of state. The Sea King rose to his feet, wavered for a moment, then took a long breath and smiled.

"Well done, Mancer," he said. "It's been too long since I last walked the halls of Meradon. Shall we?"

In all his years at sea, Tarjiaan had never seen the royal ship above the waves, and he was surprised to see that there was actually a deck where they would meet with the Imperial party. As they came out under the wide-open sky, Tarjiaan took a long breath and felt the tension in his shoulders release slightly. He closed his eyes and slowly resettled his foundations and rebuilt his facade. Outside. He was outside.

A small voice whispered in his mind: *For now.*

He opened his eyes and stifled a shudder at the sight of an Imperial ship anchored close enough to the *Chimaera* that they could have thrown rocks at each other with a decent chance of actually hitting something. As he watched, a small launch started towards the *Chimaera*, bearing six men wearing Imperial livery, a single man in black, one dark-skinned man whose robes had an almost ridiculous amount of ruffles, and a small figure swathed in saffron-yellow veils, barely visible among the men.

"She's tiny. Are we certain she's old enough?" he murmured, turning slightly towards Ikaanaji.

The Sea King snorted once. "You're sailing in circles. She's old enough," he answered. Then, softer, "She'd better be."

That did nothing to ease Tarjiaan's mind, and he struggled to keep control of himself. Facing an Imperial ship while chair-bound? He had nightmares about this. But he had to be the Sea Prince. Which meant he had to be steady. Loss of control translated into random movements of his chair, and having the chair careening all over the deck would do nothing to further negotiations, and might just end him up in the water.

"Calm yourself," Ikaanaji scolded, and Tarjiaan tried not to flinch. Was he that obvious? "They come in peace, nephew."

"With Imps, that phrase is usually followed by 'shoot to kill,'" Daanir whispered.

Tarjiaan heard Ikaanaji snort, and looked up to see his uncle's lips twitching before he resumed his solemn expression. Tarjiaan bit his lip to keep from laughing – there was a time and a place for gallows humor and it wasn't when an Imperial launch was docking the *Chimaera*. He could see clearly now how small the veiled figure was in comparison to the men around her.

Tarjiaan glanced up. "Uncle, what are my alternatives?"

Ikaanaji looked down at him. "You gave your word, Prince-Captain."

"And I will honor that, Uncle. I'm just thinking. If the girl is too young, or if she is unwilling...."

"Ah. I see," Ikaanaji acknowledged. "Do you have any thoughts?"

"If the girl is too young, I could adopt her," Tarjiaan suggested.

"A generous thought." Ikaanaji nodded, but the gesture seemed more sudden than normal. Tarjiaan wondered if perhaps the disease that was killing him was causing him to develop tics. His uncle continued, seemingly without noticing his own movement, "And if she is unwilling?"

"I would make her the offer, the same as I would any other who came to us from the Empire," Tarjiaan answered. "But I will not wed an unwilling girl, Uncle."

"Nor would I expect you to," Ikaanaji said. "But if that is the case, then this must be handled delicately. Do you think yourself capable?"

Tarjiaan coughed, startled. "Me, Uncle? I'm no diplomat, and I have no experience with this sort of thing. I thought perhaps Ilaris..."

"These negotiations are for you to do, Tarjiaan," Ikaanaji said, in a voice that allowed for no arguments. "You must be the one who lays the groundwork for this treaty. The Empire must see you as a worthy successor to me."

Tarjiaan straightened a little in his chair, but his fragile control slipped; his chair veered slightly away from Ikaanaji. Tarjiaan cursed silently and stilled the machine, bringing it back into line. Behind him, he heard Daanir clear his throat, and looked up to see the Imperial party crossing onto the *Chimaera*. The man in black approached; he looked as if he might have been old enough to be Tarjiaan's father, and was so nondescript, so completely *ordinary* that all Tarjiaan would have been able to say for certain when describing him was *brown-brown-and-brown*. He looked up at Ikaanaji and folded his hands.

"Do I have the honor of addressing His Majesty Ikaanaji Meranas?" he asked. He glanced at Tarjiaan, then looked again, clearly caught off-guard. He was silent for a moment, then continued, "And... His Highness Prince-Captain Tarjiaan Meranas?" His eyes flicked past Tarjiaan — probably at Daanir, Tarjiaan thought. What an odd thought, that Daan looked more like what an Imperial emissary expected from the heir to the Coral Throne than the heir himself. The emissary had a slight Imperial accent, and Tarjiaan realized that he'd never asked if his bride-to-be spoke anything other than the Imperial tongue.

"You do," Ikaanaji answered. "On behalf of the Kingdom of Meradon, we welcome you." He rested his hand on Tarjiaan's shoulder, and Tarjiaan saw the other man's eyes widen. So, Aanaji was wrong — the Empire didn't know the truth about him. An odd thought occurred to Tarjiaan: was the only person who called him the Cripple of Meradon his own sister?

"Thank you, Your Majesty. I am Rathsafa, and I have been authorized by His Imperial Majesty Gondarishan to speak for him in these talks, and to witness the marriage of a daughter of the royal line to your nephew." He gestured to the man in ruffles. "This is the High Priest of the Royal House. He will perform the ceremony. If we might proceed?"

"Now?" Tarjiaan blurted in shock. "You expect this wedding to happen right now?"

The emissary drew himself up, his olive skin flushing in indignation. For a moment, he seemed to be searching for the words, before slowly saying, "The ceremony must happen now. There can be no delay, or the Princess will be dishonored and shamed before our Empire."

"Tarjiaan—"

Tarjiaan urged his chair forward a few feet, hearing his uncle's warning behind him. He knew he was out of his depth. Fighting?

That he knew. Talking? He was adrift. He wanted to look to his uncle for approval or assistance, but he couldn't. The King had his expectations, as did the Empire. Tarjiaan raised one empty hand, palm to the sky, an Imperial gesture honoring their gods of Sun and Sand. "I have no objections to the ceremony. And no wish to shame the Princess. But in Meradon, marriages are a meeting of like minds, with agreement on both parts. So I would see the face of my bride-to-be before we wed. I would hear from her own lips that she consents to this bond." He looked past the emissary to the veiled woman, wondering how she could see anything through the opaque material. Standing, the girl was barely taller than Tarjiaan was seated in his chair. "My lords, I understand your ways are different. But a meeting here, in front of your own men, whose honor I would not dream of impugning, in front of your High Priest, and in front of the King and the most trusted members of his court? Surely under these conditions, it would be acceptable to make an exception? In the interests of peace?"

Behind the emissary, the priest nodded thoughtfully and said something in Imperial. The emissary replied, and they had a brief back and forth, too fast for Tarjiaan to follow. Whatever was said, it appeared that the priest agreed with Tarjiaan — Rathsafa beckoned the girl forward. The girl joined them, taking small, hesitant steps. She asked a soft question, and the emissary answered her. She took another step forward, and slowly raised the veil, revealing the form underneath. Seeing her, Tarjiaan had a hard time believing that she was as old as seventeen. Her clothing was tight cut to her body, restricting her movements while showing every slight curve. She did not raise her eyes, and all Tarjiaan could really see of her face was her forehead and the tip of her nose. Her skin was much darker than the emissary's own, and Tarjiaan wondered if his information on the Empire was faulty. He hadn't known that any of the Sualimani tribes were loyal to the Empire, or that one of their number had married into the royal house. He was distracted by movement, and watched as the girl clenched her hands in front of her body. That was when Tarjiaan realized that she was completely terrified.

She wasn't the only one.

Tarjiaan rested his hands on the carapace of his chair and spoke in hesitant Imperial, "My lady? Will you look at me?" She caught her breath and shook her head. "May I at least know your name?"

From his angle, Tarjiaan saw a flicker of pink, her tongue flashing out to her upper lip quickly before she answered, "I am Gondanikaranthia."

Gonda was the familial name, and her given name followed that. "Nikaranthia," Tarjiaan repeated. "Forgive me if I ask you to remind me more than once over the next day or so? Imperial names... I apologize, but I have trouble remembering names of more than three syllables."

As he hoped, she giggled. He ducked his head, trying to see her face. "Will you look at me now, my lady?"

"Nikaranthia," she repeated. Tarjiaan heard what he hoped was humor in her voice, but still she would not meet his gaze.

"Do you understand the common tongue, Nikaranthia?" he asked. "Did you hear what I said?"

She answered him in accented Common, "I understand."

"And I would hear from your own lips, my lady. Do you consent to this union?" Tarjiaan asked. He held out a hand for her. "If you do not wish to marry me—"

The priest snapped something in Imperial, and a guard jumped forward. He grabbed the girl by the arm, pulling her away from Tarjiaan; she yelped, clearly caught off guard, stumbling and nearly falling as the guard pulled her after him.

"My lord!" Tarjiaan started to raise his voice, and stopped when he clearly heard the girl moan. What she said was lost in the sea winds, but the meaning was clear — the guard was hurting her.

Tarjiaan reacted without thinking, drawing the force-pistol he kept hidden inside the arm of his chair and aiming it at the offending guard.

"Let her go!" he snapped. The world narrowed, and all he saw was the Imp who released the girl's arm and turned, his face going ashen.

"This? This is the honor of Meradon?" the emissary demanded in Common.

"In Meradon, we do not manhandle our women," Tarjiaan said evenly. "We allow them the right to refuse a match, or consent to one. And you, my lord, are in Meradon now. I will not allow anyone to harm an innocent. If I am in the wrong, then that is on me, and I apologize. But my lady Nikaranthia did nothing, and I will not allow her to be harmed."

Rathsafa drew himself up, looking as if he was about to say something. Then he stopped, startled; before Tarjiaan could turn to see what was causing that reaction, a small hand closed over his, forcing the pistol down.

"Please, not for me," she murmured. "You asked. I will answer. Yes, I will marry you. That is why I have come. That is my purpose, though I did not know of it until last night."

"You didn't know?" Tarjiaan asked, turning to look at her. To his surprise, she looked him in the face, revealing fine features and wide golden eyes. She would have been lovely if she hadn't been so frightened. "You have a choice, Nikaranthia. You can say no."

"I will honor my word, my lord," she said firmly. Her lips twitched, and she whispered softly, "Even if you cannot say my name properly."

Tarjiaan blinked in surprise, then smiled and slipped the pistol back into its hidden holster. He looked up at her again, noticing that she was still shivering. "Are you frightened, Nikaranthia?" he asked.

"Yes, my lord." she answered, the amusement leaving her face.

"Of me?" Tarjiaan wasn't sure he wanted to know. She bit her lip, then nodded. Tarjiaan took her hand, marveling at the fine bones in her fingers. "Are you certain that you still wish to marry me?" he asked.

"Yes, my lord." She darted a quick look at him. "Are you?"

Tarjiaan smiled, raising her hand to his lips and gently kissing her fingers. "I think we may suit each other. Now, your priest is about to have apoplexy," he murmured, for her ears alone. "Best if you go back and prepare." He let her hand fall and turned towards Ikaanaji. "Sire," he said. "I am satisfied that the lady is willing to marry me."

"Very good," Ikaanaji said, his voice clipped. Annoyed? Probably. "Then we shall prepare for the ceremony."

"If this unseemly display is complete." Rathsafa glanced at the priest, then continued, "My orders are for the ceremony to proceed immediately, so that negotiations might begin as soon as possible."

"I've no objections, Uncle," Tarjiaan said. "Save only... a delay of an hour? Time for the lady to rest and prepare herself?"

The priest nodded, and Rathsafa answered for him, "One hour is acceptable."

"And perhaps you would entertain a change of venue?" Tarjiaan continued. "One hour, and the wedding to be held there." He pointed towards the *Wave Runner*, clearly visible in the distance.

"Nephew, a word?" Ikaanaji said firmly.

Tarjiaan joined his uncle near the rear of the deck for a measure of privacy. He was fairly certain that he stretched the bonds of diplomacy to near breaking, and that his uncle was annoyed with him. But he'd warned the King that he was no diplomat. "Yes, Uncle?" he asked. Ikaanaji looked at him, and Tarjiaan realized that his uncle wasn't just annoyed.

He was furious.

"You drew your weapon," the King growled. "It's only by the blessing of the Great Mothers that you didn't destroy this entire endeavor in that one action."

"I told you I'm not a diplomat." Tarjiaan met his uncle's gaze. "Honestly, Uncle, do you think I'm going to let anyone hurt an innocent?"

Ikaanaji scowled and changed the subject. "And moving to your ship? Why?"

Tarjiaan glanced at the Tyracan ship off the starboard bow. "That ship bears thirty guns, easily. I won't rest easy until the royal ship is safe under the waves again. Even a hundred guns can't stand against the *Wave Runner*."

"Such a suspicious mind, my nephew," Ikaanaji chided. "This is a peace delegation."

"I may be suspicious, but I have cause. I know our history. I know that this entire war started with a so-called peace delegation and a marriage bid that ended in an assassination. I don't understand why you're trusting them so easily, but I'd rather err on the side of caution." He paused, and words he didn't mean to say fell out. "And truth be told, if I am to marry at your bidding, and marry a woman of the Empire at that, I would prefer to do so without also being trapped in this damned chair!"

"Tarjiaan!" Ikaanaji looked shocked at the vehemence of Tarjiaan's answer. In truth, Tarjiaan was surprised at his own words. Perhaps one drink had been one too many. He looked up at Ikaanaji, and saw Daanir, standing just beyond, his face as still as glass, looking out at the sea. Not looking at Tarjiaan at all.

As bad as this was for Tarjiaan, how much worse was it for Daanir, knowing that Tarjiaan still loved him. Had wanted to marry him. And was now marrying another.

"I apologize, Uncle," he said softly. Silently, he added, *I'm sorry, Daan.*

"Do not apologize for being honest with me, Jiaan," Ikaanaji said. "And I apologize." He paused. "We'll discuss this more later."

"Yes, Uncle." He nodded toward the Imperials. "They're waiting."

Ikaanaji cleared his throat and looked past Tarjiaan towards the emissary. "Lord Rathsafa, we will meet again in an hour aboard the *Wave Runner.*"

"As you wish, Your Highness," Rathsafa answered. Tarjiaan turned to see him escorting Nikaranthia back towards the launch.

"She's quite lovely, Tarjiaan," Ikaanaji murmured.

"I can't even imagine the stories she's been told about me," Tarjiaan answered.

"You'll prove them wrong, Jiaan," Daanir said, his voice rough. "She'll see."

"I hope so," Tarjiaan answered. Then he groaned. "Assuming I survive after I tell Marikaar that he has an hour to prepare a ship that just came out of a fight for a royal wedding."

Chapter Six
Preparations

"YOU SHOULD HAVE LET me come with you," Logiri muttered. "I could have pointed out every insult from the moment they arrived. Now you're committed, and they're laughing at you."

Tarjiaan stared fixedly forward while Logiri circled him, fussing and muttering, brushing non-existent lint from sleeves that he'd already brushed before even allowing Tarjiaan to put on the coat. He'd told Logiri about the meeting once he'd returned to his quarters on the *Chimaera*, and his aide had nearly exploded from indignation. Now on board the *Wave Runner*, with mere minutes to go before the wedding, Logiri still hadn't lost any steam. His tirade wasn't doing anything to calm Tarjiaan's nerves.

"You're not helping, you know," Tarjiaan finally said, taking the clothing brush from Logiri and tossing it onto the bed. "And having you with me would have been a disaster. If they'd realized you were Tyracan, they'd have arrested you as a traitor. I'm trying to stop a war, not start a new one."

"If the King is determined to go through with this despite the insults, then we can't give them any excuse to walk away. Everything has to be perfect," Logiri insisted.

"I think you may have taken this coat as close to perfection as it will ever get, Logiri. I also think you're more nervous than I am. Which I didn't think was possible, and which is also not helping." Tarjiaan looked down at himself, at the armor that Logiri had polished until it gleamed, at the spotless coat, at the jeweled hilt of his seldom-worn dress saber. He ran his hands down his chest and took a long breath. He could do this. "Now, tell me again," he demanded.

"The ceremony will not be very long," Logiri said. "It will be in Old Tyracan — what they call High Imperial now, because that is the language of the priests. He may repeat it in modern Imperial, but I doubt it. They want you off balance." He paused, then cleared his throat. "For a royal wedding, they may insist on a public display to prove her purity."

"A public..." Tarjiaan repeated before the words suddenly made sense. "They expect me to bed her in public?" he gasped. "Why didn't you say that before?"

"I only just thought of it," Logiri admitted. "I can't remember when it was last done – it's archaic, but it is still technically the law. Given how every little bit of this farce has been engineered as an insult to you and the Coral Throne, it is entirely possible that they will try and enforce it, if only for the humiliation factor." He scowled. "And that they're insisting on the wedding before the alliance is even sealed... it makes no sense! This is all an insult!"

"Since you've only told me that four times in the submersible, and seven... no, wait. Eight times since we came on board, yes, I know that," Tarjiaan said, turning to look in a mirror. His hair had been combed out of his usual queue, and it and his beard had been trimmed. With the gold circlet shining on his brow and the gold and pearl drops in his ear, he very much looked the part of the Sea Prince, but he had never felt more adrift. "It's not an insult if I don't accept it as such. They probably expected me to send her back in shame, and give them an excuse for another fifty years of war. Which I won't do. And I asked my Uncle why they were insisting on the wedding immediately. He says it's part of the treaty – he said that the Imperials insisted that the wedding precede the negotiations as a show of good faith."

"Because you're stopping a war, not starting a new one," Logiri repeated. "Besides, a rejected bride has no recourse in the Empire. She has no status, no honor. Her family is humiliated. Some kill themselves, to atone for their shame."

"All the more reason to welcome her in Meradon," Tarjiaan said firmly. "I'm sure that once she sees I'm not going to make a wine goblet out of her skull, she'll open up. She seems to have a spine."

"That is probably why she's unwed," Logiri asserted with a sniff. "It will take some time for her and her maids to adjust, I think..."

"Maids?" Tarjiaan shook his head. "Logiri, when they brought her over to meet me, she was the only woman there."

Logiri gaped at him, his mouth opening and closing like a fish. "You didn't tell me that!" he exclaimed. "A noble bride must be attended by at least one maid to preserve her honor. For a princess of her rank, there should be three. At least three. For her to be here without attendants...." His voice trailed off, and he shook his head. His meaning was clear — if she had no attendants, she had no honor to preserve.

"We'll find out where the other girls are," Tarjiaan said. "Logiri, will you step out for a moment? See what the status is. And stay out of sight of them, if you can. I need a moment."

Logiri bowed and left, leaving Tarjiaan in front of the crimson-framed painting on the wall: a portrait painted a lifetime ago – his father, his brother and himself. He wondered what his father would say. He wondered what Aaranji would think of the girl. If they'd forgive him for following orders. If his sister was to be believed, no. He heard a knock on the door behind him, and didn't turn to look, expecting that it was someone who had come to summon him to the ceremony.

Instead, he heard hesitant footsteps that stopped just behind him, then Daanir's voice. "You look so much like Captain Taarik," he murmured. "More like him than Aaranji ever did."

"Aaranji never got to be as old as I am now," Tarjiaan said softly. "Father always said I looked more like Mother."

"Did he?" Daanir leaned against Tarjiaan's back, and Tarjiaan caught the scent of burnt oil. "Maybe you did when you were younger."

"How would you know that? She died long before I met you," Tarjiaan said. "I was six. Seven, maybe. I barely remember her myself."

"I met her once. I was probably about six."

Tarjiaan looked over his shoulder, feeling Daanir's hair brushing against his beard. "You never told me that!"

Daanir shrugged. "I didn't know who she was until just recently. You didn't keep pictures of her around and the Captain never talked about her. Neither did Ranji. There was the figurehead on the *Marauder*, but I never really got a good look at it. You couldn't see it properly from the deck. But the King has portraits of everyone in your family. I saw one in his quarters, and Ilaris told me who she was. She came to the crèche ship once and sat with a bunch of us. She told us stories about living on land as a little girl, about how we'd all live on land someday. I don't think anyone believed her."

"But you did."

"Yeah, I did. Had to. She believed it so much, and I wanted to believe it, too. She let me hug her before she left, and she promised to come back and visit with us again, but she never did."

"Daan, that was probably right before she died." Tarjiaan sighed and rubbed his forehead. "Why do you have more memories of my mother than I do?"

"Maybe because I'm holding them for you? You always did say I was the other half of your brain," Daanir said with a chuckle. It sounded strained to Tarjiaan's ears, and was followed by a long sigh as Daanir slid his arms around Tarjiaan's waist, resting his forehead on Tarjiaan's shoulder.

"What are we going to do?" Tarjiaan asked in a low voice.

Daanir's answer was muffled, "You're going to get married. I have no idea what I'm going to do." He sighed. "I wish you hadn't told me what you planned to ask. It was easier, before, thinking you'd — I don't know. It doesn't matter now."

Tarjiaan swallowed. "I didn't know what they had planned. I wish it were different. I wish it were you."

"But it isn't."

"But it isn't." He turned in the circle of Daanir's arms, took his face in his hands, kissing him gently. "I will do my duty and you'll do yours. That's all that we can do. And you'll know that I love you. I have always loved you. That won't change." That was the truth. It hadn't changed. Despite the years, despite everything. Taking a wife wouldn't change it either.

Daanir took a shaky breath. "I love you, too. I just don't — I mean... I always expected you were going to have to marry someday for politics." The clock on the wall whined plaintively; Daanir looked at it and it went silent. "I always knew I'd have to watch you swear to someone else. I didn't expect it to hurt this much."

"You don't have to be there," Tarjiaan said softly. "Ishantar is working on the damage below-decks, and there are some problems in hydroponics. Go, with my blessing."

Daanir looked away, and for a moment, Tarjiaan was certain that he was going to object, going to insist on being at Tarjiaan's left, in the place that had always belonged to him. Would always belong to him. But he didn't. Instead, he sighed, looking back at Tarjiaan, yet refusing to meet his eyes. "I'm sorry, Jiaan," he murmured as he left; Tarjiaan had the oddest feeling that Daanir was running from him. Before Tarjiaan could follow, before he could stop him, Logiri appeared in the open doorway.

"Prince-Captain, it's time," he said.

The small group of Imperial guards standing near the mainmast laughed amongst themselves as Tarjiaan emerged onto the deck. He ignored them, looking around for saffron-yellow veils. Marikaar joined him, saluting as he approached.

"Prince-Captain." Marikaar stopped in front of him. He nodded once. "Logiri outdid himself. You clean up very well."

"Very funny." He looked around again. "Did everything arrive in time?

"Supplies from the royal pod got here three-quarters of an hour ago. We're almost ready. Stall, if you can."

Tarjiaan chuckled. "I don't think I can stall anymore. Where is she?"

"In the forecastle, with the priest." Marikaar lowered his voice. "I saw Logiri. He said you wanted him out of sight. And he said that she should have had women with her. She doesn't. So she is preparing for the wedding with the help of the officiant."

"We couldn't provide a woman to help?" Tarjiaan asked.

"Mancer Ishantar offered," he said. "She came above when the emissary brought the girl on board, and she says that she is certain that your bride has some Sualimani blood. She volunteered to assist in the wedding preparations, but they refused."

"Ishantar thinks so? I thought the same thing. I wonder how that particular match came about. Unless things have changed drastically on land?"

"You can ask the girl later," Marikaar said. "I should go and make sure things are ready." He saluted, then walked away from the crowd. Tarjiaan turned his attention back to the Imperial guards. The sight of them almost made him laugh aloud. When he'd come out of his cabin, they'd been facing each other, talking about something. Now, every single one of them was watching Tarjiaan, all of them wearing looks of wary alarm. Apparently, they were expecting Tarjiaan to attack at any moment. He needed to smooth the waters. He smiled and made his way towards them, watching as faces went slack and hands started to move towards saber hilts.

"Gentlemen," Tarjiaan said in Imperial as he came closer. "I was hoping one of you might be able to help me? If you could tell me more about an Imperial wedding ceremony? What are your practices? What should I expect?"

The guards looked at each other, now visibly confused. One of them was pushed to the forefront by his companions, and when he cleared his throat, Tarjiaan understood why. He spoke Common with only a slight accent when he answered, "To answer that, we would need to know what a Meradonese wedding is like."

"Fairly simple, to be honest," Tarjiaan answered. "We swear to each other before the Great Mothers —"

"The what?" the guard interrupted. "Great Mothers?"

"The Great Mothers Below the Waves," Tarjiaan said. "You don't know the Great Mothers?"

"That one, he's never been outside the desert," one of the other guards said. There was more than a hint of a Lastalti accent in his voice. "We tried to tell him. But he doesn't believe us."

"Well, perhaps he'll believe his own eyes." Tarjiaan turned, scanning the horizon. It was coming on to sunset, almost time for them to rise. "There!" He pointed, walking to the starboard rail. The Imperial guards clustered around him, staring in wonder as dark gray hummocks rose and fell in the water, occasionally sending plumes of water skywards.

"Sun and Sand, what are those?" the first guard gasped. "Are they monsters?"

"No! No monsters here. Those are the Great Mothers," Tarjiaan answered. "Six... no, seven of them, it looks like. Not monsters. They are the gentlest creatures under the waves. They have no teeth, you see. They strain their food from the water, and they eat nothing but small fish and shrimp. Marikaar!" he turned and shouted. "Pod off starboard! Do we have an offering?"

Marikaar appeared, followed by several crewmen carrying large tubs between them. "Already prepared, Prince-Captain. In honor of your wedding."

Tarjiaan smiled. "Thank you, Marikaar." He looked around. "Ah... my bride should be here to see this and to accept the blessings of the Great Mothers. If someone could let her attendants know?"

The first guard turned and went off toward the forecastle, and Tarjiaan watched as Marikaar and his men set up the offering, loading the contents of the tubs into capsules that would disintegrate after being fired from the cannons, "Someone should warn the Imperial ship. We don't want them to think that we're firing on them," Tarjiaan called over his shoulder.

"You'd be shooting in the wrong direction."

Tarjiaan smiled. "Uncle. *Seven* of them."

"A good sign." Ikaanaji joined him at the rail. "And I've had Ilaris inform the emissary and the Imperial vessel that we'll be making an offering. The emissary expressed some curiosity, and will more than likely be joining us."

Tarjiaan nodded, looking out at the rise and fall of the Great Mothers. One of them rolled, revealing a giant fin and leaving the Imperial guards gasping. "Uncle, it would honor me and my ship if you'd give the order."

"Thank you, Taarik," Ikaanaji said. "It's been too long since I've given proper honor to the Mothers."

Tarjiaan blinked. "Uncle?"

"Tarjiaan. I apologize. You're so much like him."

Tarjiaan leaned on the rail and closed his eyes, enjoying the sea wind in his face, letting it sooth his raw edges. "Uncle, how long before I can come back above?" he asked softly.

"The negotiations—"

"You know what will happen if I'm below too long," Tarjiaan interrupted. "If I'm in smaller spaces for too long. You're the one who had to send me away so I could fully recover. The nightmares... it's gotten no better, I promise you. I can manage a few days, but then it starts again." He looked out over the waters and sighed. "Uncle, it was bad last night, simply because of how tired I was when I reached the *Chimaera*. I'm not saying I wish to abandon my duties. I'm asking... how soon can I slip away and be in the open again, and not offend the emissary? Is there even any kind of protocol for this?"

Ikaanaji hummed softly, resting one hand on Tarjiaan's shoulder. "I think that perhaps you must create the protocol."

"That was what I was afraid you would say," Tarjiaan said. He looked over his shoulder and shook his head. "Uncle, I'm worried that I'm not... capable of this. I'm a soldier, like my father was. I told you. I'm not a diplomat. I never have been. It was never part of my training."

"A failing on all our parts, my nephew," Ikaanaji said. "You should have had all of the benefits that your brother and your cousins were granted. We made excuses because you were the sixth in line. Which should never have been an excuse." He snorted, looking out over the water. "And there's no time to teach you properly. Ilaris will be at your elbow. Use him. And your instincts are good." He paused. "Mostly. Refrain from drawing a weapon on the emissary from now on. And trust yourself, Tarjiaan. You've done well so far."

"Except for drawing a weapon on the emissary?" Tarjiaan arched a brow at his uncle, who chuckled. "I'll try to remember." He rose and turned to look back over the deck. "Where are they?"

"You sent for the girl?"

"I thought it appropriate. I'm about to be blessed by her gods. She should see how we honor ours," Tarjiaan said, noticing the fluttering saffron-yellow veil. She was with the emissary, who froze when he saw Tarjiaan, a look of panic on his face. Tarjiaan stopped a few feet from them and inclined his head in greeting. Then he held out his hand. "My lady, if I may be honored with your company? I'd very much like to explain what you're about to witness."

Nikaranthia stepped forward and slowly lifted her veil: her golden eyes were wide and wary as she looked down, then back up. Tarjiaan wondered what she was thinking. He hadn't thought about how she didn't know his armor gave him back his legs. About how she might react to seeing him standing. A chill ran down his back — how would she react to seeing him without his armor, and without the shield of the chair?

"You are so tall!" she blurted, and her cheeks darkened as her eyes dropped. Slowly, he went to one knee in front of her, trying not to frighten her even more.

"Better?" he asked, keeping his voice low. He held his hand out once more. This time, she slipped her hand into his.

"You... you should not kneel!" she protested. "Not to me!"

Tarjiaan rose slowly, his eyes never leaving hers. "You will be my wife, my lady. You will be the highest-ranking lady in Meradon. You will answer only to my uncle. To who else would I bow?"

She looked perplexed. "But... will I not answer to you? As my husband?"

Tarjiaan raised her hand to his lips, barely brushing her fingers. Her eyes widened, and her hand trembled slightly. "My lady, I will never ask you to bow to me," he answered, wishing there was some way that he could assure her that she had nothing to fear from him. Wishing for some assurance that he had nothing to fear from her. "But I will ask that you join me at the rail."

She nodded. "The guard said that there was something you wished for us to witness. And something about monsters?"

"No monsters. Come and see." Tarjiaan tucked her hand into his arm, leading her to the rail. "Uncle, may I present my bride, Gondanikaranthia?"

"Uncle?" Nikaranthia repeated. She looked at Ikaanaji, then bowed deeply from the waist. "Your Majesty—"

"My dear, it's a pleasure. But time is short. Tarjiaan, will you explain the offering while I oversee it?"

"Of course, Uncle," Tarjiaan answered. He pointed out over the water. "Do you see them, Nikaranthia?"

Nikaranthia turned and looked where he was pointing, then looked up at him. "I see... there is something very large."

"Those are the Great Mothers, the Queens of the Sea. They're not monsters. They breathe air, which is why they come to the surface. They're gentle, and they sing—"

"They sing?" Nikaranthia blurted. "How can they sing under the water?"

"I've no idea," Tarjiaan admitted. "But their song is very beautiful. And—"

"Bubble-net! Bubble-net to starboard!"

Tarjiaan froze, twisting to look up to the crow's nest and see the sentry shouting and pointing. Looking in that direction, he could see the mass of tiny fish leaping out of the water, and knew what he was about to witness. "Hold on!" he said, putting his arm around Nikaranthia and grabbing the rail with his other hand. "Hold on and watch!"

"Release the offering!" Ikaanaji called, his voice strong.

Then, without warning, the Mothers surfaced, close enough to the *Wave Runner* that Tarjiaan could have thrown a stone into the center of the pod. Massive wedge-shaped heads breaking the surface, mouths wide as they scooped up entire populations of tiny fish. Next to him, Tarjiaan heard Nikaranthia squeak as she clutched at his arm.

"Sun and Sand, they are enormous!"

Tarjiaan laughed. "They are. They're the heart of the sea, and we honor them for allowing us to live in their shadow. That they've risen now is a sign of good fortune on our wedding, my lady. And we should share in the offering." He steered her gently towards where Ikaanaji was directing the cannons. He turned and saw them approaching, and nodded towards a half-full basin that had been set near the rail.

"We saved that one for you."

"Thank you, Uncle," Tarjiaan answered. He turned to Nikaranthia as he reached down to take one side of the basin. "This won't be heavy. Take that side. We lift and pour it over the side together."

Nikaranthia nodded and lifted, and together they tipped the basin. Tarjiaan watched as her nose wrinkled as the contents slithered out of the basin and fell into the waters. Tarjiaan took the basin from her and set it down, then reached for her hand.

"Your high priest looks as if he's about to have a fit," he murmured. "Shall we to our wedding?"

Nikaranthia smiled slightly. She started to turn, then froze and pointed. "Look!"

Tarjiaan turned, and saw a great gray hump studded with barnacles break the surface of the water less than ten feet from the side of the *Wave Runner*. He grabbed the rail with one hand, feeling Nikaranthia catching his other arm as the ship rocked underneath their feet. The Mother ignored them, spouting a blast of water that carried the heavy stench of sulfur before disappearing beneath the waves once more. The sailors on deck shouted and cheered, and Tarjiaan laughed, feeling one of an endless series of knots in his chest loosen.

The Mothers, at least, approved of this wedding.

"Is that... unusual?" Nikaranthia asked timidly, wiping water from her face with a piece of her veil.

"I've been at sea since I was a boy of ten, my lady," Tarjiaan answered. He shook his head in wonder. "I've sailed these waters for more years than you've been alive, and I've never once seen one of the Great Mothers that close."

"They're breaking off," Ikaanaji said. "Well, my nephew, I'd say this wedding has been well and truly blessed. And you've added another layer to the legend of the Sea Prince."

Tarjiaan snorted, and was startled by the sound of Nikaranthia's smothering giggles behind some of her bunched-up veil.

"You sounded like her!" she bubbled. She hesitated, then stretched up and used a corner of her veil to wipe off Tarjiaan's cheek. He smiled, pleased both at the gesture, and at her boldness. Perhaps this wouldn't be so bad—

Someone behind him coughed. Nikaranthia's eyes widened, then dropped, and Tarjiaan turned to see the emissary.

"That was... truly amazing," he said. "But the High Priest wants to know if we can begin?" He turned and looked away, towards the forecastle. Tarjiaan could see the priest standing there, well out of the way of the Mother's spray, and looking annoyed.

"Does the High Priest not approve of other blessings?" Tarjiaan asked softly. The emissary's lips twitched, but he said nothing.

"Perhaps he doesn't like being kept waiting," Ikaanaji offered, his voice equally low. "It's time, Tarjiaan."

Chapter Seven
Vows

AS LOGIRI HAD WARNED him, the ceremony was in High Imperial, and Tarjiaan understood none of the lengthy speeches. Rathsafa stood next to him, prompting him for responses to questions he didn't understand, and that were asked of him so quickly that there was no time to translate. Tarjiaan wondered what he was promising – there was no protest from his uncle or Ilaris, so he didn't think he was handing the kingdom over, but he wouldn't know if he did. Nikaranthia, hidden once more beneath her veils, was asked no questions at all. She stood silent between two guards. Tarjiaan assumed the guards were standing in for her family, an assumption confirmed after an official-sounding pronouncement — one of them took Nikaranthia by the elbow and guided her across the space between them to Tarjiaan.

"Highness, your bride," he said. "She is now of your family and line."

"I accept, and thank you," Tarjiaan answered, drawing Nikaranthia to his side. He hesitated, then looked at the emissary. "Is there something I need to do here?"

"You've taken possession of her," Rathsafa answered. "That is the end. Except for the affirmation of purity—"

"Which won't be happening in public," Tarjiaan interjected, his voice low.

"The High Priest needs to verify—"

"The High Priest will have to take my word for it," Tarjiaan answered, glancing at Rathsafa. The emissary met his eyes, then looked at the priest and said something before turning back to Tarjiaan.

"Prince Tarjiaan," he asked, "is there some ceremony that you would have included before we finish? Is there something you wish done? Some ritual of your own people?"

Tarjiaan nodded. "Yes. Thank you." He cleared his throat. "If my lady would raise her veils? Or... if you would allow me the liberty?"

"You are my husband. It is your right," came the muffled answer. She didn't move. Tarjiaan waited a moment, then reached out and slowly gathered the silken material in his fingers, lifting it up and draping it so that he could see Nikaranthia. He didn't remove the veil entirely. No matter how much the garment offended him, it wasn't his choice to make. She was comfortable with it, and she might actually want it. Hopefully, she'd realized that she no longer needed to hide behind it soon enough.

"My lady Gondanikaranthia," he said, seeing her flicker of a smile and the mirth in her eyes as she looked up at him. He must have said it wrong again. He swallowed, and gathered himself, reaching for her hands. "Our ceremonies are not as... formal as your own. I, Tarjiaan, son of Aajinisa and Taarik, ask that you accept me as your husband. I swear by the Great Mothers that I will honor you and protect you, and that I will be a good husband to you, and a good father to our children." Her eyes widened. Had she not thought about children? "Will you accept me, Gondanikaranthia?"

Her mouth opened slightly, and when she finally spoke, her voice trembled. "I... I accept you, my husband."

"You can call me by name," Tarjiaan prompted gently, then softly added, "You'll probably even say it right." He winked, and she looked startled. "Your turn. What I said, just turn it around."

Her tongue flickered over her top lip. "I, Gondanikaranthia, daughter of... daughter of Masthaka, ask that you accept me as your wife. I swear by... by Sun and Sand... that I will honor you and protect you, and that I will be a good wife to you, and a good mother to our children." She stopped, then looked up again, her golden eyes meeting his. "Will you accept me as your wife?"

Tarjiaan raised her hands to his lips, kissing them each in turn. "I accept you, and gladly. Welcome to Meradon, my lady-wife."

The cheer that went up from the surrounding sailors was near-deafening, and Tarjiaan felt Nikaranthia jump in surprise. He drew her to him and put his arm around her shoulders. "I hope I don't shock you too much," he said, pitching his voice so that she could hear him. "I know we have very different customs. If I make you uncomfortable, I expect you to tell me. And you may ask me anything."

She nodded, then looked up at him. There was a light of curiosity in her eyes that Tarjiaan found incredibly welcoming. "Will you show me your ship?" she asked hesitantly, sounding as if she expected him to refuse. "I have never been to sea before this, and I was not allowed out of my room on the voyage here."

"Of course!" Tarjiaan answered. He looked around, saw the emissary standing near Ilaris and Ikaanaji. "Uncle, Lord Rathsafa, if you'll excuse us? My wife and I will be touring the ship. Marikaar?" He looked around, saw Marikaar near the railing. "Please, don't hold the festivities on our account. Serve, and we'll join you soon."

"Yes, Prince-Captain," Marikaar answered with a smart salute. Tarjiaan grinned at him and tucked Nikaranthia's hand into the crook of his arm.

"Shall we start at the top?" he asked. "And work our way down? Or start from the bottom and finish on deck?"

"And this is our ship farm," Tarjiaan announced as he opened the hatch. "This is where a small portion of our food is grown. Anything we don't catch or trade for, or bring up from the farm ships below. At the moment, there's a problem somewhere down here, so nothing is growing—"

"How can you have farms on ships underwater?" Nikaranthia asked, then stopped when she saw the inside of the bay. "Oh... I have seen pictures of farms. This is not what a farm looked like. How does it work?" She looked around at the tanks, the hanging nets and the lights, and the miles of tubing. "How does all this make plants grow?"

"I'm going to admit to only knowing the barest basics of how it works," Tarjiaan said. "I'm supposed to know everything about anything to do with the running of this ship. But growing things..." He shrugged, and she looked amused. "I can't be good at everything."

"The only one who expects that of you is yourself, Prince-Captain," Ishantar's richly accented voice came from somewhere. "We've found the problem. There is pitting on the insides of some of the tubing. That was why we had the algae overgrowth. We will need to replace the tubing, then flush the lines and start the cultures over once we're refitted." She emerged from behind a growing frame and Tarjiaan turned to Nikaranthia. Before he could introduce Mancer Ishantar, the Mancer smiled broadly and said something in her own language.

Nikaranthia blinked, then answered, very slowly, giving a basic greeting in Sualimani. Then she shook her head. "I... I am sorry. I do not speak very much. Or very well."

"You are Sualimani!" Ishantar crowed. "I thought as much when I saw you before. Welcome, little sister!"

Tarjiaan asked, "How could you tell under the veils, Ishantar?"

Ishantar grinned. "I saw my little sister's hands when she came onto the *Wave Runner*. But I wasn't sure until now. None of my people married into the Imperial family. At least, that I know of."

Nikaranthia's eyes dropped, and she laced her fingers together in front of her body. "They would not wish for me to tell you this. My mother was not a wife, nor a concubine. She was a slave, taken as such when I was very small."

"You weren't born in the Empire?" Tarjiaan asked.

"No. I am told that I was sired by the prince, and that is how my mother and I came to be taken, but I was raised as the lowest slave in the women's quarters." She swallowed and looked down. "I am sorry, my lord, for the omission. But... I am not the honored daughter they told you that I was. I will understand if you wish to refuse me."

"The fault isn't yours, my lady-wife," Tarjiaan stressed the title, and her head shot up. "And I'm not putting you aside. The Sualimani are a fine, proud people. You have a noble heritage through your mother. I think we'll suit each other just fine." He paused. "Does she live? I can request that she be sent for—"

"She attempted to escape," Nikaranthia answered. "She was executed."

"Oh, little sister," Ishantar breathed. "What was her name?"

"Masthaka," Nikaranthia answered. "Why?"

Tarjiaan nodded. "Ishantar, when you next message your mother, send her my compliments and find out what you can of my lady's family, will you? Let them know of her fate, and that her daughter lives."

"Of course. You probably have cousins, little one. Perhaps we are such?" Ishantar said. She smiled broadly. "As your kin, it should have been mine to help you with your marriage preparations. Should I help with the marriage collar for you?"

"The what?" Nikaranthia gasped. Her hand floated up to touch her throat.

"Not for you!" Ishantar protested. "For him!" She pointed at Tarjiaan. He groaned and she laughed. "Nikaranthia, among the Sualimani, the women rule," Ishantar explained. "The men are subservient. And when a woman takes a man as a husband, he wears a collar of her crafting, to show that he serves only her."

Nikaranthia looked stunned. Then she looked up at Tarjiaan. "Would you wear one?" Tarjiaan coughed, then glared at Ishantar. She burst out laughing. Nikaranthia looked from her to Tarjiaan, then shuddered. "I said something wrong?" she asked. "I often speak without thinking. It is a fault—"

"No," Tarjiaan answered, keeping his voice gentle. "No, you did nothing wrong, my lady. And if you asked me to wear a marital collar, I would. I'd just have to remember to keep my shirt buttoned."

Nikaranthia looked confused, then thoughtful. "Oh! Would it undermine your authority with your men?" she asked.

"It is a possibility," Tarjiaan answered, surprised and pleased by how quickly she'd understood. "Now, perhaps a compromise?" He glanced at Ishantar. "A bracelet is an option, isn't it?"

"A marital cuff?" Ishantar asked. "Yes, we could help you make one of those. Little sister?"

Nikaranthia looked at her, then at Tarjiaan. Then she shook her head. "Not... I cannot."

"Of course. You're right. It wouldn't be entirely proper," Ishantar said, nodding. "You should make your own. I could teach you, if you spend enough time above the waves."

"Thank you," Nikaranthia answered. She shifted slightly, glancing at Tarjiaan. Looking for him to save her, he realized.

"Shall we move on?" he asked, offering his arm. "Mancer, we'll let you get back to your duties." He looked around, wondering where Daanir was hiding. Was he watching? Nikaranthia took his arm, and he turned toward the hatch.

"Congratulations, my Prince," Ishantar called as they left. "And to you, little sister!"

Tarjiaan waited until they were back on deck before saying, "I'm sorry if that made you uncomfortable."

"I was not expecting to see anyone from my mother's people. Not that I knew very much. Mother never spoke of our life outside the women's quarters, and I remember nothing before we were brought there." Nikaranthia paused for a moment, then looked back over her shoulder. "She's so... bold."

Tarjiaan wondered for a moment if he should tell her that Ishantar was actually fairly mild-tempered for a Sualimani woman, but decided against it. She'd had enough shocks for one day. "This is the great cabin," he said as they reached the door. "When we're onboard the *Wave Runner,* these will be our quarters; this side is the day cabin, where I entertain, and meet with my officers. The bedroom and washroom are through that door."

Inside the great cabin, Nikaranthia peered into corners and wandered from place to place without any obvious pattern, going from the day cabin into the bedroom, reminding Tarjiaan of a small, curious cat he'd seen once in the floating dockyards. "You are very tidy," she said idly as she stopped in front of the red-framed picture. She studied it for a moment, then looked at Tarjiaan. She looked back at the picture and pointed, "That is you!"

"Yes, it is." Tarjiaan joined her. "A long time ago."

"How long?"

"Almost eighteen years. I was seventeen when that was painted," Tarjiaan said. "About your age."

"My age?" Nikaranthia looked up at him, her brow furrowed slightly. Then she looked back at the portrait. "You were so young," she murmured. "Who are they? The frame.... Red is mourning for your people, I know that. So this is a memorial portrait. For... is that your father?"

"That is my father and my older brother. And the memorial is for them both. They died in battle when I was nineteen." He refrained from saying what else happened when he was nineteen. She'd learn that soon enough. "Captain Taarik and his first mate Aaranji, of the *Marauder*."

"The... the *Marauder*? There actually was a ship named *Marauder*?" She looked up at him, clearly shocked. "And your father was the captain?"

"Yes. I served on the *Marauder* with him," Tarjiaan answered. He studied her face for a moment, the look that he slowly identified as mingled fascination and horror. "Nikaranthia, am I missing something? How do you know about the *Marauder*?"

"You do not know the stories?" she asked.

"Stories?" Tarjiaan shook his head. "I've heard no stories about the *Marauder*."

"They say that Imperial waters are haunted by a ghost ship called the *Marauder*, and it is crewed by two men only, by the Demon Captain and his First Mate. The ship appears in the dusk, and vanishes in the dawn, and destroys any Imperial ship that they come across."

Tarjiaan stared at her. "I've never heard that before!"

"That means that the Demon Captain is your father." Nikaranthia looked back at the picture. "He does not look like a demon. He looks... kind. And your brother – he looks very merry."

"He was. Aaranji was always laughing. And Father..." Tarjiaan considered as he looked at the picture. Then he smiled. "Father would have laughed himself sick at that story. And... you're right. He was kind. He'd have liked you."

"He would?"

Tarjiaan nodded. "You have spirit. He'd have appreciated that."

"Do you have other family?" Nikaranthia asked.

"Ah... yes," Tarjiaan answered. "A sister, and her son, who is my heir. She.... you should know: Aanaji is Aaranji's twin, and she's already made it plain what she thinks of our marriage—"

"Is that where this came from?" Nikaranthia touched his cheek. "It does not look like a battle wound, and it is still fresh."

Tarjiaan sighed. "Yes, that was my sister. I'll try to keep her away from you."

"Because your father and brother died in battle. Against my people. I am sorry, my husband. I should not drive a wedge between you and your family," Nikaranthia said.

"Aanaji and I have had our differences for years." Tarjiaan guided Nikaranthia back out to the day cabin, settling her into a chair at the wardroom table. "We're a bit like oil and water, if you understand my meaning."

"Do you think that there might be a way to smooth the way?" Nikaranthia asked. "There is a custom in the Empire, to offer the senior member of the family a marriage gift. Do you think she might accept something like that from me?"

Tarjiaan leaned against the table, folding his arms over his chest as he thought about it. "It couldn't hurt to offer. What are you thinking?"

"I am not sure." Nikaranthia folded her hands in her lap and cocked her head to one side. "They sent many things with me as gifts for you and the King. But I never saw any of it. It was all packed away before we reached the ship. We should talk to Lord Rathsafa. He knows what was brought, and may be able to make a recommendation."

"You said we," Tarjiaan said, remembering something he'd meant to ask. "Nikaranthia, I was told you'd have at least one maid. Where is she?"

Nikaranthia looked down. "Five days out of port, she did not wake. The ship healer said that it was something to do with her heart. There was nothing he could do, and she died three days later."

Tarjiaan sighed. "I'm sorry. Were you close?"

Nikaranthia shook her head. "I had never met her before. As I said, I was very low status in the women's quarters, and she was an upper servant. I am called a princess now only because they needed one to send here for the alliance, and the prince has no legitimate children, nor has he ever married. Listel was assigned to me, and she wept as we sailed. She thought we were sailing to our deaths."

"Given the stories I've heard about me, I'm not surprised. Did you think that as well?" Tarjiaan asked.

"The thought had occurred," Nikaranthia murmured. Then she peered up at him through long eyelashes. "But now... I think not."

"Good." Tarjiaan held his hand out, and Nikaranthia slipped her hand into his. He raised it to his lips and kissed her palm. "I don't want you to be afraid of me, my lady."

There was a knock on the door. Tarjiaan looked up and called, "Enter!"

Ilaris came in, closing the door behind him. "Highness, will you be joining us?"

"Yes, Ilaris." Tarjiaan rose, seeing an odd tension in Ilaris' face. "Is there something wrong?"

"Your uncle is beginning to grow fatigued," Ilaris said, his voice short. "We should return to the *Chimaera* soon. This is far more excitement than he's used to."

A soft hand came to rest on Tarjiaan's arm. "Your uncle is ill?" Nikaranthia asked as she stood up.

Ilaris answered smoothly before Tarjiaan had a chance, "The Sea King is quite old, Highness. Old men tire easily."

"We'll come and join him, Ilaris," Tarjiaan said. "My lady, you've barely had the chance to meet him. You can sit with him, and I'll bring you something to drink."

"You would act as a servant?" Nikaranthia sounded appalled. "But... I should serve you!"

"No, my dear. I'll not be acting as a servant. I'll be acting as a husband." Tarjiaan guided her towards the door.

A cheer went up as they came back out onto the deck, and Tarjiaan looked around and smiled. His smile faltered a little when he saw familiar blond hair, but he managed to keep his voice steady as he said, "The Mancer Royal is with the King?"

"He is, Highness," Ilaris answered, his voice mild. But the look in his eyes spoke volumes. Tarjiaan nodded and led Nikaranthia towards his uncle, who smiled as they approached.

"I've been wondering where you two have been," he said. "Nothing untoward, Tarjiaan? And if the answer is no, then whyever not?"

"Uncle!" Tarjiaan gasped, more shocked than angry. He couldn't remember his uncle ever being even the slightest bit improper in public. Had he been drinking? "My lady was curious about the ship." He gestured toward Daanir. "My lady, you've met my uncle. May I present the Mancer Royal, Daanir Meranas? My oldest and dearest friend, and someone I hope you will consider a friend as well." He guided Nikaranthia to sit with his uncle. Beyond them, Tarjiaan saw the emissary, who was standing within earshot and trying to look as though he wasn't listening. "Lord Rathsafa, have you met the Mancer Royal?"

The emissary smiled slightly and approached. "I have not. I cannot say I have ever before met a mancer of any rank, and I am curious."

Nikaranthia looked down for a moment, then up at Daanir. "A mancer. That is a mage, but with machines, is it not?"

Daanir blinked twice. "We don't have mages in Meradon," he said slowly and firmly. "But... I can see why you'd think it was the same. No, mages make things happen. Mancers... we help them along."

Nikaranthia looked puzzled. "What is the difference?"

Daanir opened his mouth, closed it again, then folded his arms over his chest. "I..." he stopped. Then he laughed. "I have no idea. I don't know anything about mages. So you tell me about mages, and I'll tell you about Mancers."

Nikaranthia looked down. "I do not know about mages either. Women are not allowed to know anything about magic."

"And there are no mages in Meradon," Ikaanaji said.

"If I may ask," Rathsafa said, "why not? I know of your restriction, but not why."

Ikaanaji looked up at him. "The mages of Meradon sided with the Empire, which is part of the reason why our nation was overrun. Magic was outlawed when we came below the waves. But this is not a discussion to be having. Not now, with such a joyous occasion." He smiled at Nikaranthia. "I hope you will be very happy here, my dear."

Nikaranthia bit her lip, then looked up at Tarjiaan. "I think I will be, Your Majesty."

Chapter Eight
Truth

"YOUR AIDE HAS TAKEN the princess's baggage below already," Ilaris said. Tarjiaan nodded, putting his back to the rail so he could watch Nikaranthia. She was sitting with his uncle, who was laughing and looking happier than Tarjiaan had seen him in ages.

"Ilaris, when was the last time he laughed like that?" he asked, turning back to the rail and keeping his voice low.

Ilaris glanced over, then looked out at the darkening sea. "It's been a very long time, your Highness."

All at once, the laughter cut off, and Tarjiaan heard Nikaranthia's voice raised in alarm, "Sire?" He turned and sprinted toward them, dropping heavily to one knee in front of his uncle, who suddenly looked pale and drawn.

"Uncle Ika?" Tarjiaan whispered.

The Sea King looked at him and shook his head. "I'm fine," he said. "I... grow tired. It is, perhaps, time I returned to the *Chimaera*. But you should not end the celebrations on my account." He rested his hand on Tarjiaan's arm. "It's your wedding, Taarik. You should be happy tonight."

Tarjiaan dismissed his uncle's mistake as he covered his uncle's hand with his own. "I am happy, Uncle. I'll be happier once I know you're comfortable." He looked at Nikaranthia. "My lady, would you mind if we—"

"Of course not!" Nikaranthia interrupted. Then she bit her lip and looked down and away. "I... your will, my husband."

"My will is to have you tell me your thoughts and your opinions, my lady," Tarjiaan said. He stood up slowly. "My friends, please enjoy yourselves. Thank you for celebrating with us. We will withdraw now." He looked around. "First Officer Marikaar, you should continue on to the yards for repairs at your earliest opportunity. You have the con."

Marikaar stepped forward and saluted. "Con accepted, Captain. Thank you."

"Lord Rathsafa," Tarjiaan inclined his head to the emissary. "You and your men are welcome to enjoy the hospitality of my crew for as long as you like. Just tell Marikaar when you're ready to come below, and he'll send for a submersible."

Rathsafa bowed his head slightly. "Thank you, Prince-Captain. Shall we say that the talks will begin in two days?"

"I thought you wanted to proceed immediately?" Tarjiaan asked. "I thought we would meet tomorrow–"

"I've reconsidered," Rathsafa answered. "And I think we can spare the time for you to enjoy being married before we have to go to work and I have to steal your attention from your bride."

Tarjiaan nodded, but it seemed strange. However, he wasn't going to start the negotiations with an argument. "In two days, then," he agreed. Rathsafa bowed again, and Tarjiaan led Nikaranthia away, following his uncle. Daanir was on the King's right and Ilaris on his left. Supporting him, Tarjiaan realized.

"My husband?" Nikaranthia whispered. "He is not just tired, is he?"

Tarjiaan looked down at Nikaranthia, seeing the worry in her face, the concern in her eyes. He raised her fingers to his lips and kissed her knuckles. "We'll talk in the submersible," he answered.

"And we're away, Your Majesty," the pilot called.

"Very good, Commander," Ikaanaji answered. He leaned back in his seat and closed his eyes. "It was more than four hours, was it not, Mancer?"

Daanir closed one eye and cocked his head to the side, then nodded. "Nearly five."

"You do excellent work, Mancer," Ikaanaji murmured. "But I am tired." His smile broadened. "And very happy. My dear, you are welcome in Meradon."

Nikaranthia bit her lip and looked at Tarjiaan. "You said—"

Tarjiaan nodded and tried to gather his thoughts. His head was spinning, and he knew that he still hadn't had nearly enough sleep. He rubbed one hand over his face. "Yes," he said. "Where do I start?" And what to tell her? He wasn't even certain. Tell her the truth?

"I am dying," Ikaanaji said, and Tarjiaan stared at him.

"You're just going to say it?" he gasped. "Just like that?"

"Well, it seems as good a place as any to start. I am dying."

Nikaranthia sat up straight in her seat. "No!" she blurted. "But I only just met you!" She clapped one hand over her mouth, her eyes wide and frightened. Tarjiaan rested his hand on her shoulder.

"You can speak freely with us," he said softly. "Remember, I want you to tell me your thoughts. You're not a silent shadow, nor will you be confined to women's quarters. The people will see you. They'll know you. And they'll accept you." She looked skeptically at him and he nodded. "They will. It'll take time, but they will."

She lowered her eyes, lacing her fingers together in her lap. Tarjiaan took his hand from her shoulder and rested it on her hands, looking across at his uncle. "I only just found out... this morning... how can it only be this morning?"

"It's been a long day," Daanir murmured, steadily looking out the porthole into the darker colors of the deeper sea.

"It has. But a good one," Ikaanaji agreed. "A very good one. Ilaris, will you explain?"

Ilaris nodded, stroking his chin. "The illness began... perhaps three years ago? Our physicians could do nothing to stop it, or to slow the progression. Mancer Riguaarin managed to build the breathing machines, which helped. But we couldn't reverse the damage. Then he passed to the Great Mothers, and Mancer Daanir took over. He's done incredible things—"

"And Ilaris exaggerates," Daanir interrupted.

"He does not," Tarjiaan and Ikaanaji spoke in unison. To Tarjiaan's surprise, Nikaranthia giggled.

"You sound alike," she said. "I could not tell you apart if I was not looking."

"Good thing that you can look at us," Tarjiaan pointed out. She immediately looked down, fiddling with the edges of her veil.

Daanir looked away and sighed. "I've tried to do more. To do something. The best I could do was make it so that the King could leave the machines for short periods of time. But... well, we'll see what Wilaanger says. I hope I haven't made things worse."

"The Physician Royal will be waiting when we dock," Ilaris said. "And your chair will be waiting, Your Highness."

Tarjiaan swallowed and nodded, then saw the question in Nikaranthia's eyes. "If I may ask for your patience, my lady? I'll explain about that chair in private."

She blinked, then lowered her gaze. "Yes, my husband." She paused, then turned back to Ikaanaji. "This illness is why you made the alliance?"

"I promised my people when I took the Coral Throne that we would one day return to our homelands," Ikaanaji said. "I wish to walk once more on land before I return to the Great Mothers." He gestured toward her and Tarjiaan. "This alliance, this match... that is the start of it. The start of something great, I believe."

Nikaranthia looked down at her hands, then got to her feet and walked over to Ikaanaji. She leaned down and kissed his cheek, then straightened and bit her lip. "Thank you," she whispered. Then she fled back to her chair and buried her face in Tarjiaan's arm. He smiled and reached across to tuck back her veil.

"Yes. The start of something great and wonderful," Ikaanaji murmured. He smiled and nodded. "We'll be back to the *Chimaera* soon. Tarjiaan, once you see your lady to your quarters, come and share a drink with me. I won't keep you long. And Ilaris, has a maid been assigned to my new niece?"

Ilaris nodded. "Her name is Adalia. She should be waiting in the heir's quarters. I've asked the Prince's aide to acquaint her with the rooms and with her duties, but Her Highness will have to instruct her on any specifics she might require.

Daanir looked across at Ilaris. "Adalia is one of Aanaji's maids. How'd you shake her loose?"

Ilaris smiled slightly. "I know how to handle the princess."

Tarjiaan snorted. "That makes you perhaps the one person in the entire world who does." He looked at Nikaranthia, who had turned her head so she could see, but still had her cheek resting against his arm. She looked almost relaxed, and as if she was trying not to fall asleep. He thought he knew why. "You didn't sleep last night, did you?" he asked.

She blinked and looked up. "I...no, my husband."

"Too frightened?"

She smiled slightly. "Yes. But I think I will sleep well tonight."

Tarjiaan nodded. "We'll get you settled, and you can retire. If you're asleep before I come back, then I'll see you in the morning."

Nikaranthia sat up. "But—" Her eyes widened, and her cheeks darkened. "My husband..."

Tarjiaan leaned closer. "Is patient," he said in a low voice. "If you're asleep, then it's because you need to sleep." He sat up and closed his eyes, taking a deep breath before opening them again. "To be honest, I need to sleep, too. If you don't mind, I'd rather we both rest."

She looked puzzled for a moment. "If I do not mind?"

He chuckled. "It is your wedding night, too, my wife." He turned to his uncle. "That drink? Should be tea, or I might not be able to steer my way back to my quarters."

Ikaanaji smiled. "Of course. Mancer, you'll join us?"

Daanir coughed. "I..." He looked panicked. "I... I should..."

"Daan, join us," Tarjiaan interrupted. "Please." He looked up at the vents above them as they started hissing. "We've docked."

Daanir closed his eyes. "I am honored by your invitation, Your Majesty."

"Sire, you can disembark at your leisure," the pilot called. "Wilaanger is waiting, and the Prince's chair is already prepared."

"Thank you, Commander," Ikaanaji said. "Mancer, attend me. And... Tarjiaan, may I impose on you to allow your wife to attend me as well?"

"Of course, Uncle," Tarjiaan agreed. "I'll join you in a moment."

Ikaanaji smiled as Nikaranthia rose and moved to his side, taking his arm. "Oh, to be seventy years younger," Ikaanaji said, patting her hand. "I'd have married you myself." He led her out of the submersible, and Daanir followed them. Ilaris rose, but didn't leave.

"Highness, do you need assistance?"

Tarjiaan shook his head. "No," he answered. "I can manage. Thank you." He got up and followed Ilaris out of the submersible.

Tarjiaan looked down at the green light under his hand, then back at his armor. She'd already seen the chair. Tonight, he'd have to explain the why of the chair to Nikaranthia, and see what came of it. He was dreading the conversation. Perhaps she'd be asleep before he returned to their quarters, and he'd have a night of reprieve. He took a deep breath and set the chair rolling, heading out into the corridor.

Nikaranthia smiled when she saw him, coming to his side when he rolled to a stop. She looked at the chair for a moment, frowned, then looked up.

"Oh!" she murmured. "I see."

"What do you see?" Tarjiaan asked.

"When you stand, you are too tall for the corridor." She met his eyes. "Where will it be best for me to stand? This is not protocol I know."

Tarjiaan hesitated for a moment, studying her. Her curiosity was clear, and she was obviously much cleverer than her Imperial relatives had ever given her credit for. And she had a spine hiding underneath that veil. Maybe... the conversation wouldn't be as bad as he feared?

"If you stay to my side, and a little behind, I won't run over your feet," Tarjiaan answered. "You can put your hand on my shoulder, if you like."

She smiled, turned to face forward, and rested her left hand on his right shoulder. "Like this?"

"Exactly," Tarjiaan answered. "Uncle, I will meet you in the throne room," he added, turning to look at Ikaanaji. "I'll be there presently."

The King continued down the corridor, leaning on Wilaanger's arm. Daanir followed the King and did not look back.

"If you have need of anything, Highness, please ring," Ilaris said.

Tarjiaan nodded. "I'll show Nikaranthia how to use the comms, in case she needs anything while I'm gone." He started the chair forward, moving slowly so that Nikaranthia could keep pace.

"How does it work?" she asked. "The chair. I do not see the controls?"

"Neural something or others," Tarjiaan answered. "I don't fully understand it. The best person to ask how anything works is Daanir, and I'm sure he'd be happy to teach you while I'm in negotiations—"

"I could not," Nikaranthia murmured. "Spend time alone with a man not my husband?"

Tarjiaan looked at her. "You're in Meradon now, my lady. You can speak to whomever you like. Spend time with them. Learn whatever interests you." He paused, remembering something he'd heard about the Empire and how they treated their women. His first responsibility to his wife might very well be teaching her to read. "I know you have a lot to learn, and it may be uncomfortable until you're used to our ways. But I will help you however I can. We all will." He gestured. "That door, there."

Nikaranthia stepped toward the door, only to squeak in surprise and dart back to Tarjiaan's side when the door slid open. Logiri looked almost as startled as Nikaranthia, but recovered quickly. He bowed deeply, crossing his arms over his chest in a way that Tarjiaan hadn't seen him do in years.

"Your Highness," he said. "Welcome." Then he repeated himself in Imperial.

Nikaranthia stared at him for a moment, then looked at Tarjiaan. "My aide, Logiri," he answered her unspoken question. "One of many of your people who have taken refuge with us below the waves. Logiri has been with me for nearly eleven years, and I trust him implicitly."

Nikaranthia nodded and turned back to Logiri. "I should not speak Imperial," she said. "I must practice. But... Logiri? That is not your name!"

Logiri smiled. "It's a diminutive," he answered. "My full name is Antarlogirish."

Nikaranthia's breath caught. "I... I know of your family," she said. "And... what does an aide do?"

"Remembers things I forget, corrects me when I'm wrong, and refuses to let me out of his sight if I'm not presentable to his standards," Tarjiaan answered. Logiri laughed and stepped back so that they could enter the suite. Tarjiaan stopped just inside, watching as Nikaranthia explored the sitting room.

"Your rooms are to the right, Highness," Logiri offered. "And your maid is inside, waiting for your instruction on how you'd prefer your belongings."

"My rooms?" Nikaranthia repeated. "I thought you said you did not have women's quarters?"

"We don't. But we do have the option for privacy. That is your room. The other door is mine," Tarjiaan said. "And if you wish to join me there, you're welcome to do so. But I will not compel you." He paused, feeling as if there was a shark swimming in his stomach. "If you wish to sleep alone, or if you wish privacy, you have your own bedroom."

"Also, there is a small office just off your room," Logiri added. "I've had it stocked with some essentials — pens and ink and paper and such. But since I didn't know what duties Your Highness would be taking on, it's very generic."

"Duties?" Nikaranthia repeated. She shook her head. "I am drowning."

"It's a great deal for you to absorb in a short period of time." Tarjiaan held his hand out to her. She slipped her hand into his, and he kissed her knuckles. "We'll take it slowly, and one day at a time. I'm expected by my uncle. Logiri, what would the proper protocol be when I am away?"

"It would be improper for me to remain. Adalia will remain here to assist," Logiri answered.

Tarjiaan nodded. "Thank you. If you'll withdraw, and tell Adalia I want a few moments of privacy?" He rested one hand on the carapace of his chair; Logiri blinked and arched a brow. Tarjiaan nodded, and Logiri bowed, going to the door on the right and entering the consort's suite. Tarjiaan looked down and swallowed.

"There's another reason for your own rooms," he said slowly.

"Is it also the reason you have the chair?" Nikaranthia asked, her voice quiet. "My husband, it is something that bothers you. I can see that."

He took another breath and looked at her. "The battle that killed my father and brother almost killed me. I was...injured. Badly injured," he said. He looked down, then closed his eyes and opened the carapace, revealing his legs. "The armor works... in a similar manner to the chair," he said. "It connects to my nerves, so I can move as if I still had my legs. But..."

"You cannot wear it here, because it makes you too tall for the corridors," she finished. "And... you think that I will not wish to be with you, or share your bed because you were injured?" She cocked her head to the side. "Why would you think that?"

"You don't..." Tarjiaan hesitated. "I don't disgust you?" he finished, his voice cracking slightly.

To his shock, she stared at him. For a moment, her mouth moved but nothing came out. Then she blurted, "Why would you think that?" She straightened, her hands clenched. "Who would say such a horrible thing to you?" she demanded. "Who told you that you disgusted them?"

"I..." For a moment, Tarjiaan was unable to think, unable to form words at all. All he could manage was a single letter. "I..."

"It is horrible, and hurtful and... tell me, and I will scratch their eyes out!" Nikaranthia finished. Then she stopped. "I... was it a woman? I might not be able to do it to a man. I am not tall enough."

Tarjiaan swallowed and looked at her again. "Nikaranthia—"

"Will it hurt you, if I come closer?" she interrupted. "If I sit on your lap?"

Tarjiaan coughed. "I... what?"

She didn't answer. Instead, she came closer, curled up in his lap like a friendly cat, and took his face between her hands. She met his eyes, then kissed him. Tarjiaan wrapped his arms around her and pulled her closer, not believing what was happening, afraid to let go. He shouldn't... she was too young. She was far too young.

She drew back slightly and wiped her thumb across his lip. "Within minutes of our meeting, you defended me from someone you thought was hurting me. You have been nothing but kind to me, even though my people have cost you so much." She met his eyes and smiled. "What was it you said? That we would suit each other very well?"

"You're so young..." Tarjiaan whispered.

"Not so young that I cannot care for you."

He stared at her for a moment, then pulled her close and buried his face in her shoulder, feeling her fingers as she combed them though his hair.

"Oh, my husband," she murmured. "Someone has hurt you so very badly. I am sorry." She shifted, kissed his cheek, then kissed his lips once more. "You are supposed to see your uncle," she reminded him.

"Nikaranthia." His voice sounded harsh to his own ears. "I... thank you."

She trailed her finger over his lips again. "Thank you, my husband."

Chapter Nine
Matrimony

"I DON'T EXPECT YOU to wait for me," Tarjiaan said as he left the suite. "I'm not sure how long I'll be with my uncle, and it's been a long day for you. Go to bed, and I will see you in the morning."

Nikaranthia didn't say anything as she kissed his cheek, but he saw the stubborn look in her eyes, and he was almost certain he'd find her waiting for him when he returned. Which was going to lead to a long conversation about the difference between her age and his age, and how their wedding night was going to wait until she was older. Given how she'd kissed him, he wasn't entirely certain how she was going to react to that.

He was the last to arrive — his uncle had resumed his place on the Coral Throne, and Wilaanger and Daanir were fussing over the machines, which were making soft, pinging noises.

"Tarjiaan!" Ikaanaji waved off the Mancer and the Physician. "I'm fine, the pair of you. Wil, pour a round of drinks for us. Tarjiaan, I won't keep you."

"I'm not drinking," Tarjiaan protested.

"One drink. A toast, to your wedding and to your bride."

"Half a glass, Tarjiaan?" Wilaanger asked. He went to the sideboard and started to pour.

"And water it. It's been a long day, and I don't have a tolerance for it anymore. If I drink more than that, I may spend the rest of the night unconscious."

"Which would never do." Ikaanaji smiled. "You look happy, my nephew."

Tarjiaan took a glass from Wilaanger and swirled the liquor inside it. "I think I am, Uncle," he admitted. "She... I like her. And she's nothing like I expected. Nothing like we've been given to expect from women in the Empire." He paused, looking at Daanir. "You'll like her, Daan. She's clever. And she... I asked her a question, and she got well... not angry. Riled?" He chuckled and sipped his drink. "Yes, riled is the word. I think my wife has a temper."

"And she trusts you enough already to show you?" Ikaanaji nodded. "This bodes well for the alliance."

"She trusted me enough to tell me things I think the emissary would rather we not know," Tarjiaan said. "They tried to cheat us, Uncle."

"How so?"

"She isn't an Imperial princess. At least, she wasn't raised as one. She wasn't considered a princess until whenever you proposed this alliance. How long ago was that?"

"Four months," Wilaanger answered slowly, his brow furrowing.

"Do I want to know what she was before she was a princess?" Ikaanaji inquired. "And... do you know who sired her?"

"She says that she was told her father was the prince," Tarjiaan answered. "And... I don't care who she was. She's a princess now." He sipped his drink. "I told her that I think we'll suit each other well. I think she agrees. Now... I just need to keep Aanaji away from her."

"Do you anticipate trouble?" Ikaanaji asked.

"With my sister? Always." Tarjiaan looked up at Daanir, considering their conversation from only that morning. He drained his glass, then said, "If there isn't one there already, I want a poison sniffer in our quarters."

The King looked stunned. "Tarjiaan!"

"I'll get on that," Daanir murmured. "I should have thought of it before. Especially now. I'll have one for you by morning."

"Tarjiaan, you are overreacting!" Ikaanaji snapped. "Your sister is merely dramatic—"

"My sister has been petitioning to have me removed as Heir, and you never told me. That's more than drama. And this morning, Daanir told me that he wouldn't marry me because he liked living." The moment the words left his lips, Tarjiaan realized two things — he'd had more than enough to drink, and, judging from the shocked expression on his uncle's face, his father must never have had the chance to tell the King about Tarjiaan asking to marry.

"What?" Ikaanaji demanded. "What was this? You and the Mancer Royal were betrothed? Why was I never told?"

"Uncle, I thought my father had spoken to you," Tarjiaan said. He set his glass down. "I... I apologize. I didn't know he hadn't. The morning of the attacks, I asked my father for his blessing to ask Daanir to marry me. He gave it. But I never had the chance."

A shrill alarm blared, then quieted. Ikaanaji said, "I had no idea. Why did you never ask him since? Fifteen years is a long time for such a proposal to be left hanging."

Tarjiaan looked up at Daanir, who swallowed.

"We haven't seen each other since. I was ordered to leave the below-ships," Daanir answered. "I had to go above the waves for training, because I was late coming to my gifts, and they were too strong. I had to be trained in isolation, away from everyone, for their safety. I was a danger to everyone around me until I learned control—" He looked down at his own glass, then set it aside. "They let me stay long enough to know that Jiaan was going to live."

"Who told you that bilge?" Wilaanger asked. "That's not how it's ever gone before. I knew Riguaarin for years, and other Mancers besides him. I can't think of a single one that was isolated for their training. And Riguaarin came into his gifts at twenty-three!"

"He did? I... how was I supposed to know?" Daanir demanded. "No one told me anything. All I knew...all I knew was that my prince might be dying, and I was... they told me that I wasn't his battle companion anymore."

"What?" Tarjiaan gasped. "They told you what?"

"Who told you that?" Ikaanaji demanded.

"I..." Daanir stammered. Then he shook his head. "I don't know. I don't remember his name. I only met him that once. He came to me and told me that I wasn't a battle companion anymore. That I was a Mancer, first and foremost, and I had to leave. That if I didn't, he'd order me drugged and taken by force. And... that's what they did, because I wasn't going to go. They put a limiter on me and drugged me out of my mind, and when I woke up... I wasn't here and I had no way back." He swallowed and looked down. "I never wanted to go. And I thought you never answered my letters because you thought I abandoned you, and..." Daanir smiled slightly. "I should have known. I shouldn't have doubted you. I just..." He took a deep breath. "Fifteen years of letters, Jiaan. How could none of them have reached you?"

"Uncle, why would that be?" Tarjiaan turned his head to look at Ikaanaji, who was scowling. "Why would letters have gone astray consistently, and why would I never have been able to find a crew listing telling me where Daanir was stationed?"

"You couldn't find anything?" Wilaanger asked.

"Nothing. I was starting to think that he'd died, and no one was willing to tell me. But I couldn't find a death notice either." Tarjiaan paused. "It was as if he'd been scrubbed from all official records. I finally found something, and that's why we were going to the dockyards. Part of the reason."

"There's no way that should have been possible," the King said. "And to sever the battle companion bond? That's... that's blasphemy. It should never have happened. No, there is more here than meets the eye. And I will know who is behind this." He sighed and looked at Daanir. "Falian, what did you do?"

Tarjiaan blinked and looked up at Daanir, who shook his head.

"Ika, that's Mancer Royal Daanir. Falian is ten years gone to the Mothers," Wilaanger said. "But his records are in the archives. Should I send for Ilaris?"

Ikaanaji's frown turned to a scowl. "No," he said. "No, Wil, I want you to do this. I trust you, and I know you'll do anything in your power to keep these young men safe." He closed his eyes. "I am tired."

"Rest, Ika." Wilaanger turned toward Tarjiaan, and nodded toward the door. He walked away, and Tarjiaan followed him, hearing Daanir behind him.

There was a small antechamber off the throne room, and it was there that Wilaanger led them. He said nothing until the door was closed, then sighed. "Mancer, silence the room. Video and audio. Please. This must be between us."

"I... done." Daanir looked around. "You're finally telling him?"

"Telling me what?" Tarjiaan looked up.

Wilaanger took a deep breath. "Ikaanaji's body isn't the only thing that's failing. He's been getting lost in his memories, and it's been getting worse. He has moments where he's completely coherent. And then... he sees old friends. Old faces. Fights old battles. He's fading by inches."

"He called me Taarik today," Tarjiaan said. "Several times."

"Tarjiaan, you may need to take the throne sooner than you thought," Wilaanger said, his voice low. "I will hold that day off as long as I can, but... it's getting closer, and there is nothing I or anyone can do to stop it." He paused. "I want you to keep this close to your chest. The Mancer and I know. Ilaris knows. We've been holding the kingdom together, the three of us."

Tarjiaan looked up at Daanir. "You've been keeping secrets like this? When did you learn how?"

Daanir shrugged. "I had... practice."

"Tarjiaan," Wilaanger said. "There is something else I want you to consider."

"You're not going to ask me to marry again, are you?" Tarjiaan asked.

"You have had too much to drink." Daanir sounded exhausted as he leaned back against the wall. The speakers and wires above him started crackling, and he grimaced and took a breath to steady himself. The electronics fell silent, and he snorted. "And maybe so have I."

Wilaanger sighed. Then he said, "I want you to consider naming your children by your wife as your heirs, and removing Naajir from the line of succession."

"What? But the mother line—"

"I know." Wilaanger rubbed one hand over his face. "It is only in cases where there is not an heir of the mother line that we turn to the king's own progeny. But in this case, I think that perhaps the heir of the mother line may be... unsuitable."

"The heir?" Tarjiaan asked softly. "Or the mother of that heir?"

"Ikaanaji doesn't believe that Aanaji is anything more than a child having a tantrum," Wilaanger said. "He will not hear anything to the contrary. That's why she's back on the *Chimaera*. But you and I, Jiaan, we know better."

Tarjiaan nodded. "We do. Wil, where is Naajir? She's been refusing to allow him to come above the waves. I told her that I was going to bring it to Uncle if she refused again. Is he not aboard?"

"She told us that he and his tutor remained on the *Allegiant* when she returned to the *Chimaera*," Wilaanger answered. "Which may be for the best, having him away from her."

Tarjiaan nodded. "Out of range. True."

"I'll have that poison sniffer tonight," Daanir murmured.

"We also need replace the maid that Ilaris assigned to your wife, Tarjiaan. I've sent for someone who you can trust. My grandniece, as it happens." Wil sighed again. "There are dark currents, Tarjiaan. I had been trying... we've been trying," he amended, glancing at Daanir. "But we haven't been able to see a clear course through them. Now that you're here, we have a chance." He leaned back against the wall and closed his eyes. "Ika isn't the only one who is tired. One more thing, Jiaan. I will find out who separated you and Daanir and why. I promise you that."

"Thank you, Wil." Tarjiaan looked up at Daanir. Daanir smiled at him, but it didn't light his eyes the way his smiles always had.

Finding out why would be cold comfort for both of them.

"We were manipulated," Daanir murmured as they left the throne room. "Someone got me away from you and buried me. Probably the only thing that got me out of the dockyards was that Mancer rolls are only accessible to Mancers." He wound his hands together. "Who knew that you'd asked your father?"

"Only him and Ranji," Tarjiaan answered. "I had breakfast with them that morning. I asked him then. They both approved of it. Father loved you like his own." He covered Daanir's hands with his own. "Daan, I never stopped loving you—"

"So you said," Daanir said. "But you're married now." His hands shook as he carefully drew them away. "And it's going to be hard for us to avoid each other. So... are you going to tell her about me? Before someone else does?"

"Unless you tell me not to," Tarjiaan said. "Do you want to be there?"

"That might be awkward," Daanir said, his ears the deep red of a sailor's delight sunset. "I'll bring the poison sniffer as soon as it's ready." He squeezed Tarjiaan's shoulder. "Which means I should go get to work." He squeezed again, then walked away, heading down a side corridor. Tarjiaan watched him go, then sighed and started off toward his suite. He wasn't looking forward to trying to sleep. But maybe the nightmares would leave him be tonight.

And maybe the Emperor would abdicate in favor of his supposed granddaughter, and make Tarjiaan Imperial Prince Consort. He shook his head, laughing softly as his own foolishness, and opened the door to the suite. The lights were low, and the door had closed behind him before he noticed the figure curled up on the couch. He smiled — as he'd expected, Nikaranthia had clearly tried to wait up for him. She was dressed for bed in a sleeveless nightgown sheer enough that it left nothing to the imagination. Her dark hair was shorter than he'd expected, curling close to her scalp. She looked completely at peace, and he was tempted to just let her sleep on the couch. It looked comfortable enough, if he got a blanket for her....

Then he noticed the open book in her lap.

He moved closer, and in a low voice called, "Nikaranthia?" She didn't move, and he raised his voice slightly, "Nikaranthia?"

She jerked, her entire body tensing, and when she turned to look at him, Tarjiaan was almost certain that she didn't see him. He wasn't sure what she did see, but she shrieked and threw herself off the couch. Her nightdress tangled around her legs, and she tumbled to the floor, curling around herself as she started to beg in Imperial. Tarjiaan couldn't follow her words, but he recognized the defensive posture... and saw the scars on her bare shoulders.

"Release," he snapped, and the carapace of the chair opened. He set the brakes and lowered himself to the floor, crawling toward her. Once he was close enough to touch her, he rested his hands on the ground where she'd see them if she raised her head. "Nika, wake up. Nika, you're safe. It's safe. I'm here. I won't let anyone hurt you." He repeated himself until his voice was hoarse, until he wasn't sure she was hearing him. Then she took a shaky, deep breath and looked up. She met his eyes, frowned, and pushed herself up slightly.

"You... are on the floor," she croaked.

"You're on the floor," he replied. "You needed me down here. I'm not going to hurt you."

She nodded, wiping tears off her cheeks. "I am sorry," she murmured. "I..."

"I scared you," Tarjiaan said. "I'm sorry. I was trying not to startle you. I didn't think I would frighten you so badly." He turned, seeing the book on the ground. He picked it up, and only then noticed which book she'd been reading. He licked his lips and looked down at the yellowing, hand-written pages. "I'm surprised. I thought I was going to have to teach you to read."

"You would do that?" she gasped. "But—"

"It's not against the law here," Tarjiaan interrupted. "You're not going to be punished for it." He smiled. "I was just surprised," he added, holding the book up.

"I..." She sat back on her heels and folded her hands in her lap. "My mother taught me, when I was small. The first time I was beaten, it was because one of the sentinels who watched over the women's quarters caught me. I try to keep it hidden, but I was alone and you have so many books, and I thought... but I fell asleep and..." She frowned again, then looked at Tarjiaan. "What did you call me?"

Tarjiaan blinked, then thought about what he'd said and chuckled. "Nika. It's a diminutive," he admitted. He reached across to take her hand. "I only do it to people I like," he admitted. "And...I do like you."

"Nika," she repeated. "And... you like me?" She bit her lip. "Why? You have no reason to like me."

"Daanir would tell you that I like people far too easily. He's known me... well, longer than anyone."

"But why?" she insisted. "I am one of your enemies."

"You're not my enemy." He shifted, putting his back against the couch as he considered the question. "I'll admit, I'd hoped we would...be able to at least tolerate each other. Marriage is a rocky journey if you hate each other. But I realized even before we married that I like you. You have a sense of humor. And you're clever," Tarjiaan answered. "You're curious, and brave, and you have spirit and a spine and a temper." He ran his thumb over her fingers. "I said I thought we'd suit each other well. I mean that."

"But I am—"

"No," Tarjiaan said, and she stopped talking, her eyes wide. "If you're going to say a single disparaging thing about who you were before today, don't. Nika, let me tell you what I told my uncle. I don't care who you were. You're a princess now. You're my princess, and my wife. And that's what matters to me. Anything that you might have been before today doesn't matter to me." He tugged her hand out of her lap, raised it to his lips and kissed her fingers. "What matters to me is what we have now. And what we'll have from now on."

She stared at him for a moment, then launched herself at him, hard enough to knock him sideways and onto his back. He grunted slightly as he hit, and caught her in his arms so that she didn't hurt herself. She rested on his chest for a moment, staring at him. Then she caught his face in her hands and kissed him, passionately. Desperately, as if she were afraid he'd change his mind. He held her tightly, feeling her warmth through her thin nightgown, through the layers of his clothing. Her fingers were in his hair, tugging hard enough to draw a whimper from his lips. She was too young. He had to stop....

He heard the *click-whirr* of the door mechanism, and jerked, turning to look up and see Aanaji standing in the doorway. She was dressed from head to toe in red, and her face matched her coat.

"Really!" Aanaji gasped as she stalked out. The door slid closed behind her.

"Was that...?"

"My sister," Tarjiaan finished, looking up at Nika. He sighed, and she started giggling. She shifted off of his chest, and helped him to sit up.

"I am sorry," she said. "I—"

"Nika, it's our wedding night," Tarjiaan interrupted. "Do you really think anyone thinks we're not having sex?"

"But on the floor? It is... undignified!"

"Sex is always undignified," Tarjiaan said. "If it's not, you're doing something wrong." He turned and looked at his chair. "I need to get back up."

"How can I help?"

"Release the brake... there. Move it closer and set the brake again." Once Nika had moved the chair closer, Tarjiaan lifted himself back up into the seat and sighed. "On the whole, I prefer a bed, but it wouldn't be the first time on the floor, either."

"You have had lovers?" Nika moved around in front of the chair. "I was being taught... the bedroom arts. Because they said that was all I was good for. But no one wanted me. So... if they promised you a virgin, they kept that promise, at least." She clasped her hands. "Have you had many lovers?"

"Not for quite a few years. I've been celibate for fifteen years, but before that? I had a number of bed partners, because a prince is a commodity, even the sixth prince in line, and noble-born girls think that the way to catch one is to lure them into the bedroom," Tarjiaan answered. "But I can honestly say I've only had one lover. And I will tell you about him another time."

"Him? That is allowed here?" Nika frowned slightly. "I... oh."

"Oh?"

She looked at the door. "Is that why Mancer Daanir looked so sad?"

Tarjiaan burst out laughing. "Woman, you were wasted on the Empire! Wasted!" He reached out and took her hand, pulling her close. She smiled slightly as he kissed her hand. "I have been blessed with a brilliant wife, who I like very much, and who no longer needs to hide her brilliance. And who has had a very long day and should go to bed."

She frowned. "But it is our wedding night. I thought..."

"Nika, I know what you thought," Tarjiaan said gently. "I know what everyone else will think. But... you're so young! You're young enough to be my daughter. I'm not sleeping with you. Not until you're older."

"Oh," she murmured. "I thought I had mistranslated, when you told me how old you were in the portrait. I understand now. You are... how old?"

"I am thirty-four." Tarjiaan met her eyes. "Why?"

"Tarjiaan, how old did they tell you I am?" she asked.

"I didn't see the documents, but Wilaanger told me that the marriage contract said you were a few weeks shy of eighteen. We wouldn't have accepted anyone younger. And if they had sent a... a child, I'd have adopted her, not married her." He ran his thumb over her dainty fingers. "When is your natal day? Do you know?"

"They told you...?" Her voice trailed off. "Another lie. They told you I was a princess, and they told you I was seventeen. Tarjiaan, I just turned twenty-five." She gestured to herself with her free hand. "They must have thought you would believe I was younger because I am small."

"They were right. I thought you were young enough to be my daughter. Twenty-five? That's a far more comfortable age." Tarjiaan felt himself relaxing slightly. "You've still had a very long day, Nika. If you want to sleep, I will see you in the morning."

Her jaw dropped. "You... are giving me a choice?"

Tarjiaan nodded. "Yes. Always."

She licked her lips and looked down. "May I ask a question? Two questions?"

"Please do."

She looked at him through her lashes. "You call me Nika. What may I call you?"

He smiled. "When you're ready to call me by a diminutive, the people who love me call me Jiaan."

She nodded. "Jiaan. I like that."

Tarjiaan held his hand out to her. "What's the second question"

She pointed at the door. "How do I lock that?"

Chapter Ten
Introductions

TARJIAAN WOKE SLOWLY, unaccustomed to the sensation of a warm body curled against his own. That was something entirely new. When they'd shared a bed, Daanir had always been awake before Tarjiaan. Waking with someone was nice. And he'd slept the entire night without nightmares jarring him awake. He didn't understand why, but he wasn't complaining. Without opening his eyes, he rolled toward Nika, and she settled against him with a contented, sleepy sigh. He ran his hand down her back, feeling ridges of old scars under his fingers. She'd said something about being beaten. When she was more comfortable with him, he'd ask her. For now... she hadn't asked him about his scars, so he'd give her the same courtesy.

He shifted again, tugging the sheets up and listening to the hum of the air circulators overheard. He could go back to sleep. He wasn't expected anywhere today. He had no duties. He could just sleep. And... perhaps not sleep. He kissed Nika's forehead, and her arm slipped around his waist. She didn't seem to be awake, so he let himself drift....

Until someone knocked on the door. On the bedroom door, which told Tarjiaan exactly who it was.

In his arms, Nika woke with a startled jerk; Tarjiaan tightened his arms around her, and she focused on him. She smiled, and stretched up to kiss him.

"I thought I had dreamed you," she murmured.

"You have an excellent imagination," Tarjiaan replied, and she giggled.

"Was that someone knocking?" She looked at the door. "But we locked the door!"

"And a Mancer can tell the locks to open. They're like cats. You can't lock them out." Tarjiaan raised his voice. "Daan, we'll be out in a moment."

"I have the sniffer." Daanir's voice was muffled by the door. "And Logiri's here. He's got your breakfast."

"Enough to share?" Tarjiaan asked.

"Yes." It was difficult to read his tone, muffled through the door. "More than enough for you both."

"Good. Stay." He rolled onto his back, then laughed when Nika pounced on him. She ended up laying on top of him, her chin resting on her stacked hands.

"Am I expected to parade naked before him?" she asked. "I have only my nightdress."

"In which you might as well be naked. I noticed."

She smiled. "I noticed that you noticed."

Tarjiaan chuckled and wrapped his arms around her. "You do not need to go through the sitting room. Not if you don't wish to," he answered. "That door in the corner leads to our shared bath. You can go through there to your bedroom and get whatever will make you comfortable. If you want to bathe and dress, we'll wait for you."

She arched a brow. "So... if I wished to parade naked in front of him, you would not object? In the Empire, a man would slay another man who dared look on his wife's body."

"Nika, I have trusted Daan with my life for years. I trust him absolutely, and in all things." Tarjiaan ran his hand down her back, over her hip. "That includes trusting him around you. I know him. He won't even look at you without your leave." He nodded toward the door. "Which is why he's still out there. If it was just me in here, he'd have come in. However, you should probably ask him before you parade around naked. He can be shy."

Nika looked puzzled for a moment. Then she nodded. She stretched up and kissed him, then slipped out of the bed. She stopped, looking around, then shook her head. "I am not sure where my nightdress is. No matter. I will not be long," she said, and went into the bathroom. The minute the bathroom door closed, the bedroom door cracked open.

"You can come in," Tarjiaan said. Daanir peered around the door.

"She's gone?"

"To her room to dress."

"I'll get Logiri for you—"

"Just come in."

Daanir hesitated before he stepped inside. "Do you want to dress? Or just a banyan?"

Tarjiaan sat up, running his fingers through his hair. His fingers caught on the drops that he'd forgotten about in his left ear; he grimaced and took them out. "Would you take these? I need to put the studs back in. And I should bathe. So just a banyan. Which... I'm not sure if I have one here that fits."

Daanir took the drops and put them on the dresser, then stopped before going to the wardrobe, taking out a hauntingly familiar green and gold robe, one that Tarjiaan hadn't seen since that last breakfast on the *Marauder*.

"Where did that come from?" he demanded. "That's my father's!"

"Yours now," Daanir said. "When the wreckers recovered things from the *Marauder*, you were still... so Wilaanger asked me to claim things for you. Our quarters were almost completely destroyed when they hulled the ship, so most of our things were gone. I saved what I could—"

"Which is how my books got here?"

"Which is how your books got here. I couldn't find your small lute." He stopped and held up the robe, then handed it to Tarjiaan. "This came out of the great cabin in one piece. I put it away for you, and... well, I never got to tell you. So it's been packed away in your quarters down here ever since. I found it when I moved your things."

Tarjiaan ran the silk dressing gown through his fingers. "This... this is a wonderful wedding present, Daan," he said softly. "I didn't know anything of his survived." He looked up. "He'd have liked her, Daan. She's brilliant."

Daanir leaned against the foot-board, apparently engrossed in by the grain of the wood. "Is she?"

"She was wasted on them." Tarjiaan carefully draped the robe over his chair, then shifted to the edge of the bed.

"I'll fetch Logiri," Daanir murmured, heading for the door.

"I can do it, Daan." Tarjiaan reached out, grabbed the arms of the chair, and swung himself into the seat. "I'm going to need to have this shortened," he added as he pulled the robe on and wrapped it around himself. He'd have to ask Logiri to get it appropriately altered to fit the chair. He arranged the too-long skirts of the banyan, then closed the carapace and waited for the light to glow green.

"What did you decide about telling her?" Daanir asked.

"I didn't have to," Tarjiaan answered. He smiled. "She figured it out. From a couple passing clues and the look on your face last night."

Daanir closed his eyes, tucking his hands into his pockets. "Great," he mumbled. "Well, I'll just—"

Tarjiaan nodded. "And she can read."

Daanir exhaled slowly and summoned up a weak smile. "You don't say."

"I do not read well." Tarjiaan turned to see Nika standing in the bathroom door. She was wearing a long, loose robe, and her hair was once again covered, this time by a wrap that matched the robe.

She smiled. "You weren't outside," she said. "I came to find you." She came around the bed and tipped her head to the side. "I like those colors on you."

"Thank you." Tarjiaan ran his fingers over the sleeve of the banyan. "Shall we go out?"

"I'll set up the sniffer and get out of your way," Daanir said, and hurried out of the room. Nika watched him go, then looked at Tarjiaan.

"Is this what you meant by shy?" she asked. "Am I making him nervous?"

"I think he isn't sure how to treat you," Tarjiaan answered. "Oh, before we go out, let me warn you. Don't get attached to Adalia; she's going to be replaced with someone who isn't loyal to my sister."

A mischievous smile blossomed on Nika's face. "I... may have saved you the trouble," she admitted. "She thought that I could not speak your language. She was quite surprised when I answered her insults with a dismissal."

"Nika!" Tarjiaan laughed aloud. "I wonder if that's why Aanaji came storming in last night." He held his hand out to her. "Breakfast, my wife?"

"Thank you, my husband."

They couldn't pass side by side through the door, so Nika stepped back and let Tarjiaan go first. In the sitting room, Daanir was balanced on a chair, mounting a delicately filigreed ornament over the table.

"What is that?" Nika asked, passing Tarjiaan's chair to look closer. "It is lovely."

"Poison sniffer," Daanir answered without looking at her. "Made it look nice, so no one recognizes it."

"A poison tester?" Nika walked around the table. "You have machines to do that? In the Imperial court, a poison tester is a person."

The chair Daanir was balanced on wobbled before he caught his balance again. "That's..." he paused, then looked back up. "That's the Imps for you."

"Did you design that?" Tarjiaan asked, coming closer. "It doesn't look like your work."

"Kaapi did the decorative work. She's got a good eye for design." Daanir jumped down off the chair. "Get to work, you," he said, and the box started to glow with a soft, white light. "Power source will let it run... well, almost indefinitely. If there's anything that shouldn't be in the food on the table, it'll turn red."

"Who is Kaapi?" Nika asked. "Is that your wife?"

Daanir sputtered, looking from her to Tarjiaan. "You two have got disturbingly similar minds. He asked the same thing. Kaapi is my adopted daughter and my apprentice." He looked up at the sniffer. "Logiri, it's ready."

"Good," Logiri said. "Things are getting cold. Please, be seated."

Tarjiaan moved his chair up to the table, and smiled as Nika looked at Daanir.

"Which is your place?" she asked. "Where does the battle companion sit?"

Daanir shook his head. "I'm not anymore, but thank you. It depends on their companion's dominant hand. For us, I was on the left."

Nika nodded and took the chair on Tarjiaan's right. She folded her hands on the table.

"I'm not—"

"Stay," Tarjiaan said firmly.

Daanir's jaw flexed, but he sank to the chair, fixing his gaze on the pretty bit of tech above them. "Your hospitality is uncalled for, your highnesses," he said carefully as Logiri set out the platters on the table. They sat for a moment in awkward silence. Tarjiaan glanced up at the sniffer, then picked up the cup of tea that Logiri had put in front of him.

"I am very glad to meet you properly, Daanir," Nika said.

Daanir looked down at his own hands, his ears and cheeks the same warm pink. "I... have no idea what to say to you," he admitted.

Nika nodded. "Because this place should have been yours? Men can marry in Meradon, can they not?" She glanced towards Tarjiaan curiously.

"They can." Daanir carefully inspected the cuffs of his jacket.

"I am sorry," Nika said. She paused, waiting, it seemed, for Daanir to look her way, then sighed when he did not. "You do not have to say anything. But will you listen? Because I have a question I would like to ask you."

Daanir nodded grimly. "Go ahead."

Nika unfolded her hands and rested them on the table. "I know... very little. About anything. I want to learn. So... if it will not make you uncomfortable to be with me, I would like to know more about this place. How can we breathe when we are underwater? And... and Jiaan showed me the farm on his ship. How can there be farms on a ship?" She pointed up at the sniffer. "How does that work? You can tell me? Teach me? I want to know." She paused, then grinned. "I want to know everything!"

Daanir looked stunned. For several minutes, the only sounds were the click and rattle of crockery, and the hiss of the air circulators. Finally, Daanir nodded slowly. "I... I like that you want to know. I understand that want. Now, the first thing we'd need to do is work on your reading," he said. He picked up a piece of toast and turned it over on his plate, then took a bite. "There will be a lot of it if you want to know everything," he continued once he'd swallowed.

Nika smiled. "Does that mean you will teach me?"

"When we have the time," he hedged. "I have my duties, and you're going to be busy, too."

Nika looked up at Logiri, who bowed his head to her. "Antarlogirish said that I would have duties," she said. "What duties do wives have in Meradon?"

"Anything they want to do, really," Tarjiaan answered. "Anything they've been trained to do. My uncle's late wife was a physician, for example. And as my wife, you'll have some more specialized duties. You'll make the tours of the crèche ships, for example. It's traditional for the women of the royal family to be responsible for overseeing the care of the orphaned children in the fleet. Wilaanger has been tending to it, but I think he'll be glad to hand it over. He's been handling it since my mother died, because Mother was the last of the women of the royal line other than my sister, and Aanaji won't do it."

Nika looked thoughtful. "There are no other women in the royal line? Are there any other members? Family I should meet?"

Tarjiaan shook his head. "No. I had four older cousins and an older brother, but Aanaji is the only one left."

"Oh," Nika murmured. "Oh, you said you were the sixth prince. And now you are the heir. They all... all of them died?"

Tarjiaan watched the surface of his tea ripple as his hands shook. "All in the same battle that killed my father. The battle that—" He meant to say *put me in this chair* but his voice caught in his throat, and his hand shook again, making tea slosh over the rim of the cup and onto the table. In a moment, Logiri was there, cleaning the spill, refreshing the tea. Tarjiaan took a deep breath, then jumped in surprise as Nika hugged his arm.

"Jiaan, please," she murmured. "You are hurting yourself." He turned to see her looking up at him, her eyes wide. "I will not have you hurting yourself. Not for me. You do not need to tell me this. Not now."

Tarjiaan licked his lips. "This is... you should know—"

"And you will tell me," she interrupted. "But not when you are so raw." She hugged his arm again. "Tell me about your mother. What were her duties? Was she a physician, too?"

Daanir shook his head as he became very interested in the bookshelf across the room. "Lady Aajinisa turned green when one of us skinned a knee."

Tarjiaan looked at him, grateful for the distraction. "It's not fair you remember more about her than I do," he grumbled. "You said you only met her once!"

"She was memorable," Daanir said fondly, a little frown between his brows. "She smelled good. And she sang to us."

"That's what I remember most," Tarjiaan said. "Her voice." He sipped his freshened tea and looked at Nika. "Mother was a poet, a singer, and a storyteller. She was incredibly talented. She was also the youngest of Uncle's sisters, and she was given quite a bit of leeway in terms of what she wanted to do with her life. So no one objected too very much when she fell in love with and married a common-born sea captain."

Daanir leaned back in his chair and said, "Daanir recordings. *Heart of the Sea*. Play."

Tarjiaan heard a click. Then the room was filled with music and a familiar, warm voice.

Nika sat up, startled. "Where is that coming from?"

Daanir pointed to the speaker grating in the ceiling. "I keep music recordings saved in the central core, so I can listen to them wherever I'm working. This is one of my two favorites."

"It's the anthem of Meradon under the sea," Tarjiaan added. He studied Nika, and smiled. She had her eyes closed, listening intently to the music. "Mother wrote it, and Uncle adopted it formally before I was born. You'll be expected to learn it."

"Her voice is beautiful," Nika murmured. She looked at Tarjiaan, then twisted to look at the bookshelf. "She was a poet, you said.

The book I was reading last night. It was handwritten. Not like the others. Was that her poetry?"

Daanir frowned slightly, turning to look at the bookcase. Then his eyes widened. "Wait, was she reading...?"

The song ended, and the music changed. Tarjiaan looked up in shock when he recognized both the song and the voice. His own words. His own voice, the way he remembered it.

Nika gasped, "That is your voice!" She turned to stare at Tarjiaan. "And the words... these were in the book! Is that... Jiaan, did you write this? And the rest of those poems?"

For a moment, Tarjiaan felt as if the deck under him was swaying. His face warmed. "I... used to be a passable musician," he stammered. "I haven't sung for anyone. Not since..." He paused, then turned in his seat. "How did you get a recording of this?"

"Stop," Daan told the air, touching the wall and glaring at the speaker. "Stop playing." He paused. "I wanted to be able to hear it whenever I wanted, so one night, when I asked you to play it for me, I had a recorder set up." Daanir gritted his teeth, glaring at the speaker box. "I said stop," he snapped, his voice hardening, and the song ended in the middle of a quiet rising chorus.

Tarjiaan glanced at him for a moment before sighing. "Yes, I wrote this. I wrote it for him. And I only ever sang it for him."

Nika's eyes widened. "Then I should not have heard it?"

"I'm sorry," Daanir whispered, grimacing at the abandoned toast on his plate. "It wasn't supposed to keep playing. Sometimes it doesn't listen. Sometimes, these things have a mind of their own."

Nika looked up again. "Much like a cat listens, it seems."

"I don't know much about cats." Daanir's flush was stark against his white hair and pale skin. "Do they come to know you too well? Anticipate your needs? Answer unasked questions?" He bowed his head. "If so, then the machines are very much like cats. And I should go."

"Daan–"

Before Tarjiaan could finish speaking, Nika was standing, walking around behind him to stand close enough to Daanir that he couldn't have stood without knocking her over.

"You listen like a cat. Or a machine," she said, her voice firm. "Please. You should listen now, and hear me. I am...unwelcome. I am unwanted. I am in the place that should have been yours, if Sun and Sand were fair and kind." She paused and looked at Tarjiaan. "Are the Great Mothers fair and kind?"

Tarjiaan blinked, then shook his head. "Not in my experience."

"It would be a good thing if those who have power over others were fair and kind. The Gods. Kings. Emperors. But they are not." She took a breath. "And I am here. But I will not take your place. Your place is on the left. I will be on the right. And if there is more..." She paused again. "In the Empire, wives learn to look the other way, if their husbands have... very close male friends. So long as Jiaan is happy. Because I am here now, but you were here first." She paused. "You were his first. And I respect that."

Daanir stared up at her, his expression unreadable. Once, Tarjiaan had been able to tell what he was thinking by the tilt of his brows, the flush on his cheeks. Now... he was a closed book. "No," he said finally, quietly. "However your offer is intended, Highness, it isn't yours to make."

"Then it's mine," Tarjiaan said, his voice soft. "Daan, I'm not going to pressure you into anything." He paused, then snorted. "I never could pressure you into anything. My stubborn Daan. But your place at my side, and in my heart, that's always yours and always will be yours. If you want to take it."

"But—!"

"Nika, the choice is his to make," Tarjiaan said. He took her hand and tugged her back, away from Daanir who was sitting as still as a statue. An exceptionally red-faced statue. "There are things between us that... that need to be said, that need to be understood. Questions that need to be answered. Those need time. We both need time. Now sit and eat." He looked at Daanir. "You eat, too. We invited you. Eat something more than toast."

Nika sat back down at Tarjiaan's right. "You are both stubborn," she muttered.

For a moment, there was only the hiss of the air circulators. Then Daanir snorted and grumbled, "Whale. Fish. Wet."

Tarjiaan stared at him for a moment, then started laughing.

"What?" Nika asked. "That means what?"

"The full saying is that the whale doesn't get to call the fish wet," Tarjiaan answered.

She frowned. Then she laughed. "Yes, I am stubborn, too."

"Guessing you wouldn't have survived if you hadn't been?" Daanir asked.

Nika nodded. "It is easier to lay down and die than fight to survive. But it is not in me to do that."

"It's not in any of us to do that." Tarjiaan looked at Daanir, and fought the urge to reach for his hand. "Daan, the offer is made. And we will talk. We'll find answers. And we'll figure a course from there."

Daanir flattened his palms on the table, hard enough that the table shifted slightly, and Tarjiaan was certain that he was going to launch himself from his seat and bolt. Then he relaxed. He closed his eyes and bowed his head. "I will remain until dismissed," he said quietly. "Please pass the kelp."

Tarjiaan picked up the bowl and set it down in front of Daanir. It took everything in him not to flinch. Stay until dismissed? Really?

No. Time. They needed time and answers. Just like he said. Then...

Then what?

Nika coughed gently. "Jiaan, do we have duties today?"

"Not to my knowledge," Tarjiaan answered. "Unless there's been a change? Logiri?" He turned, not seeing his aide. Not surprising – Logiri was good at taking himself out of range when there was a need for private conversation. "Logiri?"

Logiri appeared from Tarjiaan's bedroom. He bowed slightly. "Prince-Captain?"

"Is anything planned today?"

"Your uncle has requested that you and your bride join him for the evening meal tonight, but says that he understands if you wish to delay that until tomorrow." Logiri paused. "It will be a family meal."

Tarjiaan coughed. "Family... meaning he will probably insist that my sister be there as well." He sighed, learning back in his chair and rubbing one hand over his face. "Best to get it over with as soon as possible, I suppose?" He turned to Nika. "Do you object? I can't promise that she'll behave herself." He glanced back at Daanir. "She barged in on us last night. And she was dressed in mourning red."

"Making a statement without saying a word. If only she could stick to that and keep her opinions to herself, but we're talking about Aanaji here—" He sat up straight, just before the door chime rang. "Logiri, open the door! Quickly!"

Logiri looked startled, but opened the door, letting in a nervous-looking young man in the royal uniform, who kept looking over his shoulder as he came inside. As the door closed, he visibly relaxed.

Tarjiaan almost didn't recognize his nephew.

"Naajir?"

"Uncle," he said. "I hope I'm not intruding? I wanted to meet my new aunt. I apologize for not attending the wedding. I was..." He paused, and his cheeks darkened slightly. "Detained."

Chapter Eleven
Family

BEFORE TARJIAAN COULD say anything, Daanir was up and out of his chair. "Wrist! Now!" Naajir shoved his sleeve up, revealing a metal wristband; Daanir grabbed his hand and frowned. "Where are you supposed to be?"

"In my room, reviewing my lessons. Mother is busy and will be gone for at least an hour. Maybe more. I thought it was worth the risk."

"What risk?" Tarjiaan asked. "What are you doing here? Wil said you weren't on the *Chimaera*." He stared for a moment, then rolled back from the table. "Daan? Is that a locator?"

"Just a... there. Right, that's fixed." Daanir looked up. "Sorry. Yes, it's a locator. He can't fart without Aanaji knowing."

"It's the reason I'm not topside," Naajir said. "I want to be. I know I'm supposed to be. I've tried to be, and after the last time, Mother—" He stopped, pushed his sleeve back down. "Not the time or place. I did want to be there for you, Uncle. I want to know you better." He glanced at Daanir. "The Mancer tells me all about you."

Daanir shrugged uncomfortably. "He spends enough time with me. I have to talk to him about something."

Tarjiaan raised one hand. "I need you both to reel in that line and cast it again. What am I missing? Daan, my sister can't stand you. She's allowing Naajir to spend time with you?"

"She doesn't know," Daanir answered. "I tell the locator to show that Naajir is wherever he's supposed to be when he shows up in my lab. Which I just did. Usually, I plan for it," he added with a frustrated look at Naajir. "And to answer the next question, your uncle doesn't know. Neither does Wil. I don't know how Aanaji got him on board with no one the wiser, but no one knows he's onboard but me, I don't think. And Kaapi. She's the one who brought him to me."

Naajir nodded. "The king doesn't know I'm on the *Chimaera*. I think she's got him believing I'm on a crèche ship somewhere."

"That's what Wilaanger said last night." Tarjiaan looked at Daanir. "And you haven't told him why?"

Daanir blinked. "You're asking me why I haven't sailed into Hurricane Aanaji?" he asked. "Jiaan, I told you. I like living. This is her boy. I have no doubt she'd find a way to kill me horribly if she found out I was helping him. Over the years, I have learned how to keep a secret, if it really counts."

Tarjiaan ran one hand over his face. "I... Naajir, sit down. This... I'm not sure what to do with this." He gestured. "Sit."

"Please," Nika added.

Naajir bowed again and took a seat, nodding his thanks as Logiri put a cup of tea in front of him. He picked up the cup, took a sip, then wrapped his hands around it and stared into the depths of the drink. Then Logiri coughed — Naajir flinched, looked up, then slowly relaxed and took another sip of tea.

"Naajir," Tarjiaan said. He paused, considering his words. He has a feeling that if he said the wrong thing, the boy would flee. And he understood the feeling, and the source of it. "You may not think this is the time or the place, but I want you to tell me what is going on," he said. He reached across Nika and rested his hand on his nephew's arm. "You may not believe this, but I understand. I want to help. Let me help."

"You just got married," Naajir murmured. "You shouldn't be worrying over me."

"Yes, he should," Nika said and added her hand to Tarjiaan's.

Naajir looked at her. "You're nothing like what I was expecting," he said softly. He nodded. "Mother... ever since we came to the *Chimaera*, she's changed," he said slowly. "All my tutors were left behind on the *Allegiant*. She told me that from now on, I'm only going to be learning what she wants me to know, doing what she wants me to do. She wants me to depend on her for everything. I've heard her say it—"

"To who?" Tarjiaan asked.

"I don't know," Naajir admitted. "I was... well, I was locked in my room. I could hear her, but I don't know who she was talking to. I know her plans are to have me eventually ascend the Coral Throne while she rules through me. And I don't want that." He bit his lip, a firm scowl settling at the corners of his eyes. "I won't be a puppet. But there was no one here for me to turn to. Not until Mancer Daanir." He picked up his cup and drank again. "And... I'm sorry, Uncle. I shouldn't be putting this on you. I really did come to congratulate you." For a brief moment, Tarjiaan saw his brother's face.

"You look so much like Aaranji," Tarjiaan said. "I had no idea."

Naajir scowled. "My mother says that all the time," he grumbled. "I'm not him. I'm me. And I'm tired of her holding it over me that I'm not him."

Tarjiaan squeezed Naajir's arm. "Let me think on what I can do, Naajir. And thank you for coming to me. For trusting me."

"I have an idea," Nika said, turning to look at Tarjiaan as she drew her hand back. "You will be starting negotiations soon, no?" Tarjiaan nodded, and she looked back at Naajir. "How is your handwriting? And do you speak Imperial?"

Daanir looked at her curiously, then smiled. "Oh. Oh, that's good. The treaty is the King's highest priority right now. That might actually work."

"You want me to request Naajir as... what? My secretary?" Tarjiaan considered the idea, then looked at Naajir. "I like this idea, but I won't request it if you have doubts about it. So, what are your thoughts? If I request it of Uncle, and couch it that you'll be learning the diplomatic process, I think we'll practically have a royal writ ordering it. He's already told me that he regrets that I never had the training my brother and cousins had, because I was sixth in line and no one thought I'd need it. He won't want to make that same mistake again."

Naajir blinked. "I... Mother refused to let me learn Imperial, but... Kaapi is learning, and she lets me read her books. And I remember everything I read. I'm sure my accent is horrible, though."

Nika laced her fingers together, then spoke in Imperial, "It is very nice to meet you, nephew."

Naajir bit his lip, then haltingly replied, "And to... to know... ah..." He stopped and frowned. "I haven't learned the word for aunt," he said in Common.

Nika repeated his words, adding in the missing one. "Now you say it," she added.

"Please say it again?"

She said the phrase again, and Naajir nodded and repeated after her. She nodded and patted his arm.

"Your accent is not bad." She glanced at Tarjiaan and smiled, for a moment looking like pure mischief. "It is better than your uncle's."

"You should get back to your room," Daanir said. "If we don't know for sure where your mother is or how long she'll be gone-"

Naajir hurried to his feet. "Thank you. I... I wasn't thinking. I should go back."

"I'll do what I can, Naajir," Tarjiaan said. "Will we see you at dinner?"

Naajir frowned. "Dinner?"

"There is a family dinner tonight," Logiri said. "Ordered by the King."

"Who you said does not know you are here on this ship," Nika murmured. "I wonder... Jiaan?" She turned and smiled sweetly. "I do not know much, but the impression I have gotten is that battle companions are considered family. Is that so?"

Daanir dropped his gaze. "I haven't been that for years, your Highness, as I—"

"And I say again, you were wasted on the Empire, my wife," Tarjiaan breathed. "If they'd realized what a mind you have, Meradon would have been in serious trouble. Yes, battle companions are considered family. The vows are considered as binding as marriage vows. Unless you formally renounced them." He turned to look at Daanir. "I didn't ask you. I should have, but... I don't know. I think I was afraid of the answer. When you never got an answer from me, did you renounce your vows?"

Daanir bowed his head, jaw flexing. "No," he murmured, gazing at Tarjiaan steadily. "But they told me you had, because...."

And there it was. That explained why Daan was pushing him away. He took a deep breath. "No, Daan. I never renounced my vows. And I never blamed you. I told you that. Renouncing you would have been like renouncing breathing." He held his hand out and pulled half-forgotten words from the depths of his memory. "I shall be as your strong arm. As the sword in your hand, the shield at your back. The...... you know, I never thought I'd have to say the entire blasted litany again. I think I've forgotten most of it. I'll go find my notes if that will convince you that I mean what I say."

Daanir snorted softly and took the offered hand, ducking his head. "I stand before the Mothers and swear myself to you, that I shall be your companion for so long as we both shall draw breath. I shall be as your strong arm. As the sword in your hand, the shield at your back. Your life is mine to protect, as my life is yours. From this moment until I return to the Deep, I so vow." He looked up. "You got that phrase wrong when we first said it, too. Captain Taarik made you say it again. I remember."

"I remember being nervous enough to puke my breakfast up," Tarjiaan admitted. "I remember being terrified that you would say no when they asked the question."

"Question?"

Tarjiaan jerked in surprise; he somehow forgotten Nika sat at his right, that Naajir was still across from him. "Before we swear as companions, we're asked the question – do you come before the Mothers of your own will to bind your life and your honor to this man, and stand as his battle companion? It's the last question before the vows, and I had managed to convince myself that Daan was going to say no."

"Because I refused to eat...something the night before. I forget what." Daanir lifted a brow. "I had to see if I could say no to you. I had to know that I could, if I was going to stand behind you." He smirked slightly. "You had more than enough people around you always saying yes."

"It was that awful seaweed soup Father's cook made." Tarjiaan bit his lip, trying not to laugh. If he started laughing, he wouldn't stop.

Daanir lightly traced Tarjiaan's knuckles with his thumb. "Jiaan, after all these years, you're sure you still want me? There are better choices."

"There was never a better choice. Not for me." Tarjiaan tugged Daanir closer, pressing their joined hands to his heart. "Daan, you belong on my left. You always have."

Daanir smiled slightly, a look that quickly shifted to a frown. "I'll need to get back into practice, then. I wonder if Kaapi knows which cabinet my old kit is stored in." He paused. "I wonder if it still fits."

"After fifteen years?" Logiri chided. "You'd be better off being measured for new armor, and a new set of weapons. You've grown and changed over the years."

"He's right," Tarjiaan agreed. "Your old kit won't be right for you anymore. Maybe set it aside for Naajir to train?" He smiled at his nephew, who turned pink.

"Something new, then," Daanir murmured. "You're going to split my loyalties until you're crowned, my Prince. I'll have to practice that subtlety until then."

"I'll try not to distract you too much," Tarjiaan said. "Your duties to my uncle are more important." He let Daanir go and rested his hand on the table. "So we'll see you at dinner tonight. A little late, perhaps?"

"And with an unexpected addition," Daanir added. "Come on, Naajir. I'll walk back with you." He paused. "For the record, your notes are on the top shelf of the bookcase. Blue binding."

"And," Logiri continued as they left, "if I may be so bold? The Mancer Royal isn't the only one who needs to be measured. Her Highness should as well."

"Measured?" Nika squeaked. "For *armor*?"

"For the royal uniform," Logiri answered. "Dress and informal, Captain?"

Tarjiaan nodded. "Will you arrange that, Logiri? You'll have to find out if there's a seamstress on board."

"I will find out and make the arrangements as soon as possible," Logiri said, bowing. "I can't imagine that they'll have anything ready for this evening, but I highly doubt anyone present at the dinner will understand the significance of Her Highness' existing clothing."

Nika sat upright next to Tarjiaan and said something in Imperial, too quickly for Tarjiaan to translate. Logiri bowed deeply in response, then left the table and the cabin without a word. As the door closed, Tarjiaan turned to look at his wife, who was staring at the tablecloth. "I missed something," Tarjiaan said softly. "Nika?"

Nika folded her hands on the table. "Antarlogirish has recognized the... insult that I am to you. One far worse than offering you a slave in place of a princess."

"It's not an insult if I don't take it as one, Nika," Tarjiaan said. He rested his hand on Nika's, feeling her shaking. "And you are a princess. You're my princess. Now, tell me?"

"What I wear... I dress as what I was intended to be. I told you how I was trained... it was because I was to be a Palace harlot."

Tarjiaan stared at her for a moment. "You were a virgin. They swore to that. And you told me that you were. Not that I care one way or the other, but—"

"I was," Nika agreed. "I never completed the training. Because no one was willing to be my first." She paused. "It was another mark of my... unsuitability. Another level to the insult. I was the harlot no one wanted." She worried her lip, peering up at him. "Will you change your mind now?"

Tarjiaan squeezed her hands, then picked up one and kissed her palm. "Nika, my only concerns about marrying you were if you were willing, and how young they told us you were. Knowing you're twenty-five? That's a much more comfortable age."

"Comfortable?" she repeated. "Jiaan, in truth, if they had not sent me to you, I would have been strangled as useless baggage at the next new moon. Twenty-five is not a comfortable age when you are a harlot in the Empire. It is ancient."

For a moment, Tarjiaan felt as if the brakes were off on the chair, and he was skidding down a steep slope. "You're serious? You'd have been killed?"

Nika hesitated, "When a harlot gets too old, or is otherwise unappealing to the men of the court, they are disposed of. I was nothing. I was worse than nothing. I was too old. I spoke my mind too often. I was too... too bold. I was unattractive—"

"I don't think any of that is true," Tarjiaan interjected, stopping the breathless recitation of her perceived flaws.

"Thank you. But back ho... back in the Palace, I was considered a failure as a slave, as a harlot, and as a woman. I thought they were taking me to sea for the sailors to use, and that I would be killed before they went back." She bit her lip. "How much have I just damaged the negotiations?"

Tarjiaan picked up his cooling tea and sipped it, then slowly shook his head. "I'll have to speak to my uncle and Ilaris. But I'm not sure if you damaged it or gave me ammunition." He paused and set down his empty cup. "I don't understand how they thought they'd get away with so many lies." He rolled back from the table. "Any one of those invalidates the treaty."

"Perhaps they did not expect me to trust you so quickly?" Nika suggested. "After all, I am the only one who could tell you that they were lies."

Tarjiaan turned her words over his mind, studying them. Wondering.... "Nika?" he asked slowly. "Yesterday you were terrified of me. Why do you trust me so much so soon?"

Nika smiled and stood up, coming to stand next to Tarjiaan's chair. As he looked up at her, she took his face between her hands and gently kissed his lips. "Because before you even knew my name, you were ready to fight the gods themselves to protect me. And because even knowing that my people are your enemies, you trusted me enough to let me see the heart of you, and the pain. You trusted me with your truth." She ran her thumbs over Tarjiaan's cheekbones. "They had me terrified of the Sea Prince, the Butcher of Meradon. But I have met Tarjiaan, and I like him very much. And I trust him."

She leaned down and kissed him again, then let him go. "I think I want a bath," she said. "Will you join me?"

"In the bath?" Tarjiaan tried to force his brain into a new course. She held her hand out.

"Yes, in the bath," she said. "Unless you have duties to attend to? If you do, then I will wait until you are ready."

Tarjiaan took her hand and tugged her closer. "Today, Nika, our only duties are to each other."

Knocking woke Tarjiaan from sleep, and he rolled onto his side to see that he was alone in his bed.

"Nika?" he called. The door opened, and Logiri came in. He didn't look straight at the bed, going instead to the closet and giving Tarjiaan a chance to pull the sheets over himself.

"The Princess sent for me," Logiri said. "She thought it past time that you prepare for dinner."

Tarjiaan blinked, looking around. "How long did I sleep?"

"It's been several hours, her Highness said. She thought if you were sleeping so deeply, you must need it, and let you be," Logiri answered. He paused, then added, "Captain, if I may be familiar?"

"After as many years as you've been with me? You can be as familiar as you like, Logiri." Tarjiaan propped himself up on his elbows. "Go ahead."

To his surprise, Logiri turned toward him and smiled. "It's good to see you happy, Tarjiaan. I can't say I have ever seen you so... content."

Tarjiaan grinned and sat up. "You make me sound like a cat."

"And if she strokes you the right way, I fully expect to hear you purr."

Tarjiaan burst out laughing. "Perhaps." He glanced at the door to the bath. "Where is she?"

"Her new maid arrived earlier, and they are going through the Princess' wardrobe and picking out her clothes for this evening." Logiri hesitated. "Did she explain...?"

"She did, and I'll be discussing what she's told me with my uncle and Ilaris." Tarjiaan reached out and picked up the banyan, running his fingers over the silk. "I don't understand how they expected to get away with one lie after another."

Logiri answered, "They underestimated her. And they underestimated you. Which they seem to have a habit of doing. Now, shall we prepare you for dinner?"

Tarjiaan nodded. "I'll need to bathe."

"Again?" Logiri glanced at the door to the bath. "Your towels were wet, and there was water all over the floor in the bath. I'd assumed that you already... oh..." For the first time in Tarjiaan's memory, Logiri looked flustered. "Well, then. I'll fetch fresh towels."

Tarjiaan and Logiri went through the motions with the ease of long years of practice, and he was ready quickly, guiding his chair into the sitting room. Nika was sitting on the couch, clearly relaxed, chatting with a handsome woman of Tarjiaan's own age, and who he recognized at once.

"Chel?" he said. "You're Wilaanger's grand-niece?"

She turned to him, bowed, then laughed and held out her hands. "It's good to see you again, Captain. I thought you knew?"

Tarjiaan took her hands and tugged her closer, hugging her. "I had no idea. But it shouldn't surprise me. We lost a fine medical officer when you left us. And I told you that you were not allowed to call me captain." He turned to Nika. "Chel served as ship's physician on my first command. I can't even count how many lives she saved."

"You are a physician?" Nika asked. "And... you are willing to act as my maid?"

Chel smiled. "Uncle Wil thought you needed someone you could trust. When he explained, I agreed to come. My research can keep, and Lysson is happy so long as he's where I am. He's writing a new concerto, Jiaan, and he wants your opinion."

"I look forward to hearing it," Tarjiaan said. He held his hand out to Nika. "Shall we? And let me see what you're wearing."

Nika turned in a circle. The green gown was close in color to the royal green, and her short hair was again covered by a wrapping in a similar green. The bodice of the gown was still form-fitting, but Tarjiaan could see panels of gold fabric that loosened the skirts and allowed for more ease of movement. "This is lovely. Nika, you look magnificent. And the alterations... your work, Chel?"

"A joint effort. Her Highness sews with a good hand," Chel answered. "Once I understood what we were trying to do, it was a simple matter of cutting the gores and adding the contrast. I rather like the effect."

Nika looked down at herself, running one hand over her bodice. "I adore it. And Lady Cheladra was telling me that I could even wear trousers if I wished? I have never worn trousers."

"You wouldn't wear them for a formal dinner, but yes, you can wear them," Chel said. "I've added trousers to the list of things my lady is to be measured for." She stepped back. "Now, we shouldn't keep you."

Nika kept her left hand on Tarjiaan's right shoulder as they made their way toward the throne room. She had a casket tucked under her right arm.

"Nika, what do you have there?"

She squeezed his shoulder. "A gift for your sister. Cheladra and I went through the gifts and jewels that were sent with me, and she helped me pick this. Is she truly a physician?"

"A very gifted one," Tarjiaan answered. "She came back below the waves to marry, and to work on medical research."

"And her husband is a composer," Nika added. "Is that why he wants your opinion?"

Tarjiaan smiled. "He's far more gifted than I ever was."

"And yet he wants your opinion," Nika murmured. "My husband, if I am not allowed to hide my brilliance, then neither are you. I would like to hear you."

Tarjiaan looked forward toward the doors to the throne room. "I'm going to have to ask for patience there, Nika. I haven't sung in years. And I don't have an instrument down here."

Nika squeezed his shoulder again. "Then I will wait. You changed your earrings. Do all men wear earrings here?"

"Not all." Tarjiaan touched his usual gold studs. "These are badges of honor for sailors. They show that I've sailed through what we call a ship-killer storm."

"And you have done this four times?" Nika brushed her finger over his ear, making him shiver. "That is impressive."

"The silver show I was crew on a ship that did, twice. The gold are from when I was captain. And four isn't that impressive," Tarjiaan admitted. "I know men and women who have more. My father had fourteen gold."

"All in one ear?"

Tarjiaan chuckled. "Seven in each ear. He used to joke he'd have to put the next one in his nose because he was out of space in his ears. Shall we?"

Chapter Twelve
Invitation

A LONG TABLE HAD BEEN set up in the throne room, set with linens as white as seafoam and bordered with the royal green. Ikaanaji was already in his place at the head of the table, and he smiled as Tarjiaan and Nika entered. He wasn't attached to the larger machines, which stood dark behind the Coral Throne.

Wilaanger met them as they entered. He smiled and bowed. "Your Highness, it's a pleasure to meet you," he said. "I am Physician Royal Wilaanger, and I welcome you to Meradon." He gestured toward the table. "The King is in good spirits tonight," he said in a low voice as he escorted them.

"He's away from the machines. Why?" Tarjiaan asked.

"He insisted," Wilaanger said. "He wants to sit at the table with the family. And fighting him on it would make things worse. This... this will make him happy, and he might actually eat something." He paused, and Tarjiaan stopped, waiting for recognition. His uncle looked as if he were asleep, but after a moment, he stirred and opened his eyes.

"You're here," he murmured. "Come, sit."

Tarjiaan guided his chair to the empty place on the king's right, noticing that the king was wearing his cloak of state. The smaller support device must have been underneath. As he took his place, Wilaanger held Nika's chair for her. She thanked him and sat down next to Tarjiaan, setting the casket on the table next to her. Ikaanaji beamed at her, then picked up a box and passed it to Tarjiaan.

"I'm so pleased you've joined us," Ikaanaji said. "Now, before anyone else joins us. Tarjiaan, this is for you to give to your bride. Aajinisa left it with me to give to you when you married. I should have had it at the wedding, but I forgot."

Tarjiaan looked down at the box, then passed it to Nika. who turned the box over in her hands, then set it down and opened the catch to lift the lid. Inside, nestled in a bed of pale silk, was a pendant on a chain. The pendant was a small, gold disk, engraved with a compass rose. There was a sapphire set in the center of the rose, and each point was set with a matching, smaller sapphire. Tarjiaan stared at it for a moment, then looked up.

"I remember this," he said. "I remember Mother wearing it."

"Your mother never took it off," Ikaanaji said. "It was the first gift your father ever gave her. She wanted you to have it for your bride." He smiled. "His first gift to you?"

Nika ran one finger over the face of the pendant. "My husband has given me his respect and my freedom. Those were his first gifts to me. But this... this means so much." She looked up — there were tears on her cheeks. "Jiaan, help me put this on?"

Tarjiaan took the pendant out and opened the clasp on the chain. He lowered it over Nika's head, watching as she smoothed her hand over the pendant on her breast.

"Uncle, thank you," Tarjiaan said, turning back toward Ikaanaji. "I had no idea that Mother left anything to me."

"Aajinisa loved you all very much, and she left something for each of you." He paused, then nodded. "There were other things, but I can't recall where they are. I'll have Ilaris look into it. Now, where is Aanaji?"

Wilaanger said. "Ika, are you certain that having Aanaji here tonight is wise?"

Ikaanaji sniffed. "Where my niece is concerned? There's no wisdom, only emotion. But this is family." He paused again. "But perhaps you should tuck the pendant away, my dear Nikaranthia."

Nika looked down, then slipped the pendant into her bodice. "I am aware that she considers my very presence here an insult," she said. "I do not want to add fuel to that fire." She rested her hand on the casket. "I brought a marriage gift, as she is the senior member of my husband's immediate family. Do you think it will cause strife? I have no wish to cause you more trouble."

"I think it will hardly hurt to try," Ikaanaji answered.

Tarjiaan glanced toward the doors, then asked, "Do you think she'll actually attend, Uncle?"

"I told her that if she did not attend, then she was to spend her time packing," Ikaanaji answered. "Now..." He stopped as Ilaris slipped into the throne room.

"Her Highness, the Princess Aanaji," the Chamberlain announced as Aanaji swept into the room, stopping inside the door as she waited to be recognized. She was once again dressed head-to-toe in red, and Tarjiaan heard his uncle growl softly.

"What is the meaning of this?" Ikaanaji demanded, and Tarjiaan heard an ominous beeping from beneath the cloak. Wilaanger hurried to his side as Ikaanaji snapped, "How dare she—?"

"Uncle," Nika said softly. She reached across Tarjiaan and rested her hand on the king's arm. "Please, do not tax yourself."

Ikaanaji scowled as he looked at her and Tarjiaan. "I will not have her insult your marriage so—"

"It is no insult if I do not take it as such," Nika interrupted. "Is that not so?"

Ikaanaji's eyes widened, and he coughed. "Jiaan, your father used to say that."

"That's who taught me. And I've said it to Nika," Tarjiaan said. "I should have warned you, Uncle. We both knew that Aanaji was dressed in mourning. She... interrupted us last night."

"Interrupted?" Wilaanger murmured. "Oh, Jiaan..."

Tarjiaan had to stop himself before he laughed aloud at the scandalized tone of Wilaanger's voice, or the shock on his uncle's face. Nika looked at him, and he could see the mirth she was trying to hide. "Don't you worry about us, Wil," he said. "She more than paid in sheer embarrassment for what was just a minor inconvenience."

"To be fair, she probably did not expect to find us on the floor," Nika added. Tarjiaan stared at her, hearing his uncle's delighted laughter. She winked at him, then nodded ever so slightly at his uncle.

Tarjiaan leaned closer. "You did that on purpose?" he whispered.

"He was too angry," she whispered back. "Now he is not. And the frightening noises have stopped. Is there a machine under his cloak?"

Tarjiaan realized that she was right, and wondered why he hadn't noticed that the beeping had stopped when his uncle had started laughing. He kissed Nika's fingers, then turned back to his uncle. "Uncle, you know as well as I that my sister is... fond of theatrics," he murmured. "This is all for show. And if she doesn't get the reaction she wants, she'll stop."

Ikaanaji raised brow. "So, you are counseling me to ignore her?"

Tarjiaan shrugged slightly. "There's the added bonus that ignoring her will annoy her to no end." He reached out and picked up a glass of water, raising it to his uncle before taking a sip. Ikaanaji snorted, and gestured to Ilaris.

"And you say you've no gift of diplomacy," Wilaanger murmured.

"This isn't diplomacy," Tarjiaan replied, setting his glass down as Ilaris escorted Aanaji to the table. "This is my sister."

Aanaji took her place across from him. "Uncle," she said without pleasantries. "I want it recorded that I object to this farce of a marriage."

Ikaanaji sniffed, then turned to Tarjiaan and Nika as if Aanaji hadn't spoken at all. "Nikaranthia, my dear, have you formally met your husband's sister?"

Nika hesitated, then ducked her head. "I have not," he answered slowly. "Although we did have a short encounter, I was not in a position to be formally presented."

Aanaji actually blushed, whereas Nika looked to Tarjiaan like the picture of innocence. She smiled as she raised her head. "You are the senior member of my husband's immediate family. So I have brought a marriage gift for you, as is our custom."

"A... a gift?" Aanaji stammered. "You... brought... a gift? For *me*?"

Nika rose and carried the casket around the table to Aanaji. "I understand this is hard for you. Tarjiaan has told me what my people have done to your family. I understand that I am... unwelcome. I hope that we may, at some point, at least tolerate each other?"

Aanaji stared at her, then reached for the box. Nika bowed as Aanaji took it, then returned to her chair. Tarjiaan reached for her hand and kissed her fingers again, and she smiled and slipped her hand free to caress his cheek.

"You're already besotted," Aanaji murmured. "It's been a day. Not even a day."

"And we suit each other quite well," Tarjiaan replied, turning toward his sister. "What is the gift? Nika didn't show me."

Aanaji unfastened the clasp and raised the lid of the box, gasping in surprise. "Is this... is this a singing sphere?"

"You know of them?" Nika replied. "Yes, it is."

"Truly?" Ikaanaji murmured as Aanaji took the fist-sized metal sphere out of the box and rolled it between her palm. As it moved, the sphere chimed sweetly. "Nikaranthia, this is a wondrous gift."

"I've read about singing spheres, but I've never seen one," Tarjiaan said. "Is it true that it takes a single craftsman their entire life to master the skill to make one?"

"I have heard the same, but I do not know. Have you asked Antarlogirish?"

"Logiri?" Tarjiaan asked. "I wouldn't have thought to ask him."

"The Antar family are renowned craftsmen for the Emperor, and the secret of the singing spheres is theirs." Nika gestured toward Aanaji and the gleaming sphere in her hands. "It was perhaps one of his brothers or uncles who made this."

Aanaji looked up. "Do Imperial women not learn these skills?"

"Not the metalwork, no," Nika answered. "Antar women are weavers, and their work is such that only the Emperor is allowed to wear it."

Ikaanaji held his hand out, and Aanaji passed the sphere to him. He turned it, then held it up. "Exquisite," he murmured. "Nikaranthia, this is a lovely gesture."

"Thank you," Nika murmured. "I hope it may smooth our way to tolerance?"

Aanaji arched a brow and took the sphere back from Ikaanaji. She put it back into the casket and closed the box. "I will...consider," she said. "You say you understand?"

"I have seen the portrait that Tarjiaan keeps in his quarters on his ship. And he has told me a little about your father and your brother," Nika answered. "I would like to know more." She paused. "I would like to know you, if you'll allow it."

"I will consider," Aanaji repeated.

Tarjiaan picked up his water glass and glanced at his uncle, who looked bemused. The smile faded from his face as the throne room door opened, and Ilaris came in.

"The Mancer Royal Daanir Meranas," he announced. "And His Highness Prince Naajir."

Tarjiaan was torn as to who he wanted to watch more — his uncle, or his sister. The look on his uncle's face was one of sheer delight. His sister, on the other hand, was a picture of pure rage.

"What is he doing here?" she demanded.

"Which he?" Tarjiaan asked. "My battle companion or my nephew?"

"Aanaji!" Ikaanaji sounded elated. "You brought your son home to us!" He smiled and held his hand out. "Naajir! Come here and let me look at you!"

Naajir glanced at Daanir, then approached the table, skirting around the side of the table where Tarjiaan and Nikaranthia were sitting, stopping next to Tarjiaan's chair.

"Sire," Naajir said, and bowed. Ikaanaji laughed.

"You're to call me Uncle, Naajir," Ikaanaji said. "You've grown. Which seems a silly thing to say. Of course you've grown. Now, sit. Join us. And... Mancer, join us." He waited until everyone was seated — Wilaanger at the foot of the table, Daanir on Nikaranthia's right, and Naajir next to his mother. "This is as it should be," the Sea King said. "The entire family... this is as it should be." He gestured, and servants started moving around the table, carrying platters and pitchers.

The meal was oddly pleasant, possibly because Aanaji was unusually silent. Naajir slowly warmed and relaxed, until he was chatting easily with Nikaranthia, answering her questions.

"I have been told that I may choose to have duties overseeing orphaned children?" Nika said. She turned toward Ikaanaji. "And that this was the former duty of your wife and your sisters? Is this correct?"

"It is," Ikaanaji confirmed. He laid his fork down next to what looked to Tarjiaan to be his untouched plate and gestured toward Wilaanger. "Wil has been undertaking those duties, and I'm certain he'll be happy to assist you however you need if you decide to take that on."

"I think I may, if you think I will not frighten them?" Nika turned to look at Wilaanger, then turned back to Ikaanaji. "I am... very different from your people."

"Not so different," Wilaanger said. "I know that Imperial bloodlines tend to stay within themselves, but in Meradon, we see the wisdom of diversity. Ika, your... grandmother, was it? Was Sualimani?"

"Our grandmother," Ikaanaji corrected. "She looked on you like her own."

"You are that close?" Nika asked. She paused, looked at Tarjiaan, then at Daanir. Then she turned back the King. "Sire, was the honored Wilaanger your battle companion?"

Ikaanaji's eyes widened, and he glanced at Tarjiaan, who smiled. "I didn't tell her," he said.

Across the table, Aanaji sniffed. "You are completely besotted."

"Why shouldn't he be?" Wilaanger asked. "Shouldn't a man love his wife?"

"Or a wife love her husband?" Nika added. Tarjiaan stared at her, and she smiled.

"Uncle." Tarjiaan tore his gaze from Nika to face the king. "I was thinking about the negotiations, and our discussion about my training. And about my lack of training."

Ikaanaji sobered. "Yes?"

"I should like to request that Naajir attend the negotiations as my secretary." Out of the corner of his eye, Tarjiaan saw his sister sit upright. "I thought I'd have to send for him, but since he's here, that will make things easier. He will be able to learn the diplomatic process firsthand, and he'll have firsthand knowledge of the treaty agreements—"

"Because he'll have been there when they were made," Ikaanaji finished. "That's a marvelous idea, Tarjiaan."

"Uncle..." Aanaji's voice was strained. "I don't think my son is ready..." Ikaanaji looked at her, and she fell silent.

"Why would he not be ready, Aanaji?" he asked. "He is Tarjiaan's heir, and will be the Sea Prince when Tarjiaan sits on the Coral Throne. His education should have reflected this. Why, then, would he not be ready?" He didn't wait for an answer. "Ilaris!"

Ilaris appeared as if conjured. "Sire?"

"I presume that the young prince is quartered with his mother," Ikaanaji said. "See him installed in his own quarters. Near the Heir's suite, so that Tarjiaan can better supervise him. Have a schedule of lessons and duties prepared, and tutors assigned, if there are not tutors already in place. Make certain that they understand his lessons are to be arranged around the negotiations. If the young prince is not ready, then we will remedy that lack swiftly." He rested his hand on the tabletop. "Tarjiaan, you are now Naajir's guardian—"

"Sire!" Tarjiaan gasped. He looked across to see the stunned look on Aanaji's face, certain there was a matching expression on his own. Aanaji recovered first.

"So be it," she said. "For the good of Meradon. Isn't that right?" She rested her hands on the table and stood up. "Sire, if I may withdraw?" She didn't wait for permission, turning and walking away from the table, her back straight as a ship's mast. Ilaris followed her out into the corridor.

"Uncle, that's...I wasn't expecting this," Tarjiaan said. "I... I have given no thought to anything other than having Naajir at my side in the negotiations. We'll need to discuss what else he needs. What lessons, what duties. I... I am a bit unmoored."

"You can leave that to me," Daanir offered with a quick half-smile. "You've a lot on your plate already. Kaapi has the full complement of tutors, and they can take on another student. Having them work together will be good for them. You just get through the negotiations and worry about the rest later." He glanced at Naajir. "If that works for you, Highness."

"Thank you, Daan." Tarjiaan nodded. "We'll talk later."

"And will Naajir be included in this conversation?" Nika asked. "He is a young man, not a child. Should he not have a say in his future?"

"I think I had forgotten that Naajir is no longer a child," Ikaanaji admitted. "You're right. He should be part of the conversation. And I am curious. Naajir, what would you like?"

"I..." Naajir stammered, looking at Nika with something very close to adoration. "I get to have a say? I... no one has ever asked me what I want!"

Nika smiled. "I understand that feeling."

"I..." Daanir stopped and cocked his head to the side. "A submersible just docked." He leaned forward and looked up the table. "Sire? Should I go—?"

Ikaanaji held up his hand. "Ilaris!" he called. The Chamberlain appeared in the double doors.

"Sire," he said as he bowed. "Is this about the submersible? I was just coming to tell you. It's from the *Wave Runner*. There's a storm on the surface, and First Officer Marikaar sent the emissary below out of concern for his health."

"Concern for his health?" Tarjiaan repeated. Then he realized what Ilaris meant. "Oh. How badly was he seasick?"

"The First Officer didn't say," Ilaris answered. "I'm about to go and meet him."

"I'll come with you, Ilaris," Wilaanger said. "If he was sick enough to send below, he may need more than a bed to lie on. I'll see to him." He followed Ilaris out of the throne room.

"So, you decided that you're going to take on the crèche kids?" Daanir asked after Ilaris left. "That's a good thing. A lot of them, they're young enough that they don't remember their mothers. Wilaanger takes good care of them, but he can't...well...mother them." He paused. "Are you even old enough to mother them? You barely look older than my daughter."

"Thank you," Nika said. "I am flattered you think so." She looked down at herself. "It is because I am small, I think. I just turned twenty-five."

Ikaanaji frowned, and there was another alarming beep from the folds of his cloak.

"I was going to tell you, Uncle," Tarjiaan said quickly. "Nika told me yesterday, and I have no complaints." He glanced at Nika. "Twenty-five is a much more...suitable age for my bride, I think. I don't feel quite so much as if I robbed the crèche."

"Is there anything else that they lied to us about?" Ikaanaji asked.

"We may be about to find out," Daanir said. He frowned. "They're coming here. They've bypassed the way to the suites and they're coming here."

"Oh." Nika sat up. "I... May I be excused?"

"What's wrong?" Tarjiaan asked.

"I... He is coming here, and I am not veiled. I..."

Tarjiaan nodded. "I'll take you back to our suite—"

"You'll do no such thing," Ikaanaji snapped. "It's unnecessary."

"Uncle," Tarjiaan protested. "We'll be there and back in a few minutes."

"You will remain," Ikaanaji insisted. "You will be here when he arrives. I have spoken." He sniffed. "Veils. Honestly, Aajinisa. It's no time for jests."

Daanir eased from his seat. "I'm just... going to check the oxygen levels there." He knelt by Ikaanaji's chair, moved the cloak, and rested his fingers on the machine.

Tarjiaan swallowed. "Uncle, this is my wife, Nikaranthia. Who is used to wearing a veil. If we may be excused?"

Ikaanaji scowled. "I said no, Taarik."

Chapter Thirteen
Revelations

TARJIAAN SWALLOWED, bowing his head slightly. "As you wish, Sire," he replied, and was surprised that his voice sounded almost normal. He turned to Nika, who looked confused and hurt. "Change places with me." He paused, then added, "So you won't need to raise your voice for Uncle to hear you."

She frowned slightly, looked past him, then at him. Did she understand what he was offering? After a moment, she nodded, and stood up. Daanir jumped up and took her chair out of the way, letting them rearrange themselves so that Nika sat at the King's right. Tarjiaan took her place at the table, and watched as she realized that she was hidden from view by his body and the chair. She relaxed slightly and rested her hand on his arm.

"How long will it take them to get here?" Naajir blurted. His cheeks colored, and he looked down at the table.

Daanir frowned, then nodded, going back to his seat. "Another minute. Maybe. They're walking quickly."

"How do you know that?" Nika asked.

"There are sensors and cameras all through the corridors of the *Chimaera*," Daanir answered absently. "I ask them and they tell me." He was gazing into the air above their heads, gaze flicking back and forth as he picked up a glass of water.

"The way that you talk to the machines—" Nika asked, "Can anyone learn their language?"

"There's more to it than that. I simplified it." Daanir cleared his throat, drinking his water in a gulp. "A lot. And... no. It's something in here." He tapped his temple, then his chest. "It's something you're born with. Most realize it early on. I was... distracted." Tarjiaan squeezed Daanir's shoulder. Daanir's smile was fleeting as he sat up straighter. "They're here," he murmured.

Tarjiaan let his hand fall, just as the doors opened and Ilaris entered, leading the Imperial emissary. Wilaanger followed behind, and stepped to the side as Ilaris announced, "Lord Rathsafa, emissary of the Serene Emperor Gondarishan."

Lord Rathsafa bowed slightly. "I apologize for the intrusion, Your Majesty," he said. "But this could not wait." He paused, then drew himself up. "Your Majesty, I would like to claim sanctuary for myself and my crew. I have heard that you offer a haven to those who wish to remain as part of Meradon beneath the waves. I beg that courtesy."

Ilaris straightened behind him, his jaw tensing. "You what?" he hissed.

"Come closer," Ikaanaji ordered. "And repeat that."

Rathsafa took three steps forward, then dropped to his knees. "I wish to claim sanctuary for myself and for my men. I beg your mercy, Your Majesty. I–"

"What about the treaty?" Tarjiaan asked. "The alliance?"

Rathsafa raised his head. "There...there was no treaty. The Emperor... he may now know that I am here, and that has forced my hand. There..." He took a deep breath and rubbed one hand over his face. "May I start at the beginning?"

Tarjiaan realized that there was a soft beeping coming from his left, one that was increasing in frequency. "Uncle, you said that this treaty was mine to do. I think that means that this is also mine to do. May we withdraw?"

"No," Ikaanaji growled. "I wish to hear this story before I grant or deny sanctuary." The beeping started to grow almost frantic, then quieted as Daanir lowered his head, his hand hovering low in the direction of the Sea King. Daanir met Tarjiaan's eyes, and Tarjiaan could see the alarm there.

"Then we should do this in a civilized manner," Tarjiaan said quickly, turning back to his uncle. Ikaanaji scowled, then nodded, and Tarjiaan tried not to sigh visibly. "Ilaris," he said, "bring the... bring Lord Rathsafa to the table."

Rathsafa got to his feet and followed Ilaris to the table; Ilaris drew a chair free and stood back, eyes narrowed as if he was witness to something distasteful. Tarjiaan coughed to draw Ilaris' attention, then shook his head slightly. Now was not the time for the Chamberlain to show how little he favored the policy of accepting refugees. Ilaris sniffed once, but his expression moved to one of cold neutrality.

Rathsafa didn't seem to notice the exchange. "Thank you," he said. He looked around and folded his hands on the table. "From the beginning. My name... I was not named Rathsafa when I was born. My wife named me Rathsafa when she granted me her collar. She knew that I wished nothing more than to be free of my past, so she renamed me as her first gift to me." He paused. "The name I bore before, the name I wish that I never had to hear again, was Gondanadarish."

Tarjiaan heard Ilaris hiss again, and felt his own stomach lurch. This had gone from a summer squall to a hurricane in a heartbeat.

"Nadarish is the name of the Emperor's son," Ikaanaji said. "I attended his naming ceremony."

Rathsafa shook his head. "Nadarish was the son of the Queen of Lastalt, by her husband Prince Consort Gondarishan. By right of birth, he should have been King of Lastalt, and that's all. But... Gondarishan had other plans." He looked at Ikaanaji. "The false emperor Gondarishan murdered his mother and sisters to secure his place on the Tyracan throne, and then murdered his wife — my mother — Queen Tishaya."

"There are many who believe that," Ikaanaji murmured. "But there was never any proof."

"I still have no proof," Rathsafa agreed somberly. "Only my understanding of how these events unfolded, and my... conviction that he must be stopped. That this so-called Emperor must be defeated before he destroys everything. I have been working to this end for years. Building alliances in secret. Given the chance and the means, the Lastalti people will stand behind me as my mother's son, and some of the Sualimani tribes have offered aid in memory of my wife, who was imprisoned to try and control me, and who was slain by Gondarishan himself when I tried to free her and our child. We lack only the might of Meradon, and the legend that is the Sea Prince. I'd hoped that I would have a full army ready before I approached you, but I had to move sooner than I had expected. And now, I am forced to alter my plans once more." He raised both hands, palms to the sky. "I swear this to be the truth, by Sun and Sand."

Tarjiaan took a sip of his water, trying to force his thoughts into order. He thought he knew why the plans had changed, but he had to be sure. "Your wife's name was Masthaka, wasn't it?" He looked to his left, at Nika's ashen face. "And Nikaranthia is your daughter."

In answer, Rathsafa unfastened the buttons on the high collar of his shirt. He laid it open to reveal the marital collar underneath. "My wife was Masthaka. She helped me escape the Palace when she was there as an attendant to the Sualimani queen. She married me and gave me a home. Gave me hope. Gave me children, twins who were my joy. And Gondarishan destroyed that home, that hope, and that joy. I thought them all dead, but two years after I was brought back to the Palace in chains, I found my wife and our daughter imprisoned in the harem as slaves. I had plans laid to try and free them, but those failed, and cost Masthaka her life. I never knew what happened to our son," he said softly. "Last year, I discovered my father's plans for my daughter, and I couldn't... I had to act." He looked across the table. "Do you know how much you look like her?"

Nika hugged herself, shaking her head. "I... I do not understand. What plans? No one had any plans for me."

Tarjiaan put his arm around her, pulling her to his side. "They were going to kill her, she told me."

Rathsafa shook his head. "No. Or at least, not immediately. I learned what he intended, and I set this voyage into motion, because I had to save her." He closed his eyes. "I failed Masthaka, and she was executed for my failure. But... Tarjiaan, I need you to understand the woman you have married."

"I don't care about her past—"

"Not her past. Not the lies that they made her believe. My daughter's true bloodlines." Rathsafa pointed at Nika. "Your wife is the eldest born and only living *legitimate* child of the rightfully born Lastalti King. She is the last daughter of the bloodline of the Tyracan Queens. And through her mother, she is related to the Sualimani Queens." He took a deep breath. "What I learned – what forced me to act now – was that Gondarishan was going to have me killed, and he was going to take my daughter as his wife."

"By the Mothers," Wilaanger murmured.

Nika didn't move. Tarjiaan could feel her shivering in the circle of his arm. "So it is my bloodline that is important to you," she said.

"Not your bloodline," Rathsafa said. "You're her daughter. I couldn't save her. I tried. I tried to get you both away. I failed her. I failed all of you. I never found your brother, never knew what happened to him. The Emperor killed your mother in front of me for my failure, and swore that if I so much as breathed wrong, he would do the same to you. He told me that to my face, right before I spit in his." He gave a soft, satisfied smile. "One small achievement, and the last time I stood in his presence. I was as much a prisoner in the Palace as you were."

Nika swallowed, then demanded, "Have you any idea how many of the women I trained with longed for a swift death?"

"Have you any idea how often I wished for the same?" Rathsafa closed his eyes. "But I wasn't going to leave you. You were all I had left to fight for, so I tried to protect you as best I could. I had... small victories. You were as safe as I could make you. And when I found that I could no longer protect you, I brought you to someone who, I hoped, would do better than I had."

Nika clasped her hands tightly in her lap. "You brought me to someone who might aid you in taking back your throne—"

"I don't want the throne!" Rathsafa's voice rang and echoed through the throne room. "I have never wanted the throne." He paused and looked away. "All I wanted was to serve my wife and raise my children. He denied me that. He denied me my life. Now... I just want the nightmare to end." He looked up. "There are documents, signed and witnessed and in the hands of the Sualimani Queen, swearing to my marriage to Masthaka, and that you are the legitimate daughter of that union. And should Sun and Sand smile on me for once in this forsaken life of mine and this venture succeeds? Then the Lastalti throne is yours. The Tyracan throne is yours. If you want them. And I would not have told you this much so soon, but the High Priest... he told me that he planned to commune with his brethren. I didn't know they could *do* that. Not over this distance. I... I stopped him. But they will wonder why he doesn't respond. And they will look more closely at why he was here to begin with."

"You stopped him?" Tarjiaan repeated. "You... did you kill him?"

"No. He is in a lead-lined cell on our ship," Rathsafa said heavily. "There's one on every ship, in case a mage loses their grip on reality during their practice. It dampens their abilities." He took a deep breath and let it out slowly. "That is... my entire truth. I have nothing left. No more secrets. I will abide by your decision, Your Majesty. If you want me in irons, then call your guard. I ask only for mercy for my men, who have served me in the hopes of one day living free under the sky." He hesitated. "My daughter, I don't expect you to forgive me. I don't expect you to do what I cannot."

Nika nodded slowly, then softly asked, "What was his name? My brother? I do not remember him."

Rathsafa looked down. "Your brother's name was Ysnavin. Your name, before they took it away and renamed you in the harem, was Ysnika. Your mother named you both in honor of her mother, Ysnia."

"Ysnia?" Wilaanger repeated. "Queen Ysnia?"

Rathsafa nodded. "Masthaka was her fourth daughter, sired by her third husband."

Silence, broken only by the hum of air circulators and the distant rumbling of engines. Ikaanaji rested his hand on the table, breathing deeply enough that Tarjiaan heard something beep beneath his cloak.

"This is a... heavy burden you have placed on us," Ikaanaji murmured. "We must consider." He paused. "What name will you have us use?"

Rathsafa looked stunned at the question, and hesitated before answering, "Rathsafa. That is the name of the man I wished to be."

"Ilaris, take Lord Rathsafa to his suite. He will be confined to quarters while we deliberate." Ikaanaji gestured. "That is all."

Rathsafa rose. He bowed deeply. "Thank you," he murmured, and followed Ilaris away.

"Well, that's bilge in the drinking water, isn't it," Daanir muttered as the door closed behind them. He was looking at Wilaanger, who sat in stunned silence, his face unreadable.

"I do not know if I can believe him," Nika said quietly. "I do not know if you should, my husband. He has lied about many things."

"And what if he wasn't lying, and the Emperor does get word about what's happened?" Daanir asked as he glanced between Tarjiaan and the king. Tarjiaan met his gaze with a sinking feeling. If it was true, they'd not only lost a chance at peace, but lit a fire under the ongoing conflict. "We need a way to verify some element of what he said," Daanir muttered to himself. "Any element. I can look through the rolls and see if anyone is any closer to decrypting their transmissions."

"We need information faster than that." Tarjiaan rubbed his forehead. "Talk to Ishantar. I asked her to speak to her mother, to find out more about Nika's mother, and to tell them about her. She'll be able to find out if there are such documents."

"Does Mancer Ishantar have connections to the Sualimani Queen?" Nika asked. "A daughter of the royal house serves on your ship?"

"She's not very close to the throne," Tarjiaan answered. "Third grand-niece. It may take time. Ishantar's family is on the southern coast, and the Royal Court is itinerant." He frowned. "It's... high summer on land. They'll be north, and inland, if they haven't changed their patterns. But Ishantar's mother will know how to find them, and will be able to get us some answers."

"And then what?" Wilaanger asked. "Holy Mothers, I thought we were going to see an end to this war."

Tarjiaan nodded, closing his eyes, trying to think. It was like trying to navigate through fog. "I want to hear more of his plans," he said, rubbing his fingers between his brows. "I don't think we know enough."

"You believe him, don't you?" Daanir asked.

Tarjiaan shook his head. "I don't know." He turned to Nika, then reached for her hand. "This... I don't know."

"What if he is telling the truth?" Naajir asked.

"That's none of your concern," Ikaanaji snapped. "This dinner is over. Go to your room."

Naajir rose, then hesitated by his chair. "I don't know where that is," he said softly.

"Go to Kaapi," Daanir said. "She's supposed to be working on her history lessons tonight. You can doss with us until you're settled in your own rooms."

Naajir bowed toward Ikaanaji, then fled the throne room. For one brief moment, Tarjiaan wished he could do the same.

"All our plans." Ikaanaji's voice was harsh. "To bring our people back to land, to stand once more on our own shores. All of them are ruined." He turned to glare at Nika. "This is all your doing."

"What?" Nika gasped. "I... no!"

"Uncle!" Tarjiaan protested. "She didn't know any more than we did!"

Ikaanaji ignored him, pressing his hands on the table and pushing himself up to his feet, looming over Nikaranthia, who sat frozen in her chair. Tarjiaan saw his uncle tense, and reacted – grabbing Nika, pulling her across the carapace of his chair and into his arms as the chair shot away from the table, just in time to avoid the shower of glass and water and cutlery as Ikaanaji swept his arm across the table. Daanir and Wilaanger both jumped up – Daanir moved to stand between the King and Tarjiaan, while Wilaanger went to Ikaanaji's side.

"Ika, stop it!" Wil grabbed the King's arm. "She's done nothing! It's not her fault! Sit down!"

"I will not sit! Where is Ilaris?" Ikaanaji looked around. "Ilaris! I want this woman sent back to her people."

"No!" Tarjiaan shouted. "You are not sending her away!"

"All our hopes for peace are shattered, because of her!" Ikaanaji pointed one wavering finger. "She will be banished—"

"She will not!" Tarjiaan had to raise his voice to be heard. It cracked at the strain, but it stopped Ikaanaji cold. "Nikaranthia is my wife. I swore to her by the Great Mothers, and if you are banishing her, then you are banishing the both of us."

"Jiaan, no," Nika whispered. "No."

He tightened his arms around her. "Uncle, sit down and calm down," he said, his voice firm. "You're behaving worse than Aanaji."

"I..." Ikaanaji looked around, clearly confused. "What... Wil? Wil?" He lowered himself back to his chair, and the silence of the room was broken only by a thin wail from a hidden machine.

"Wil—" Daanir took a step forward, only to be waved off by the Royal Physician.

"I know how to get him back into the machines," Wilaanger said. "See to your companion." He rested his hand on Ikaanaji's shoulder. "I'm here, Ika."

"Wil? Are we going home soon?" Ikaanaji's voice sounded small, like the voice of a lost child. "I'm tired. I want to go home."

"Soon, Ika," Wilaanger said, his voice calm and gentle. He took Ikaanaji's hand. "Come with me. You can rest." He coaxed Ikaanaji back to the throne, helping him to sit. "Let me get your medicine. Then you can sleep."

"Wil, I want to go home." All at once, Ikaanaji started crying. "I want to go home!"

Wilaanger sighed and put his arms around the king. "I know, Ika. Soon. We'll go soon."

Tarjiaan couldn't look away. He felt as if he was seeing something that he shouldn't have – something that felt deeply disturbing. He jumped when a hand closed on his shoulder. "Come with me," Daanir said softly.

Tarjiaan followed Daanir out into the corridor, saying nothing. In his arms, Nika was shivering.

"What was that?" she whispered. "What just happened?"

"I'll explain once we're... where are we going, Daan?"

"Your rooms." There was a faint flicker in his eyes, and his fingers on the wall left a trail of sparks as they moved. The lights beneath cameras blinked off as they approached and buzzed back to life once they were past. The door opened a few feet before they reached it and shut as soon as they were inside.

"I realize there's a lot to take in and consider right now, Jiaan," Daan muttered.

"Great Mothers," Tarjiaan breathed. "My head is spinning. But... if Rathsafa was wrong, if the High Priest got word of our location, every ship in the Imperial army will be underway as soon as the tide turns. The fleet must be ordered to move." He let Nika go, helping her onto her feet. "And... and he can't. Not now. Which means... I have to. But... Daan, I... I don't think there's precedent for an heir to give orders in place of the King. Not in Meradon."

"I can buy us some time," Daanir was still, his eyes on something neither of them could see. "Make it a Mancer's order. Move the ships by force. The navigators might make noise about it, but at least we'd be out of range for them to argue."

"You'll burn your brains out," Tarjiaan said. "And you'll be charged with treason regardless. No. I... we need Ilaris and Wil. Can you send for them? Discreetly?"

"Wil is going to be busy." Daanir blinked a couple of times, returning to them from wherever he'd been. "During times like this... it can take a while."

Tarjiaan turned to look at Nika, who'd gone to sit on the couch. She was quiet, her hands clasped in her lap. She met his eyes, then looked down.

"I am... fine," she murmured.

"You're not. I don't think anyone in this room is fine," Tarjiaan said. "Daan, how... does that happen often?"

"More often than it used to. It's always at night. Real night, not ship's night. Not sure why, but it gets dark above the waves, and he goes dark below. He won't remember it tomorrow."

"And I'm not likely to forget," Tarjiaan answered. "Right. Send for Ilaris, will you? Someone needs to give those orders, and they need to be given now."

Chapter Fourteen
Orders

THE DOOR CHIMED, OPENING of its own accord. Ilaris looked around as he came inside, clearly looking for whoever had opened the door for him. He saw Daanir, bowed his head slightly, then bowed more fully to Tarjiaan.

"Your Highness? You sent for me?"

Tarjiaan took a deep breath and tried to ignore the feeling that sharks were circling in his gut. "Ilaris, my uncle is... indisposed. And given that we may have an immediate threat to our people, I am assuming command of the fleet until such time as my uncle has recovered." Tarjiaan paused, watching as Ilaris' face went ashen.

"Highness—"

"I am aware that this is treason, Ilaris," Tarjiaan said. "But under the circumstances, I can do nothing else. Are the command codes all still the same?"

Ilaris swallowed and nodded. "Yes, Highness."

Tarjiaan nodded, closing his eyes and mentally reviewing the highest priority codes. "For immediate transmission on all channels, highest priority and highest security. For the below-ships, issue Code Deep Scatter. Is that understood?"

"Deep Scatter," Ilaris repeated. "Understood. And for the above ships?"

"Code Great Migration," Tarjiaan answered. "In addition, I want you to message Marikaar directly. Tell him to make for the floating

170

dockyards. They are to act as escort for the dockyards from there, as instructed in Great Migration."

"And what of the Imperial ship?" Ilaris asked. "You don't mean to allow them to sail, do you?"

Tarjiaan shook his head. "I... don't like that I have to give this particular order," he said. "Ilaris, order Marikaar to put the crew to the question, as we would any Imperial ship. Any who do not swear to Meradon are to be held as prisoners of war, with all due courtesy. But only the crew. There is a prisoner on the Imperial ship. Marikaar is to leave them where they are." He took a deep breath. "Then he is to sink the ship with all prisoners on board. Tell him to use the same method as our last battle. He'll know what that means."

"Jiaan!" Nika gasped, barely audible. "You cannot—"

Tarjiaan shook his head. "Nika, there's no choice. This is one man balanced against the safety of all of Meradon. I cannot order the High Priest freed. I cannot have him taken prisoner on the *Wave Runner*, not knowing that he can reveal their location at any moment. And I cannot bring a mage to the below-ships." He sat up straighter and met Ilaris' eyes. "By my hand and seal, and the authority granted to me as the Sea Prince and heir to the Coral throne. You have your orders, Ilaris."

Ilaris bowed deeply. "Your Highness."

The door closed behind him, and Tarjiaan slumped, covering his face with his hand. He shook his head and breathed, "Fuck."

"Your father and your brother would have been lining up to wash your mouth out," Daanir murmured. "Here. Best I can do."

Tarjiaan looked, and saw the tumbler in Daanir's hand. For the first time in a long time, he found himself craving the numbness found in the glass. He took it and sipped the drink, then looked at it. "What is this?"

"Something I learned in the dockyards. They called it bilge. It grows on you." Daanir sipped his own drink. "It's strong if you're not used to it, so I cut it."

"This is cut?" Tarjiaan took another sip. "Daan, if this was in the bilge, it would eat through the hull! If I spill any, there'll be holes in the deck!"

"I don't remember you being a lightweight when it came to drinking."

"I don't drink anymore." Tarjiaan rolled to the table and set the glass down. "I need my wits about me. I doubt I'm sleeping tonight." He sighed. "Nika, I'm sorry. If there was another way, I'd take it. But I have to protect our people." He closed his eyes and went searching for his next thought. "Daan, I need to know when Wilaanger is available."

"I'll send him your way when he comes back on the system," Daanir nodded.

"He is a priest," Nika said, staring at her hands. "Killing him is blasphemy."

"I know." Tarjiaan took a deep breath. "But if he contacted his brethren on land, and told them our current coordinates? Every ship under the Emperor's command will be on their way to these waters with mages and depth bombs, and possibly constructs, and they will destroy any ship they find without a moment of hesitation. I promise you, his death will be quick. It's more mercy than he'd give either of us." He paused. "If there was a way to avoid this, I would. But I have to think of Meradon. There are children on this ship, and on all the below-ships of Meradon."

"Depth bombs?" Nika frowned. "What is a depth bomb?"

"Nasty pieces of ordnance," Daanir answered. "I haven't gotten my hands on one to see how it works, but they drop them from above, and the bombs lock onto anything large enough to be a below-ship, and they blow it to pieces. But they're not smart. They lock on to anything over a certain size. I've seen Great Mother carcasses after getting hit by one. You could sail a dinghy through the hole."

Tarjiaan gestured. "This ship? If it's punctured, even the smallest hole? It will implode. Explode inwards. Everyone on board will die." His world wavered for a moment, as the weight of his own words came crashing in on him. He shuddered, and his voice shook as he finished, "Your life is in the balance here. Daan's life. Naajir's." He swallowed. "People you haven't even met yet. The children in the crèche who you'll be tending to. Men and women and children who just want to live their lives. An entire nation of people who are relying on me to keep them safe. You want me to choose the man who would see them all dead over them? I cannot... I will not trade all of their lives for his. I wouldn't even trade my sister, and she hates me." He pressed his hands down on the carapace of his chair. "I thought this was over. I thought... there was a treaty. An alliance. The war would be over. No more senseless killing. I let myself hope..." He shrugged. "Maybe that was my mistake."

"But if he is left behind, he will not know anything to tell the others," Nika insisted. "Or... perhaps I could speak with him—"

"First question – would you have me leave him on an empty ship? There won't be a crew. A single man alone on a ship like that? That's a death sentence, too. A slower, painful one, at the mercy of the winds and the weather and the Great Mothers. Second question – if you did talk to him, would he even listen to you?" Tarjiaan asked. "To a woman? To a woman he thinks is a slave?"

"I do not know," she admitted. "Perhaps he would not. But if there is a chance, is it not worth it to avoid yet more bloodshed?"

"He's a mage," Daanir said. "They can control people, can't they? If we let you near him, how would we know if you were still... you? Is that a risk you'd be willing to take? To have him take over your mind and have you kill Jiaan in his sleep?"

"Oh, now there's a lovely thought," Tarjiaan sputtered. "Thank you. I hate it." He turned back to Nika. "There's already going to be bloodshed, Nika. The Emperor sent ships out after me. Hunting me especially. The last attempt in my life was the day before I met you. And let me tell you something you may not know, and that I didn't know until then. You told me the story about the *Marauder*. And you told me you've heard stories about the Butcher of Meradon. Have you heard the ones that say I leave no survivors?"

Nika nodded, her eyes wide.

"They're not true, and I can prove it. I have sent thousands of sailors back to the Empire. I lost count a long time ago, but there are records of every man who ever stayed under the waves, and every man who sailed back to the Empire. Thousands... and yet I was told by an Imperial officer the day before I met you that he's never met anyone who survived an encounter with me, or heard of anyone who had. Why do you think that is?"

Nikaranthia wound her hands together tightly. "Because the Emperor would not want them to know they could leave his navy," she murmured, not looking at him.

Tarjiaan took a deep breath. "Nika, people will talk. Gossip travels faster than any ship. How would he have stopped them from talking?" He shook his head. "The only way to stop a man from talking is to stop him from breathing. If I let that ship sail back to Imperial waters, there won't be a single man left alive to tell the tale. Nika, for the good of Meradon—"

"They would say the same, would they not?" she demanded. "Do you imagine that there is a single one of the Empire's generals who does not believe that the cruelty they inflict on others is for the good of their people? Is that what you want to be? Ruthless and cruel, as they are?"

Daanir finished his glass and poured another. "People die. The sea is dangerous. We don't have to like it to know the course that works in the current."

Tarjiaan sighed and rubbed his forehead. "I don't want to argue with you, Nika. I am going to do what I have to do to protect our people. You don't have to like it. I certainly don't. But if protecting the lives of people who look to me to defend them from the Empire makes me ruthless and cruel? So be it." He turned to Daanir. "Is Wilaanger available?"

Daanir shook his head with a grimace. "Nothing."

Tarjiaan growled softly, his chair shifting slowly from side to side. His stomach was churning, and he had a headache growing behind his eyes. This was nothing he knew, nothing he'd ever been trained for... and he still had to do the best he could for his people. And now his wife thought he was no better than the men he was trying to protect his people from.

Was he?

"I need to breathe," he muttered. "I need a moment. Excuse me." He turned the chair toward his bedroom.

He heard Daanir sigh as the door closed between them. Then there was silence. He leaned forward, resting his forearms on the carapace of his chair and letting his head hang. No, there wasn't going to be any sleep for him. Not tonight. He needed to talk to Wil, to see if his uncle was going to recover, and if not, what arrangements needed to be made. He'd need to find out from Ilaris if there was any precedent for an invalid king to be removed from the throne while still alive, or if he was going to have to usurp his uncle's throne for the good of Meradon. He needed to plan the next steps, determine where and when the fleet could reassemble, and if they would bring the battle to the Empire or stay in hiding. He needed to talk to Rathsafa, find out what he was planning, and decide if he believed what he was told. He needed...

The door opened behind him. No one spoke, and the silence grew heavy and uncomfortable.

"His name was Antivar. That Imperial officer I mentioned," he said without turning, saying something so that he didn't scream. "He was nineteen, and he... he was born to the sea. I could tell. He had so much promise. He was terrified of me, but he stood up to me and told me that I should kill him and let his men live. He thought I was going to make his skull into a wine bowl. Can you imagine?" He paused, but there was no response. "I asked him to stay. I wanted him to stay. I wanted to see the officer he could be. He told me he wished he could, but the Emperor had his mother as a hostage against his return. That's... probably my fault. They're keeping hostages so they don't lose more officers to Meradon. I promised him a place if he could find his way back to our waters. A place for both of them." He closed his eyes and shook his head. "I don't think I'll ever see him again. Because I showed him mercy. Because I gave him a choice."

"The choice." Daan amended quietly. "Taking skulls as wine bowls? That's a grim reputation to have."

"It is one of the milder ones I have heard," Nikaranthia murmured.

Daanir huffed, "Drinking from a skull is mild?"

"The Emperor is said to have two himself. Gilded goblets, the heads of his enemies." Nikaranthia folded her hands as she stepped closer to Tarjiaan. "Perhaps you can offer this choice to the priest—"

"We don't house mages. It's too dangerous," Daanir answered before Tarjiaan could. "The mistake has been made before. It's in the records." He sighed. "He's right, my lady. It isn't a pleasant choice, but it's the only option we have." Daanir squatted in front of Tarjiaan's chair. "Wil's heading to the clinic. Shall I detour him before he heads back to the throne room?"

"Please," Tarjiaan answered. "Gilded skulls of his enemies? Well, I suppose I know what my fate is, if the Emperor gets his hands on me."

"Do not say that!" Nika gasped. "He would not—"

"Wouldn't he?" Tarjiaan turned his full attention on her. "Nika, right now, I am the greatest enemy that the Emperor has, and not because of the might of Meradon. If it was just our tech and our ships? We aren't a threat to the Empire. Our tech and our ships aren't enough to do more than hold the line against the sheer number of people he's willing to throw against us, but he's running out of people and resources, isn't he? We could wait him out – wait until the Empire falls apart under its own weight, and return to Meradon then. We've waited this long, held the line this long – what's one more generation? But he's not willing to give us that time. He sees the end coming, just as much as we do, and he's not willing to let us go. He's sending ships looking for me specifically. He's afraid of me for the same reason your father wants me as an ally – the legend of the Sea Prince. People will follow the Sea Prince, because he is a symbol of hope. If the Emperor defeats the legend? He'll prove to the entire world that he's unbeatable." He paused. "And I'm not a legend. I'm just a man. And when I do die, and I stand before the Great Mothers to be judged? All I'll be able to say is that I did my best with the gifts they gave me."

"That's all any of us can say," Daanir said. "Wil in two minutes."

"Thank you." Tarjiaan held his hand out to Nika. She hesitated, then slipped her cold hand into his. "Nika, I need you to consider something. You're my wife—"

"I had noticed," she interjected, her voice sharp.

He snorted. "And I noticed you noticing," he replied, and saw her lips twitch. "That means someday... a year... a month... a week... I don't know when, but someday, you will be Queen of Meradon. The people of Meradon will look to you to guide them, as much as they look to me. And Mothers forfend, if anything happens to me before Naajir reaches his majority, you will be Regent. That means these choices that aren't choices? They will be yours to make. You'll have advisors. You'll have people to support you and help you and make certain you have all the information possible, but the choices will be yours. And you'll have to live with them, for the good of Meradon." He paused, closed his eyes, and made another decision. "You have a choice, though. A choice that I never had. If you feel that this is... untenable. If you feel that you cannot bear the burden, then I will release you from your vows and take you to Sualiman myself. You'll be free to live with your mother's people, free to learn who you are outside of the Empire, and free of your responsibilities to Meradon. Or, if you want, you can remain in Meradon, on one of the other below-ships. Perhaps find someone to build a life with."

"You said that if I was banished, you would come with me," she whispered.

"I did, and I would," Tarjiaan answered. "But I won't force you to stay if you don't want to be here, Nika. I won't make you stay somewhere you don't want to be. I won't force you into a role you don't want. And if you choose one of those options and leave me? I will miss you."

"You'd need to wait a month," Daanir blurted. "Just in case."

Tarjiaan glanced at him, then coughed. "Oh. Ah... yes."

Nika looked from him to Daanir, frowned, then rested her hand on her belly. "I... you do not think...?

"It's possible," Tarjiaan answered. "Unless...do women in the Empire have ways to block conception?"

"Several," Nika answered slowly. "It is encouraged in the women's quarters. But I have not used any of them. There was no need."

Tarjiaan nodded. "Then you have some time to decide what you want," he said. "Nika, I'm likely to be busy all night. I don't expect you to stay up, unless you want to observe and learn from what we're doing. Send for Chel so you can get ready for bed, and while she's here, you can ask her about what contraception is available to you now." He closed his eyes. "And we should have Logiri in. I'm going to need tea."

"You've your call light." Daanir nodded to Tarjiaan's arm. "You can—" He glanced over his shoulder as the door opened.

Wilaanger looked as exhausted as Tarjiaan felt, his large kit slung across his shoulders. "If it isn't an emergency, your Highness, can I return to you in a few hours–"

"I won't keep you long, Wil," Tarjiaan said. "Go sit. Breathe. I'll be right there." He touched the button to call for Logiri, then asked Nika, "Do you remember how to use the comms? Your call light for Chel?"

"I can show her—"

"I remember." Nika stared at her hands.

"Just in case," Daanir offered quietly.

Nika nodded slowly, not looking at either of them.

"Nika." Tarjiaan held his hand out. "I've dropped an entire tidal wave on you. I know it's a lot, and I'm sorry. Are you going to stay, or are you going to go to your room?"

She took his hand, squeezed it gently, and crossed into the bathroom as she had just that morning, shutting the door behind her.

Daanir rubbed the back of his neck. "One thing at a time."

Tarjiaan nodded. "Just keep swimming." He rolled out of the bedroom and into the sitting room. "Wil, thank you for coming. I have some questions, and I need answers now because that will determine what I do next."

Wilaanger lifted his weary gaze. "About?"

"My uncle." Tarjiaan rolled up to the table and rested his hands on it. "Wil, based on the potential threat caused by the High Priest being able to communicate with the other mages on land, and seeing that my uncle is in no condition to give the orders, I've taken command of the fleet and ordered Deep Scatter and Great Migration." He paused. "How long do you think he will be... indisposed, Wil?"

The healer shook his head slowly. "Your Highness, it isn't so simple as that. And this... Tarjiaan, this is treason! You can't—"

"I know what I've done, Wil. I've weighed our options, and I've made the choice for the good of Meradon. I have issued this order, and this order alone, because it was an emergency. Or would you rather have our ships be where the Empire will find them when they come in answer to the High Priest's call? There are Imperial ships in the water already, and we have no way of knowing how long we have before they reach us. Is that a gamble you're willing to take? Because I can't. I swore to protect the people of Meradon. This is the only way I can." He met Wilaanger's eyes. "Wil, you've already told me that you and Ilaris and Daan have been handling things. And Daan told me that it's been happening more often."

"The Mancer Royal swore an oath—"

"As did I," Tarjiaan snapped. "I swore to defend this kingdom with everything I am. And you're withholding vital information that I need to do that. Now I need the truth. You told me that you and Daan and Ilaris have all been ruling in my uncle's name. Am I going to have to do the same? Issue orders in his name and hope for the best? And why wasn't I recalled when things started getting this bad? Or at least informed? Why am I only finding out how dire things truly are now?"

Wilaanger's cheeks were flushed. He sat ramrod straight, gripping the strap of his medical kit. "Your Uncle," he enunciated slowly, his fury scorching the air around him "my King, wanted to spare you for as long as he could. He gave us instructions, when he could, on what he saw as the best path forward for Meradon and we saw those instructions fulfilled. His word, his law; that is the way of the sea."

Tarjiaan nodded. "That is the way of the sea," he agreed. "And tomorrow, I will see him and I will tell him myself what I ordered and why, even though I doubt he'll remember what happened tonight. And I will abide by his wishes, because he is my King." He paused, swallowing and looking away. "Wil, what would you have me do?" he asked softly. "I have to protect our people. I have to uphold my oaths." He turned back to the older man. "I'm lost. I'm doing the best I can, but I don't think even Ilijiaan would know what the right course would be here, and he was actually trained as Sea Prince."

"He would have known not to try to pry the trident from his uncle's hand," Wilaanger chided. "I never thought you could do this, your Highness. This... Tarjiaan, I don't know how I can protect you. Or if I should."

For a moment, Tarjiaan wanted to scream. Wanted to shake Wil, to rage at him, to make him see that all he was doing was trying to protect his people. How was that wrong? How could his uncle hold that against him?

But it wouldn't do any good. If he did this, Wil wouldn't see him any anything other than a traitor.

And he couldn't bear losing another father.

"Daan, have the orders been sent?"

Daanir paused, then shook his head. "Not yet. It would take time to get them set—"

"Cancel them." Tarjiaan bit the words off and spat them out. "Cancel the orders. I will see my uncle in the morning. Thank you. That is all." Without another word, he turned and went back to the bedroom, closing the door behind him.

Chapter Fifteen
Truth

HIS MOUTH WAS DRY ENOUGH to hurt. His back hurt, too. He focused on that, focused on the pain. It made the hunger fade away. At least he could think again – whatever drugs she'd been giving him had worked their way out of his blood. But now he could feel the pain. And he could think, and he could feel the walls closing in. The tiny room was barely bigger than the cot to which he was strapped. For his own safety, she'd told him. He was broken now. Broken and helpless, and he needed to be protected.

Where was she? Was she coming?

His mouth was so dry.

The door slid open, and a large figure stood outlined in the doorway. He knew that figure.

"Tarjiaan?" Wilaanger dropped to his knees next to the cot. "Great Mothers, boy, what has she done to you?"

"Wil." Tarjiaan relaxed. He'd been found. He was safe. Then he heard his sister's voice.

"Honestly, Wil, just leave it. We don't need it anymore. There's a true heir now. A perfect strong little boy."

Tarjiaan frowned. "Aanaji?"

Wilaanger smiled. "Aanaji has had her baby. A perfect little boy. He'll make a fine king someday." He rose, and Tarjiaan tugged weakly against the straps as Aanaji came into view. She looked different. Slender, and older, with gray in her hair.

"Please, help me," Tarjiaan *whispered. He tasted blood as his lips cracked.*

"Leave it," Aanaji *said, resting her hand on Wilaanger's arm. "We don't need it anymore. We never needed it." She turned and left. Wilaanger looked at Tarjiaan, shook his head, then left the room. The door slid closed behind him, plunging the tiny cell into darkness.*

No!

No!

Tarjiaan!

"Tarjiaan!"

Cold water drenched Tarjiaan, shocking him awake. He rolled, pushing himself up onto his hands, and saw...

"Nika?"

She was holding a pitcher, and she looked... Great Mothers, she looked terrified.

"You were *screaming,*" she said, her voice shaking. "I could hear you through all the doors. Then I could not wake you." She looked down at the pitcher in her hands. "I could not think of anything else–"

"I... thank you." Tarjiaan wiped water from his face and shifted. "I'm sorry. I–" He jumped when Daanir's voice rang out.

"Jiaan?" Daanir skidded through the doorway, half-dressed in his underthings and a shirt, with a gun belt slung over his shoulder. He had his force-pistol gripped tightly in one hand. "Step away from him."

Nikaranthia dropped the silver pitcher with a clatter. "He wouldn't wake up," she gasped. "I had to do something."

Daanir exhaled sharply, nostrils flaring, as he scanned the room. "What happened?" His voice was no less strained, but had lost the threat of violence. "The sensors told me there was screaming–"

"A nightmare," Tarjiaan interrupted. "I had a nightmare. I'm sorry. I frightened you both."

Daanir leaned against the door-frame. "A nightmare." He holstered the pistol, rubbing his hand over his face.

Nika joined Tarjiaan on the bed, heedless of the wet sheets. She wrapped her arms around his shoulders. "You do not need to apologize for this, my husband. You are safe. You are well."

Tarjiaan sighed, letting the pressure of her arms around him ground him, pulling him back into himself. "I do need to apologize, because I didn't warn you. I should have. Nightmares... when I have to be below, I get them. Frequently. Not this bad. Not usually." He shifted, putting his arm around Nika. "Daan, I'm sorry. I roused you out of bed, didn't I?"

"Not the first time. Won't be the last." He shook the tension from his hands and rolled his shoulders. It was such a jarring reminder of how he'd always been after a fight, Tarjiaan could have laughed in relief. He heard the outer door open again, and Daan looked over his shoulder. "Stand down," he called. "He's fine."

"What was it?"

Tarjiaan tensed at the sound of Wilaanger's voice. "Why is he here?" he asked in a low voice.

"It sounded bad," Daanir muttered grimly, crossing into the sitting room. The door slid shut behind him as he heard Daanir saying, "False alarm. I must have—"

The door sealed, muffling the rest of his words. Nika smoothed her hand down Tarjiaan's back. "You do not like it below? Is this not where most of your people live?"

"It's where most of our people live, yes," he answered, hugging her more tightly to his side. "But...I can't stay here long. It's...I should explain all of it. It's part of what I was going to tell you this morning. And if I'm explaining it, then Daan should hear it, too. He was there for the beginning. But he doesn't know what came after." He turned toward her, and kissed the top of her head. "Thank you. I'm sorry I frightened you." He took a deep breath and looked down at himself – he hadn't bothered to strip more than his coat before lying down, so he was wearing his sweat-stained shirt and rumpled trousers. "They're here. Best to do it now, I suppose." He shifted away from Nika, toward the edge of the bed.

"You are still shaking," Nika said. "I can feel it. You are making the bed shake. How can I help?"

Tarjiaan's mind rebelled – he didn't need help. He could do it... but he didn't have to. "Brace the chair?" he asked.

It took two tries before Tarjiaan felt steady enough to swing from the bed into the chair. He closed the carapace and met Nika's eyes. She looked worried.

"I'll be fine, Nika," he said. "Let's go out."

Wilaanger was wearing a banyan over battered trousers, and his gray hair was loose from its usual queue.

"I'm sorry," Tarjiaan said.

"Nightmare, Daanir said?" Wilaanger frowned slightly. "The attack?"

Tarjiaan sighed. "The closet," he answered. Wilaanger blanched.

"Closet?" Daanir folded his arms over his chest.

"I'll explain." Tarjiaan gestured to the couch. "Wil, you know all this. Go back to bed."

"Once I'm certain you're fine." Wilaanger took a seat on the couch. "As fine as you get down here, that is."

Tarjiaan smiled. "Which isn't." He paused, collecting his thoughts. "Nika, you wanted to know why I don't like being below. It's because I can't manage in small spaces for very long. Enclosed spaces are..." He paused, trying to think of the right word. "Suffocating? No, that's not it. Smothering. Everything presses in and..." He stopped, hearing the catch in his own voice. "That's why I stay above. Uncle knows. Wil knows, too."

"Because of the *Marauder*?" Daanir asked softly.

"That's only part of it," Tarjiaan answered. "The rest... is Aanaji. You wanted to know why she'd been banished. She...." He stopped again, hearing his heart hammering in his ears as panic strangled him silent.

"Do you want me to tell them what I know?" Wilaanger asked. He waited for Tarjiaan to nod before leaning forward to rest his elbows on his knees. "Daan, keep an ear on the alarms for me?"

"Already listening. It's quiet."

Wilaanger nodded. "The court was in... quite a state after... after everything. Losing so many, losing Captain Taarik and Prince Ilijiaan... Ilijiaan wasn't even supposed to be out there! He was the Sea Prince. He was supposed to be out of harm's way. But he was as stubborn as the rest of the royal sons, and he insisted that he had to serve above the waves. The *Vagabond* was a total loss...." He paused, then shook his head. "Those were devastating losses, and we were not... we weren't paying attention. This can be laid at my feet as much as anyone else's."

"I've never blamed you," Tarjiaan said.

"I blamed myself. I should have been paying closer attention, and it almost killed you." The physician took a deep breath. "Tarjiaan was released from the hospital wing into the care of his sister. Aanaji had some healer training, although she had never applied herself seriously. She knew enough to take care of Tarjiaan, I thought." He rubbed one hand over his face. "The next thing I knew, it was two months later, and Aanaji was in labor. Aanaji never had an easy pregnancy. She lost two before Naajir. So it didn't surprise me that when she went into labor with Naajir, everything that could go wrong did. And when I finally had her stable, and her baby was safe and healthy, I realized that I had no idea where Tarjiaan was. I'd seen her reports, but I hadn't seen him. So I went to her quarters to see who was tending to him in her absence."

"No one," Tarjiaan murmured. "No one knew where I was. No one came looking for me. She drugged me and left me strapped to a cot in a closet, alone in the dark. I couldn't get out, I couldn't help myself, and I had no one to help me. All I really remember is the dark, and her telling me that it should have been me to die. I was deformed. Disgusting. I was a mockery. A broken, crippled thing that — I should have had the decency to die with the *Marauder*. I should do them all the favor of dying so I wouldn't be a burden on them anymore and so that no one would be forced to look at what I was." He paused, his eyes itching. Burning. He shook his head. "There was more like that. Worse than that. Until Wil found me. But by then... the damage was done."

Daanir frowned.

"No, I wasn't going to tell you," Tarjiaan answered the unspoken question. "I don't think I could have told you. I was... well, you saw me before the *Chimaera* surfaced. And that was just from sailing too close to the memories. I couldn't tell you the whole of it. Not and still be functional."

"Sometimes, I think Tarjiaan survived just because of sheer stubbornness," Wilaanger said. "You saved his life, and he was not going to give up that gift so easily. The physical damage was extensive. Some of the bedsores went to the bone. Infection set in and... it was a near thing. There were three separate surgeries, and it took months for him to heal completely."

"I... I saw scars," Daanir stammered. "I didn't know—"

"There are still some places where I don't have much sensation." Tarjiaan looked down at his hands. "Then there was the withdrawal, and what came after. I started drinking to excess to control the cravings for whatever it was she'd drugged me with, and it wasn't long before I was a complete drunkard."

"And surprisingly good at hiding it," Wilaanger added. "It took months to dry you out after I found out."

Tarjiaan shrugged. "Now? I don't drink anymore, except for one night a year. Drinking is only something else that would trap me. I know that if I fall back into a bottle, I won't come out. I've drunk more in the past few days than I have in years, and Daan, you and Wil saw how hard it hit me." He took a deep breath. "I can't... I can't be helpless again. Be trapped again. The armor helps, but I can't wear it below. I... I can put on the facade of the Sea Prince. I can show people that, be who I need to be. And on the surface, it's true. I know my worth. I know that I am... more than a thing. That I am not helpless. That Aanaji was wrong. But even after all this time, down deep, some part of me still believes her."

"That was why you were afraid to show me your truth," Nika murmured.

Tarjiaan couldn't look at her. If there was pity in her eyes, it would shatter him. He knew it. "She told me, over and over, that no one was ever going to want me – not the way I was. That the only reason anyone would want me was because they either felt sorry for me or because they wanted the throne. And you... when I asked you if I disgusted you, you threatened to scratch her eyes out. You didn't even know who told me that, and you were ready to fight them." He heard Daanir snort and dared to look up. His battle companion stood by the wall with his head bowed. Without the oil slicks, his white hair hung shaggy over his brow, nearly hiding his eyes.

"I am more ready to fight her now," Nika asserted, pulling Tarjiaan's attention from Daanir. "She should not have been allowed to return, nor been entrusted to the care of another after what she did to you."

"I argued with Ikaanaji over that," Wilaanger said. "Over leaving Naajir with his mother. He insisted that she should be allowed to keep the child, as a mercy after having lost her father and her twin. Never mind that she almost killed her younger brother." He paused.

"Perhaps that was when the... the mental decline began. I'm not certain."

"It doesn't matter," Tarjiaan said. "With Naajir under my care now, it's one that we might have seen an end to already. Wil, I'll want your help, if you will? He might need the same sort of care I did." He frowned. "Where is he? He didn't know where his quarters were."

"He still doesn't," Daanir muttered. "He's dossed out on the floor in mine." He paused. "And he's still asleep."

"Good. I'll get him sorted out tomorrow." Tarjiaan leaned back and rubbed one hand over his face. "That's all of it, I think. That's everything I didn't tell you. Either of you." He took a deep breath and let it out slowly in a long sigh. "I'm sorry I woke you all. I'm sorry I've made a mess of things. You should all go back to bed."

"And you?" Nika asked.

Tarjiaan shook his head. "I doubt I'll sleep again tonight. I'll find where Logiri hid the kettle and make some tea—"

"You will what?" Nika sounded shocked.

"I am perfectly capable of making tea!" Tarjiaan replied. "Even if Logiri does think it's a scandal when I do."

"If you are going to stay up, then I will make the tea." Nika stood up. "Where do I look for the kettle?"

"Daan, you've poked around in here more than I have," Tarjiaan said. "Is there a steward's pantry? I haven't looked, and I honestly didn't pay attention yesterday when we had breakfast."

"There is." Daanir gestured toward a corner. "The door is part of the panel, so it's hidden if you don't know to look for it. Your Highness, I'll show you how the kettle works. It's probably not what you're used to." He led the way to the corner and touched a control – the door slid open.

"Jiaan?" Wilaanger said. "Are you going to be all right?"

"You tell me, Wil," Tarjiaan replied. He took a deep breath. "You know, there are no negotiations now. Maybe I should just take Nika and go back to the *Wave Runner*... stop looking at me like that," he said as Wilaanger scowled at him. "If you all had been honest with me from the outset, things might be different now. And speaking of being honest, you knew I was looking for Daanir. I talked to you about it, and about not being able to find him. Why didn't you tell me he was here?"

Wilaanger looked blank. "I..." he stammered. Then he looked puzzled. "I... remember that conversation. I remember how frustrated you were. And I remember how happy I was when he was assigned here and I found out he was safe, and I was going to tell you. But... for the life of me, I can't remember why I didn't!" He frowned. "I did some looking into the records last night while your uncle slept. I can't find anything either. At least, not under my own authority." He hesitated, then shook his head. "If you'd spoken to your uncle about this, you'd have had an answer. You wouldn't have liked that answer."

"And why not?" Daanir asked from behind Tarjiaan. He rested his hand on Tarjiaan's shoulder. "What do the records say?"

"That Daanir Nessunre was killed in the line of duty seven years ago." Wilaanger shook his head. "But that record is only visible when I use Ikaanaji's authority to search. Under my own authority? It's the same as what Tarjiaan found. Or didn't find. There's no record of Daanir Nessunre at all."

"Except in the Mancer rolls, and those are only available to Mancers," Daanir said. "I... Riguaarin said something that struck me as funny, back when I first came on board. He said he was surprised no one had snapped me up for a berth in the fleet. It made no sense to him that I was as good as I am, and not on a ship. I never thought about why, but if there's no records for a ship captain or their mate to see, then they can't request someone, can they?"

Wilaanger spread his hands wide. "That's all I've had the time to find," he said. "It's a start. And it tells me that this was no accident.

The redundancies on the rolls... it shouldn't be possible to just wipe someone's records clean."

"Who could?" Tarjiaan asked. He closed his eyes, thinking. Not liking the answers.

Wilaanger confirmed his suspicions. "Another answer you won't like," he said. "The only person who can bypass the redundancies without setting off security alerts is your uncle. Which makes no sense!"

"Unless someone borrowed his access," Daanir murmured. "These days? You do it. I do it. Ilaris..." His voice trailed off. "Wil, why didn't the King ask Ilaris to do this search? It makes sense for him to do it. The records... that's his job."

"You were there. You heard him," Wilaanger said. "He trusted me to do it—"

"Which implies that he didn't trust Ilaris," Tarjiaan interjected. "I don't understand why he wouldn't. Ilaris has been there... I don't remember a time when he wasn't at Uncle's elbow."

Wilaanger leaned back on the couch, folding his arms over his chest. He shook his head slowly. "I..." He stopped, then shook his head again. "No."

"You know something?" Daanir asked.

Wilaanger looked up. "Speaking as a battle companion, if I asked you to betray Tarjiaan's confidence, would you?"

Daanir reeled back as if he'd been struck. "Of course not! I... oh."

"I'm not asking you to betray my uncle," Tarjiaan said. He paused, then let his still-simmering frustration speak, "Even though you seemed fine with accusing me of doing just that."

Wilaanger scowled. "Tarjiaan—"

"I didn't do anything that you and Daan haven't done, and don't tell me you haven't, because you already admitted to it. I just did it on my own authority, and not borrowing my uncle's. And I can't help but feel that the real heart of your problem with my doing it is that I didn't go through you or speak to you first." Tarjiaan shook his head. "We're doing the best we can, and we need to work together. I'm not going to argue with you about this. Hopefully, however many hours between my orders and his won't come around to bite us." He sighed. "Wil, go to bed. Uncle will need you, and I shouldn't be keeping you awake."

Wilaanger scowled. "I'm only trying to protect Ikaanaji–"

"And I'm only trying to protect Meradon," Tarjiaan snapped. "We have the same goal, so why aren't we working together? After all, my uncle *is* Meradon."

Wilaanger visibly deflated. "He is Meradon. Now," he said in a low, sad voice. "But he's always been my Ika. Even after he married Alyaan, he was my Ika." He looked past Tarjiaan. "You understand, I think."

Daanir closed his eyes, his brow creased with sorrow. "I understand."

Tarjiaan looked up at Daanir, then at Wilaanger. "And I had no idea. Wil–"

"Why would you have known?" Wilaanger asked. "It's not something we discuss. I just..." He paused and looked past them, and Tarjiaan glanced over his shoulder to see Nika setting cups on the table. "I hope you have a happier end than we did," Wilaanger finished softly. He stood up, tugging his banyan closed. "I'm going back to bed. No more excitement, Jiaan."

"Will you have a cup before you go?" Nika asked. "I found a calming tea in the cabinets. I think it is something we can all use."

Wilaanger turned to her. "How did you know?"

"I know a little of herbs and their properties," Nika answered, folding her hands in front of her. "I recognize the scent of the herbs." Then she smiled. "And the teas are all labeled."

"You can read?" Wilaanger said. "I'm surprised. Yes, my dear. I would like some tea."

Nika smiled. "Come and sit, and I will pour. Daanir? Jiaan?"

"Thank you, but I should go back before the kids wake up and find me gone," Daanir answered. He turned to Tarjiaan. "No more nightmares."

"I'll do my best," Tarjiaan said. "Thank you. I'm sorry I frightened you."

Daanir smiled. He hesitated, then looked at Nika. Tarjiaan wasn't sure what exactly passed between them, but eventually Daanir breathed a quiet sigh and leaned down to kiss Tarjiaan gently on the lips. "You're forgiven," he murmured. "I'll check in with you in the morning." He nodded to Wilaanger, bowed slightly to Nika, and left.

Silence, until Wilaanger cleared his throat. "I've seen the Tyracan high tea ceremony," he said, taking a seat at the table. Tarjiaan joined him as Nika began to fill teacups. "It's quite the elaborate ritual, and very lovely. Nikaranthia, do you know it?"

"I know it," Nika replied. She turned the full teacup in front of her and slid it across the table to Wilaanger. "The art of serving tea is a skill we were taught in the women's quarters. There are five different tea ceremonies, and we were required to learn all of them. I was never of the status to be allowed to perform the full, formal tea ceremony, but I do know it."

"Ika has a Tyracan tea service. It was a gift, and I don't think it's ever been put to proper use," Wilaanger said. "I'm certain he'd appreciate seeing the ritual once more."

Nika slid a teacup to Tarjiaan, then poured a third and sat down facing Tarjiaan. "I would be honored to share tea with the King," she said. "But not tonight."

Tarjiaan chuckled. "No, not tonight." He picked up the tea and sipped it. "Thank you," he said. "I've never seen a tea ritual. I've read about it."

"I will show you," Nika said. "I will show you all five, if you wish. After you have rested."

Wilaanger drained his cup. "And that is my signal to leave. We'll talk tomorrow, Tarjiaan."

Tarjiaan nodded, sipping his tea as Wilaanger left. As he finished, Nika stood up and came around the table.

"Come to bed," she said, taking his hand.

"I was–"

"I know what you said you were going to do," Nika interrupted. "And if you do not sleep, how will you be able to face your uncle in the morning? Come to bed." She smiled. "And before you say you cannot because your bed is wet, you will come to my bed."

"Nika, I–" Before Tarjiaan could say more than two words, she stepped closer and kissed him.

"Come to bed," she murmured, her breath tickling his lips. "I will keep the nightmares away."

Chapter Sixteen
Betrayals

SOMEONE WAS KNOCKING, and Tarjiaan woke in an unfamiliar bed with a warm weight on his chest. It took him a moment to remember where he was and to realize that the weight was his wife, sprawled on top of him.

"Highness? Are you awake?" Logiri's voice was muffled by the closed door.

Nika raised her head. She looked around, her brow furrowed. Tarjiaan smiled and traced the line of her cheekbone with his fingers.

"Did you sleep well?" he asked in a low voice.

"I should be asking you that question," she answered. "Did you?"

"Yes. You kept the nightmares away." Tarjiaan glanced at the door as Logiri knocked again. "I'm awake," he called. "What is it?"

"Highness, the Mancer Royal is here. He says it's important."

Nika shifted off of Tarjiaan. "Your shirt is on the chair," she murmured. "I will get it." She got out of bed, coming around to his side with his shirt in one hand, and her robe in the other. "May I help?"

"Thank you." Tarjiaan pushed the blankets out of the way and sat up. He'd slept in his trousers, and he took the shirt and pulled it on, leaving it hanging open as Nika shifted his chair into position and set the brake the way he'd shown her. She stepped back as he swung into the chair and closed the carapace, putting on her robe as he waited for the light to glow green. Then she opened the door for him and followed him out of the bedroom. In the main room, Daanir was pacing, his hands moving with restless energy. He stopped when he saw them, and his brows rose.

"You slept?"

"Surprisingly, yes. And surprisingly well." Tarjiaan looked up at Nika. "I'm feeling better. Will you have breakfast with us?"

"Ah... no. I came because I need to leave, and I wanted you to know." Daanir started moving again. "Wil and I were called to the crèche ship. Something happened, Wil said. He took the message this morning. They said it wasn't dangerous, but they need a healer and a mancer, and we're the closest ones. And...well, I thought that since it's not dangerous, and since Her Highness might be taking on the crèche kids, it might be a good idea if she came with us. She can see the crèche, get an idea of what she'd be getting herself into if she decides to do it."

Tarjiaan blinked. "You and Wil? Can you both leave?" He glanced over at Logiri and decided on discretion. "Given our talk last night?"

Daanir grimaced. "I know. I don't like it, but there doesn't seem to be another option. Other than...well, you. You'll be with the King all morning, and you can insist on it being private. We'll be as quick as we can. A few hours, maybe, and if it runs longer, Wil says he'll come back before me and send the submersible back. My work usually takes longer than his anyway. Once we're all back, the three of us can talk to the King, tell him what Wil found. And we'll see where we go from there." He tucked his hands behind his back and turned to Nika. "You'll have time to dress and eat before we go, if you're coming."

Tarjiaan turned to Nika. "Do you want to go?" he asked. "Like Daan says, I'll be with my uncle most of the morning. You could spend that time here with Chel, but I'm not certain when I'll be back."

Nika frowned slightly. "I... is that allowed? For me to go with them?"

Tarjiaan fought the urge to remind her yet again that she was no longer in the Empire. She knew that, but it would take time to really understand. Instead he tried a different tack. "Nika, if we were in the Empire, would you hesitate to attend some function with my father if I couldn't attend with you?"

She looked startled. "I... no. Your father would be the head of your family. If he requested my attendance, and you agreed, I would be obligated to do so."

Tarjiaan shook his head. "Not what I asked. Assume you have a choice."

Her lips twitched. "In the Empire, I would not. But to answer the question that I think you are trying to ask, it would be acceptable for a wife to attend a social situation with her husband's father."

Tarjiaan nodded. "Wilaanger has been acting in place of my father since my own father died," he said. "And you know that you're safe with Daanir. If you want to do this, you have my leave and my support." He reached for her hand and kissed her fingers. "And I want to hear all about it when you come back."

Nika squeezed his hand, then turned to Daanir. "How long do I have to get ready?"

Daanir tipped his head back. "Don't dawdle. And Chel is on her way."

"You called her?" Tarjiaan asked.

"No. I just noticed she left her quarters." He looked back at the door, which opened to reveal Chel in the corridor. She looked startled, then noticed Daanir.

"Oh, that explains it," she said. "What's is it?'

"Her Highness is going to accompany me and Wilaanger to the crèche ship, and we need to be ready to leave soonest," Daanir answered.

Chel nodded. "All right. Timing is everything – I have the first of your royal uniforms." She patted a bundle under her arm. "Shall we get you ready, then, your Highness? And have you eaten?"

"Please," Nika answered. "And not yet."

"Right. Logiri, will you put together a tray for us? We'll be ready soonest." Chel followed Nika into her room, closing the door behind them.

"Sorry to steal your wife for the day." Daanir grinned. "So, I can't stay for breakfast. How about supper?"

Tarjiaan laughed. "Bring Kaapi. I want to meet her."

"She wants to meet you," Daanir admitted. "She told me this morning that she and Naajir went into the submersible docking bay last night to see your armor when she was supposed to working on her lessons. She's heard about it, and she's seen my early design sketches, but she's never seen it up close. They both promised me that they didn't touch it." He paused. "What you said last night, about your armor helping? How long have you been wearing that set? It looks like my original design sketches."

"That's because it is. Falian worked from your designs," Tarjiaan answered. "He thought they were brilliant. There have been some minor adjustments made over the years for fit and comfort, and the padding has all been replaced a few times, but it's mostly still the same. Why?"

"Because it's tech that's nearly fifteen years out of date," Daanir answered. "And we can redesign it. Something lighter, more compact. Something you could wear down here." He spread his arms wide. "It won't be quick, but Kaapi already has ideas—"

"She's going to design it?" Tarjiaan asked.

"She's good. I think she's spending the morning sketching and talking out ideas with Naji. And she told me she was shocked I let you wear something so out of date. Like I had a say in it." He grinned.

"If it's up to her, you'll have new armor every year, with all the latest technology."

Tarjiaan laughed. "I never was one for the latest fashions. That was Ranji. Remember his red armor?

"I remember your father's reaction to the red armor," Daanir answered. "I think the mildest word he used was ridiculous."

"So do I, and I agreed. It was ridiculous." He looked over at the table. "I'm not interested in the latest fashion, but I'll take the latest technology. Do you have time for a cup of tea before you go?"

Daanir shook his head. "No. Wil needs me in the throne room. Tell Chel to bring Nika to bay four, will you?"

Once he was gone, Tarjiaan went to the table. Logiri had already poured a cup of tea for him, so Tarjiaan sipped it while Logiri took a laden tray to Nika's door. When Logiri came back, Tarjiaan set his cup down.

"I need your discretion, Logiri. And your expertise."

Logiri arched a brow, tensing just enough that Tarjiaan noticed. "I hear nothing. But I am available however you need me, Prince-Captain."

"Nothing like that, Logiri. I need you to find out what suite they're holding the emissary in, and check on his status. See if he needs anything, and that he's being treated with all courtesy." Tarjiaan rested his hands on the table. "You know nothing."

"My head is as empty as the vast mother desert," Logiri agreed.

"There is no alliance. The emissary claims to be acting against the Emperor. He gave his name as Rathsafa, but he confessed that his real name is Gondanadarish, and that Rathsafa is the name his wife gave to him on their marriage... Logiri?"

Logiri had gone ashen, bracing himself against the chair. "Gondanadarish? Nadar? Nadar is here?"

"You know him?" Tarjiaan blinked. "And well enough to use a diminutive? That means you'd be able to confirm that he is the Prince?"

Logiri nodded slowly. "I... yes." He stopped. Closed his eyes. Then he drew himself up and nodded once. "Is there anything else you would have me do once I confirm his identity and see to his needs?"

"Use your best judgment," Tarjiaan answered. "And your best discretion." He glanced at the door. "Logiri, if what he says is true, Nika is his daughter."

Logiri went still. He turned and looked at the closed door. "I... yes. I can believe it. Yes." He bowed, visibly composing himself, then bowed again. "I will report later, Prince-Captain. May I serve?"

"Please. I need to get my thoughts in order. Oh, and Logiri, my bedding will all need to be changed."

"I noticed something amiss this morning," Logiri admitted, not looking up as he filled a plate. "Sweet rolls or toast?"

"Sweet rolls, thank you." Tarjiaan picked up his tea again. "Nightmare. Bad one, and Nika couldn't wake me. She threw a pitcher of water on me, and... well."

Logiri gave him a long look, then asked, "And are you feeling able to meet with your uncle this morning? Is it something that can wait?"

"It has to be done, and it has to be done soonest," Tarjiaan answered. "I'll need my court uniform."

"Of course. I'll see to it while you eat." He set the plate down in front of Tarjiaan, refilled his tea, then bowed and disappeared into Tarjiaan's bedroom. Tarjiaan looked down at his plate, then left the table to fetch a pen and paper from a cabinet. He made notes as he ate – his orders for the fleet, his reasoning for doing so, why he'd given those orders and why he'd walked them back. The work soothed his still-frayed nerves, and he started laying out new plans, new ideas that he wanted to discuss with his uncle, getting engrossed enough in it that when Nika combed her fingers through his disheveled hair, he jumped.

"I did not mean to startle you," she said as he turned toward her. "We are going to leave, and I did not want to go without saying goodbye." She kissed him and smoothed her hands down the front of her coat. She was wearing the royal colors – the coat was long and dark green, and she wore it over a long black skirt. "Am I... is this good?"

"You look wonderful," Tarjiaan said. "Chel, Daanir said to meet him in bay four. If you would?"

"Actually, I'm going with my lady," Chel said. "If Uncle Wil and the Mancer Royal are working, she'll need someone to show her around." She smiled. "Shall we?"

Nika nodded, kissing Tarjiaan again before she and Chel left. Tarjiaan looked down at his notes, then at his empty plate and cup.

"Logiri, I need to get ready."

When Tarjiaan entered the throne room, he got the distinct impression that his uncle had been waiting for him.

"Good morning, Uncle," he said as he approached. He stopped a measured distance from the throne and bowed. "I was hoping we might be able to talk this morning? If you're feeling well enough?"

"I am fine," Ikaanaji said. "And I was going to send for you." He paused, and only then did Tarjiaan notice Ilaris, standing in the shadows cast by the machines behind the throne. "I'm told that you attempted to usurp my throne?"

"And that is why I came to speak to you this morning," Tarjiaan answered. "I wanted to explain to you my decision, my reasoning for doing so, my reasoning for canceling those orders, and hopefully convince you that the orders that I gave were correct, and to give them yourself." He opened his hands, palms to the sky. "My thoughts are only ever on the good of Meradon, Sire."

Ikaanaji snorted. "You betrayed your oaths to protect Meradon for the good of Meradon?"

"I did not!" Tarjiaan protested. "May I explain?"

Ikaanaji nodded once. "Proceed."

Tarjiaan took a deep breath and bowed again. "At dinner last night, when Rathsafa revealed that the High Priest could communicate with the mages on land, we realized–"

"We? Who is we?"

"The Mancer Royal and myself, Sire. We had much the same thoughts," Tarjiaan answered. "If the High Priest revealed our current coordinates, he could relay that to the forces on land, and bring every ship in the Imperial Navy into our waters. They are already out, close enough that they found me not even two days ago. We would not have much time to act. Last night, you were... indisposed, and so I gave the orders to initiate Deep Scatter and Great Migration so that none of our ships would be anywhere near here when the Imperial ships arrived. I also ordered that the *Wave Runner* take on board Rathsafa's crew, then destroy the Imperial ship. When the Physician Royal pointed out how gravely I overstepped my authority, I canceled those orders."

Ikaanaji scowled slightly. "Where is the Physician Royal? And the Mancer Royal? Why are they not here?"

"The Mancer Royal informed me that they were needed on the crèche ship this morning. Since the reason that they were summoned was vital but not dangerous, they brought Nikaranthia with them so that she might start her duties overseeing the crèche children."

To his surprise, Ikaanaji smiled. "She's a delightful girl," he said.

"She says that she'd like to share tea with you, Sire," Tarjiaan said. "She knows the Tyracan tea ceremony."

"Does she?" Ikaanaji smiled. "That will be pleasant. Now, you realize that you overstepped your authority. That does not change the fact that you did it."

"And I would do it again, Sire," Tarjiaan said. He drew himself up. "I will keep my oath to defend Meradon with everything that I am. As meager as that might be. And if that includes asking forgiveness instead of waiting to ask permission? I will do so."

Ikaanaji snorted. "You changed your mind, though."

Tarjiaan considered his response, then opted for the truth. "Wil yelled at me," he admitted. "He accused me of trying to take the trident from your hand, when all I thought I was doing was defending the fleet." He shook his head. "He told me I was a traitor, and that he would not be able to protect me from you if I betrayed you. And that is why I rescinded the orders. Because I could no more betray you than I could get out of this chair and walk out of this room."

"And do you think you need protecting, Tarjiaan?" Ikaanaji asked. Tarjiaan met his eyes and shook his head.

"No, Sire. Not from you. Because you understand the choices that have to be made to protect our people."

For several minutes, the only sounds were from the machines and the air circulators. Ikaanaji looked away, toward the viewing ports along the side of the throne room. Tarjiaan sat still, feeling the sweat running down his back. Whatever happened now, it would be for the good of Meradon.

"I can see no fault in your reasoning," Ikaanaji finally said. "Save only that you allowed Wil to change your mind. When you take your place in this throne, Tarjiaan, the decisions are yours and yours alone. You cannot allow others to sway your rule." He paused, then smiled and added, "No matter how much their opinion matters to you."

"Great Mothers willing, it will be a long time before I take my place in that chair, Uncle."

Ikaanaji smiled. "Good. You're calling me Uncle again. It's always strange when you call me Sire. Ilaris, carry out the orders that Tarjiaan issued last night."

"Yes, Sire," Ilaris said, coming forward. "If I may be excused to do so?" He bowed when Ikaanaji gestured, then walked out of the throne room.

"The emissary Rathsafa..." Ikaanaji said. "We must come to a decision about what is to be done with him."

"I may be able to confirm his identity, Uncle," Tarjiaan said.

Ikaanaji looked surprised, then thoughtful. "Your aide. The Tyracan refugee. You trust him in this?"

"He's been with me nearly eleven years, and he hasn't killed me yet," Tarjiaan said, making his uncle laugh. "I trust him. And he says that he knows the Prince. Once we confirm that he is who he claims to be, then we can see what his plans are."

"If his claims are true, if he is the Imperial Prince, and if your wife is indeed his daughter, then you are now heir to the Imperial throne as well as the Coral throne."

Tarjiaan coughed. "I..."

"You hadn't thought about that?"

"Honestly, Uncle? I wasn't thinking any farther ahead than this meeting and possibly supper tonight!" Tarjiaan laughed. "I have no desire to warm the Imperial throne. For one thing, I don't think I have it in me to gild the skulls of my enemies and use them as drinking bowls."

Ikaanaji snorted. "Heard that one, have you?"

"Nika confirmed it," Tarjiaan said. "Uncle, I apologize for... acting beyond my authority. But I would do it again if necessary."

"And I will make it so that it is not beyond your authority," Ikaanaji said. "Once Wil returns, we will decide how best to do that." The doors opened, and Ilaris came back into the throne room.

"Have matters been settled, Sire?" he asked.

"They have," Ikaanaji answered. "Ilaris, will you bring the tea? My head aches."

"Uncle?"

Ikaanaji grimaced as he shook his head. "It is nothing. Wil can find nothing wrong, which means it's probably the noise." He gestured to the machines behind him. Ilaris nodded and left, coming back a few minutes later with a tray that he set down on a table near the wall. He brought a cup to Ikaanaji, then another to Tarjiaan before returning to his place by the wall.

"Have you seen to Naajir yet?" Ikaanaji asked. He sipped his tea and grimaced. "Ilaris, you let this steep too long. It's bitter."

"I haven't seen him this morning. I came to you first," Tarjiaan answered, sipping his tea. It was indeed bitter, but refusing to drink with his uncle would have been insulting, and the last thing he wanted to do was raise his uncle's ire. He took another sip. "Naajir spent last night with the Mancer Royal. He's friends with Daanir's daughter, I'm told."

"How is that possible?" Ikaanaji asked. "Didn't he just come aboard the *Chimaera*?"

"I don't know, Uncle," Tarjiaan answered. Now that the potential conflict was over, he felt exhausted. His coat was too warm. He...

Ikaanaji's cup fell to the floor and smashed into pieces as he slumped in the throne. Tarjiaan stared for a moment, feeling as though his wits were adrift.

"Uncle?" He tried to tell his chair to roll forward, but it didn't want to obey him. Neither did his arms. "Ilaris? Something's wrong."

"Nothing is wrong, Your Highness," Ilaris answered. He walked past Tarjiaan, going up to the throne. He stopped next to Ikaanaji, then turned and gestured. Tarjiaan could hear footsteps behind him, but it was as if they were coming from a long way away, down a dark corridor.

The last thing he saw was Ilaris smashing one of the machines.

Warm wind, and the smell of the sea. He was asleep on deck. Why was he asleep on deck? Tarjiaan blinked, and looked up at full sails and taut lines. His mind felt foggy, and his head was cold. It took him a moment before he registered that the sails above him were canvas, and not the thin metal solar sails that rose over the *Wave Runner's* decks. That the voices he heard around him...

Imperial.

He pushed himself up, steadying himself with his hands. He already knew what he'd see – he was on board an Imperial ship. It was underway. He was alone. No armor. No chair. Even his coat was gone, and he'd clearly been searched – his trouser pockets were turned out, his shirt untucked. He shook his head, and realized that his head was cold because his hair had been shorn close to his scalp. He remembered the throne room. The bitter tea. Ilaris, smashing the machines.

Was his uncle dead?

Ilaris, what have you done?

"What is this?" He spoke the words in careful Imperial, not expecting an answer, but hoping for at least a reaction. He looked around, seeing men that he recognized from his wedding. None of them would look at him. The man closest to him turned red and turned away.

"So, the mighty Sea Prince at last falls." Tarjiaan recognized the voice of the High Priest. He turned and looked up at the man, who smiled coldly at him. "I'm told you were going to have me killed."

There was no reason to lie. Not anymore. "A merciful death. Quick and clean. Will you offer me the same courtesy, Holiness?"

"Sadly, I cannot." The High Priest gestured to the surrounding men. "My Emperor wants your death for himself."

"And my skull as a drinking bowl?" Bravado was all he had left. He was not going to panic in front of his enemies. And grief would come later.

Assuming he had a later.

The High Priest sniffed. "Once, he may have been satisfied with that, but now? He has other plans for you." He grimaced. "They are... distasteful, and I will spare you the details. But you are to be delivered to him alive and as unharmed as can be managed."

Something thumped on the deck behind him; Tarjiaan turned to look, and for a moment, it didn't make sense. A metal box, oblong, and about half as tall as a man. One of the sailors swung the front open, and inside, Tarjiaan saw shackles.

Bravado shattered. "No!"

"There are spells embedded in the box to sustain you," the High Priest said. "You will come to no harm..." He paused, looked at Tarjiaan, then shook his head. "No physical harm. I'd wondered... but no matter. My Emperor has spoken. Take him, and seal the box."

Chapter Seventeen
Sabotage

NAAJIR FOLDED HIS LEGS to sit on the floor next to Kaapi, his own work forgotten in his lap as he tried to see her drawings.

"Do you think they'll let you design the new armor?" he asked.

"I do better design work than Daanir," she answered without looking up. "He says so. So maybe we can work together on it. I do the outside and he does the inner workings. You heard him before he left – we're invited to dinner."

"You'll like my uncle," Naajir said. "And my new aunt. She's... she's nothing like my mother said. And..." He looked up as the door chime rang, suddenly cold as the camera told him who was on the other side. "Kaapi...?"

"She can't get in. Daanir told the door she's not allowed... wait. How... she's overridden the lock!" Kaapi dropped her drawing pad and got to her feet as the door slid open. Naajir's mother glanced over her shoulder, then rushed inside and slapped the door control. When the door sealed, she slumped against it, breathing hard. Naajir slowly got up, staring at her – ever since they'd come back to the *Chimaera*, she'd been cold. Distant. But now? He'd never seen his mother so... disheveled. And the look in her eyes...

She was *terrified*.

"Mother?"

"Naji," Aanaji breathed his name. "I need for you both to listen to me. This... I don't have much time. He's distracted, but he won't be for long." She fished in her pocket and took something out, then held out both hands. "Here, take these."

"Data disks?" Kaapi took one and held it up. "What's on it?"

"They're identical," Aanaji said. "And it's vital that at least one of these reaches the Mancer Royal. Do you understand?" She shuddered and looked at the door. "I don't have much time. Your name is Kaapi. Is that right?"

Kaapi nodded, her eyes wide.

"Your father is a good man. And he loves my brother. I know that. You need to give him that. Tell him... tell him I'm sorry. Tell him that he has to find Tarjiaan and save him. That the future of Meradon rests on him now. He has no reason to believe me, but the explanation is on the disk. And if he loves my brother, he'll listen." She turned to Naajir, stepping close enough to put her hand on his shoulder. "Naji, I'm sorry. I am so sorry. Listen to me. I know what you can do."

"What?" Naajir stepped back. "I..."

"You hid it well, but I know." Aanaji smiled slightly. "I saw you, when you first broke through, when you made the lights dance in your room. I did my best to hide it from... from others, because it might save your life. You both need to hide. Do you understand?"

"No," Kaapi answered. "But... we'll do it."

"Mother, what is it?" Naajir asked. "What's happened?"

She shook her head. "There's no time. The explanations are on the disk. There's no mancer on board right now, so there's no one who will be able to find you if you hide from the machines. Hide, and stay hidden until the Mancer Royal comes back. Trust him. Trust only him." She looked at the door again, then pulled him closer and kissed his forehead. "I'm sorry. I love you. Now go hide!" She touched his cheek, then turned, rushing out the door. Naajir started to follow, but Kaapi caught his arm.

"Kaapi, let go!"

"No!" Kaapi tugged him back. "Something is wrong. Can you hear it?"

Naajir closed his eyes and listened to the machines, the way Daanir had taught him. Now that he was paying attention, he could hear it – a concerto played out of tune. "I hear it."

"Something is broken, and it shouldn't be. Something is really wrong. We need to do what she said." Kaapi looked up, her face scrunching. "The cameras won't see us now. Let's go."

Nika sat down next to Chel and watched as Daanir and Wilaanger entered the submersible. Daanir was frowning. The expression didn't suit his face at all. He looked better when he was happy. Smiling. Not glowering.

"Tell me again," he said, sounding annoyed, "why we needed to be here? There was nothing here that a competent engineer could have handled, and they didn't need you at all."

Wilaanger shook his head. He looked puzzled. No... he looked confused. "The message this morning said we were needed. I don't understand it."

Daanir's scowl deepened. "I never saw this message. Why did they send it just to you? If they needed me, they could have sent for me directly. You're not my assistant to take messages for me." He tipped his head back to look at the ceiling. "It doesn't make sense. And I should have asked these questions earlier."

Wilaanger shrugged. "When we get back to the *Chimaera*, I'll show it to you." He turned to Nika and Chel. "And what did you think of the crèche?"

Nika smiled. "The children are very happy. They are well cared for. I like the attendants, and I think we will work well together. And they were not frightened of me."

"I told you they wouldn't be," Chel murmured. "Children are far more accepting than adults."

Nika nodded. "It reminded me very much of the children's area in the women's quarters in the Palace, before they send the boys away."

"Send the boys away?" Daanir looked at her. "Boys go where?"

"It depends on their status," Nika answered. "Highborn boys go to the upper apartments, where they will be tended to by tutors. Lowborn boys go to the servants quarters to learn service. And slave children and those without living parents are either taken to the slave quarters or sold."

"Sold?" Daanir stared at her. Then he snorted. "I'd have been sold."

"There are no slaves in Meradon, I thought?" Nika asked.

"That's right," Daanir said. "No slaves. But a lot of orphans. Most of the kids you met today have lost their parents. Like me. I don't remember mine at all."

"You grew up like that?" Nika thought about it for a moment. "And now you serve the King, and will serve the next King as well. That is so much more than what an orphan in the Empire could attain."

"I was lucky," Daanir said. "I got lucky when I was picked for battle school. And I was good enough to catch Captain Taarik's eye. Then... well, then I became a Mancer."

"And you were good enough to catch Riguaarin's eye," Wilaanger said. "Daan, don't hide your light under a barrel."

Daanir snorted and tapped the badge on his chest. "As if I could."

"I mean it's not luck that got you this far," Wilaanger said with a laugh. "It's skill and determination."

"And stubbornness," Chel added. "Jiaan told me once you were as stubborn as the sea is deep."

Daanir laughed. "You've met the man. I had to be. Once—" He stopped. "What...?" He turned in his chair. "Commander, what's the reading on the pressure gauge?"

"It's in the green, Mancer," the pilot called back. "All systems showing normal. Is something wrong?"

Daanir swung out of his seat, heading forward, toward the control. "There's something–"

He was halfway to the controls when the panel in front of the pilot exploded in a shower of sparks. Daanir dove forward, pulling the pilot from his chair and taking his place. Wilaanger and Chel both jumped up, dragging the pilot toward the empty space at the rear of the submersible.

"Daanir?" Wil shouted.

"Not now!" Daanir's voice was strained, and Nika could see metal flying around him like a swarm of bees. And she remembered Tarjiaan's words: *This ship? If it's punctured, even the smallest hole? It will implode. Explode inwards. Everyone on board will die.*

There was nothing she could do to help Daanir, so she turned to Wilaanger and Chel. "May I help?" she asked.

Wilaanger looked up at her and shook his head. "I'm afraid not."

"Is... is he dead?"

Wilaanger nodded. "Daanir, what happened?" he called. "And... is it over?"

"It's stable," Daanir answered. "And...there was something in the controls that shouldn't have been there."

Chel looked up from covering the body. "Sabotage?"

Daanir shook his head without turning. "I... either that or the engineers are incompetent. And I know the engineers."

"Who would want to kill you?" Nika asked.

"Might not have been me—"

"Daanir, the target was you, or Uncle Wil, or both of you," Chel pointed out. She frowned. "They sent for both of you."

"And someone was expecting me to pilot. I usually do." Daanir grimaced and turned back to the controls. "And we both know who benefits. Back to the *Chimaera*, double speed." His hands danced over the controls, then stopped, hovering over one spot. Nika heard his breath catch. "Get do—!"

The panel exploded — a shower of sparks and smoke and flames. Daanir jerked, then went limp. Nika dashed forward, grabbing his coat and tugging him away from the controls with a strength she didn't know she possessed. Chel rushed in to take Daanir's place, doing something with the controls and using language that Nika wasn't sure she should have known. But it didn't matter. Daanir flopped on the deck, his face and chest a mass of blood. She touched his throat, and could feel his pulse fluttering like a bird's wings.

"Daanir!" she moaned. Wilaanger across from her, trying to clear away the blood, trying to get Daanir's coat open. There was nothing she could do. She could hear her own heartbeat pounding in her ears. He couldn't die. He couldn't. It would shatter Tarjiaan into pieces that would never be mended. Jiaan needed him.

She needed him.

"No. Please. Do not leave us," she whispered as she touched his cheek. "Please." Something warm filled her chest, her core, some heat within her that spread out and down her arms, flowing from her hands into him. Metal fragments dragged themselves out of wounds and fell to the deck. Lacerations closed, skin reformed, and she felt warmth returning to limbs that had already started turning cold. He took a deep breath. Another. Then he opened his eyes.

"Not... not leaving," he croaked. "Nika..."

"Your Highness," Wilaanger whispered. "You saved him!"

"I..." Nika looked at the healer, who was staring at her in awe. She wanted to protest, to tell him that she couldn't have. She was a woman. It wasn't her. But the darkness grabbed her and dragged her under before she could answer.

Nika woke to the sight of Daanir's face framed by dazzling lights She had to squint, raising one hand to shield her eyes. The room dimmed, enough that she could see the roof of the submersible. She could hear the machines, the faint hum of the air system. It sounded oddly normal.

"How are you feeling?" Daanir asked quietly.

"I... do not know. I... Fine," she whispered. Carefully, she opened her eyes a little more and looked at him. The parts of his face that had been torn apart were a little paler than the rest, but he looked otherwise unharmed. She sighed in relief. "You are all right."

"Thanks to you, I'm told."

She bit her lip. "Water?" He handed her a cup and helped her to sit up, steadying her as she sipped. She looked at him again and realized what she'd done. What it meant. Her hands shook, enough that water splashed over the edge. "Please," she whispered. "You cannot say a word about this. About what happened. Any of it. Please."

Daanir looked puzzled. "What? Why? You saved my life, which means you saved the King's life." He looked at her. "You're shaking. What is it? What are you afraid of?"

"Women are not allowed to be mages," she whispered, terrified. "Not in the Empire. And there are no mages in Meradon. They are outlawed. You told me that. I will be sent away! I cannot... I cannot lose him... lose you... I—"

"Highness, it's all right. You're not a mage." Wilaanger moved into view.

"But I... I used *magic*..."

"It's not the same, and healing magic is not outlawed." Wilaanger took her hand.

Nika stammered. "Healing... but it is magic. How is that not the same?"

Wilaanger shook his head. "It is and it isn't. Yes, it is magic. No, you are not a mage. At least, not under the laws of Meradon. You, my dear, are a healer. You have the Sualimani healing gift. I have a touch of it, but not nearly enough to do what you just did." He smiled. "You'll be an incredible physician once you're trained."

"A healer. I... I could be a physician? Like you?" She stared at him, then looked down at the water. "I could save lives?"

"You'll be a considerably better physician than me," Wilaanger assured her. "And yes, you could save lives."

"Could I... could I save the king?" Nika whispered. "Is that something I could do?"

Silence, and she looked up to see Daanir staring at Wilaanger. The physician had gone pale.

"I..." he stammered. "I don't know. Without training, it may do more harm than good, but..."

"But she saved my life, didn't she?" Daanir whispered. "Didn't she? With no training. She told my body what to do and it did it. Like I do with the machines. Like I did with the machines, to save Jiaan. She just did the same thing for me."

Wilaanger nodded. "She did. And... Nikaranthia, we can try. We'll talk to Ika. He may not agree. But we can try."

She bit her lip and looked down at her cup, then drained it in a swallow. "Jiaan calls me Nika. I would like it if you would, too," she said. "All of you. Please."

"We're coming up on the *Chimaera*," Chel called from the pilot's seat. "Taking us into bay six."

"Six is empty?" Daanir frowned. "It wasn't when we left."

"It's empty now," Chel answered. "Will you take us in? You're a better pilot than I am."

Daanir patted Nika on the shoulder and got up, making his way forward. A moment later, Chel came back and took a seat facing her.

"You can read, you told me? Good. I have some introductory texts you can have," she said. "Basic training for emergencies. We can start there."

Nika stared at her. "You will teach me?"

Chel smiled. "Yes. Nika, I like you. And you make my Captain happy, so I like you even more. This? He's going to burst, he'll be so proud."

Nika felt her face warm and looked down at her hands. "You think so?"

Chel reached across the space between them and rested her hand on Nika's. "I know it. I can't wait to see his face when we tell him."

"It will probably make his day better," Daanir added. "Considering the meeting he was going to have with the King this morning. Right, we're docked. Just hold until we equalize, and we'll be able to go find some answers."

Nika looked back toward the door, and noticed the floor was empty. "What happened to... what was his name? I was not introduced to the Commander."

"His name was Taliki, and we sent him to the Deep," Wilaanger answered. "I'll contact his mother once we're settled."

"I would like to offer my condolences, if I may?" Nika said. She looked up as hissing came from the vents overhead. "Is that–?"

"We're clear," Daanir said, coming toward them. He paused and frowned. Then he looked at Wilaanger and drew his pistol. "Something isn't right. Wait here."

The moment he stepped out into the *Chimaera*, the machines swarmed Daanir's senses, screaming and crying like small children, clamoring for his attention. It was overwhelming enough to make him stagger.

"Enough," he said aloud. "Enough! I can't hear you all when you all sound off at once!"

Slowly, the systems eased into their regular rhythms, their usual harmonies. Except... there was a voice missing. No. No, there were two voices missing, and a hole where there shouldn't be. He looked up at the ceiling, trying to make sense of what he was hearing...

"Wil?" he called over his shoulder. "Keep the sub hot. We may be leaving real fast."

"What is it?" Wilaanger asked.

"Nothing good. Stay here. I'll be back." He paused, then looked back to the armor waiting against the wall for Tarjiaan. The clips holding it popped free one by one, and the armor marched forward and into the submersible like half of a marionette. "Secure that," he added. "I'll be back."

The corridors were silent, even more than they should be, and Daanir gently dimmed the cameras as he passed. There was no one in the Heir's suite. No one in his own rooms. Where were the children? He didn't dare go and check the throne room – he knew what he'd find there. But how...?

Cameras were dimming in an intersecting corridor, hiding whoever was coming toward him. He recognized the touch of that power and started to run. As he turned the corner, he saw them, and heard Kaapi gasp something he never thought he'd hear:

"Papa!"

She hit him hard enough to knock him back a few steps, and her control over the cameras dropped. He took over, hiding them as he hugged his daughter tightly.

"I'm here," he whispered. "You're safe. I've got you. We're getting out of here." He blinked, looked around. Naajir looked close to tears. "Naajir? What happened?"

"I don't know!" Naajir wailed. "Mother got through the locks you told not to let her in, and she gave us data disks and said to find you and give them to you. That... that the future of Meradon rests on you, and you need to find Uncle Tarjiaan and save him." He pulled a disk out of his pocket and handed it to Daanir. "Something is wrong. Something is really wrong, and she's scared and she told us to hide." He frowned and looked up. "And... and something is wrong with the machines. They're out of tune."

Daanir nodded slowly. There were a million questions buzzing in his mind, but he knew there was no time. The sensors were warning him – there were guards coming closer. Given everything else he was seeing in the machines, he was certain they weren't coming to welcome him back.

"Bay six," he said. "Now."

Kaapi took off running, and Naajir followed. Daanir tucked the data disk into his breast pocket and ran after them, whispering an apology as he forced enough power into the surveillance cameras to short out the entire internal security system. From somewhere behind him, he heard an alarm – not the all-hands klaxon to battle stations, but the sharper siren that warned of fire. He paused by a maintenance panel, touched it, and shorted out the external sensors as well. That should keep the guards busy, and would let the sub get out of range.

Wilaanger was standing in the door, and backed out of the way as the children both ran into the entry. Daanir followed them, telling the door to seal behind them. As it slid closed, more alarms started to sound.

"What's happening?" Wilaanger demanded. "Daanir, what's going on?" He looked at the door. "We're leaving. What about Tarjiaan? And Ika?"

Daanir swallowed, then looked at the children. "Belt in. It might be rough."

Kaapi grabbed Naajir's arm and tugged him into the submersible. Daanir took Wilaanger's arm and tugged him away from the open hatch.

"It's all fucked, Wil," he whispered. "And... the King's machines are silent."

Wilaanger's face went pale. "No."

Daanir swallowed again and showed Wilaanger the data disk. "Aanaji... she rousted out the children, told them to hide. Gave them the disks and told them to tell me that we have to save Tarjiaan."

Wilaanger looked at the disk. "What's on here?"

"Answers, I hope." Daanir tucked the disk away. "Once we're underway. For now, we move."

Chapter Eighteen

Escape

DAANIR TOOK OVER THE controls, taking the submersible out of the *Chimaera* and into the dark waters. He needed to put some distance between them and the royal pod before...

Before what?

He looked up as a hand settled on his shoulder. "Tell me what happened," Wilaanger said.

Daanir shook his head and dug the data disk out of his pocket. "No idea. Naajir? Kaapi? Give us the whole of it."

"She opened the door, Papa," Kaapi answered. "She got through your lock. And she gave us the disks and told us to give them to you. She said they were the same, and we were to give them to you. She said..." She paused, her nose wrinkling as she thought. "She said you had no reason to believe her, but the answers are on the disk."

"And she said you had to find Uncle Tarjiaan and save him," Naajir added. "And that the future of Meradon was on you now. Daanir, she was terrified. She said she didn't have any time, and she'd distract him. I don't know who she meant, but she was scared of him." He paused. "And she said to tell you that she was sorry."

Daanir looked up again, and this time noticed the slight figure standing in Wilaanger's shadow.

"Find Tarjiaan?" Nika asked. "Where is Jiaan? You did not bring him back with you. That means you could not bring him back, or we would never have left. Where is he? What happened?"

Daanir looked at the controls, at the sensors. "We're clear. Let's get some answers. Wil, play the disk."

Wilaanger slid the disk into the reader, and stepped back to make room for the others. Daanir turned his chair to face the screen, which lit up to show the throne room. As they watched, Tarjiaan entered and greeted the King as he approached. He came to a stop before the throne, bowed, and said, "*I was hoping we might be able to talk this morning? If you're feeling well enough?*"

They watched as the audience continued, as Tarjiaan explained himself, as he defended his decisions and his reasons for reversing them. Daanir heard Wilaanger snort when Tarjiaan admitted that the reason he'd changed his mind was that Wil had yelled at him.

"I hadn't thought my opinion would hold that much weight," Wilaanger murmured.

"He thinks of you as a father," Nika said. "Of course he values your opinion."

Wilaanger snorted again, then blinked. "His aide would be able to identify the Prince?"

"I hope Antarlogirish will be safe," Nika said. "And... Rathsafa. I hope he is safe. I...I have so many questions I want to ask him."

Daanir nodded, watching the screen. Ilaris left to issue the King's orders, then came back. He served tea. They talked about Naajir...

The King collapsed. Tarjiaan called for help, and Ilaris came into view... followed by Imperial guards.

The video stopped as Ilaris started to destroy the machines. The screen went dark, then lit up again to reveal Aanaji. She licked her lips, glanced to the side, and took a breath.

"*My mind is my own, for the first time since I came back to the* Chimaera," she said. "*I... I have been under Ilaris' control since I was fifteen, since my mother died. Since Aaranji went to the* Marauder *to serve with our father, and Tarjiaan went to the crèche. I was alone, and... I was easy prey. I know that now.*" She glanced to the side again and took another deep breath. "*Ilaris is a mage. He hides his power, but he can take control of my mind and twist it, make me do things that I would never do otherwise. I have betrayed Meradon a hundred times over. The codes necessary to reveal the movements of our ships – I know how to access them without being detected. I know how to transmit them, and I have done so over and over again. Every ship of Meradon that's fallen to the Imperial fleet, every life lost, all of them can be laid at my feet.*" She paused again, and tears started rolling down her cheeks. "*The death of the* Marauder *was my fault. My twin's death was my fault. That Tarjiaan survived at all... the Mothers were kind in their way. And I repaid that kindness by torturing him and leaving him to die, and by separating him from the man he would have married.*"

Daanir stopped the playback. "She knew?" he whispered. "How...?" He looked up at Wilaanger. "She hid that she was accessing codes and transmitting them. She somehow hid all of this from Riguaarin and from me. How?"

"The same way she deleted your existence from the rolls?" Wilaanger suggested. "And got through your locks?"

Daanir frowned, then looked past him, to where Naajir and Kaapi stood side-by-side. "Naji?" he asked. "Is your mother a mancer? She never showed any signs of it where I could see. As a matter of fact, I was sure she didn't understand anything about how anything worked. But if she was hiding it... I don't know. Naji?"

Naajir shrugged slightly. "I don't know," he said. "I get it from somewhere, I suppose. And I don't know..." His face paled. "I... Wilaanger, is Ilaris my father? He's... he's had control of my mother since she was my age. She never married. And she never told me who fathered me."

Wilaanger frowned, then sat down. "I don't know," he answered. "She never told anyone who sired any of her children. She refused testing to find the reason for her miscarriages–"

"Her what?" Naajir's voice was shrill.

"She never told you that, either?" Wilaanger rubbed one hand over his face. "Finish the recording, Daan. Then... then I'll tell you what I know. All of it. It makes no difference. Not anymore." He gestured to the screen, and the silent, grainy image of Aanaji. "Run it."

Daanir nodded and restarted the recording. Aanaji looked sad and lost.

"*I have done terrible things. If he controls me again, I will do more terrible things. But Ilaris doesn't appear to be able to control more than one mind at a time. He is attempting to control the King. He's attempted it before, and I think... I don't know, but I think this is why my uncle is dying. Why his mind is slipping away. And perhaps... I may share the same fate.*" She looked away from the camera, then back. "*And if I can stop him now, and save Tarjiaan? Then I will welcome that fate.*" She looked down, then shook her head. "*I have to finish. There's so much I want to say, and I can't. I have to get this information into the right hands. But I will end with this – Naajir, you are the one good thing that's come to me from all of this. My Naji. My little mancer. I know. I've always known. You used to make the lights dance over your cot when you were small. I watched you, and I kept it hidden so that he would never know. I'm sorry if you ever thought it was wrong, or that I would disapprove. I just wanted you safe. And I know the Mancer Royal will keep you safe.*" She took a deep breath. "*Daanir, if you're seeing this, I am sorry. Aaranji messaged me to tell me that Tarjiaan asked to marry you. And because I knew, Ilaris knew. When we knew that Tarjiaan would live, he ordered you both separated. He wanted Tarjiaan isolated, so he could be controlled, and it infuriated him that he couldn't take control of Tarjiaan's mind the way he could mine. And now he's decided that since Naajir is the right age, he can move on. Tarjiaan can't be controlled, so he has to be removed.*" She bit her lip, and her voice shook. "*Find him. Save him.*" She jumped, looked to the side, and the recording ended.

Daanir drummed his fingers on the console, his mind racing. Then he turned to Wilaanger. "There wasn't a message this morning, was there?" he demanded. "Ilaris has been in your head, too."

Wilaanger went pale. "What? I..." He swayed, then leaned forward and covered his face with his hands. "I... it makes sense," he said, his voice muffled. "Tarjiaan asked me why I never told him when you came onboard the *Chimaera*, when I knew he was looking for you. I was going to tell him... and I didn't." He lowered his hands. "You can't trust me—"

"He can't control more than one at a time." Daanir gestured toward the screen. "Aanaji would know better than anyone."

"Do we trust her?" Wilaanger asked.

"Do we have a choice?" Daanir replied. "I don't think we do. And I think she's telling the truth on that disk. If she's right about him only being able to get one person at a time...Ilaris was trying to control the king, and we were away from the ship. You were out of range, so I think you're safe. For now." He frowned, looking out the forward view-port. "I don't think he's tried to control me. Or maybe he has? How would I know?"

Wilaanger shook his head. "He may not be able to control someone more powerful than he is."

Daanir shrugged. "Perhaps. We don't know, so we'll be careful. What's the rest of it?"

Wilaanger leaned back in his chair, looking distant. In the silence, a small hand settled on Daanir's shoulder; he looked up to meet Nika's eyes, then reached up to touch her hand.

"We'll find him," he said softly.

She nodded, squeezing his shoulder in a surprisingly strong grip. "Did he poison them? Was there no... sniffer to warn them?"

"There are three in the throne room," Daanir said. "He must have disabled them. He had to have done it immediately after we left, or I'd have known. It wasn't poison, I don't think. I hope."

He considered it, then shook his head. "It wasn't poison. Aanaji wouldn't have told us to go after Jiaan if it was poison."

"And yet...the King is dead, isn't he?" Nika asked softly. "Ilaris smashed the machines."

Daanir closed his eyes and nodded. "If not yet, then..."

"Ika is dead," Wilaanger said. "My Ika is dead, and I failed him." He sat up straighter. "I will not fail Jiaan. So... what I know. What you need to know. Ika and Alyaan... their marriage was... tense?" He paused, then nodded. "Tense is a good word. At the best of times, it was tense. At the worst of times? Alyaan would take a tour of the fleet crèche ships and be gone for weeks. This was in the early days of the war, and the war in their quarters was nearly as destructive." He shook his head. "Ika's intended bride died in the attack on Meras City. His marriage to Alyaan was one of convenience and alliance – her family was powerful, and Ikaanaji needed all the support he could muster in the early days, because so many wanted to submit to the Emperor and return to land. Her family supporting his rule... it saved the Kingdom. But it destroyed my Ika." He looked around. "Chel, some water please?" Chel brought him a cup, and he sipped before continuing. "As much as they presented themselves as a loving pair in public, in private Alyaan was jealous and spiteful. She never forgave him for loving Tallistri, no matter that she was dead, no matter how hard Ika tried to honor Alyaan as his wife. And she purely despised me." He snorted. "It's a good thing there were never any children. But... during one of those extended tours, Ika took a mistress. I warned him not to. I confessed my feelings and I offered him... anything and everything I had. But he never was interested in men. He wanted... comfort. He wanted someone to care about him. He was... desperately lonely. And he found solace with Larina." He paused, then sighed. "Larina was Ilaris' mother."

"Great Mothers..." Daanir breathed. "Ilaris is the king's son?"

"So Larina claimed," Wilaanger answered. He spread his hands wide. "But she refused to allow the tests to prove it, and she died shortly after she made the claim, when Alyaan returned to the *Chimaera* after one of her tours."

"Conveniently?" Chel asked.

Wilaanger shrugged. "Perhaps. Alyaan refused to allow the boy to remain on the *Chimaera*, so Ilaris was raised in the crèche, and only adopted into the king's household after Alyaan died." He frowned. "I knew Ilaris was... bitter. But this? I had no idea—"

"The King knew, though," Daanir said. He slumped in his chair, looking out at the darkness, seeing the ghostly reflections in the glass. The future of Meradon was on his shoulders... and was standing behind him, embodied in a frightened boy and a woman who he didn't think had yet realized that she was Queen. "The King knew," he repeated. "And he tried to warn us. He tried to tell us not to trust Ilaris."

"What do we do now?" Chel asked. "Where are we going? We can't go back to the *Chimaera*, can we?"

"No," Daanir answered. "Or to any other ship in the fleet." He paused, then waved at the console – the screen lit up again, showing Ilaris and the Imperial guards. "Those guards...Nika, were they from the ship you came in on?"

Nika came closer, peering at the screen. "I... perhaps? I could not see very well through the veil. But the only Imperial ship in the area was my... was Rathsafa's ship. They would have had to come from there."

Daanir nodded. "It makes sense. Which means those were the men that followed Rathsafa, and to whom Jiaan wanted to put to the question. They might help us, given the chance."

"Then we are going after them?" Nika asked. Daanir could hear the hope in her voice, and silently cursed himself for having to shatter it.

"We can't," he said, and watched her face fall. He gestured. "This tub has no weapons, and limited air." He closed his eyes, tapping into navigation, figuring a course. Their top speed. The distance. How much air was in the tanks. He didn't like the answer, but it was their only hope. "We're going after the *Wave Runner*," he finished. "That's our only hope of getting Jiaan back. And if the orders were given, then they've already set out for the floating dockyards. We'll have to catch them."

"We can't hail them, can we?" Chel asked. "The *Chimaera* would be able to intercept the signals if we use the comms."

"The *Chimaera* might be able to intercept the signals," Daanir corrected. "The same with the other ships of the pod, or if any other pods are left in the area." He paused, considering it. "Maybe. If they were looking for signals. If someone was paying attention to the comms. If a million little things were all lined up properly. But... we can't take that risk, because luck doesn't always favor the right people. We have to run silent and dark, and hope they don't guess that we're going to make for the *Wave Runner*."

"That's a very big hope," Wilaanger murmured.

Daanir nodded. "It is, but it's the only one we've got. Now, I can't tell if Ilaris actually issued those orders. Not from here. But we have to assume that the *Wave Runner* is en route to the floating dockyards, and moving at her top speed."

"Which we can't match," Chel said. "How are we going to get to them before our air runs out?"

Daanir shook his head. "I don't know."

"Wilaanger, can you put us to sleep?" Nika asked. She rested her hands on Naajir and Kaapi's shoulders. "You do not need us. If we sleep, will we use as much air?"

Wilaanger scowled, narrowing his eyes. He didn't say anything, and Daanir turned his attention back to the controls.

"It won't reduce the air consumption by much," Wilaanger finally said. "A fraction, if that. You may not be breathing as deeply during sleep, but you are still breathing." He drummed his fingers on the arm of his chair. "Daan, what about the emergency gear? There should be enough breathers."

Daanir closed his eyes and shook his head. "We don't have enough." He opened his eyes again and looked around. "Wil, what if we drop the oxygen percentage to... eighteen—"

"Absolutely not!" Wilaanger interrupted. "Nineteen five. You *know* that, Daan. Anything under, and you risk deficiency, and impaired thinking."

"What about the scoops?" Chel asked. "We can surface and recharge using the scoops. I know it takes forever, but... no, we can't be on the surface that long, can we?"

"No weapons, and no way to hide," Daanir said with a nod. "It's a last resort option, but it's far more dangerous than I like. We have to stay below, if we can." He closed his eyes, trying to order his thoughts.

"Daanir, you did not eat breakfast with us. Have you eaten at all?"

Daanir looked up at Nika. "I'm fine."

"You are not." She folded her arms over her chest. "You are going to take care of us, yes? Then I am going to take care of you. It is all I know how to do. So..." She paused and looked around. "Is there food?"

"Emergency rations," Chel answered. "I'll show you."

The walked away, and Daanir started to turn toward the controls, pausing when he noticed Wilaanger looking wistful.

"What's wrong?"

"An old man's maundering," Wilaanger answered. "Wondering what it might have been like if Alyaan had possessed even a fraction of Nika's generous spirit. If anything would have been different."

He smiled. "Wondering just how you three are going to change Meradon."

"It's not us three," Daanir protested. "It's the two of them, and we still have to save Tarjiaan." He glanced over his shoulder, then lowered his voice as he leaned toward Wilaanger. "Wil, I'm not going to complicate things. Right now, I need to focus on protecting my Queen and my Sea Prince, and try to find a way to save my King."

"When you put it that way..." Wilaanger replied. He sat up straight as Nika came back, carrying a bowl.

"I do not know what this is," she said, handing the bowl to Daanir. "But Chel says that it is edible. So eat." She paused, folding her hands in front of her. "Daanir? When we were...discussing... was it only last night? It seems so long ago. Tarjiaan said that if I was Queen, and something happened to him, that I would have to make decisions. This is what he was talking about, is it not?"

Daanir looked down at the unappetizing gruel in the bowl. It would sustain him, but it the taste was truly awful. He nodded. "Yes, Your Majesty," he answered. "And I've been remiss. I should—"

"Do exactly what you are doing," Nika interrupted. "I do not know enough to make the decisions. Tarjiaan said I would have advisors. At this moment, I have three. All of whom know so much more than I do. Please proceed as you think best, and I will learn as we go." She clenched her hands, then rested one on his shoulder. "I will take care of you, because you are the best hope we have to save Tarjiaan and Meradon. Lady Aanaji was right. Meradon is in your hands now."

Daanir nodded. He reached out and rested his hand on the console. "Course laid. We won't catch the *Wave Runner* before the dockyards, but we'll catch them." He held up his bowl. "Better make one of these for each of us," he added. "It's going to be a long trip."

Chapter Nineteen
Occult

NIKA COULDN'T REMEMBER the last time she'd been this tired, but she'd sworn to take care of Daanir, and the man didn't seem to sleep unless he collapsed where he was sitting. He sat in the pilot's seat, watching the controls; she sat next to him, curled up in the other seat and watching the patterns of lights as they reflected in his eyes. This was the third time that they'd needed to surface to refresh the air, a process that they only did under cover of darkness, and which took most of the night. Each time, she'd asked him questions to keep herself awake, and they'd talked, long into the night when the others were asleep, passing the hours as the submersible bobbed on the surface of the waters like a cork and the machines did whatever they were doing to replace the air so they could dive and continue on. He explained what they were doing, but it was so far beyond Nika's understanding that she'd given up trying to follow, and just rode the waves of his passion. He'd been so nervous when they'd met, so reserved every time they'd sat down together. The most emotion she'd seen from him had been when he'd thought Tarjiaan was under attack.

But now? He was animated, excited, talking about the machines and their functions with enthusiasm and humor. He was irreverent and unguarded, and she realized that she was seeing the man that Jiaan had fallen in love with. But he was still stretched too thin, and if he cracked, they'd never succeed. She shifted in her seat and smiled, resting her cheek on her hand. He glanced at her, and arched one pale brow.

"I've lost you completely, haven't I?" he said. "What didn't you understand?"

How to answer? Nika tipped her head to the side as she thought, then answered, "The bit at the end."

Daanir nodded, looked at the console, then back at her. "Which bit?"

"The part after 'it is a simple process, really,'" Nika answered, and watched his eyes widen. He clapped his hand over his mouth to muffle his laughter, but it was still loud enough that Nika looked back at the rest of the compartment where the others were sleeping. No one seemed to hear Daanir, who had doubled over in his seat, his shoulders shaking.

"Daanir?" Nika reached out and touched his shoulder. "Breathe."

Daanir nodded, sitting up and taking a long, shaking breath. He wiped his face, looked at her, and snorted with laughter again.

"I didn't wake anyone, did I?" He twisted in his seat. "Doesn't look like it."

"I do not think so," Nika said. She closed her eyes for a moment, taking a deep breath, then looked at him again. He seemed more relaxed. Good. "I think you needed that release."

"I think I did," Daanir agreed. He wiped his face again, scratching the new growth of beard that he hadn't bothered to shave off, then shook his head. "That... I can't remember when I last laughed that hard. Years."

"The light is blinking," Nika murmured, pointing at the console. "You said that it would when the tanks were full, no?"

"I did." Daanir rested his hand on the console, falling silent for a moment. Then he nodded. "We're full. Let's get closed up and back underway. The *Wave Runner* is out here somewhere."

"Where do you think they might be?" she asked as the submersible dove once more.

"They're not with the floating dockyards, so I'm not sure. Once we're at a cruising depth, we'll backtrack the route they'd have taken. We'll find them." He glanced at her. "Ready to try?"

Nika blinked. "I... you were serious?"

"You're the Sea Queen. Stands to reason you should know how to pilot. At least the basics, and a submersible is easy."

"You said that process was simple, too," Nika reminded him, making him snort. "I think your definitions of simple and easy are very different from mine."

Daanir nodded. "Fair. How about this, then? Piloting a submersible this size is easier than piloting a ship, or a below-ship like the *Chimaera*." He gestured to the controls. "I'm right here, and I can take over if you're out of your depths."

"We are underwater," Nika muttered under her breath. "I am already out of my depths." Apparently, her voice carried better than she thought, because Daanir broke down in laughter again. He recovered more quickly this time, scrubbing one hand over his face.

"You need to rest," Nika said softly. "You need to sleep. Really sleep, not just for an hour."

"I'll sleep when we reach the *Wave Runner*," Daanir said. He closed his eyes and shook his head. "I'm curious. Have you gotten Jiaan to laugh like that yet?"

Nika thought about the few days she'd had with her husband. "No," she finally answered. "Not yet. We barely had any time. He has laughed, but not to that extent. Why?"

Daanir shook his head. "Just wondering. He used to laugh like that all the time. I was wondering if he still did."

"Will you tell me more about him? About what he was like growing up? I want to know everything. And you have known him...

how long?" Nika rested her chin on her hand. "How long have you been Jiaan's battle companion?"

Daanir looked thoughtful. "That's actually several questions with different answers. When we took the oath, he was about to turn eighteen, and I'd just turned seventeen. But we've been training together since I was ten, and he was eleven." He snorted again. "Jiaan was the only one who was willing to take the crèche brat as a training partner. Possible because he'd been in the crèche himself, but it was the best thing that ever happened to me. So, I've known him twenty-four years. I was his battle companion for just over a year before the *Marauder*, and then I didn't see him again for fifteen years. So... I'm not sure what to tell you about what he was like growing up. He's a different person now. We both are."

"Tarjiaan is thirty-four," Nika said. "You have been together almost longer than I have been alive."

Daanir chuckles. "When you say it like that, it makes us sound like a pair of ancients."

"I just... I am jealous, I think. You have so much history with him. So many memories. He is my husband and I barely know him. And I..." She paused, then whispered, "And I am so afraid I will not have the chance to know him the way you do. That three days are all I will ever have of him." She looked down, her throat tight, her eyes burning. "It is not fair."

Movement, and she looked to see Daanir kneeling next to her seat. "You're right," he said. "It isn't fair. But we're going to get him back. We're going to get to the *Wave Runner*, and we're going to get him back." He took her hand, running his thumb over her fingers. "I seem to remember someone telling me that it'd be nice if the gods were fair and kind, but they aren't. And that's right. The gods aren't fair. Or kind. If they were, we wouldn't be here. We'd be back in the *Chimaera*, figuring out where the three of us go from here."

"So what do we do?" Nika asked. She tightened her grip on his hand. "How do we change things?"

"We fight back," Daanir answered immediately. "We push back. We don't just let things happen. We don't lay down and die." He paused and smiled. "Someone also told me that it wasn't in her to do that."

"You are using my own words against me," Nika protested.

"Are you giving up?" Daanir asked. "Or are you going to keep fighting? For him? When we find him, he's going to need you. You've been good for him already."

"He is going to need both of us," Nika corrected. "You are on his left, remember?"

Daanir smiled. Then he kissed the back of her hand, his new facial hair tickling her skin. "And you're on his right," he added. "Now, am I teaching you to pilot this thing or not?"

"Easy," Daanir crooned, leaning over the back of Nika's chair. "Keep it slow. We'll show up on their sensors as a Great Mother if we don't push our speed."

Nika nodded, slowing the submersible. "Are we close enough that they will see us?"

Daanir straightened and moved to the other seat. "We're within their sensor range, but not close enough for me to get into their systems. Take us up, slowly."

"How slowly?" Nika asked, touching the controls to take them toward the surface. Learning to pilot the submersible had been surprisingly easy, and she found that she enjoyed it. It was another kind of freedom to look forward to — she could go where she liked, when she liked. "How fast does a Great Mother rise?"

"Maybe you should ask them?" Chel said from behind them. She came up next to Nika and pointed at their sensors. "Pod rising to meet us."

"What?" Daanir twisted to look, then blinked. "I've never seen them do that before," he stammered. "I...anyone? Naji, you've been studying their songs. Is this... normal?"

"No. They'll swim along with the below-ships," Naajir said. "And sing to them. But they don't usually swim alongside submersibles. Something about the different vibrations from the engines. It doesn't sound like their songs, so they don't... well, they don't see the subs like they do the below-ships."

Nika looked at the sensors again, touched the controls, then drew back. "Daanir? Will you take over?" she asked. "I think I may not be a good enough pilot yet to match them without hitting one, and that would be horrible."

"Yeah, I'll take the controls." Daanir's hands danced over the console. As Nika sat back, she turned to see his lips moving, although she couldn't hear what he was saying. His eyes never left the sensor screen, and there was something very much like awe in his eyes. She reached across and rested her hand on his arm, and saw his slight smile.

"The Great Mothers are favoring us and our mission," she said. "That is what this means, is it not? They are escorting us, and hiding us from view."

"I..." Daanir glanced at her. "I have no idea. But I like the course you've set, so we'll sail it. Right, let me pilot — it's a little more complicated when we're in a pod." He turned back to the sensor and the controls, and Nika turned to look at Naajir.

"Tarjiaan told me that they sing. You are studying their songs?" she asked. Naajir smiled broadly and nodded.

"Yes. It's how they talk to each other," he said. "And there are patterns to the songs, and each pod has different variations and a different melody. I'm trying to see if there's a way to translate it, but I can't get the algorithms right. It may not have a one-to-one correlation to Common. I'm still working on it."

"I do not know what an algorithm is," Nika admitted. "I do know that Jiaan said they sing, and that it is very beautiful." She turned in her seat. "You are a musician, too? You must be, to understand that much about their songs."

Naajir blushed slightly. "My mother... when it was just us on the *Allegiant*? She was different. She encouraged me. When I was small, she encouraged me to learn music, that it was in my blood from my grandmother. And when I sat down at a light-harp for the first time and played it like I was born knowing how, she told me that following Uncle Tarjiaan's example of being a music prodigy wasn't a bad chart to sail."

"She said that?" Daanir looked over at them. "Truly?"

"She did," Naajir said, nodding enthusiastically to emphasize his words. "I started music lessons when I was four, and I play flute, viol, small lute and the light-harp. The small lute is the most recent, but I wanted to learn it because Mother has a recording of Uncle Jiaan playing, and... well, I wanted to be him when I grew up."

"I want to hear you play," Nika said. "I told Jiaan the same thing — that I want to hear him play. I never thought to ask him how many instruments he plays."

"Six," Daanir answered, turning back to the sensors. "The last I knew, it was six."

"Flute, viol, chitarra, small lute, double-neck lute and light-harp," Naajir added. "Mother said he was one of the only people who still played double-neck." He smiled when Nika looked up at him. "It has twice as many strings as a small lute or a chitarra, and it's *hard*. I tried it, but my hands weren't big enough. Mother said I had to get my growth in." He shrugged slightly. "When my mancer gifts broke through, I started mixing music and mancery, and I started studying the songs of the Great Mothers. But then we were called back to the *Chimaera* and I stopped pretty much everything, because Mother... well, she changed." He sighed. "And now I understand why she changed. Because it wasn't really her." He paused. "We're going to get her back, too, aren't we?"

"We are going to try," Nika said. "We are definitely going to try. We have too many people left behind on the *Chimaera* to not go back for them." She looked over at Chel. "We will go back for them," she repeated, thinking of Chel's husband. She hadn't even met him yet. And Rathsafa... what would Ilaris do to the man who claimed to be her father? Was he even still on the *Chimaera*, or had Ilaris handed him back over to the Empire when he'd given them Tarjiaan? What about Logiri? Or Adalia? Adalia hadn't even liked her, but Nika was loath to surrender even her life to the desert winds.

"Nika, I think you're right," Daanir said softly. "The Mothers are hiding us. The *Wave Runner* isn't alone up there."

"Any sign of who?" Wilaanger asked.

"I..." Daanir paused, then looked at them. "There's no tracking bug. And I'm not sensing any tech other than the *Wave Runner*."

"The Imperial ship?" Nika whispered. "We... Jiaan is up there." She looked up at the roof of the submersible, her mind racing. "I... have they taken the *Wave Runner*, too?"

Daanir took a deep breath. "We have to assume so," he said softly. "And...I'm not sure what to do now, other than staying with the pod until it's safe to rise to the surface."

Nika tipped her head back and closed her eyes, trying to think. They were so close! "Mancers are not mages, you told me," she said slowly. "But... can Mancers speak to other Mancers, the way mages can speak to other mages?"

"Is that something we can do?" Naajir asked. "I've never heard of it, but I'm not all that advanced yet."

"It's not something I've ever heard of a Mancer being able to do," Daanir answered. "People? No. Machines, yes." He frowned slightly, then smiled. "Which means it's time for me to talk to the *Wave Runner*."

"Will she talk back, Papa?" Kaapi asked. "Or... oh, you mean you're going to get into the systems and see what they say?"

Daanir nodded. "Chel? I need you to take over for me."

"I will move." Nika stood up and let Chel take her place. "Daan, what do you need?"

He stopped in the middle of getting out of his chair and looked at her, and she realized what she said. She felt her cheeks warm.

"I... I apologize..."

"Don't you dare," Daanir said. He came around the seats and stopped in front of her, then rested his hands on her shoulders. She looked up at him, and he met her eyes and smiled. "Don't apologize for treating me like a friend," he added. "Now, what I need? A place to lie down. And possible some pain killers once this is done. I haven't tried to reach this far before. It might not work."

"If it does not work, we will rise with the pod and try again," Nika said. "But I think it will work. The pod being here, at this depth, it is unusual, no?"

"And for this long? Yes," Naajir answered. "They need to surface to breathe.

Nika smiled at him, then turned back to Daanir. "That tells me that the Mothers want us to succeed. So this is right. Do what you need to do, and then we will go as we need to go."

Daanir nodded, then went and stretched out on one of the couches. "Kaapi, be ready for a data dump," he called as he closed his eyes. "I'm going to pull what I can from the systems and the sensors without getting caught. And see if I can reach Ishantar or one of the other mancers up there."

He fell silent, looking as if he were asleep.

Nika stepped back, watching him, then turned to Wilaanger. "I did not think to ask him. How long will it take him to get this information?"

Wilaanger sighed. "I don't know," he admitted. "It will take as long as it takes."

Nika nodded. "Then we should start to make plans for what happens next, depending on what he finds." She moved over to seat by the viewing port. The water was dark, but she thought she could see large shadows that were darker.

"Your Majesty?"

Nika looked over her shoulder. "You don't need to call me that, Wilaanger."

Wilaanger smiled. "I do. Because you are my Queen. And more importantly, I want to." He sat down across from her. "What are you thinking?"

"I suspect that the Imperial ship has taken the *Wave Runner*," Nika answered. "Probably using Jiaan's life to do so. Which means that the *Wave Runner's* crew is either imprisoned, or enslaved." She frowned slightly, pleating her skirt between her fingers. "Jiaan is not on the *Wave Runner*. He is somewhere on the Imperial ship. They would not put him where his crew could reach him."

Wilaanger nodded slowly. "That makes sense. And makes things complicated. We can get on board the *Wave Runner*. We won't have as ready access to their ship."

"Then that is a problem we must solve," Nika said. "We have to find out where they are keeping him, and how we can get to him without risking his life." She paused, closing her eyes and trying not to yawn. "If Sun and Sand and the Mothers are kind to us today, Daanir will find that information."

"Your Majesty, you should rest," Wilaanger said. "We can't lay any solid plans while Daanir works, so lay down. Nap." Before she could protest, he held up one finger. "Consider that an order from your physician."

"Would that work with Jiaan? Or his sister?"

"No," Wilaanger admitted. "But it would be nice if there was one member of the royal family who heeded the royal physician with minimal fuss."

Nika couldn't help it — she laughed. Then she stood up. "Very well," she said. "I will listen. This time." She passed his chair, pausing to rest her hand on his shoulder. "But do not get used to it."

Chapter Twenty
Subterfuge

FOR A MOMENT, THE IDEA of reaching across the expanse of the deep to tap into the *Wave Runner*'s systems was terrifying. Every Mancer in training heard the stories about that one Mancer who overextended and got lost in the machines. But there was no choice. They had to know what was happening. So Daanir closed his eyes and reached, past the systems of the submersible, looking for the familiar mechanical mind of the *Wave Runner*. He'd told Jiaan the truth — he'd designed the *Wave Runner* from the kelson up, pouring all of his new skills and all of his power into a physical representation of his love. He knew every seam and rivet of the ship in much the same way that he knew every freckle and scar of Jiaan's body, and he wasn't entirely sure which he loved more. But honestly, they were the same entity in his mind — you couldn't separate the Sea Prince from the *Wave Runner*. The King had been wrong to even try.

He reminded himself to breathe, and reached further, feeling the slight tension in the back of his neck. The headache would be worth it if they came out of this with Jiaan safe. It would all be worth it... and his mind brushed against the *Wave Runner*'s central core. There were even legends about powerful mancers that could bond with their ships, and their ships would speak to them in words. He never believed the stories, but that didn't stop him from talking to any machine in the vicinity.

"Hello, my lovely. It's been a long time."

The ship welcomed him, with a definite sense that she recognized her creator and was happy to see him. There were other Mancers who had told him that they'd felt the same from their own creations, and there were the stories about the Mancers of old, who could have full conversations with their ships. He'd never known anyone who'd actually gotten an answer, but he knew he wasn't insane. Or at least, no more insane than any other Mancer. He petted and praised the *Wave Runner*, then asked for the information that they needed, passing it on to the submersible and Kaapi. Recordings, readings, security logs. Tarjiaan's logs, and those of his First Mate.

"My lovely, can you report to Ishantar? Let her know that we're here?"

An image rose in his mind — Ishantar, locked in a holding cell, a broad metal collar around her throat. His gorge rose — a *limiter*. They'd put a limiter on her, locking her powers inside her head. She'd go mad if they didn't get to her soon.

"What else can you show me, my lovely?"

Another image. The priest who'd presided over Jiaan's wedding, walking the decks of the *Wave Runner* as if he owned her. He was clearly furious about something, but Daanir couldn't tell what. Then the image faded, and he felt a gentle push...

[Go back.]

The shock — the *Wave Runner* actually talked to him! — was enough to snap him awake, shaking and gasping. The lights were too bright, and there was something wet on his face. He tried to sit, and fell back whimpering as his head nearly exploded.

"Easy," Wilaanger whispered. "Dial the lights down, Chel."

"Drink this," Nika said in a sweet, low voice. A cup pressed to his lips, and he tasted something overly salty-sweet and vaguely medicinal. He recognized it as what mancer trainees all called *mancer juice*, and drained the cup. It moved away, only to be replaced by a damp cloth wiping his face.

"Let that work," Wilaanger said. "Nika, that tonic helps even out the salts in his blood. It'll help with the headache I'm certain he's got, and it'll help him recover faster. You can give him another cup in a few minutes."

Daanir grimaced and shook his head, wincing. "Don't have a few minutes," he growled through gritted teeth. "*Wave Runner* is taken. The mage is on board her. Ishantar is locked down—"

"Limiter?" Wilaanger sounded appalled.

"Yeah." Daanir took a deep breath. "Dumped a pile to the sub's systems. Kaap?"

"I've got it all, Papa."

Daanir smiled and closed his eyes. "Good girl," he murmured. "More juice?"

"Nika, give it to him. Small sips, Daanir. Don't gulp it. You'll be sick. Here, let's see if you can sit up." An arm slid under his shoulders, and Wilaanger helped him to sit up. His head didn't spin too badly, but it was enough to make him groan.

"Daan, drink." Nika sat down on the couch next to him, offering him the cup once more. He let her feed him the juice, and realized that her leg was pressed against his, and that he was very conscious of the pressure, of her warmth. Of how close she was. Of how much he enjoyed her just being there. He hadn't felt this way since his days at Jiaan's side....

Sweet Mothers under the waves, how had he gone and fallen in love with Jiaan's wife?

He shuddered, and she touched his hand. "Daan, what is wrong?" She frowned. "Your heart is racing. What is it?"

"You... you can tell?" Daanir stammered. "I..." At a loss for words, he took the cup from her and drained it.

"Daanir, I told you small sips," Wilaanger chided.

"We don't have time to coddle me," he said. "We need to go through the information. We need to see where Jiaan is, and if there's anything in there we can use—"

"Mancer Ishantar destroyed the solar sails," Naajir called. "When the *Wave Runner* was captured. That's why the ships haven't moved. The mage is on the *Wave Runner* now, and he keeps threatening them to make them repair things, but they're not cooperating and he can't make them work." Naajir turned to face them. "Ilaris can control minds. This mage can't?"

"But Ilaris can apparently only control one at a time," Chel offered. "My lady, do you know anything about how mages work?"

"Not much," Nika answered. "It was forbidden for women to be mages, or to even know about how magic works. Perhaps he also cannot control more than one as well?"

"Which means the rest of the crew is still as willful and stubborn as their captain," Wilaanger added. "And I think we now have proof that the mage can't control a Mancer. Otherwise, he'd force Ishantar to undo whatever she did."

"Well, that's comforting to know." Daanir rubbed his hand over his face. "I'm feeling steadier."

"Just stay there, and we'll bring the information to you," Kaapi said. "I've got the projections. On screen, sight and sound?"

"Please," Nika called. "The earliest one to start with?"

"Yes, ma'am." Kaapi turned back to the controls, and the forward screen glowed for a moment before showing an image of the Imperial ship docked alongside the *Wave Runner*, close enough that there was a gangplank stretched between the two ships. As they watched, Marikaar appeared, stopping at the foot of the gangplank. A moment later, the High Priest crossed onto the *Wave Runner*.

"*Holiness*," Marikaar said, bowing slightly. "*You honor us. But... how did you even* find *us?*" He straightened, then jerked, his face turning red as his hand crept up to touch his throat.

"*Hear me!*" the priest announced, his voice booming. "*This ship is now under Imperial command, and you will accompany us as a prize of war. The life of your captain depends on your cooperation. Do you understand?*"

A shot rang out, and the priest gasped and staggered back. Marikaar fell back, gasping for air. Then he drew his own pistol and ordered, "*Repeat that!*"

The priest had one hand clasped over his injured arm, his sleeve drenched with blood. "*Your captain is in our custody,*" he growled. "*If you value his life, you will cooperate and follow my orders.*"

The screen went black, and Naajir turned toward them. "There are more recordings. It looks like the priest held them in place so they couldn't sail away, and their forces overran the ship. The commanding officer ordered the sails scuttled when they knew they were taken."

"Holding them the way they did during the attack before Jiaan was called below," Daanir said. "Right. There are Imps on the *Wave Runner*. Now what do we do?"

"Papa, come look at this?" Kaapi called. "I have still images of the Imp ship, and there's something that doesn't make sense."

Nika stood up, leaving Daanir's thigh feeling oddly cold where she'd been touching him. He stood up, reaching out to catch the bulkhead as his head spun. Wilaanger took his arm.

"Once you do this, you're laying back down," the healer said. "You pushed too far."

"It'll be worth it," Daanir replied. "If we get Jiaan back, it'll be worth it." He nodded toward the controls. "Let's go."

His legs felt as if they were two different lengths as Wilaanger steered him toward the controls, and he found himself clinging to the back of Chel's seat as if they were caught in a raging storm. Kaapi looked up at him and her brow furrowed.

"Papa?"

Daanir smiled and reached down to squeeze his daughter's shoulder. "I'll be fine, Kaap. Show me what you see?"

Kaapi touched the console, and the screen glowed again, showing an image of canvas sails and rigging. She pointed at a large box dangling from one of the yardarms. "That shouldn't be there."

Daanir frowned and nodded. "You're right. It shouldn't. What..." His stomach lurched, and he heard Nika moan next to him. "You... you got it?" he asked without looking. "You see it?"

"Jiaan," she whispered. "Jiaan is in that box!"

Daanir coughed, trying to force his voice to stay steady. "Wil... did Ilaris know about Jiaan's problem with small spaces? We never talked about it, and Jiaan didn't say."

Wilaanger sighed. "Yes. We'd discussed it, trying to find ways to make Tarjiaan comfortable when he needed to come below. After the last time... well, nothing we tried worked, and I insisted to Ika that he not be called below unless it was absolutely necessary. That was four years ago."

Daanir nodded slowly. "And you never discussed it around me because no one talked about Tarjiaan around me." He frowned, then leaned against the seat. "I... how do we get to him?"

"We have bigger problems," Chel said. "Daanir, we need to refresh the air, and we're almost out of supplies. And don't think I haven't seen you slipping your rations to the children." She looked up. "We thought we'd be fine once we got to the *Wave Runner*. But we can't stay here."

"Why not?" Nika asked. "We cannot surface without being seen. But can we not get on board the *Wave Runner*? This craft, it is the one that brought us to the *Chimaera*, is it not? So there is a place on the *Wave Runner* to dock."

Daanir looked at her. "Nika, what are you thinking?" he asked. "The Imps control the ship."

She looked up at him and smiled. "No, they do not," she said. Then she reached over and tapped his chest. "You do. They will never know we are there. You can make it that way."

Daanir blinked, then grinned. "And they'll never look for us under their own noses, will they? If they're even looking for us at all." He turned, and his knees buckled — he caught himself on the back of the seat before he fell.

"Daan, lay down," Nika said. "We can plan while you are horizontal. We cannot if you are unconscious."

"Lean on me," Wilaanger added. He helped Daanir back to the couch and handed him another cup. Daanir leaned back against the cushions and sipped the mancer juice slowly, trying to think.

"If we get on board, I can hide us. From sensors and physical search." Daanir drank more of the juice. It was starting to taste bad, which meant that it was working. It only tasted good when you needed it. "I'll show you."

"I can pull up the schematics—"

"No, I have to physically show you," Daanir said. "There are tunnels and crawlspaces not on the plans, and internal doors that you can't find unless you're looking for them. An entire network of mancer access panels. They run the entire length of the ship. We'll have access to everything and they'll never know we're there."

"So we get on board, get into those tunnels and... send the submersible out to follow like a baby seal?" Chel asked. "There'll be nothing for them to find."

Daanir nodded. "We can get to Marikaar, tell him that we're there. Let him know that we're going to take the ship back. And..." He finished his juice and set the cup down, leaning forward and resting his elbows on his knees. "And we're getting Jiaan back. We'll think of something. But we have to get him out of there."

"But first, we have to finish saving ourselves," Nika said. "And we have to save the ship. Chel, how much air do we have left?"

Daanir knew the answer before Chel spoke, but he stayed silent and let her answer. "Two hours at our current usage," she called.

"Then we have a little over an hour for you to rest, Daan," Nika said. "Try to sleep. I do not think that we will have much time for sleep once we get on board."

"But—" Daanir froze when Nika folded her arms over her chest and looked at him. She arched a brow, and he chuckled and lay down on the couch, setting the cup on the floor.

"Jiaan would love seeing you like this," he murmured.

"Then we will have to make sure he does," she answered, sitting down. "Now sleep!"

Nika waited until Daanir was gently snoring before she got up and moved away. The others were all gathered around the controls, the children were standing behind the seats — Naajir behind Wilaanger, and Kaapi behind Chel. Kaapi turned as Nika joined them; the girl smiled and threw her arms around Nika, tightly enough that Nika squeaked.

"Thank you!" Kaapi whispered, her voice shaking. "For taking care of him and making him listen. He doesn't take care of himself, and he doesn't always listen to me when I try."

Nika caught her breath and hugged the child back, amused despite herself that Kaapi was almost as tall as she was. "You are welcome, Kaapi," she replied. "I promise that I will do my best to make him listen and take care of himself. We must all take care of each other, no?"

"Yes." Kaapi agreed. She stepped back and sniffled, wiping her face with one hand. Then her eyes widened. "I... your Majesty... I...."

"No," Nika took Kaapi's hand. "You did nothing wrong, and I am not angry. And I do not want you to treat me any differently than you have been."

"But you're the Queen!" Kaapi protested.

"And you are family," Nika replied. "That is more important than crowns or thrones." She squeezed Kaapi's hand, then looked at Naajir. "That holds true for you, too."

Naajir grinned. "I know."

"Good. Now, what do we know?"

"Not much," Wilaanger admitted. "We've been sifting through the recordings and readings that Daanir grabbed." He paused, and Nika realized that he was studying her with an odd look on his face.

"Is something wrong?" she asked.

Wilaanger chuckled and shook his head. "No, nothing is wrong... your Majesty." He looked down at the controls. "Chel, pull up that one recording."

"There's a recording in here that we don't think Daanir meant to pull. It's nothing to do with anything, but it was in the middle of the captain's logs. It appears to follow on a log he'd just made." Chel's hands danced over the controls, and the screen brightened. Nika recognized the room — Tarjiaan had called it the great cabin, and said it would be theirs when they were on board. He was seated at his desk, his coat was off and his shirt unbuttoned, and he was going over papers that he took from the desk. He got up and walked away, his footsteps heavy as he moved around outside of the camera view. When he came back, he was carrying an instrument.

"That's a double-neck lute," Naajir whispered.

Nika nodded, unable to look away as she watched Tarjiaan doing... something. Plucking strings and turning pegs. Tuning the lute, she realized. Finally, he nodded, looking back at the papers, and started to play. It was like no performance Nika had ever seen before — he'd stop, mark something on the page, play parts over and change them. Then he played the entire piece through without stopping.

"*Well?*" he said without turning.

"*I did not think you'd noticed me come in,*" Logiri said from out of sight. "*I've brought your tea. And it's quite lovely, Prince-Captain. I don't think you could improve on that any more than you already have. That arpeggio in the third measure is delightful. Like sparkles on calm water.*"

"*I'll make a musician out of you yet, Logiri.*"

Logiri laughed as he came into view, carrying a teacup that he set on the desk. "*A musician? No, I doubt that. But an appreciative and educated audience? That is what I am. And happy to be that. Have you decided on words for it?*"

Tarjiaan shook his head and set the lute aside, picking up the tea. "*Not yet. I think I might leave this as an instrumental, but the words may come.*" He sipped the tea and looked at the papers again. "*I'll make a clean copy of this and send it below tomorrow.*"

"*Very good, Captain. I... Tarjiaan, were you meaning to record?*"

Tarjiaan turned in his chair. "*What? I... no, I must have forgotten to turn off the recorder after I made my log entry.*" He reached out and touched something, and the screen went dark.

"He's composing," Wilaanger said. "I had no idea he was still composing." He turned, and his eyes widened. "Daanir."

Nika turned to see Daanir standing behind her, one hand resting on the bulkhead. He looked pale, and she was certain that it had nothing to do with his efforts, and everything to do with the recording.

"You could have waited for me," he said softly. "I woke up hearing the lute, and I knew it was him and... you could have woke me up."

"We didn't know what it was," Chel replied, turning her seat around. "I'll play it again."

"Please do," Nika said. She went to Daanir's side and took his hand, holding it as the recording started over.

"He said he hadn't played..." Daanir murmured as it finished, then paused. "No. He said he hasn't *sung*. Not since...." He stopped and shook his head. "Right. Let's get moving."

"Are you ready for this?" Wilaanger asked. "Have you rested enough?"

"I'm ready, and I'm done resting." Daanir tapped Chel on the shoulder; she surrendered her place at the controls to him. He rested his hands on the console. "Let's go get him back."

Chapter Twenty-One
Concealment

DAANIR BROUGHT THE submersible into the bay and stopped the engines. He wanted to sit for a moment, to let himself recover from another extreme use of his power. But they had no time. "Right. The systems won't show us for now, but I can't hide us that way forever. Let's move."

"Where are we going?" Kaapi asked as he stood up. "And... what about the armor? Are we taking it with us?"

"I don't think we have a choice," Wilaanger said. "We can't risk losing it if something happens to the submersible."

Daanir nodded slowly and looked at the armor, considering what it would take to bring it with them and how drained he already was. What he was still going to have to do. "I..."

The clips holding the armor in place popped, one after the other, and the armor moved forward.

"We can handle the armor," Naajir said.

"We?" Daanir turned — Naajir was standing behind Kaapi, his hand on her shoulder. "What do you mean we?"

"It's something we've been working on, Papa," Kaapi said. "We were going to tell you when we got it right. We can work together."

Daanir stared at them. "You... you can mesh your gifts? I was taught that wasn't possible. How...?" He stopped and shook his head. "No. We don't have time. You can tell me later. Do not push yourselves, understand?"

From behind him, he heard Nika mutter, "Whale. Fish. Wet."

He turned and pointed a finger at her. "And you. Stop that. If I fall over now, we're all done for. The hatch we're heading for is in a storage compartment halfway down from the docking bays. I've dimmed the cameras in the corridors, and there's no one around, but if anyone comes down and I don't catch them before they get to us, we're right out in the open. So we have to move."

"Lead on," Wilaanger said. Daanir nodded and led the way to the hatch, checking the external sensors in the docking bay as he unsealed the submersible. There was no one in the bay, or in the corridors leading to the bay, but he drew his pistol anyway. They paused in the bay long enough for him to launch the submersible, with the automatic pilot set to remain below the *Wave Runner*, then he led them out into the ship. The empty corridor seemed to echo far louder than it should, making the heavy footsteps of the armor sound like cannon shots. When he'd been working in the yards, overseeing the building of the *Wave Runner*, he'd been able to walk this corridor in seconds. Now it seemed to take hours, and he could feel sweat trickling down his back by the time he reached the door. He opened the door and stepped out of the way, keeping watch down the corridor as Nika entered the compartment, then Chel.

"There's no room in there for me and the armor," Wilaanger said. "Give me the pistol and go open whatever you need to open."

Daanir glanced down the corridor, then nodded and passed his pistol to Wilaanger, slipping past him and into the compartment. "That's something I didn't consider — having six people in here," he muttered as he moved crates away from the back corner. The hidden panel slid out of the way at his touch, and he stepped back. "Right, inside and turn right. There's a place to stop and rest ahead on the left. You'll know it when you see it. Go."

This time, Chel went first, with Nika following her. The armor marched through the space after them, and the children followed.

Wilaanger closed the compartment door as he came in, and handed Daanir his pistol.

"What about the crates?"

"I'll get them before I close us up." Daanir went to the door and rested his hand against it, hearing the locking mechanism engage. Once the door was locked, he holstered his pistol and started moving the crates back into place, tugging them into position as he followed Wilaanger into the passage. The panel slid closed, and Daanir sagged against the opposite wall.

"Daanir, you need to rest," Wilaanger said, his voice pitched low. "You can't keep pushing like this."

"Do I have a choice?" Daanir asked, his voice equally quiet. "Neither of the children are strong enough to do what needs to be done. Although... combining their gifts? Wil, I was taught that wasn't possible!" He shook his head and ran his fingers through his hair. "I'll rest when Jiaan is safe."

"You'll rest now," Wilaanger said. "Or you'll make a mistake and we'll none of us be safe." He folded his arms over his chest. "Don't make me put you to sleep, Daan."

Daanir scowled at him, but any impact it might have had was broken by a yawn. "Fine. I'll rest. We'll all rest. And food. There are stable rations stored down here, and a tap into the drinking water." He straightened. "This way."

Nika was waiting in the passage for them, and she looked up at Daanir and sighed. "You're going to lay down right now," she said, taking his arm.

"Food first," Daanir protested. "I need to eat. We all need to eat, and there should be plenty." He gestured for Nika to precede him, following her into the compartment. This room had long benches for sitting or lying down along both walls, and a small sanitary station in a corner closet. When he'd designed the ship, and had to explain these passages and rooms to his superiors, he'd told them that these were rest areas for mancers tasked with maintaining the ship. In truth, they were for him, created in his hopes of one day being the mancer tasked with maintaining the ship. These were his hiding spaces, places where he could retreat and be alone with his thoughts. It was an extravagance that he'd never had before — privacy was something no crèche child ever really had, nor any young sailor on a ship of the fleet. This area was going to be his and his alone.

That one impulsive decision years ago was going to save all their lives.

"That bench opens," he said, pointing to the left-hand wall. "There should be ration packs. They're old, but ration packs are supposed to last forever. Water spigot in the closet is fresh water. Water in the basin is reclaimed for washing, not drinking." He slumped down on the right-side bench and leaned back, closing his eyes. The systems were pinging and fizzing along his nerves, trying to get his attention. "I hear you," he muttered. "Not now."

"Daan?"

He opened his eyes to see Nika standing in front of him, holding a ration pack. "Eat this," she said, "then sleep. Who were you talking to?"

"The *Wave Runner*," Daanir answered. "She wants my attention." He took the pack and tore the wrapping open, pulling out a ration wafer and starting to eat. Despite everything, the taste of the wafers made him smile.

Across from him, Wilaanger opened his own pack; he took a bite and chewed it, then made a face. "I always forget how tasteless these things are."

"That's because they're not food," Chel said. She broke one of hers in two and popped a piece into her mouth. Once she'd swallowed, she added, "I can't think when I ate these last, myself."

Daanir chuckled and finished his first wafer. "You can always tell who was never in the crèche," he said. "We grew up on these." He held up his pack. "This is my childhood. Sometimes, they're all the food we had when the hydroponics couldn't keep up. And they do have a taste."

"They taste like lemon," Kaapi added, coming to sit next to Daanir. "Papa keeps them in our quarters, because we both like them, and sometimes regular food makes me sick."

"Sick?" Chel repeated. "What...?"

"Kaapi can't have milk or cheese," Daanir answered. "And we didn't know because she'd never had it before she came to me."

"I remember that," Wilaanger said. "And I never gave it any thought, except that I didn't understand how that was never found before. The crèches are supposed to have first pick from the farm ships. Those children are the future of Meradon...."

"Keywords there are *supposed to*," Daanir interrupted. "I didn't come up in the royal crèche. Neither did Kaap. If we were supposed to have fresh produce and real food on the table? I don't remember it. Not after Lady Aajinisa died. We had dried or preserved, if we got actual food at all." He shrugged. "Somewhere between what you ordered to happen, and what actually happens? The good stuff got shunted off to some noble table somewhere, and someone made a profit on it. It's something that needs fixing, but right now, it's the least of my worries."

"It is something I will see corrected," Nika said. "Now that I know it is a problem. It is a problem in the Empire, as well. The powerful want what they want, no matter who suffers for them to have it." She looked down at her ration pack. "They do taste like lemon. It is very pleasant. They remind me of the biscuits that are served during the tea ceremony. But these are a meal and not a confection?"

"Each pack is a full meal. The wafers contain everything your body needs," Wilaanger said. "They're nutrient dense, but... bland.

And make sure you drink plenty of water when you eat them if that's all you're eating."

Daanir looked down, trying to focus on eating his wafers, trying to ignore the *Wave Runner*. "We need to figure out the next step," he said as he finished his last piece. "How we're going to take *Wave Runner* back, and how we're going to get Jiaan off the other ship."

"The first step is that you need to rest," Nika said. "You are fraying at the edges, like a poorly made tapestry. You need to sleep. We cannot do anything else until you are rested, because anything we do will depend on you. No?"

Daanir started to turn, then jumped as Kaapi elbowed him. "Kaap!"

"She's right, Papa," Kaapi said. "You need to sleep. We can't do what you do. We're not strong enough yet, and the *Wave Runner* doesn't know us. You can hear her. I can't. I don't think Naji can, either. So you have to listen." She paused, then sighed and added, "Please."

"Thank you for remembering your manners," Daanir replied. He hugged her to his side and looked around. "Right, I'll curl up in a corner."

"Will you be able to sleep with all of us in here?" Chel asked.

Daanir grinned. "Crèche boy," he replied. "I can sleep anywhere. You don't even have to keep your voices down." He kissed the top of Kaapi's head, then went over and stretched out on the floor, his face to the wall. The moment he closed his eyes, *Wave Runner* tugged hard at his mind.

"What is it?"

The answer was two images. The first was a view of the sky, and the low, seething clouds on the horizon, alive with lightning. The second were the readings from the ship's systems, warning of the severity of the storm coming toward them.

"Oh, fuck," Daanir growled as he rolled over and scrambled to his feet. "We're out of time."

"What is it?" Wilaanger asked, getting to his feet.

"Ship-killer storm!" Daanir turned and looked up. "I need Marikaar," he said aloud. "Get his attention. Show him how to get here." He leaned against the wall and closed his eyes, trying to think.

"Daan?" Nika's hand was warm on his arm. "I have a question."

"What?" Daanir answered without opening his eyes.

"Can we use the submersible to get to the other ship, and get to Jiaan?"

He blinked and looked at her. "What? I... wait." He frowned. "I... maybe? We'd need to get on board without being seen. Which might mean punching a hole in the side of the Imp ship." He arched a brow at her when she nodded. "And you thought of that already? And you're comfortable with that idea?"

"Comfortable?" Nika repeated. She shook her head. "No. But you were there when Jiaan told me that if it came to this, if it came to the point where I had to make these decisions, that I would have to choose for the good of Meradon. And that is where we are. I understand now. I understand how unfair I was. And I know that I must choose for the good of Meradon." She paused and bit her lip. "I choose his life. Your life. I choose the lives of the people on this ship. I choose... us. All of us. All of Meradon."

Daanir smiled. "He's going to be so proud of you," he said. "And, for the record? I'm proud of you. Right, let's figure this out. The sub has no weapons." He stopped, hearing movement in the passage. "That was fast." He drew his pistol and moved to the door, waving the others out of the way. The door slid open, revealing a man roughly the same shape as a barrel on legs. He saw the pistol and raised his hands.

"Are you alone?" Daanir asked.

"Yes," Marikaar answered. "Lord Meranas? And... Your Highness? What... *how*? How did you get here?" He looked over his shoulder. "They say you murdered the king. The reports we've had... they say you've gone mad."

"Later, Marikaar," Daanir said. "What you need to know — the King is dead, and I didn't do it. I wasn't even on board the *Chimaera*, and I can prove it. Ilaris is a traitor, and we need to move because there's a ship-killer storm on the horizon. And the Imps have Tarjiaan."

Marikaar nodded. "I knew they had the Prince-Captain. What about Logiri?"

"No data," Daanir answered. "Alive, I hope. But my priorities were saving the Queen and the Sea Prince."

"The Sea..." Marikaar looked past Daanir. "This is Prince Naajir?" He bowed slightly. "Highness. I've been wondering when we'd meet."

"Commander." Naajir nodded his head slightly. "I wish I could say it was a pleasure, but it's not. Tell me what I can do to help."

"We need to take this ship back, and we need to get Tarjiaan, and we need to do both now. We have a bare bones plan involving a submersible, but it has no weapons." Daanir took a deep breath. "And we need to get Mancer Ishantar out of that limiter collar before it fries her brains. Ideas?"

"You tapped into the systems?" Marikaar asked. "You must have, to know that. There's something I haven't entered into the logs yet, because I haven't been able to make an entry where that priest couldn't hear me." He looked up. "The storm isn't the only thing on the horizon. The Imperial fleet is out there, at the very edge of sensor range. One ship in closer, but I'm not worried about a single ship. And... well, we were going to take out as many of them as we could before we died, but we were taking the *Wave Runner* back tonight. We're going to sink the Imp ship and I've been praying that my Captain forgives me, but it'd be a cleaner death than anything those bastards have planned for him."

"You would kill your Captain?" Nika asked, coming up next to Daanir. "Marikaar, *why*?"

"Ma'am, given what they've done to him already?" Marikaar said, bowing to her. "It would be a mercy." He looked up. "Look, back when I first came on board, I had a long sit down with Quentas, who was first mate before me. And he told me to take care of his captain, and all the things I needed to know to do that, and there was a strong hint that if he caught wind of me not taking care of Tarjiaan? That he'd come back up here and see how many times he'd get my arse to skip before I hit land. And if you'd ever met Quentas, you'd know he could do it." He paused. "Our Prince-Captain, he hides inside that armor, but we all know he has his shadows, and sometimes they get the best of him. The entire crew knows. We don't talk about it, but we do what we can to keep him safe from himself. But now... they told us what they did to him. I know where he is. That box... I've been on deck of a night, and I could hear him. I won't ever tell him that once we get him free. But I've *heard* him, and right now? Death would a blessing for him." He bowed again. "Ma'am."

Nika nodded slowly. "Thank you, Commander," she murmured. "Pray to your gods and mine that it does not come to that."

"It's all I've been doing," Marikaar said. "Now, we've got a window, but it has to be now. He's gone back to his own ship. Something to do with communing with the mages on the other ships. He'll be gone an hour or so. Maybe more, because of the storm. The ship is as ready for the storm as we can make it. And we're ready to rise."

Daanir nodded. "Wil," he said without turning. "You and Chel get to the infirmary. Take Kaapi and Naajir with you."

"We want to help!" Kaapi protested.

"You will." Daanir turned to look at his daughter. "Once Mancer Ishantar is free, you're both assigned to her." He turned back to Marikaar. "How long before that storm hits?"

Marikaar frowned. "It's moving fast. You want to wait for it to hit?"

Daanir grinned. "I want it on top of us. I want it to hide the sound of gunfire over here. You get the ship secured and underway. I'll get the Captain." He looked at Nika, seeing her looking up at him. "Ready to test your piloting?"

Her eyes widened, and he watched her grow an inch as she stood up straighter. "I can do this."

"Good," Daanir said, nodding. His mind was racing. "Marikaar, got anything that will punch a hole in a wooden hull?"

"Right, that storm is just about on top of us," Daanir said. "We'll launch in a moment, and it's not far to the other ship. How are you feeling?"

Nika looked up at him, rubbing her hands over her skirts to dry her palms. "I am terrified. And I am not certain which terrifies me worse — that we will fail, or we will succeed."

Daanir nodded. "I understand that. Now, before I forget, take this."

Nika turned to see him holding a pistol out to her. "Daan, I do not know how to use that!"

"You're going to learn. Because I'm leaving you unguarded while I'm on that ship, and if something happens to you, Jiaan will never forgive me. Stand up."

Nika got out of her seat and came around to stand with Daanir. He handed her the pistol; it was oddly heavy in her hand.

"Use both hands," he said. "And do not put your finger on the trigger unless you're going to shoot. You do not point this at anything you don't intend to kill. Understand?"

"Yes." Nika's mouth was so dry it hurt, and she bit her lip and tried to remember how to breathe. "What do I do?"

Daanir smiled and moved behind her, putting his arms around her so that his hands were over hers. "If someone comes up through the hatch that isn't me? You put your thumb here — that's turns off the safety. Then you point the barrel at them and squeeze the trigger. I set this for a wide blast, so you'll hit whatever is in front of you."

Nika nodded, trying to focus on the heavy pistol in her hands, but far more aware of Daanir's warmth at her back, the strength of his arms around her. She took a deep breath and blurted out the first question that came to mind. "How... how many times can I shoot? If there is more than one?"

"This one? You can shoot until the barrel melts." Daanir rested his hand on her shoulders. Then he moved away so abruptly that Nika had to step back to keep her balance. She lowered the pistol and looked at him, at his red face. He seemed to be trying to look everywhere but at her, and she realized that she wasn't the only one feeling the heat.

"Daan?"

He swallowed, then met her eyes. "Nika...I... I shouldn't. I can't....you're his *wife*!"

"And you were his before I ever was," Nika said gently. "You stand on his left, and I will be on his right. And once he is safe... then we will see what else we are. I think he will not object. I know I do not. But I do not know your answer. Nor will I, until we all talk together."

Daanir smiled slightly. "Then I'd better get to work." He closed his eyes. "Storm is close. Take us out, Nika."

Chapter Twenty-Two
Escape

"THIS WILL NOT FLOOD the submersible?" Nika asked, looking at the hatch in the floor.

"It's not actually open to the water," Daanir answered as he took off his boots. He felt oddly calm, as if this were a drill he'd done dozens of times. As if all their lives didn't hinge on his getting this right the first time. The only time. "When I get down there, I'll close the top hatch here, and open the lower hatch. The water will fill the space, and I'll swim out. When I come back, it'll happen in reverse." He took off his coat and tossed it onto the couch. "I may have to take over the controls and bring the sub to me when we get out, so if she starts doing things you don't tell her to do, it's me." He sat down and dangled his legs through the hatch. "Give me the bomb?"

Nika nodded. She went over and picked up the box that Marikaar had given to them, bringing it back to Daanir. He lowered it into the compartment and took a deep breath.

"Checklist — I've got the breather." He touched the device that dangled around his neck. "I've got an extra breather for Jiaan. I've got the bomb...."

"Your pistol?" Nika asked.

He smiled. "I've got a pistol and a knife. I don't think I'm missing anything." He took a deep breath. "Wish me luck?"

Nika knelt next to him, and before he could say anything, leaned in close and kissed him gently on the lips. "Good luck," she whispered. "Bring him back to us."

Getting into the Imperial ship was easier than Daanir thought it would be — no one appeared to notice the explosion that blew a gaping hole in the hull, and he saw no one as he slipped through the dark hold and found his way up to the deck. Once he was there, he understood why — the Imps were all focused on the fighting taking place on the *Wave Runner*. He could hear shouting and shooting, punctuated with the loudest thunder he'd ever heard, and no one was looking in his direction. Not that anyone would be able to see him — the rain was coming down in heavy sheets, and he couldn't see more than an arms-length ahead of him in any direction. He found his way to the rigging and started climbing, rough ropes digging into his hands and feet. How long had it been since he'd climbed the rigging? He couldn't remember. It didn't matter. What mattered now was getting to the box swinging from the spar. He couldn't hear anything from above him except for thunder, and fear started to twist his guts as a gust of wind left him clinging to the ropes, watching as the box swayed and danced. Too late, he realized the one thing he'd forgotten to plan — how was he getting Jiaan *down*?

He couldn't turn back. He'd never have another chance at this. He started climbing again, and reached the spar from which the box dangled. He took a deep breath and started working his way out along the spar. As he got closer, he could hear moaning that didn't sound like the wind.

"Jiaan," he breathed. Then he raised his voice, trying to be heard over the storm. "Jiaan! I'm here!"

No response. He wasn't sure if that was good or not. He inched further along the spar — the box was so close...

The ship pitched and rolled, and Daanir grabbed the spar before he went flying off. The box swung wildly... and one side swung open. For a moment, Daanir's heart stopped — then he saw inside the box. Saw Tarjiaan, chained in place, his face gaunt and pale enough to nearly glow in the darkness. For a moment, it didn't seem as if he was seeing anything. Then he blinked, focusing on Daanir.

"Daan?" His voice sounded as if it had been shattered into a million pieces.

"I'm here," Daanir called. "I'll get you out." He moved closer to the chain. He'd have to somehow get to the manacles holding Jiaan in place, and get him out. Was Jiaan strong enough to hold on while Daanir climbed down the rigging? They'd find out. He reached for the chain, and as he did, every hair on his body rose. His skin started to tingle, and he recognized the sweet, metallic smell and the taste of electricity right before the blinding flash and the deafening cannon-shot of thunder. He screamed. At least, he thought he screamed. He could feel himself falling...the entire spar was falling.

Tarjiaan was falling.

"No!" Daanir grabbed onto the falling spar, riding it down. The ship had rolled once more, and they were heading for the water. He fumbled at the breather and shoved it into his mouth just as the cold water claimed them.

Nika sat at the controls, watching the dials and screens, wishing that she knew what they meant. It had been ages since Daanir had gone, and she wasn't certain at all what was happening, or how much longer it would be. She glanced back at the hatch in the floor, then at the reading that showed that the compartment underneath was still full of water. It would stay full, Daanir said, until he flushed it once he came back. Sun and Sand, let that be soon!

All the lights on the control board flared to life, and the submersible started moving. Nika reached for the controls, then stopped. Daanir had said he might do this. He was bringing the submersible to him. It was almost over. She touched the button that Daanir had shown her, the one that showed what was happening outside the submersible. The water was dark, but there were things moving in it, things slowly sinking like shadows in ink. She couldn't tell what she was seeing, but something hit the top of the submersible with a heavy thump and a screech of metal on metal that made her yelp and stare warily at the ceiling, waiting for it to burst inwards the way Tarjiaan had said a craft like this would if it was punctured. Nothing happened, even though there were other, smaller thumps. Then she heard something else — a pump whirring to life, and she hurried to the hatch. As she dropped to her knees, the hatch opened; Daanir appeared, gasping for air.

"Help!" he croaked. "Help me get him out! He needs you!"

Nika was already moving, grabbing Tarjiaan's tattered shirt with both hands and pulling; Daanir pushed from below, and together they managed to get Tarjiaan out of the water and onto the floor of the submersible. He wasn't moving... or breathing.

"I lost the breathers," Daanir gasped as he lifted himself out of the water. "We hit the water and I lost the breathers. We need to get him breathing on his own."

Nika stared at him. "What do I do?"

"Breathe for him. Cover his mouth with yours and breathe. I'll take care of the rest."

Nika nodded and took her place on Tarjiaan's left, leaning over him and covering his mouth with hers. She blew hard into his mouth as Daanir started pressing on his chest.

"Keep going!" Daanir grunted. "Keep breathing. Don't you dare leave us, Jiaan!"

"You are not allowed to leave us!" she added. "I have barely been a wife, you are not allowed to make me a widow!" She covered his mouth again and started breathing, aware of his chest rising and falling. Chel had told her about this, about breathing for a sailor who'd drowned to try and bring them back. It was simple, even someone without the healing gift could do it, so everyone in Meradon was trained in the technique.

But Nika hadn't been trained yet. Was she doing it wrong?

Was she killing him?

Panic flared, and with it, her fledgling power. She felt it rush from her the way it had when she'd saved Daanir's life, heat flowing out of her and into Tarjiaan, warming his cold body, drying the water in his lungs. He took a gasping, shuddering breath. Then another. He started coughing.

"Roll him onto his side," Daanir gasped. They moved him, and held him in place when he vomited up water. When he finally fell still, Daanir helped her lay him back down.

"He'll be all right," he said, wiping water from his face. "He'll be fine. And...you healed him, didn't you? I could feel it."

"I have no idea what I am doing yet," Nika said. "But... I think so. I think I helped."

Daanir reached across Tarjiaan, took her hand, and pressed a kiss into her palm. "Thank you. It... it all went wrong, Nika. I had no way to get him down. I didn't think of it. I knew they had him up there but I didn't think of how I was getting him down. And the storm... the spar was hit by lightning."

"And *that* is how you got down?" Nika gasped.

"And that's how I lost the breathers," Daanir replied. "The strap on mine broke when we hit the water, and the other one... I don't even know. My trousers are torn right down the side, and the pocket is gone." He gestured, and Nika noticed his tattered clothes, and the long length of pale thigh streaked with livid red burns.

"You were burned!"

Daanir looked down at himself. "Am I? I didn't feel it. Probably the lightning. But electricity... it knows me. It plays rough, but it knows me. It won't be the last time I get an electrical burn." He groaned as he got to his feet. "Now I feel it. But I'll be all right. You're not going to faint again, are you?"

"I do not think so, no," Nika said. She reached out and ran her fingers over Tarjiaan's ragged beard. "He is so thin. His earrings are all gone. And his hair... they cut off his hair. Why?"

"Humiliation, maybe?" Daanir said with a shrug. "It doesn't matter. It'll grow back. Let me get a blanket so he doesn't get chilled, laying there wet. Then I'll get us back to the ship."

"Something hit the top of the submersible, but it did not make a leak, and we did not explode," Nika said.

"Well, that's good," Daanir said. "It's a long swim back." He looked up. "Dent in the hull. Nothing major." He shook out a blanket and held it out to her; she took it and wrapped it around Tarjiaan, then took his hand. The skin of his wrist was raw.

Nika winced. "I will need medical supplies. This must be wrapped."

"We don't have a lot here, so do what you can," Daanir said. He handed her the box of medical supplies. "We'll get him to Wil and Chel the minute we're back on board. They'll be able to tell you what else needs doing, and show you how to do it." He sat down in the pilot seat and touched the panel. "Hailing the *Wave Runner*. Anyone hear me?"

The speakers crackled to life. "*We hear you, Mancer!*" Marikaar's voice sounded jubilant. "*The ship is ours! Tell me you've got him?*"

"We've got him, and we'll need a litter waiting for us at the docking bay. He's in bad shape." Daanir glanced back at Nika. "Your Majesty? Orders?"

Nika licked her lips. "Get clear of the Imperial ship," she said. "And... Tarjiaan was going to order it destroyed. Do whatever it was that he was going to order."

"*Ma'am?*"

"How you ended the last battle, Tarjiaan said," Daanir added. "He said you'd know what it meant. The orders... Ilaris never sent them, but those were his orders."

"*Understood, Mancer. Once you're on board, we'll get clear, and then we'll blow her to bits. Marikaar out.*" The speakers went quiet, and Nika sighed and stretched out on the deck next to Tarjiaan, resting her hand on his chest. It rose and fall gently, as if he was asleep.

"If he wakes screaming," she said softly, "I do not have a pitcher of water to throw on him. But he is already wet, so I do not think it would work."

"If he wakes up screaming, we'll mob him," Daanir answered without turning from the controls. "He used to like that."

Nika raised her head and looked at Daanir's back. "Mob him? That means... what?"

"Lay on top of him. Hold him down. The weight helps him relax." Daanir looked back at her. "You barely weigh anything. But it'll help, I think, if we both do it. If we're both here for him."

Nika nodded, shifting closer and resting her head on Tarjiaan's shoulder. "We will both be here for him." She closed her eyes, hearing the engines coming to life as Daanir took them back to the *Wave Runner*.

"Yes," she heard him say. "We will."

The moment the submersible powered down and the hatches opened, people flooded into the tiny space. Tarjiaan, still unconscious, was bundled onto a litter.

"Go with him," Daanir said to Nika. "If he wakes up and he doesn't see either of us, he'll panic."

"I am going to have them take him to his own bed," Nika said. "It will be familiar, and it may help when he wakes." She paused. "Where is his armor? Still in the hiding place?"

"I'll check. And if it is, I'll send it to your cabin. That's good thinking." Daanir nodded. "Go on. Get him taken care of. I'm going to go help Marikaar."

Nika nodded and ran after the litter bearers, leaving Daanir alone in the quiet submersible. He sat down in the pilot seat and finally let himself think about what had happened.

She'd *kissed* him.

Maybe he was wrong. Maybe it was nothing. It could have been just a kiss for luck....

No, he was sure. He was sure how he felt, and given what she'd said? He was pretty certain that he wasn't alone.

As soon as he was able, he was going to have to sit down with Tarjiaan. Given Nika's initial invitation, he was fairly certain that she was right, and that Tarjiaan wouldn't object... but Daanir having feelings for Nika hadn't been part of the equation then. Or maybe they had. He'd never been very good at equations involving actual people — numbers were much simpler.

He tipped his head back, closing his eyes. He needed to move, to get topside. Who felt what for whom wouldn't mean anything if the Imps sent them to the bottom of the sea.

"We'll figure things out," he said aloud. "But we need to be alive to do it. So get moving, Mancer." He took a deep breath and got up, leaving the submersible and heading for the deck.

"Mancer!" Marikaar shouted as Daanir walked out into the wind and rain. "We've got a problem."

"What?" Daanir turned, and saw the Imperial ship. It was listing, but it was still there. "We're not moving?"

"That's the problem," Marikaar said. "The mage is still holding us here, and we can't get clear. We're dead in the water. The bastards scuttled some of the mechanisms in the weaponry. Main deck force guns are useless, and so's the rail cannon. We're readying the powder cannons, and Ishantar and the young prince and your girl, they're working in the starboard gun house, making sure we've got something we can do other than throw rocks."

Daanir nodded. "Right. I'll get them firing. Be ready to deploy the foresails and a jib. Enough to move us. Was the Captain's armor moved to the great cabin?"

Marikaar blanched. "That was unnerving, if you don't mind my saying so. The armor walking on its own, marching nice as you please into the great cabin and straight to the rack in the Captain's room." He paused. "It won't do that usually, will it?"

Daanir chuckled. "No. That was probably my daughter. It's her sense of humor. But it needs to be where Tarjiaan can see it." He looked up at the sky. "We need to get underway. Get to the helm, Commander."

"Mancer, take this," Marikaar said, holding out a communications earpiece. "Signal when you're ready."

For safety's sake, the gun house was separated from the rest of the ship by heavy metal bulkheads and secure hatches. Because of that, Daanir couldn't hear Ishantar swearing in Sualimani until he was actually inside.

"Mancer Ishantar, language," he called as he closed the hatch behind him. "Report."

Ishantar looked up, clearly startled. "Mancer Royal, I... I should not have been using such language around the children. I apologize."

"We didn't understand it," Kaapi said. Naajir snorted.

"I did," he said softly. "My mother swears the same way."

"You didn't tell me that!" Kaapi protested. "Papa, I want to learn Sualimani!"

"Later, Kaap. Report, Ishtantar," Daanir repeated.

"The blasted Imps went at the loading mechanisms with a sledge. We cannot bring the shot up to the powder cannons." Ishantar gestured at the silent guns. "The power cells on the force guns are gone, and I don't know where."

"Right, so we focus on the powder cannons." He went and crouched next to one, resting his hand on the top of the mechanism that would bring the shot up from the powder magazine in the belly of the ship. "The chain is broken on this one. What about the others?"

"The shaft is dented on this one, and smashed completely on the third," Ishantar answered.

Daanir nodded. "Right. Can't fix those fast. So... Naji? Kaap? You ever hear the term powder monkey?"

"No, Papa," Kaapi answered. "What is that? What's a monkey?"

"Small animal, lives in trees?" Naajir said "I think? Or was that a cat? I forget."

Ishantar laughed. "Yes about the monkey. Cats live on the ground."

"And that's not important right now.," Daanir said as he stood up. "Powder monkeys are what we used before we had the loading chutes, or on ships that didn't have them. Youngest, fastest members of the crew were powder monkeys. I was a powder monkey when I came up, and right now, so are the both of you. Along with any other crew members who are small and fast. You're going to physically bring the shot up from the magazine. Physically and carefully. Understood?" He turned the comms on with a thought. "Marikaar! I need the starboard magazine manned now. The force cannons are inoperable, and the loading mechanisms for the powder cannons are too badly damaged. We're doing this the old way."

"*Understood, Mancer. The quartermaster is on the way to the magazine. Gunners will meet you in the gun house.*"

Daanir nodded and turned to Ishantar. "Show them the way, recruit anyone else can to run. I'll check the guns over, make sure they're not going to blow up in our faces. Then go get to work on the rail cannon."

"Yes, sir." Ishantar led the children out, and Daanir went to work. By the time the last of the cannons were cleared, the first ones were loaded and ready, and the gunners were waiting for the word.

"Right," Daanir said. "Let's teach them to swim!" He turned on the comms. "Marikaar! On my mark!"

"*For Meradon and the King!*"

Daanir nodded. "For Meradon and the King! Fire!"

Chapter Twenty-Three
Destruction

A DISTANT EXPLOSION drew Tarjiaan from sleep. What was he hearing? And... where was he? The last thing he remembered was the box. But now... the feel... the smell...

His own bed? His quarters on the *Wave Runner?*

What had happened? He felt weak. Sick. He was bare under the blankets. That wasn't right. He didn't sleep nude when he was on board, in case he needed to roust out of bed fast. Had he been ill? Had everything — the planned alliance, the betrayal, the box — had all of it been a fever dream?

Another distant explosion. He opened his eyes, blinking until his vision cleared.

There was a woman sleeping in his chair. He blinked again.

"Nika?"

At the sound of her name, she jerked, sitting up straight. She looked around, and her eyes widened when she realized he was awake.

"Jiaan!" She scrambled out of the chair and onto the bed, throwing her arms around him and bursting into tears. He pulled her close, closing his eyes and holding tightly to her as she clung to him.

It hadn't been a dream. All of it was true. His uncle was dead. Meradon was betrayed. Another explosion shook the *Wave Runner* and forced him to revise the thought — Meradon was under attack. And he....

He could still feel the box, hear the echoes of his own screaming. Trapped and helpless.

Aanaji had been right.

No. He pushed the thought away with an effort that left him shaking, feeling sick.

"How did you get away?" he stammered as Nika's tears slowed. His voice was shaking, jagged as broken glass. He coughed and tried again. "You were on the crèche ship. You couldn't have known what happened. How did you get away? And... how did you know? How did you find me?"

"Ilaris tried to kill us," she whispered. "The submersible was sabotaged. But Daanir saved us, and... Jiaan, there is so much to tell you!" She raised her head and looked at him, then kissed him hard enough to push him onto his back. He could feel the fear and the relief radiating from her, and he wondered if she could feel the same from him. He held tightly to her until she drew away. "I was so frightened," she whispered, her breath tickling his face. "I thought I was going to lose you. I thought I was going to be a widow before I was properly a wife. I thought I was never going to see you again. Then we found you, and we saved you, and we are never letting you go ever again." She buried her face in his shoulder, and he could just barely hear her muffled voice. "I love you. So much. I did not realize how much until I thought I had lost you. I did not think I would ever get to tell you." She pushed herself up. "I should let Marikaar know. He will tell Daanir. And I should tell Wilaanger. He left something for you for when you woke — a tonic. Let me help you—"

"I think I can manage sitting up."

Nika got off the bed and went to the comm in the corner. As she reported to the others, Tarjiaan tried to sit up. To his surprise, it took him three times before he could manage the simple movement. He was breathing hard by the time he was sitting up, and the sound of blood rushing in his ears was almost enough to drown out the sound of shouting and fighting outside the door.

"Nika, how long has it been?" he asked as she came back to the bed. "I'm not entirely sure I could get out of bed right now if you fired me from a cannon." She filled a cup from a large bottle, but didn't offer it to him. Instead she cocked her head to the side, her brow furrowed.

"I... may have lost count," she admitted. "We spent a long time in the submersible. I think it's been about twenty days."

"Twenty?" Tarjiaan looked down at his hands, at how the bones stood out. "He said there were spells on the box to sustain me. To keep me from dying in there. They never opened it—"

"You... they did not *feed* you?" Nika said softly. She set the cup down and went back to the comms. "Wilaanger, I need you or Chel immediately."

The comms crackled, and Chel's voice replied, "*On my way!*"

"Nika, what are you thinking?" Tarjiaan asked. "And why do I think it means I'm not getting that?"

"Because you are right," Nika answered. "I am not sure if you should have this, so I want a real physician to see to you. I do not know enough." She wrapped her arms around herself. "The famines in the Empire... it is known that when people are deprived of food for too long, it can be dangerous to feed them. The shock can kill them." She grimaced. "It... amuses the Emperor."

Tarjiaan sighed. "Why does that not surprise me?" He paused, repeating what Nika had said in his mind. "Real physician?"

"Not someone who has only just begun their studies," Nika amended. She looked down. "Wilaanger says that I have the potential to be a very good physician. He..." She paused. "You will not be angry with me?"

Tarjiaan blinked. "Nika, if Wil says you'll be a great physician, he's not lying. Why would I be angry at that?"

She hesitated, then blurted, "Because it is magic! I am... I have power...and I saved Daanir's life, and I saved yours, and I do not know how, and magic is outlawed in Meradon and I do not want to leave!"

Tarjiaan's jaw dropped, surprise drowning the panic he could still gnawing at the edges of his thoughts. "You... you have the Sualimani healing gift? Nika, that's wonderful!"

"But—"

"Wil didn't explain?" Tarjiaan looked over at the door as another explosion shook the ship. "Nika, before you answer that, tell me what's happening. We're under attack. What's happening right now?"

"Right now? Nothing you need to worry about," Nika said. "Which is what Marikaar, Daanir and Wilaanger all told me to tell you if you woke before this was over. They are handling things. And truly, I could not tell you what was happening right now. I am in here." She turned toward the door as someone pounded on the day cabin door.

"It's me!" Chel shouted from outside. "Let me in!"

To Tarjiaan's shock, Nika went to the table and picked up a pistol. She carried it to the door, unlocked it, and left the room, coming back a moment later with Chel. She locked the bedroom door again once the physician was inside.

"Well, it's good to see you awake," Chel said. "Although you have looked better, Your Majesty."

Tarjiaan shuddered. "Don't call me that," he said softly. "Not... not yet."

Chel smiled sadly. "I'm sorry, Jiaan. How are you feeling?" She took out a small medical scanner and brought it to the bedside.

"Right now? I don't think I could win a fight against a jellyfish. And Nika says it's been twenty days?"

"Twenty-three," Chel corrected. She studied the scanner, then nodded. "You were right to call me, Nika. That cup... is that the tonic?"

"Yes. I was not certain it was safe to give it to him yet," Nika answered.

"You understand refeeding syndrome?" Chel smiled. "Good. Start with about half that cup. Do you have a small sandglass or a timer?"

"On the desk in the day cabin," Tarjiaan answered. Nika left, coming back with a sandglass.

"Half a cup, every time you have to turn the glass, Nika. And watch him carefully through the first two doses." Chel looked at the scanner again. "If he tolerates that, then we'll move on to something more substantial. Nika, I'll leave this with you, and I'll show you how to use it." She paused, arching a brow at Nika.

"I told him," Nika said. She sat down on the edge of the bed and took Tarjiaan's hand. "You and Wilaanger were right."

Chel chuckled. "I told you," she said. "Now, I don't have the healing gift, so I don't understand it. But you'll be able to support him more just by doing what you do. If you need support, you know how to get me. I need to get back to the infirmary."

"Chel, how bad is it?" Tarjiaan asked.

Chel frowned slightly, shivering as another explosion sounded. Then she sighed. "You're not going to settle if I don't answer that question," she finally said. "I know you. So... we're stuck. The storm has eased, so that's helping, but the mage is holding us in place, and we can't break free. Ishantar has been working on the rail cannon, but the Imps did something to it when they took the ship. And they stole the power cells from the force cannons, and smashed the loading mechanisms for the powder cannons. Daanir is running the starboard gun house with powder monkeys, one of whom is your nephew." She frowned. "Once we're able to move, Marikaar will deploy the canvas sails. Ishantar says that she scuttled the solar sails when the Imps took the ship."

"Naajir is here?" Tarjiaan looked at Nika. "How?"

"Chel, where is the recording?" Nika asked.

"Daanir has one of the disks. Naji may have the other," Chel answered. "It doesn't matter. They're both inaccessible right now."

"Then I will explain what I understand, and we will show the recording to Tarjiaan once we are safe. Show me how to use the scanner."

Once Chel was gone, Nika sat down on the bed next to Tarjiaan, handing him the cup. "Only half," she said. "And I will tell you what I can." Tarjiaan sipped the tonic and waited as she gathered her thoughts. "There was nothing in the crèche ship that required Daanir or Wilaanger. When we were returning to the *Chimaera*, the control panel exploded and killed the pilot. Daanir took over, and there was another explosion. He was so badly burned, and..." She paused, then rested her hand on his blanket-covered thigh. "I knew that if anything happened to him, it would break your heart. I begged him not to leave us... and the power answered."

Tarjiaan covered her hand with his own. "Thank you."

She smiled slightly. "There will be no half-truths between us, my Jiaan. I did not want him to die because it would have broken my heart, too. I love him, as much as I love you."

For a moment, Tarjiaan couldn't think of a single thing to say. His wife... in love with the man he loved? "That..." he started. Then he laughed. "That's a relief. Truly. And I am not surprised. He's very easy to love, once he stops arguing with you about how he isn't."

Nika laughed. "Truth. We got back to the *Chimaera*, and Daanir made us wait while he went out. When he came back, he had Naajir and Kaapi, and each of them had a disk that your sister gave them." Her hand underneath Tarjiaan's shook slightly. "Tarjiaan, Ilaris is a mage. He has been controlling your sister for years. Your sister confessed to everything, and said that she thinks that Ilaris can only control one person at a time. So when he was trying to control your uncle, she was free to help the children escape. And Daanir believes that he was also controlling Wilaanger."

"That... Uncle Ika was complaining of a headache, right before Ilaris gave us the drugged tea," Tarjiaan murmured. "I wonder... but there's no way to know. Not now." He set the half full cup aside. "What did she say? What did she confess to doing?"

"She confessed to betraying Meradon. To providing access to the Empire that allowed them to attack ships." Nika paused and turned to look over her shoulder. At the portrait, Tarjiaan realized, and he suddenly knew what she was going to say. "She said that the *Marauder* was her fault. That every ship to fall to the Empire was her doing."

"His doing," Tarjiaan said softly. "Ilaris forced her." His head was spinning, and he didn't think it had anything to do with how ill he was, or the effects of the tonic. "He..."

"He... may have forced her in more ways than that," Nika said softly. "She said that this started after your mother died. Your brother went to serve with your father, and you went to the crèche. She was alone, and vulnerable..."

Tarjiaan held up his hand, and wasn't surprised at how much it was shaking. "Ilaris is Naajir's father, isn't he?" he asked. "Ilaris raped my sister."

"She did not say it, but I think you and I and Wilaanger may be of the same mind," Nika said. "There is more. Do you want to know, or wait until you are stronger?"

"Nika, I don't think I'm ever going to be strong enough for this. What else is there? What else did she say?"

Nika got up and walked around the bed, turning over the now-empty sandglass and picking up the cup. She handed it back to Tarjiaan. "Drink the rest of this. Slowly," she said. "I am probably going to forget things. But for now... let me think. She was the one who separated you and Daanir. Your brother told her that you were going to ask Daanir to marry you, and because she knew, Ilaris knew."

"And it was Ilaris' doing that she almost killed me when I was in her care?" Tarjiaan asked. "I can't... Nika, I don't understand what he's doing! Why he's betraying Meradon. He's been at my uncle's side since I was a boy. Why...?" His voice trailed off as she looked away, and he coughed. "You... you know?"

"Wilaanger told us who Ilaris truly is," Nika said softly. "That he is the king's own son."

Tarjiaan shook his head and winced as the motion made his head feel as if it was going to spin right off. "No, that can't be right. My uncle had no children."

"By his wife, he had no children," Nika said. "But there was another woman, and Wilaanger will be able to better explain that part. When we are safe and you are well." She looked thoughtful, then smiled. "One more thing."

Tarjiaan sipped the tonic and nodded. "What else?"

"Naajir is a Mancer."

Tarjiaan coughed on the tonic. "He's what?"

"Naajir is a Mancer. And he and Kaapi can work together. They are the ones who brought your armor here." She gestured to the wall, and the armor waiting on its rack. "When you are stronger, it is waiting."

Tarjiaan finishing the tonic and put his cup down, tipping his head back against the headboard. "I think...it may be some time. But I can't wait that long."

"For now? You will rest, and you will heal." Nika rested one hand on his bare chest. "Jiaan, there is a very good chance that they think you are dead. And I think we should let them, until you are able to prove them wrong."

Another explosion, but this one sounded different. More distant. Tarjiaan frowned at the wall, wondering what was happening to his ship. His people.

His kingdom.

Mothers of the Deep, he was *king*.

"I'm not ready for this," he whispered, grabbing fistfuls of the blankets that covered his lower body. "I was never supposed to be king. I'm only here because I was all they had left. I'm a ship captain, like my father. That's all I ever wanted to be." He took a deep breath. "Now... Nika, I...."

She covered his hands with hers, gently teasing his fingers free until she could hold his hands. "I know, Jiaan. And I understand. I am frightened, too. This... we were neither of us prepared for this. But now... we must take up the mantle because there is no one else, and we cannot do otherwise." She paused, and sighed. "I understand what you mean now about the hard choices. And I think we can make them, together." She met his eyes, letting go of one of his hands so she could cup his cheek. "You are not alone. You have me, and you have Daanir. We will take care of our people. And we will take care of each other."

Tarjiaan swallowed, feeling his throat aching. His eyes were burning, and Nika must have seen something because she pulled him into a tight embrace, running her fingers over the back of his neck, over his short hair. His mental walls crumbled at her touch; her voice was soft and comforting as he cried in her arms, cried until he was exhausted.

"You need to drink more," she murmured. "Then you should sleep. I am here." She got up, gave him another cup of tonic, watched him drink it, then helped him settle back on the bed, drawing the blankets up. To his surprise, she sat on the bed next to him, her back against the headboard.

"Sleep, Jiaan," she said, stroking his shoulder the way he would have petted a cat. "I am here."

Daanir leaned back against the wall of the gun house and closed his eyes. "Report?" he called, hearing the comm crackle to life in his ear.

"*Things just got interesting,*" Marikaar replied. "*Can you hear the cannon fire?*"

"Yes. Someone is a lousy shot," Daanir answered.

"*Because they're not shooting at us,*" Marikaar answered. "*That's an Imperial ship firing on the one that's holding us, but they're not going to last long once the rest of the ships heading for us catch up. The one that was ahead of the others. And I think I know what ship that is.*"

"The one that Tarjiaan sent home?" Daanir asked. "Can we do anything for them?"

"*If we can break the mage's hold, we can get out of here. Then we can cover for them so they can follow us.*"

Daanir rubbed his face, then scratched his cheek, feeling the short scruff of beard along his jawline. "Tell me that Ishantar has the rail cannon working?"

"*She says it's close.*"

"Close isn't going to get us out of here. Tell her I'm on my way up." He looked around and pointed at the closest gunner. "You! You're in charge now! Kaap! Naji! You're with me!" He turned and headed out of the gun house, hearing the sounds of running footsteps behind him.

"Where are we going?" Naajir shouted.

"The rail cannon. We're going to help Ishantar get it working." Daanir stopped and turned, waiting for the pair to catch up with him. "Listen to me," he said. "It's going to be dangerous up there. If it gets bad, you're both to get to the great cabin and shelter in place with Tarjiaan and Nika. Understood?"

Kaapi nodded, then looked at Naajir. "Naji should go anyway," she said. "I can help. He needs to be safe."

"I don't need to be coddled!" Naajir snapped. "I want to help."

Kaapi scowled at him. "You're the heir—"

"My mother is a traitor," Naajir interrupted. "Do you really think they'll let me inherit anything? Besides, if we don't get this ship moving, there won't be a throne for me to inherit." He looked at Daanir. "I want to help," he repeated. "What can I do?"

"Let's go find out," Daanir answered. He drew his pistol and led them out onto the deck. He could hear the distant boom of cannon fire, and the closer, sharper snap of force pistols. The fighting seemed to be focused on the starboard side, which made sense, so he led the children toward the port side and up the back of the rail cannon mounting. Ishantar was underneath the machine, swearing in two languages. She glanced over at them, then grimaced.

"Report, Ishantar," Daanir ordered, going to crouch next to her. He rested one hand on the cannon's mechanism and winced. "Oh, they savaged this."

"That is putting it mildly," Ishantar said. "And getting it to work may be more than any of us can do."

"Can we get it to fire one shot?" Naajir called. Daanir looked up to see that Naajir was standing where he could see out to starboard, to the other ship. "If she has one shot in her, we can end this."

"What do you see, Naji?"

"There's someone giving orders on the Imp ship. I think it's the mage." Naajir looked back at them over his shoulder. "One shot and it could be over. Do we have one shot?"

Daanir looked at Ishantar, who frowned, looked up at the rail cannon, then nodded.

"She'll never fire again after, but I think we can get one shot out of her."

"Then let's make that shot count." Daanir stood up, letting Ishantar crawl out from underneath the cannon. "Kaap, Naji, let's get to work."

Chapter Twenty-Four
Flight

"COME ON... COME ON... yes, that's the way...." Daanir winced as a shower of sparks rained down on him, but the connections held, and the lights glowed bright green. "Got it! It's holding! Kaap, report!"

"Green here!"

"Green!" Naajir called. "It's holding! Gauges are steady!"

Silence, and Daanir rolled out from underneath the cannon and looked down the line toward the controls, where Ishantar was stationed. "Ishantar? Tell me you're green?"

"Still red!" Ishantar called. Daanir got to his feet and ran down toward her, his feet skidding on the wet grating.

"Right, then the problem is between the board and that connection," he said as he joined her at the panel. He frowned, looked out at the Imperial ships. At the single ship who was trying to help them, and who was already badly damaged. At the storm that seemed to be growing in fury once more. "Ishantar, take the children and get under cover. I'm going to force the connection."

"What?" Ishantar grabbed his arm. "You can't do that!"

"I can, but it'll be... explosive." Daanir grinned. "Tarjiaan would tell you my failures are usually explosive. But we can't wait anymore. Those ships are coming, that storm is coming, and the ones who are trying to help us can't wait for us to get this right. It needs to be done now." He looked out at the Imperial ship, seeing the High Priest on

286

the deck. "I've got a target. It's time to teach him to swim." He looked back at Ishantar. "Get the kids. Get to shelter." He turned back to the console and rested one hand on it. "Marikaar?"

"*I hear you, Mancer.*"

"There's about to be a very large boom, and it might take out the ally ship along with the Imps. We can't reposition, and we only have one shot at this, so have rescue teams ready to go for that ally ship." He glanced to the side, saw Ishantar and the children down on the deck, running. "On my mark." He turned his attention to the console, setting the cannon for a broad beam, and tracking the High Priest. He could feel the bad connection, like an aching tooth. Relatively easy to reroute it...*there!* "Five... four... three...two... one!"

The ship shook as an explosion rocked the decks. Tarjiaan jerked awake, pushing himself up. The moment he moved, Nika scrambled out of the bed, running to the table and grabbing up the pistol. She touched the comms.

"Marikaar, what was that?" she demanded.

"*Rail cannon, Ma'am,*" Marikaar answered. "*And... you're about to hear another big noise... now.*"

Tarjiaan looked up at the loud snap. That sound, he knew.

"The sails," he said. "The canvas sails. We're free?"

"*Captain! Good to hear your voice!*" Marikaar sounded honestly overjoyed. "*We're free. The Mancers got one last shot out of the rail cannon, and blew it to bits to do it. Now... what?*" There was a buzz of unintelligible noise, then Wilaanger's voice sounded through the comms. "*Nika! I need you now!*"

"What is wrong?" Nika asked. "Tarjiaan needs me—"

"*The cannon exploded. And Daanir fired the cannon.*"

Tarjiaan heard the words, but they didn't make sense. Then Nika moaned. He looked at her, at her stricken expression, and he knew.

"Go," he croaked. "Nika, go!"

She stared at him for a moment, then brought him the pistol, laying it on the bed. She kissed him, then ran and unlocked the door, leaving it open as she rushed out. Tarjiaan pushed himself upright and picked up the pistol, hoping that his hand wouldn't shake too badly if he had to use it. The door swung gently, back and forth, the hinges squeaking softly. Then someone knocked.

"Uncle Tarjiaan?" Naajir peered around the door. "They... they told us to come here. Can we come in?"

"Who is we?" Tarjiaan asked. Naajir stepped into view, his arm around the shoulders of a girl his own age. Both of them were soaking wet, and the girl was crying; Tarjiaan realized who she had to be. "This is Kaapi?"

"Yes," Naajir answered. "And...." He looked back over his shoulder, and his breath caught.

"Come in," Tarjiaan said, trying to keep his own composure. Daanir was hurt, and he was trapped in his bed, unable to be with the man he loved. Moving automatically, he checked the pistol, set the safety, and laid it aside. "Close the door behind you."

"The fighting is over," Naajir said, taking Kaapi to a chair and sitting her down. He went back and closed the door. "I... should I lock the outer door?"

"I don't think it's necessary," Tarjiaan answered. "Naji... how bad is it?"

Naajir paused, looking at Kaapi. "Uncle, do you have a handkerchief? And...towels? Maybe?"

"Handkerchief in the press, there, and towels in the washroom." Tarjiaan pointed. Naajir walked behind Kaapi, then met Tarjiaan's eyes and shook his head before going into the washroom. Tarjiaan fought to keep his expression neutral, but the need to do something was overwhelming. Enough to override the one rule he'd made for himself.

"There should be a nightshirt in the press as well," Tarjiaan added as Naajir brought towels out of the washroom. "Toss it to me. And... there's a folding wheeled chair in that cabinet. I'll want that."

"You... Uncle?" Naajir took out the folded nightshirt and brought it to Tarjiaan, then went and handed a handkerchief and a towel to Kaapi. "What are we doing?"

Tarjiaan pulled the nightshirt on over his head, arranging it so that he was decently covered. "I need to be out there," he said. "And I'm not recovered enough to wear my armor." He looked at the armor on the rack. "I'm honestly not sure how I'm going to get into my armor when I am recovered."

"I can tell it to lie down," Naajir said as he pulled the wheeled chair out of the cabinet. He unfolded it and brought it to the bed. "This is clever. And... I've never seen you wearing your armor. I've only seen you in your powered chair."

"Papa says we're going to make you better armor," Kaapi said softly. "He said I could help. We could help." She scrubbed the handkerchief over her face. "We're going out there, aren't we?" She stood up. "In case..."

Tarjiaan closed his eyes and took a deep breath, forcing his fear down to protect her heart. "We'll be there when he wakes up," he said. "He's got the best healers Meradon has ever known at his side. And Nika, who'll be better than they are once she's trained. And I'm told she's already saved his life. We'll be there when he wakes up, and I'll help you yell at him for scaring us."

As he'd hoped, Kaapi giggled. "How can we help?" she asked.

Tarjiaan forced a smile, then turned to Naajir. "There are brakes on each wheel. Set those, and steady it." He paused. He could count the number of people who'd seen him without his armor or without the carapace of his motorized chair on the fingers of one hand. He only used this chair in his quarters, late at night. His crew had never seen him...

And he had no choice. If he didn't go, he'd never forgive himself. He pushed back the blankets and moved to the edge of the bed. Naajir held the chair steady as Tarjiaan eased himself from the bed to the seat.

"Uncle?" Naajir said. "You're shaking. You shouldn't be out of bed."

"There's a pitcher and a cup on the table." Tarjiaan pointed. "Fill the cup halfway and give it to me. Kaapi, my dear? There's a blanket on the chair. May I have it?"

Naajir handed him a cup. "What is this?"

"I'm not sure what it is," Tarjiaan admitted. "They just told me to drink it." No time to sip — he drained the cup in a swallow and set it aside, taking the blanket from Kaapi. He covered his legs, then put his hands on the wheels. Before he could start moving, Naajir stopped him.

"Uncle, let me help," Naajir said. "I don't want you getting worse. That would stretch the healers too thin." He rested one hand on Tarjiaan's shoulder. "You're going to take care of the rest of us. Let us take care of you."

Tarjiaan looked up at his nephew, and saw again his brother looking back at him. He reached up and patted Naajir's hand. "Your uncle would be very proud of the man you're becoming."

Naajir looked at the portrait, then squeezed Tarjiaan's shoulder. "I'd rather the uncle I have be proud of me. Not the uncle I never met."

"Oh, I am," Tarjiaan said. "Now, let's go. I need you both to keep me from being a coward and changing my mind. We're going."

Naajir pushed the chair out onto the deck. The skies overhead were angry gray, and Tarjiaan was certain that he could feel the lightning in them. He grimaced.

"We need to get this ship underway," he said softly. "There's another storm coming. It's going to be worse than the last one."

"Captain?" Tarjiaan turned as Marikaar came toward them. "I... Captain, should you be out of bed, sir?"

"I need to see Daanir," Tarjiaan said. "Did they take him to the infirmary?"

Marikaar shook his head. "They've got him over there," he answered, pointing toward the still-smoking hulk of the rail-cannon. "The Physician Royal didn't think he should be moved. Captain, you don't look well. You should be in bed—"

"He saved my life, Marikaar," Tarjiaan said, his throat tight. "Today, and on the *Marauder*. I'm not letting him—" His voice failed, and Marikaar frowned.

"He's the one?" he said softly. "The one you've been looking for?"

"How do you know that?" Tarjiaan asked.

"We know a lot more than you think, Captain," Marikaar said. "I didn't realize that was him. I'll clear the way. Naajir, take care—"

"Captain?"

Tarjiaan turned at the familiar voice. "Antivar!"

The young officer smiled. His face and his uniform were streaked with soot and blood, and he still had the hilt of a shattered sword in one hand. His other arm was around the shoulders of a young man with Sualimani-dark skin, dressed in ragged clothes. Tarjiaan recognized him as the young man that the Imperial refugees worked so hard to keep him from looking at too closely the last time he'd seen them. "Captain, I'm so happy to see you. Although... if I may, you don't look like you should be out of bed."

"That's what I was telling him," Marikaar said. "But this is important. Captain Girantivar, did your ship have a healer?"

Antivar straightened. "You need one?"

"Honestly, we need six," Marikaar answered. "There's a good man fighting for his life, and—"

"Ivar?" The young man next to Antivar stood up straighter. He didn't look at any of them, never raising his eyes from the deck. "I help?"

"Navi, go with the big man," Antivar said. "He won't hurt you." The look he gave Marikaar carried heavy tones of *"you'd better not."* Marikaar grinned.

"He's safe with me, Antivar."

Antivar nodded. "Thank you. Navi, do what you can. Help the good man." He looked at Marikaar. "His mind is broken, but it somehow made his healing stronger."

Marikaar nodded. "Come with me, lad. Let's see what you can do." He took Navi by the hand and led him away. Antivar stayed where he was.

"They told us they had you... and I couldn't... you were so kind." He smiled slightly. "My men agreed. We're yours, Captain. If you'll have us."

"Did they all come through it?" Tarjiaan asked. "And... Antivar, what about your mother?"

Antivar looked grim. "When... when we were on our way back, we were intercepted by the rest of the fleet. I asked one of the ship mages to bespeak the priest in our village, to tell my mother that I was safe. And the answer we got back was that she had taken ill and died a month after we sailed. I have no one left on land."

Tarjiaan shook his head. "I'm sorry, Antivar. May the Mothers sing her name forever."

Antivar smiled slightly. "She'd like that. Thank you, Captain."

"Uncle Captain?" Kaapi said, her voice hesitant. "Can... can we go?"

"Naajir, please?" Tarjiaan said. Naajir started pushing again, and Antivar followed. Kaapi looked at them, and when Tarjiaan nodded, she ran on ahead.

"Are these your children, Captain?" he asked. "And... do you mind if I attend you? Navi is... special. We're protective of him."

"He's the one you all were hiding from me when I met you before," Tarjiaan said. "I'd noticed you playing a shell game with him as the pea."

Antivar chuckled. "Well... yes."

"Marikaar will take care of him. And please, stay. Thank you, Antivar." Tarjiaan tried to see through the people, but couldn't. "You didn't answer. Did all of your men make it through?"

"Yes. Sun and Sand were kind." Antivar paused, then added, "For a change." He walked in front of them and raised his voice, "Make way for the Captain."

His crew turned, looking shocked as they parted to let him through. As they saw him in his chair for the first time. Inside the circle of people, he could see Wilaanger's broad back as he knelt over a bloody body.

Daanir's body, unnaturally still.

He didn't realize that he'd made a sound until he felt Antivar's hand on his shoulder.

"Navi will do everything he can to save him." He paused. "He's your... friend?" Antivar asked. The way he stressed the word *friend* spoke volumes, and the sympathy in his eyes said more.

"Yes."

Naajir shifted the chair, and Tarjiaan could see past Wilaanger. Nika knelt across from the older healer, and Marikaar brought Navi around to kneel next to her before going off with an Imperial sailor. The young healer looked up, revealing startlingly pale gold eyes in a face that had been horribly scarred. He nodded slowly, no doubt at something Wilaanger said. He looked at Nika, then grabbed her wrist, pressing both their hands to Daanir's chest. With his other hand, he gestured to Wilaanger, who rested his hand on top of theirs.

"Who is the lady I'm going to have to apologize to?" Antivar asked. "He doesn't always remember manners anymore."

"My wife," Tarjiaan answered.

Antivar sputtered. "Your... your *wife?*"

Despite himself, Tarjiaan smiled. "She knows, Antivar. She said that it's something that wives accept in the Empire?"

"Maybe?" Antivar said hesitantly. "I've never had a wife."

Tarjiaan nodded, watching the healers work. He couldn't see the extent of the damage, couldn't tell if what they were doing was working. But he could see Daanir's face, see that his terrible pallor was fading, growing warmer as the color returned. As he watched, Kaapi knelt down at Daanir's head, reaching out to touch his cheek.

"No touch," Navi snapped. Kaapi jerked back, her eyes wide.

"Sorry," Antivar called. "But he's right. Don't touch. You'll interfere with the healing."

Kaapi nodded, clasping her hands in front of her.

"Uncle..."

"Go ahead," Tarjiaan said. "I'll set the brakes."

Naajir disappeared into the crowd, coming out behind Kaapi. He knelt down next to her and put his arm around her shoulder. She leaned into his side, and he kissed the top of her head. Tarjiaan blinked, and heard Antivar chuckle.

"Betrothed?"

"Not that I know of," Tarjiaan admitted. "But clearly, there are things I don't know." He paused, trying to distract himself from the worry, from the painfully slow process. From how naked he felt from being unarmored on his own ship. "Antivar, tell me about Navi." He looked up. "He called you Ivar."

Antivar's face turned red. "I... ah..." He paused and closed his eyes. "He was a ship slave, because of his healing abilities. We... we were close... close friends..."

"You're safe here, Antivar," Tarjiaan murmured. "So is he. And he's no longer a slave."

Antivar nodded. "I... I've been in love with him since the moment I met him. He's kind, and funny, and so, so smart. I promised him that I'd buy him, free him, once I had the rank to do it. Then... we... we were almost caught. He put himself in harm's way to save me, and he refused to confess to the captain who he was protecting. The captain beat him near to death with a belaying pin, and when he finally woke, he was like this. We... the whole crew have been taking care of him ever since. He was on loan to the *Fury* — our current ship — when we attacked you, or we'd have lost him with the *Sea Witch*." He paused, then added, "Healing slaves are kept in chains in the infirmary. Thistintal... the one with the patch, over there, with the big man? He's my first mate, and he took an axe to Navi's chains to get him safely out when you beat us. Istin, report!"

"Prince-Captain." Marikaar came through the crowd, followed by the Imperial sailor with the eyepatch. "First Mate Istin and I have confirmed that everyone is off Girantivar's ship. Permission to get underway."

"Granted, Marikaar. And you have the con until I'm recovered enough to take it back."

"Commander, use my men as you see fit," Antivar added. "We're yours to command now." Marikaar bowed deeply. Then he walked away, shouting orders. Crew members ran in various directions, and the group surrounding Daanir dwindled away. Tarjiaan unlocked the brakes and put his hand on the wheels, moving the chair around to better see. Daanir's color was definitely better, and what Tarjiaan could see of his skin showed no injury. He'd grown a beard since Tarjiaan had last seen him. It suited him, and Tarjiaan couldn't wait to tell him that.

"Tarjiaan, what are you doing out of bed?" Chel asked as she came to stand at his side.

"I needed to be here," he said without looking at her. "We needed to be out here. What happened? How badly was he hurt?"

"I didn't see," Chel answered. "I was with a patient in the infirmary, and I came as soon as I was able. But... who's that young man?"

"Our ship healer, Ma'am," Antivar answered. "He's very good."

She nodded. "He and Nika could be twins, couldn't they?"

Tarjiaan blinked. "I... *what*?" He looked up at Chel, then back at Nika and Navi. Looked past the scars... "Fuck me sideways..."

"What?" Antivar asked. "What is it?"

"What's Navi's full name?" Tarjiaan asked, his voice low.

Antivar hesitated, then shook his head, his words stumbling as he answered, "As long as I've served with him, he's always been Navi. Why?"

Tarjiaan studied him for a moment. Antivar knew more, but he wasn't going to say, because he wasn't sure of how safe *safe* actually was. Understandable. "A long story that isn't mine to tell. And it may be nothing. But... I'll explain when I can." He sat up straighter as Wilaanger shifted to sit on the deck, pulling his hand away. Once he moved, Tarjiaan could see the extent of the damage to Daanir's clothes... and the unmarked skin beneath the blood-stained rags. "Wil?"

Wilaanger looked up and frowned. "What... never mind. You had to be here. I understand. And... who is this young man and can we keep him? He is by far the best healer I've ever known."

Antivar chuckled. "Navi is our ship's healer."

Wilaanger looked over his shoulder. "And... oh, you're the captain of the other ship."

Antivar shook his head. "Not a captain anymore. I'll be proud to serve the Prince-Captain of Meradon. Will this man live?"

"Thanks to your Navi. He directed the healing beautifully," Wilaanger said. He turned to look at Navi, and a speculative look passed over his face. "Navi. I... I'm sorry, but I have to ask. Is your full name Ysnavin?"

Both Nika and Navi looked up sharply. Navi shook his head, scrambling back, slipping on the wet deck. "No! Not!"

"Navi?" Antivar hurried around to kneel next to Navi, who twisted and buried his face in Antivar's chest.

Navi shook his head. "Not," he whispered, his voice just barely audible. "Hurt."

Antivar winced. "I understand. We're safe now, Navi. Safe." He looked up at Wilaanger. "I'll explain. But he'll need to lie down now." He smiled at Nika. "And so will you, my lady."

"Chel, does he have to go to the infirmary?" Tarjiaan asked.

"We can move him to the great cabin. Especially since Nika will be there to keep an eye on him. And as for you, Captain, you need to be laying down, too." She looked up. "We're going to get rough. Let's get things and people secured. Ishantar! Take Naajir and Kaapi down to the mancers quarters, will you?"

"And see Antivar and Navi settled in officers' quarters," Tarjiaan added, his voice low. Chel patted him on the shoulder.

"I'll handle things, Captain. Take your wife and go back to bed. We'll bring Daanir along shortly."

Wilaanger slowly got to his feet, walked around Daanir and held his hand out to Nika. "Your Majesty?"

"What?" Antivar squeaked. "I... *what*?"

"Antivar, we'll sit down and explain everything later. All of us," Tarjiaan said. "Take Navi so he can rest." He looked around, at his crew, afraid of what he'd see in their eyes. Disdain? Pity? Disgust?

He wasn't expecting the pride. The relief.

"Good to see you back, Prince-Captain," one of them said. "Welcome home. Now listen to the healer. Get yourself back in fighting form. We need you."

A ragged round of cheers and agreement, and Tarjiaan felt something sharp and painful in his chest ease and fade.

His crew knew him. They knew who he was underneath the armor.

He was their captain.

That was what mattered to them — that he could lead them into battle and out again. That he survived, and kept surviving, and that he would make sure they did as well. That the Sea Prince would bring them home.

"Get to your posts." He raised his voice to be heard. He tipped his head back, watching as the sails swelled overhead. "We're not home yet. Those other ships are coming, and so is that storm. This isn't over yet."

"Are these your children, Captain?" he asked. "And... do you mind if I attend you? Navi is... special. We're protective of him."

"He's the one you all were hiding from me when I met you before," Tarjiaan said. "I'd noticed you playing a shell game with him as the pea."

Antivar chuckled. "Well... yes."

"Marikaar will take care of him. And please, stay. Thank you, Antivar." Tarjiaan tried to see through the people, but couldn't. "You didn't answer. Did all of your men make it through?"

"Yes. Sun and Sand were kind." Antivar paused, then added, "For a change." He walked in front of them and raised his voice, "Make way for the Captain."

His crew turned, looking shocked as they parted to let him through. As they saw him in his chair for the first time. Inside the circle of people, he could see Wilaanger's broad back as he knelt over a bloody body.

Daanir's body, unnaturally still.

He didn't realize that he'd made a sound until he felt Antivar's hand on his shoulder.

"Navi will do everything he can to save him." He paused. "He's your... friend?" Antivar asked. The way he stressed the word *friend* spoke volumes, and the sympathy in his eyes said more.

"Yes."

Naajir shifted the chair, and Tarjiaan could see past Wilaanger. Nika knelt across from the older healer, and Marikaar brought Navi around to kneel next to her before going off with an Imperial sailor. The young healer looked up, revealing startlingly pale gold eyes in a face that had been horribly scarred. He nodded slowly, no doubt at something Wilaanger said. He looked at Nika, then grabbed her wrist, pressing both their hands to Daanir's chest. With his other hand, he gestured to Wilaanger, who rested his hand on top of theirs.

"Who is the lady I'm going to have to apologize to?" Antivar asked. "He doesn't always remember manners anymore."

"My wife," Tarjiaan answered.

Antivar sputtered. "Your... your *wife*?"

Despite himself, Tarjiaan smiled. "She knows, Antivar. She said that it's something that wives accept in the Empire?"

"Maybe?" Antivar said hesitantly. "I've never had a wife."

Tarjiaan nodded, watching the healers work. He couldn't see the extent of the damage, couldn't tell if what they were doing was working. But he could see Daanir's face, see that his terrible pallor was fading, growing warmer as the color returned. As he watched, Kaapi knelt down at Daanir's head, reaching out to touch his cheek.

"No touch," Navi snapped. Kaapi jerked back, her eyes wide.

"Sorry," Antivar called. "But he's right. Don't touch. You'll interfere with the healing."

Kaapi nodded, clasping her hands in front of her.

"Uncle..."

"Go ahead," Tarjiaan said. "I'll set the brakes."

Naajir disappeared into the crowd, coming out behind Kaapi. He knelt down next to her and put his arm around her shoulder. She leaned into his side, and he kissed the top of her head. Tarjiaan blinked, and heard Antivar chuckle.

"Betrothed?"

"Not that I know of," Tarjiaan admitted. "But clearly, there are things I don't know." He paused, trying to distract himself from the worry, from the painfully slow process. From how naked he felt from being unarmored on his own ship. "Antivar, tell me about Navi." He looked up. "He called you Ivar."

Antivar's face turned red. "I... ah..." He paused and closed his eyes. "He was a ship slave, because of his healing abilities. We... we were close... close friends..."

Chapter Twenty-Five
Pursuit

SOFT...

Warm...

Daanir sighed, half-awake, half-asleep, hearing the distant chime of bells. Three bells. Early. Why was he awake this early? And where was he? A soft, warm bed wasn't someplace he usually woke up, and a warm companion in that bed was something that never happened anymore. He tried to remember how those two things had come about, but everything before he woke up was darkness and fire. Which meant that he if wanted answers, he had to wake up all the way. He opened his eyes, saw dark, curling hair, and stared in shock, his entire body tensing. Nika sighed and moved closer, putting one arm over Daanir's ribs. His brain seized, refusing to restart.

How had he ended up in bed with Tarjiaan's wife?

Another arm slid around him from behind, and he heard a familiar chuckle. "Stop fretting," Tarjiaan murmured as he kissed Daanir's bare shoulder. "I'm very well aware of where you are and who you're with." He chuckled. "We never did this, did we? I can't remember us ever having a third in the bed."

Daanir turned his head to see Tarjiaan leaning over him. His short hair and the empty holes in his ears were startling – they looked *wrong*. But his Jiaan was awake and alive. "I... but... no... we... but...you're all right? I... the last I saw you was when they took you out of the sub. I... I lost the breathers, and you weren't breathing

299

when we pulled you into the sub. We had to breathe for you. You were... it was bad."

Tarjiaan nodded. "I think I'm still a long sail from well. But I'll get there, thanks to you both." He kissed Daanir's shoulder again. "Nika told me some of it. Not all. You can tell me the rest later. And you're in better shape than I am right now, which is impressive. You should be dead, and I owe Wil, Nika and a young Imperial healer a very deep debt of gratitude that you're not."

Daanir frowned. "I..." Then he remembered. "The rail cannon."

Tarjiaan nodded and rested his forehead against Daanir's back. "I don't remember you being suicidal, Daan. Could you not do that again? Please?"

"It was necessary," Daanir said softly. "And... wait... I remember now. The other ship, the Imp ship. If I didn't get that shot off, we were all going to die. Did they get out?"

"They're safe. We took them aboard. Good thing, too. You wouldn't be here without their healer." Tarjiaan paused, then added, "You made me do something I've never done, Daan. Something that's scared the piss out of me for years." Daanir turned toward him, tipping onto his back and waiting for Tarjiaan to continue. "Because I wasn't going to not be there for you. I didn't know if they could save you, and if I wasn't there... I'd never forgive myself. But I could barely get out of bed, let along wear my armor." He raised his head and met Daanir's eyes. "You needed me. So I used my chair."

"You..." Daanir blinked. "I don't follow. What chair?"

Tarjiaan rested his hand on Daanir's chest. "I haven't willingly let anyone outside a very small handful of people see... me. Not for years. Not since I could make that choice. There was always the armor, or the powered chair. There was always something to hide behind. Which meant that no one really saw me as I was. As I am. For... call it twelve years now. The only ones who have seen me like this in that time are you, Nika, Wil and Logiri. And for the longest time, it was just Wil and Logiri. There's been no one in my bed since you. I had no one I was brave enough to be that... vulnerable with. Not until you came back to me. And then Nika came to me." He paused. "The chair I'm talking about is the one that I keep in here for when I'm out of my armor. No one but Logiri has ever seen me use it before last night. I went out on deck where they were working on you. It didn't matter who saw me. I needed to be there. With you." Tarjiaan smiled, and the expression was somehow different, somehow... softer. Before Daanir could understand why, Tarjiaan leaned down and kissed him. "I love you, Mancer mine," he whispered against Daanir's lips. "I've always loved you. And I wasn't going to let you leave without being there. If Nika and Navi hadn't pulled you back, my kiss would have been on your lips when the Mothers came for you." He shifted, wincing slightly as he moved. "And before you protest about being in this bed with both of us, part of it is practical. She needed to monitor both of us—"

"In her sleep?"

"Who says I am asleep?" Nika murmured. She opened her eyes and raised her head slightly, smiling at him before stretching up to kiss him lightly on the lips. She drew back and frowned. "Something is wrong?"

"I... I shouldn't be here," Daanir stammered. "I..."

"Why not?" Tarjiaan asked. "Daan, we both know what we have. And I know how Nika feels about you. She told me. The only thing I don't know is how you feel about her."

Daanir shook his head, feeling a surge of panic. "No, I... I shouldn't be here. I... I don't get to be here. I don't *deserve* to be here. I'm not... let me up." He tried to sit up, but Tarjiaan leaned onto him, pinning him down.

"Daan, stop," Tarjiaan said. "You're not making sense."

"Jiaan, his heart is racing. I think he is panicking," Nika said. "Let him sit up. Daanir, sit up. Breathe. And talk to us." She shifted, and

Tarjiaan moved, letting him sit up. He drew his knees up to his chest and wrapped his arms around them, curling into a ball. He heard Tarjiaan moving next to him, then arms encircled him from both sides, holding him tightly.

"You get to be here because we want you here. You are exactly where you are supposed to be," Tarjiaan said softly. "You've been part of my heart for half our lives, Daan. There is no other place else where you belong."

"What does it mean that you do not deserve to be here?" Nika asked. Her cheek on his shoulder burned like a brand. "I do not understand."

Daanir took a deep breath, and let the poison out. "That I don't deserve this. I don't deserve you. Because I'm a hopped up nobody who fucked his way into a position that never should have been his. That I failed my prince because I never should have been the one at his side. That it was my fault, and my punishment was being buried in the worst station in Meradon so I didn't damage anyone else. That I should be grateful..." He stopped and shook his head.

"I... I never said that. I never said any of that. That's not what happened," Tarjiaan said. "I... who fed you that bilge, Daan? Who told you that fleet of lies?"

"I—"

"Daanir." His voice was quiet. Even. Furious.

Daanir shivered. He heard the anger, like distant thunder. "Commander at the station. Maintenance Station Six. That's where I was sent for training. I was there four years before I was sent to the dockyards."

Tarjiaan hummed softly, his arms falling away. "Station Six... station..." He paused. "And who is the Commander at Station Six, Mancer Royal?"

The tone in Tarjiaan's voice made Daanir raise his head. Tarjiaan was sitting up next to him, frowning slightly. He, like Daanir, was completely naked. But even so, this wasn't Jiaan.

He was in bed with the Sea King, and the Sea King was not pleased.

"I..." Daanir swallowed. "Why do I think you know this already? His name is Ishian."

"I thought so," Tarjiaan said. "I just wasn't sure he was still there. Do you know who he was before he was banished to Station Six?"

"Banished?" Daanir blinked. "I... he... he told me that he was a decorated battle veteran."

Tarjiaan snorted. "The only decorations he ever had was when he shit his breeches. He's a coward who deserted his companion, his post and his position, and he was court-martialed and banished. The only reason that he wasn't executed was that my brother pled for clemency." Tarjiaan glanced toward the portrait, then looked back at Daanir. "He's the reason Ranji didn't have a battle companion. Because he was Ranji's battle companion, and he deserted his post and his place and almost got Ranji killed. There were even rumors that he tried to defect to the Empire, but those were never proved. Everything he told you would have been better directed to his own reflection."

"I... I never knew that," Daanir said softly. "No one ever told me why Ranji never had a battle companion."

"It was before either of us came above. He wouldn't have told me, either, except I was a pest." Tarjiaan grinned, and Jiaan was back. "It was right before you and I swore to each other, and I wanted to know why he didn't have someone at his side if it was such an important ceremony. And I wouldn't let it go, so he finally told me. Told me to keep it to myself, because it wasn't something he was proud of."

"It does not sound as though it was your brother's fault," Nika said.

Tarjiaan nodded. "It wasn't his fault. It was his shame, that he'd chosen so badly, that he hadn't seen the truth behind Ishian's pretty face." He nudged Daanir with one elbow. "He said he'd tell you. He wanted you to understand why he was so hard on you when we were training. Something else he never had the chance to do?"

"No." Daanir rubbed one hand over his face. "He never told me I... Jiaan, I don't know what to do with this. I..." He snorted. "You told us about still hearing Aanaji's voice, about how no one would ever want you. And that part of you still believed it. Remember?"

Tarjiaan's eyes narrowed. "I remember."

"I hear him," Daanir leaned back against the headboard. "Ishian. I hear him telling me how I failed you. How no one was ever going to want me on their ship or at their side with that failure hanging over me. That I was lucky to have him, lucky that he wanted me on his station." He paused. "In his bed. And... and since I was already telling myself I failed you... it wasn't hard to convince myself that everyone else thought so, too. My trainer certainly agreed. And not getting any replies... then being told you'd renounced me... that just hammered it home. I had nothing to prove Ishian wrong until...what, not even a month ago? Riguaarin helped, but... I've been waiting for someone to tell me they've figured out that I'm a fraud and a failure and send me back to him."

"I can prove you didn't fail anyone," Tarjiaan said softly. He put his arm back around Daanir's shoulders. "If you want to hear it?"

"Prove it?" Daanir turned and looked at him. "How?"

Tarjiaan smiled. "You and I are both still here. And Meradon is still here."

"But—"

Tarjiaan shook his head. "I'm not done. That... that construct. That thing destroyed almost half of the Meradon above-ships. You know as well as I do that there was nothing we had that could stop it. Except for you. You saved Meradon, and you saved me. When it hit the *Marauder*, you saw how to beat it, and you gave me the tools to do it. You didn't fail, Mancer mine. You saved the kingdom. You stopped the invasion. You should have been heralded as a hero."

Daanir stared at him for a moment. "You've lost your mind. Jiaan, I almost got you killed."

"I'm still here," Tarjiaan repeated. "If you hadn't given me the tools to stop that construct, we would both be dead, and Meradon would be seafoam and memory."

"Construct?" Nika said. Daanir turned to look at her. "I... was it an Executioner? The Emperor sent an Executioner out here?"

"Is that what they're called?" Tarjiaan asked. "It was... Mothers below, I can still see the thing when I close my eyes. Twice as tall as a man. Heavily armored. Rounded helmet—"

"That is an Executioner," Nika said with a nod. "They are usually saved for land battles. I saw a demonstration of one in the Arena once. They cannot be stopped. Just one can put down an entire rebellion." She squeezed Daanir's arm. "You *stopped* one?"

"We stopped one," Daanir jerked his thumb at Tarjiaan. "I saw the flaw, and I powered up his armor to punch through it. But... we didn't know... and I failed..."

"You didn't fail, because I am still alive and Meradon is still free," Tarjiaan said. "Nika, that is how I lost my legs. Those things... they have something inside, some kind of liquid. I punched through the armor and ripped out the power source, and it fell backwards on top of me. Whatever liquid was inside ate through my armor." He reached up and touched the round scar on his collar. "This was from it dripping on me. The rest..." He took a deep breath, his arm around Daanir tensing. "I don't remember much. Pain. That's all."

"I found you," Daanir said. He closed his eyes, picturing every tiny detail of the destruction on the *Marauder's* decks. "I found the Captain...and Ranji. The only way I knew it was Ranji was that ridiculous red armor. I went looking for you, and I found you underneath that thing. I pulled you out and your legs were..." His voice caught, and he curled up again, pulling his knees in tight. "You were bleeding out and all I could think was that I had to save you. I couldn't save anyone else, but I had to save you," he whispered. "I... the machines answered."

"Your power woke the way mine did," Nika murmured. She leaned in next to him and rested her cheek against his shoulder. "When it was needed. When we had to save the people we love."

"You haven't answered, you know." Tarjiaan leaned into Daanir's other side. He ran one hand up and down Daanir's arm, making him shiver.

"What was the question?" Daanir asked. He tried to remember the entire conversation, but it was a blur. "I... did you ask me a question?"

"Just needing to know something." Tarjiaan took one of Daanir's hands in his. "I know how you feel about me. I've know that for years. I never doubted it, not once in all the years apart. I hope you know how I feel about you?" He waited until Daanir nodded. "And I know how Nika feels about you, because she told me. The only question..."

"Yes," Daanir said softly. "And I was scared to my bones that you were going to use my guts for bait if I ever said a word."

Tarjiaan looked at him in shock, then burst out laughing. Daanir chuckled, then stopped, watching as Tarjiaan kept laughing, as his face turned red. As tears started to leak from his eyes.

"Is this what you were talking about?" Nika asked. "About how he used to laugh?"

Daanir nodded. "Yes. And...more so. Jiaan? Jiaan, you need to breathe!" He grinned, hearing Nika starting to laugh. "Jiaan!"

Tarjiaan waved one hand, still laughing. "Bait?" he wheezed. "Bait? Really?" He blinked and wiped his face. "Oh... oh... and what I just thought of... Daan, you're favored male number two."

"I'm what now?" Daanir asked. He glanced at Nika. "Did that make sense to you?"

"No." Nika reached across Daanir to poke Tarjiaan in the ribs, making him yelp and laugh again. "Explain."

Tarjiaan nodded. "I... Daanir, you didn't remember our lessons about the history on land before the war? About the reign of the Tyracan queens?"

Daanir frowned, trying to remember. "I... don't think I was paying attention," he admitted. "History never interested me. What did I miss?"

Tarjiaan nodded, shifting around so that he was sitting with his back against the headboard, his shoulder pressed against Daanir's. Daanir leaned into him, then put his other arm around Nika. She drew the blanket up over them as Tarjiaan started to talk.

"The histories call us the Four Sisters — Tyraca, Lastalt, Sualiman and Meradon. The Desert Queen, The Lady of Forest and Fields, The Maid of the Mountains, and the Heart of the Sea. Meradon was the odd one out of the sisters, because we've always been ruled by a king. Lastalt was ruled by the oldest child, male or female. But Tyraca and Sualiman have always had queens, and they traced lineage through daughters. And... in Tyraca and Sualiman, the queens keep men the way that the Emperor keeps women. In Sualiman, the men are subservient, but in Tyraca, the Queen's husbands were equal partners who served on her Council. There was a word for them, in old Tyracan. I forget what it was, but it translated to *favored male* and they were numbered in order of... well... acquisition. So... since you have your arm around the last daughter of the Tyracan royal line, it makes sense that we're her favored males."

"And I had you first, so you are favored male number one?" Nika asked. She hummed softly, resting her head on Daanir's shoulder. "This... makes things easier, I think. Since our children will not be in the line of succession for Meradon. It will not matter which of you sires them."

"Ah..." Daanir glanced at Tarjiaan. "It might matter. Remember?"

Tarjiaan frowned, then nodded. "Oh. Yes. Wil suggested... but Naajir...."

"Made a good point on the submersible, after we found out," Daanir interrupted. "His mother admitted to being a traitor to the crown. She was coerced, but... do you think the people of Meradon will accept him as Sea Prince if it gets out what Aanaji did?"

Nika took a deep breath. "We are getting ahead of ourselves. This is something we have time to discuss. We have more pressing matters now. We should get dressed, since we are all awake. Daan, I very much doubt that Kaapi slept last night—"

Daanir sat up, the comfortable languor of being caught between the pair of them gone in an instant. "I... I didn't even think about her!" he stammered. "Where is she?" He tried to scramble out of the bed, but Tarjiaan grabbed his arm.

"Easy. You don't need to go running out naked. Ishantar took charge of her and Naji, and they're bunking in mancer quarters. And Wil is going to want to see you before he lets you do anything." He let Daanir's arm go and sat back. "Nika, should I assume I'm not allowed to get dressed?"

Nika turned to him, giving him a long, appraising look before getting out of the bed and going to the table. She came back around the bed with a medical scanner. "Daanir, would you move, please?" she asked, studying the screen.

Daanir nodded and got up. "Where are my clothes? Since I'm not allowed to go running out naked."

"Your rags, you mean?" Nika asked without looking up. "They were being held together by blood. We will find something for you.

Tarjiaan, you are going to want to meet with your crew today, I assume?"

"You assume correctly, my wife," Tarjiaan answered.

"Then you may dress, but no armor." She frowned at the scanner. "But only if Chel confirms what I think I am reading here. You are far more recovered than I would have expected."

Daanir came around the bed and looked over Nika's shoulder, then triggering the scanner to show the last set of readings. He whistled softly. "What were you saying about Nika monitoring in her sleep?"

Tarjiaan frowned. "I... I think you said it, actually. Why?"

"Because the differences between the first readings on this thing and the second are enough that I'd think they were for two different people," Daanir answered. He held his hand out, and Nika handed him the little machine. He turned it over, examining it, letting it burble and chime in his head. "It's calibrated correctly. Jiaan, you shouldn't be as healthy as you are. And... if Nika keeps on doing whatever she's doing? You'll be back to normal tomorrow. Maybe the next day."

"That is not an excuse to overreach," Nika added, taking the scanner back. "You will listen to Chel and Wilaanger."

"Yes, Ma'am." Tarjiaan drew the blanket up to his waist. "Did either of you hear the bells? What watch is it?"

"Three bells," Daanir answered. "Not sure what watch, though. It's either the middle of the night, or just about dawn." There was something odd about Tarjiaan. Something different...

He wasn't the only one to notice. Nika stopped in the middle of buttoning her shirt. "Tarjiaan, are you feeling well? You seem... different." She looked at Daanir. "Do you see it?"

"I'm fine," Tarjiaan answered. "Better than I expected. Why?"

"There is something—" Nika started. Then Daanir realized what it was.

"You're you," he blurted. Tarjiaan arched a brow.

"Who else would I be?"

"No, I mean... you're the way I remember you. You're laughing. You're teasing us. You're... you're not hiding."

Tarjiaan smiled. "I... I was thinking about this, before I fell asleep. There's no reason for me to hide. Not anymore. Not after I showed my entire truth to my crew last night, and they welcomed me back." He looked down. "I was convinced that she was right. No, that wasn't Aanaji, was it? That was Ilaris, saying that no one would want me. That no one would ever follow me. That the only reason they did was that all the other heirs were dead and I was all they had. But you two... you've fought for me. Came close to dying for me." He gestured toward the door. "My crew were ready to die for me. For us. And when I went out on deck last night and they saw me without armor, when they saw me... they welcomed me home." He took a deep breath. "I may not be... entirely out of hiding. There are still going to be times when I need to hide. Especially once this is over, and I'm not distracted by keeping us all alive. But with you both? I know that I don't have to." He looked down, then back up. "I love you both. And we have work to do. Nika, when you call Wil, see if he can find something for Daanir to wear? As much as I appreciate the view, it's distracting."

Chapter Twenty-Six
Challenge

TARJIAAN WAS PUTTING on his shirt when Wilaanger and Chel arrived.

"Good morning," Wil called as he came into the bedroom. "Things are calm for the moment, and the Imp ships are closer but not in range. We have breakfast for you. Chel is setting the table. And I have something for Daanir to wear. And they somehow had a pair of trousers to fit me. I'm rather surprised. I'd expected to have to wear a sail with a hole cut in it."

Tarjiaan chuckled. "Daanir is in the washroom. I think I've managed to talk him out of shaving, but he's washing up."

Wil nodded and went to the other door, knocking and passing a bundle inside. Then he came back to the bed and looked at Tarjiaan.

"You look better than I'd give you credit for. Where is the scanner? And where is Nika?"

"Also in the washroom, and the scanner is..." Tarjiaan looked around. "There. There's a box in the top drawer there. May I have it?"

Wilaanger stopped moving, turning to look at Tarjiaan. "Nika..." he said in a low voice. He glanced at the washroom. "And Daanir..."

"And me," Tarjiaan added. He wasn't certain what Wilaanger's response would be, and was surprised when he burst out laughing.

"Did... did Daanir tell you?" he demanded. He picked up the scanner, then got the box out of the drawer and handed it to Tarjiaan.

"About what?" Tarjiaan looked at the washroom door. "Right now, he's fretting over Kaapi. Is she out there?"

"Ishantar put her and Naajir to work as soon as they'd eaten something. I'll send for them." Wilaanger glanced at the washroom door again. "On the submersible, I said something to Daanir. Wondering about how things might have changed if your uncle's wife had been anything like your Nika. If Ika had been anything like you. Wondering how the three of you were going to change the world. Daanir told me that it wasn't the three of you — it was you and Nika, and he was on the outside."

Tarjiaan opened the box and started replacing his earrings. "We showed him the way in," he said. "Where he belongs. And convinced him that it was his place. And to answer what you're going to see in the scanner, Daan says that he thinks Nika is healing me in her sleep."

Wilaanger's brows rose, and he turned on the scanner. A moment later, his brows rose higher, and he glanced at Tarjiaan.

"I think you may be correct," he said slowly. "Which... that may be dangerous for her. I'll have to see if Navi can help train her. I don't know enough." He laid the scanner down.

"When you talk to that healer, tell him that she's possibly been healing both of us," Daanir added as he came out of the washroom. "But I don't know how bad I was before." He looked down at himself and the plain trousers and shirt he now wore. "Thank you for this. Where's Kaapi?"

"I'll send for her," Wilaanger said. "And do I get to say I told you so?"

Daanir smiled. "This once, yes. And thank you. Did you say there's food?"

"Food first. Then people who want to see you and the captain," Wilaanger answered. "I'll let you finish." He nodded and left, and Tarjiaan looked over his shoulder.

"I do like the beard, Daan. It suits you. Now, where's Nika?"

Daanir hesitated for a moment before answering, "Feeding the fish."

Tarjiaan sat up, twisting to look at the door. "What? She's sick?" He turned back. "Wil?"

Wilaanger appeared in the doorway. "What is it?"

"Nika's sick."

Wilaanger frowned slightly, then looked back. "Chel, would you...?"

"Of course." Chel came into the room. She took the scanner off the bed, then went to the washroom and tapped gently on the door. "Nika? May I come in?"

The door opened, and Chel went inside. Tarjiaan looked at Daanir. "She was fine. She didn't say anything was wrong."

Daanir nodded. "She was washing up. Then she turned green and... well." He shrugged. "She says it's just being on the ship, but that's not her. She was as steady as if she were born to the sea the entire time we were coming after you. And we had to top the air tanks three times, which meant we were like a cork for hours." He frowned and folded his arms over his chest, then blinked and looked at Wilaanger. "Oh..."

Wilaanger chuckled. "Perhaps. Wait for Chel," he said.

"What?" Tarjiaan asked. "What is it?" He turned to look at the washroom as the door opened, and Nika and Chel came out. Nika looked slightly ill, but she was smiling.

"Jiaan." She came around the bed and into his arms, wrapping her arms around his neck.

"Nika, are you all right?" he asked. "You didn't say you were feeling sick."

She drew back, her smile wider. "I am fine," she said. "Better than fine. I..." Her voice faded, and she hugged him tightly. All at once, Tarjiaan *knew*.

"Great Mothers," he breathed. "You're pregnant?"

She nodded, her hair rubbing against his cheek.

"It's very early," Chel said. "You may have shot her down with your first salvo. And before you ask, it's not unheard of for some women to be taken with a touch of pregnancy malaise this early. Once Nika has something in her stomach, she should be fine. But she's perfectly healthy, and there's no reason to think that she won't stay that way." She smiled broadly. "Congratulations, Jiaan."

Tarjiaan nodded, unable to find his words, unable to believe the news. Unable to isolate a single thing in the hurricane squall of emotions raging through him. He buried his face in Nika's shoulder and tried to make sense of it all. Shock. Awe. Elation. And... complete, overwhelming terror.

"Jiaan?" Nika said softly. "Are... please tell me you are happy?"

Tarjiaan drew back and looked up at her. She was crying, and the look on her face was one he hadn't seen there since their wedding, when she was still so afraid he would reject her. He reached up and wiped her tears away with his thumbs. "Nika, I am... so many things right now. Yes, I am happy. I am... Mothers below, I don't think happy is a big enough word." He started laughing, and wasn't sure why. "I... I never thought... this is something I never thought I'd have." He looked over at Daanir, who was leaning against the wall, smiling. "Daan, I'm going to need help. I don't know how to be a father."

"I'm not going to be any help at first," Daanir answered. "When I became a father, mine was old enough to talk back. Babies... I don't know anything about babies."

Tarjiaan held one hand out, and when Daanir took it, pulled him closer. "We'll learn. We'll all learn." He took a deep breath. "But first... we have to survive. Nika, are you feeling better? You need to eat."

"We all need to eat," Nika replied. "Finish dressing and come to the table." She leaned down and kissed him, then stepped back. "Chel, I have so many questions."

"Good thing that I have answers. We'll talk." Chel held her hand out, and escorted Nika out of the room. Tarjiaan looked up at Daanir and Wilaanger, and burst out laughing.

"I..." he sputtered. "A baby. I..." He stopped, took a deep breath, then looked at the portrait on the wall. His father's image looked back at him, but there was no wisdom there. No advice. There was nothing there but paint and memory.

"Scared?" Daanir asked, sitting down next to him.

"Terrified." Tarjiaan leaned into Daanir's side. "I don't know how to be a father," he said softly. "But I know what I don't want. I don't want my child to have the same upbringing I did. I was ten before I really knew my father. He wasn't there when I was small. He wasn't there when my mother died because he was in battle. I don't want that for my child. I don't want to be the stranger who comes into their life maybe once a year. I'm going to be there for them, and for Nika. And... I have nine months—"

"Ten," Wilaanger corrected. "Minus roughly three weeks."

"Nine months," Tarjiaan repeated. "I have nine months to root a traitorous mage out of the belowships, save my sister, secure my throne, and... possibly end this war." He took a deep breath and blew it out. "First things first."

Daanir nodded, then smiled slightly. "Breakfast?"

"Breakfast. Would you get my chair?"

Wilaanger and Chel left once Tarjiaan, Daanir and Nika were seated, with Wilaanger promising to bring the children back once he'd located them. Tarjiaan sat at the head of the table, with Daanir on his left and Nika on his right. They had both shared a long look before coming to the table, then Daanir held Nika's chair before moving to sit facing her. Tarjiaan looked from Nika to Daanir, wondering if he'd missed something. Then he remembered their first breakfast together and grinned.

"Your place is on my left?" he said, looked at Daanir.

"And hers is on your right," Daanir agreed. He set a large bowl of rice porridge in front of Tarjiaan. "Now eat. You need it. None of your clothes are going to fit right."

Tarjiaan frowned, thinking back over what little he knew and the great deal that he didn't as he mixed smoked fish into his bowl. "I... what happened to Logiri?" he asked. "Do you know?"

Daanir shook his head. "He wasn't in the Heir's suite when I went through the *Chimaera*. That's all I can tell you. You want the pepper sauce?"

"Please. Before I went to see my uncle, I asked Logiri to look in on Lord Rathsafa," Tarjiaan said. He mixed pepper sauce into the bowl, took a bite, then sipped his tea. "He said he knew the prince from before, and could confirm if Rathsafa was telling the truth."

"Do you think Ilaris would hurt them?" Nika asked. "I mean, my... Lord Rathsafa would be a valuable hostage, no?"

Tarjiaan considered the question while he ate, then nodded slowly. "They both would be, to be honest. You said you knew of the Antar family, that they were craftsmen of some renown? The Emperor would want to make an example of someone of rank."

"They are highly skilled craftsmen." Nika bit her lip. "There are also rumors that they are not only craftsmen. But I do not know the truth of them. Eat, Tarjiaan. It will be cold."

"I'm eating, and you should, too." He took another bite. "What rumors?"

She didn't answer immediately, finishing the last of her own breakfast. "They are craftsmen of great renown, and their works command high prices. The piece that I gifted to Aanaji would cost enough to pay the annual taxes of several small villages," she said. "Because they are so renowned, and because their works are so costly, the nobility catered to them, hoping to win the honor of being allowed to purchase even a small piece. Part of that was hosting members of the family at estates and parties. Having even a journeyman Antar metalsmith as a guest was considered something of which to boast." She paused again, then added, "But they may have been more. It is believed by some that the Antar family are the Emperor's spies...and assassins."

Daanir sputtered around a mouthful of food. "Assassins? That... wait..." He turned in his chair to look at Tarjiaan. "He is, isn't he? And you knew! And you were making jokes about it!"

Tarjiaan nodded. "I knew. He told me himself when I asked him to be my aide, and I made certain that my uncle knew. Uncle Ika thought I was insane, but once he'd interviewed Logiri, he approved my choice."

"How did you know he was not going to try to kill you?" Nika asked.

"At first? Because he swore that he wasn't sent for me," Tarjiaan answered. "He was escaping the Empire. He'd been ordered to kill someone, and he wasn't allowed to refuse. So he ran." Tarjiaan paused. "After that? About a year after he became my aide, one of the Imperial refugees came to us sick. They called it Desert Fever, and it went through the ship like a tidal wave. Every Meradon-born sailor caught it, including me. And Logiri took care of me until I was well. He'd had it before, and couldn't catch it again." He smiled slightly. "He could have killed me and no one would have ever been the wiser. He didn't. He's been a good and true friend for a long time. And who better to protect me from an assassin than someone who was an assassin?"

"How many attempts did he stop?" Daanir asked.

"Three." Tarjiaan shook his head. "He's proven himself time and time again to be a good friend."

"And he is a good enough friend that he has heard you play," Nika said. "When do we get to hear you?"

Tarjiaan stared at her for a moment. "I... how did you know about that? Did he tell you?"

"I don't think Logiri would tell us water was wet if you told him to keep it to himself. No, I grabbed all the recordings I could when we were still in the submersible," Daanir answered. "Including your logs. And there was a recording mixed in with them—"

"Which I thought he deleted," Tarjiaan interjected. He leaned one elbow on the table. "That..." He paused, then shook his head, looking down at his calloused fingertips. "It was over a year before I picked up an instrument again. It took that long before my hands stopped shaking from the drugs and the drinking. I didn't think I was ever going to play again. Then Wil brought me a small lute." He smiled slightly. "My mother's small lute. He asked my uncle for it and left it where I could see it. It took... perhaps a month of seeing it before I picked it up and started playing again. All of my callouses were gone by the time I did. I had to start over."

"You told me that you have not sung," Nika said.

"I haven't. And I'm not sure I can." Tarjiaan tapped his throat. "Once I was in Wilaanger's care, he found that there was vocal cord damage in addition to everything else. He wasn't certain if it was from fumes from the construct fluids or from screaming."

"I... I though you grew into that rasp. That I just hadn't been here to hear it change. You can't sing?" Daanir looked stricken. "I... no, that's not fair!"

"I don't know if I can or not," Tarjiaan admitted. "I haven't... I was afraid to try. I can still compose. Other people can sing the words I write." He reached out and rested his hand on Daanir's. "Be patient with me. I...I'll try. Once we're through this."

"There will be time for singing later," Nika said. "Time for many things later. But for now, we have so much to do, do we not?"

Tarjiaan took her hand and kissed her fingers. "Truth. But I'm not entirely certain what I'm able to do. I know what I want to do. I want to get back into my armor and get back out on deck. But am I ready for that?" He let Nika's hand go. "I need a report on the rest of the Imperial fleet, and on the storms. There were going to be more storms. I could taste them. I need to talk to Wil and see where I am."

"Taste storms?" Nika repeated. "You can do that?"

Tarjiaan shrugged. "It's what my father called it. When you live or die by the winds and the waves, you learn to read them. Read the weather, and know how to react to it. I think it was one of the first things he taught me when I came on board the *Marauder*."

"If there are more storms coming, then I should go help with repairs," Daanir said. "Wil said he'd be back with Kaapi. I—" He sat up straighter as the door opened and Wilaanger looked inside.

"Good. You're finished. You have visitors." He came inside, followed by Kaapi.

"Kaap." Daanir stood up and came around the table, and was immediately knocked back by Kaapi, who threw herself at him and started crying. He hugged her tightly, murmuring, "I'm sorry. I'm fine now. I'm not leaving you. I promise."

Tarjiaan turned away to given them a modicum of privacy, and saw Naajir in the doorway. He held his hand out, and Naajir came to the table. He put down a book he was carrying, hesitated, then leaned down and hugged Tarjiaan tightly.

"You look better, Uncle," he said as he straightened. He turned, but his lip, then asked, "Aunt Nika...?"

"Of course!" Nika opened her arms and hugged the boy, then gestured to the seat next to her. "Sit. You have been helping Mancer Ishantar this morning?"

Naajir sat down next to her, and Kaapi took the chair facing him, next to Daanir. "There are a lot of repairs that need to be done," Naajir said as he slid the book across to Kaapi. "And there's another storm on the horizon, and there are more ships following us, and..."

"And let's let Marikaar make his own report, shall we?" Wilaanger said as he sat down next to Naajir. "He's on his way, as is Ishantar. And Antivar asked if you might be available. He didn't say why, though."

Tarjiaan nodded. "Wil, I was hoping to be able to get back into my armor and back out on deck. I want to see how much damage we sustained, and get a sense of what we're facing."

"Marikaar still has the con," Daanir murmured. "Let him command."

Tarjiaan scowled at him, then took a deep breath. "I just want to see!"

Someone knocked at the door, and Marikaar and Ishantar both came inside. Marikaar smiled when he saw Tarjiaan. "Captain! You're looking well!"

"Thank you." Tarjiaan gestured to the open seats. "Sit. I want to know what's happening." He looked at the door. "Where's Chel?"

"Back in the infirmary, seeing to the injured," Wilaanger answered. "Now, first things first. Naajir? Do you have the disk?"

Naajir nodded and went into his pocket. "I... this is the only one left, isn't it? Daanir had his in his coat pocket."

"I took my coat off in the gun house," Daanir said. "It's probably still there. But we should make a copy of this."

"We'll copy it once we play it. I want Marikaar and Ishantar to see what we facing once we're through this."

"Captain, meaning no disrespect, but we need to focus on what's happening now, not next." Marikaar rested his hands on the table. "Whatever is on that disk can wait. What we're facing now? There's another storm bearing down on us, and it looks to be worse than the last. And the Imperial ships that survived the last storm are bearing down on us, too. I can't tell which of them will overtake us first."

"Who is at the helm?" Tarjiaan asked.

"Destirian," Marikaar answered. "She's good, but she's not you." He paused, then sighed. "Captain, are you well enough to take the helm? You're the closest to a Reckoner this fleet has seen since... well, since your father."

"A Reckoner?" Tarjiaan laughed. "Reckoners are a myth, Marikaar."

Marikaar snorted. "There's no such thing as myths. Not for sailors. You know that. And it's not a myth that you took the *Sea Wolf* into a ship-killer and out the other side. Twice. You've got the earrings to prove it."

"The *Sea Wolf*?" Daanir asked. "What's that?"

"My first command," Tarjiaan answered. He pointed to the wall, where a framed drawing of a ship hung. He smiled, remembering those early days. "She was a corvette. Probably about fifty years past her prime, and only eighteen guns on her. She was mine for five years, and I loved that little ship. She retired with honors and went to the Mothers six years ago."

"A corvette?" Daanir turned to look at the picture. "They gave the Sea Prince a *corvette*?"

"I asked for her," Tarjiaan said. "She had just lost her captain, and she had a solid first mate. I sat down with him and he agreed that this was what I needed. I was twenty-two. I was the youngest captain in the fleet, and I was a captain only because the Heir is always a captain. I hadn't earned my stripes, I was shoved into them. So I needed to learn, and learn fast. And I needed to prove to myself that I could. I'd only just learned to use the armor, and I needed to know that I was going to be able to be the Sea Prince." He shook his head. "The *Wolf* was a good ship, and Mentiras was a fantastic first mate. He was just what I needed to get steady and set my course when I was still completely unmoored. He went on to take command of the *Wolf* when I was given the *Wave Runner.*"

"Mentiras?" Daanir said. "Wait... I know him. He commands the floating dockyards now. He's a wonderful commander."

"He is, and it will be good to see him again," Tarjiaan said with a nod. "Once we're through this. Wil, am I healthy enough to take the helm?"

Chapter Twenty-Seven
Reckoning

"WHAT IS A RECKONER?" Nika asked as Daanir and Ishantar carefully examined Tarjiaan's armor.

Tarjiaan nodded, thinking back over his early history lessons. "There's a specific school of magic that each kingdom was known for. The Sualimani healing gift, for example. Lastalti magic was plant-based. In Meradon, it was Reckoning. A Reckoner knows the sea, the currents, the stars, and can read them like print on a page. They know where they are at all times, and they know where anything around them is as well. It was a mostly passive magic, from what I was taught. It was supposed to run especially in the royal line, but if it ever existed, it died out generations ago." He looked over his shoulder. "How is the armor?"

"It doesn't look as if it's been tampered with, but I still want to go over it," Daanir answered without looking up. "There are some refinements I can make in connections. It won't take long. Ishantar, look at this."

"Tarjiaan." Wilaanger drew Tarjiaan's attention back to the table. "I don't think this is wise. You're still not entirely recovered."

"Do we have a choice?" Marikaar asked. "Wilaanger, I wouldn't ask if I didn't think it was necessary. Between the storm and the Imp ships... if we don't use everything in our arsenal, we're not coming through this. We're already down most of our weapons and the solar sails."

"There's no way to get those back before the storm?" Tarjiaan asked.

"No, Captain," Ishantar said from behind him. "We'll need parts that we don't have. I worried that the mage would force me to undo the damage, so I made it so that I couldn't."

Tarjiaan frowned. "Understandable. Inconvenient, but understandable." He met Wilaanger's eyes. "Wil, if we had any other choice, I'd take it. I don't think that we do. I can recover while the ship is in dry dock. We'll be berthed for... how long, Daan?"

"At least a month. Maybe more." Daanir came back to the table. "Assuming we make it through the storm and the Imps." He rested his hands on Tarjiaan's shoulders. "Kaap? What are you working on?"

"Designs," Kaapi answered. "I couldn't sleep." She looked down at the book, then at Tarjiaan. "Designs for you. But they're not really ready yet."

"May I see?" Tarjiaan asked. "Or are they "your eyes only" not ready?"

Kaapi blushed slightly, then pushed the book toward him. He picked it up and started turning pages.

Armor. Pages and pages of armor designs.

"Kaapi, these are extraordinary," he said, tipping the book so Nika could see.

"I really like the sixth page," Kaapi said, sounding more eager. "Yes, that one. It's the most compact, and I think it'll work well in the below-ships, and..." She stopped as Tarjiaan held up one finger.

"It's a beautiful design. Very elegant. I do like it, but there's one thing you didn't take into account." Tarjiaan put the book down and turned it, tapping the design. "Human hips. They don't bend this way."

Daanir leaned over his shoulder. "Yours did," he murmured. Tarjiaan choked, hearing Nika burst into laughter. Tarjiaan looked up at Daanir, who smiled innocently at him.

"Not in front of the children," Tarjiaan muttered. He swallowed and looked around the table. Marikaar looked as if he were fascinated by the grain of the tabletop, while Wilaanger just looked amused. Tarjiaan went through the rest of the designs, stopping at one of the later ones. "Daan, look at this."

Daanir leaned over his shoulder again. "Kaap, this one... number seventeen. That's not your typical work."

"Naji helped on that one."

"You two work very well together," Tarjiaan said, looking up to see that his nephew had turned slightly pink. "I like this one. Think you two can refine it?"

Kaapi squeaked in her excitement. "Really? You really like it? We can really design the new armor? Papa said we might help, but..."

"Kaapi, you and Naji already did design the new armor. Now it needs to be refined," Tarjiaan said. He looked up at Daanir, then smiled as an idea occurred to him. "You're my battle companion again."

Daanir arched a brow. "Yes, we determined that."

"And you stand on my left. You're part of me, as much as Nika is, and I'm not going to hide that. You're part of the royal family. That means that your daughter should be recognized as part of that as well."

Daanir blinked. "I... wait. What... what are you saying?" He straightened and went to stand behind Kaapi. His hands on her shoulders weren't fond, though. They were protective. "You... are you saying you want to adopt my daughter?"

Too late, Tarjiaan realized that he'd rushed in without thinking. He held up both hands. "No! I'm sorry. I went too fast. Daan, I can't adopt her. She's *your* daughter. I'm not stealing her away from you.

But she should be recognized as being part of the royal family, to reflect your rank and your place at my side." He paused. "Unless I missed it? Has Kaapi already been recognized as a royal fosterling?"

"Me?" Kaapi whispered. "But... I'm not anybody. I'm not important."

"Kaapi, you are very important to us," Nika said gently. "Although, Jiaan, I think you could have waited and discussed this with her and Daanir privately, instead of surprising them with it and getting things muddled." She rested her hand on Tarjiaan's arm. "You should take the time to think about this," she added. "And to decide if this is what you want."

Kaapi looked up. "Papa? I... is that... may I?" She frowned. "Will you still be my father? This won't undo that, will it?"

"No, Kaap. It won't." Daanir smoothed Kaapi's hair. "It'll be like you have another father and a mother. Three parents, instead of just me."

Nika nodded. "If you want us?" she added.

Kaapi stared at them, her eyes wide. She bit her lip and looked across at Naajir. "I..."

"Do it, Kaap," Naajir said. "It won't change anything."

"It won't?"

Naajir grinned. "Not a thing. Do it."

Kaapi looked up at Daanir, who had a puzzled expression on his face. "Papa, may I get up?"

He stepped out of the way, and Kaapi got up and came around the table to Tarjiaan. He pushed back from the table, set the brakes, and waited.

"What do I call you?" Kaapi asked. "Because I can't call you Papa. It would be confusing."

"We'll decide that later," Tarjiaan said. "That's a yes?"

She grinned and hugged him, pushing the chair back slightly. "That's a yes," she answered. She let him go, then went and hugged Nika.

"Captain, I'm going to take the children off now, and get back to work," Ishantar said. "So you can get back to your planning." She looked at the design and nodded. "That is a nice design. The armor will be very functional. Kaapi, tell me about it as we go."

Kaapi took the notebook, and she and Naajir followed Ishantar out of the great cabin, all of them talking animatedly. Tarjiaan waited until the door was closed before he turned to Daanir.

"I'm sorry," he said. "I didn't mean to make you think I was stealing your daughter. She should be recognized as a royal fosterling, the same as you were."

"We just can't make it official until we do what we need to do," Daanir said. "Your armor is ready. Are you?"

"Let's find out."

Being back in his armor felt strange. Tarjiaan stood up, then looked down at himself, trying to understand what was different.

"Something wrong?" Daanir asked, walking around him. "Is it uncomfortable? It looks like it's fitting properly. I was worried it wouldn't, with how much weight you've lost, so I adjusted it."

Tarjiaan shook his head. "It's comfortable. It seems to fit fine. Adjusted how? Are you going to have to let the armor out again?"

Daanir chuckled. "No. I adjusted to so that it adjusts itself. It'll change as you do. It's a variation on the padding that cushions your legs, and it'll react in real time as you need it. I'll make sure that the new armor has the same mods."

"That is very clever," Nika said. "Jiaan, do you know what is bothering you?"

"I'm not sure," Tarjiaan answered. He ran his hands over his torso and down onto the waist of the armor, and heard Daanir's breath catch. He arched a brow, and Daanir laughed.

"You need to stop petting yourself," he said. "If you don't, I'll give in to temptation and start petting you myself. Then we'll never get out on deck."

Nika giggled as she came into the bedroom from the day cabin. "I would very much like to see that."

Tarjiaan wondered if the shocked expression on Daanir's face matched his own. "Nika!"

She burst into laughter, which didn't stop when he bent to kiss her. Her giggles made kissing more interesting, and Tarjiaan was smiling when he straightened.

"Do..." Daanir's voice cracked, and he coughed and cleared his throat. "Ah... do you want your coat?" He paused, bit his lip, then added, "And do I get one of those? Two? Two of those?"

"One each?" Nika walked up to him and tipped her head back. Daanir bent to meet her; Tarjiaan leaned against the wall and watched them, watching the heat crawling up Daanir's throat, the way Nika caught the back of his neck with one hand to control the kiss. His hand spread out over the small of her back, pulling her closer. One of them moaned softly — Tarjiaan wasn't certain who. But Nika drew back slightly, running her thumb over Daanir's lips.

"My turn?" Tarjiaan asked softly. They both looked at him, and their matching grins were almost feral.

Daanir let Nika go and approached Tarjiaan. "Your turn," he agreed, but he didn't stop, pushing Tarjiaan back against the wall with his body. Tarjiaan towered over him, until Daanir grinned and the armor moved without a thought from Tarjiaan, spreading his feet and bending his knees until he was nose to nose with Daanir.

"That's better," Daanir murmured. Then he leaned into Tarjiaan and kissed him, his hands wrapping around Tarjiaan's upper arms and pinning him in place. It was far more aggressive than Tarjiaan ever remembered Daanir being before, and this time, he was the one to moan, then whimper as the armor suddenly became far too restrictive.

Daanir drew back, his brows raised. "Oh... I... um... we never thought of that." He looked down, his hands relaxing on Tarjiaan's arm. "Ah... I should... there's a panel, isn't there? I thought there was."

"What is wrong?" Nika came up next to them, frowning slightly. She looked at them, then blinked. "Oh. I... is this something you did not know would happen? Neither of you knew?"

Daanir looked at Tarjiaan, and the both of them started laughing. Daanir let Tarjiaan go, releasing his control over the armor so that Tarjiaan could stand up. Tarjiaan coughed, then stepped away from the wall, moving slowly.

"Excuse me," he said as he headed to the washroom.

"Need help?" Daanir asked. He smiled, sweet and uncomplicated.

"Go and help," Nika urged, gently pushing him after Tarjiaan. "I will go and... distract the others so no one comes looking for you." She smiled at Tarjiaan and left the bedroom, closing the door behind her.

"Do you still want the washroom?" Daanir asked.

"We're alone," Tarjiaan answered. "And I'm not sure I can walk that far."

Nika heard laughter behind her, but didn't turn. She pointed at each spar in turn, reciting the names that Marikaar had taught her.

"I... I think that was all?" she finished. "Have I got them?"

"You're very quick, my lady," Marikaar said. "I could make a sailor out of you in a month."

"I have only just learned to pilot a submersible," Nika said. "I do not think a ship of this size is anything I wish to attempt." She looked up at the big man next to her. "Not yet."

"That's the spirit, my lady," Marikaar said with a laugh. "Wilaanger, the Captain's Lady is a fine one."

"Marikaar, show your queen a little respect," Wilaanger replied with a sigh.

"Ah, she'll have enough people bowing and scraping once they get back to below. Up here? She's my Captain's Lady—" He turned and smiled. "Speaking of... Captain! Good to see you up and about. That issue with your armor is squared away?"

Tarjiaan paused and looked at Nika, who smiled and nodded. He smiled back. "Yes, Marikaar. Thank you. The Mancer Royal put things right. Now, show me what we're looking at."

"Come up to the helm." Marikaar led the way to a set of stairs, and up to the deck atop the great cabin. Marikaar had brought her up here earlier; he'd called it the quarterdeck, showing her the wheel and explaining the way the ship was steered. When the solar sails were in place, he had told her, there were engines deep in the body of the ship that drove them forward. Now, they were dependent on the winds. As were their pursuers. Tarjiaan went to the rail, taking something from Marikaar. Looking past them, Nika could see sails on the horizon, clearly visible against the angry, gray clouds. Lightning flashed, and she heard the deep rumble of thunder as Daanir came up next to her.

"How can you tell how bad the storm will be?" she asked.

Daanir shook his head, resting his hand on her back. "I never got the knack of it," he admitted. "Jiaan can do it. So could Ranji. I... well, it's going to rain. That's the best I've got. The sensors tell me what I need to know."

Nika nodded. "Is he a... a Reckoner?"

"The Mothers might know, but I don't. If he is, he's the first in generations. I think he just had a real good teacher in his father. Captain Taarik could sail a leaky bathtub into a storm and come out in one piece." He nodded toward where Tarjiaan was talking with Marikaar, gesturing out over the water. "From what Marikaar said, Jiaan is that good, too."

Nika nodded, looking out at the other ships. "The ships are very close, are they not?"

"They're smaller and lighter than we are, so they'll run faster before the winds. But they're at a disadvantage with the storm," Tarjiaan called over his shoulder. He looked back and smiled. "Come up here, both of you. I want you to hear this."

Nika and Daanir both joined him at the rail, falling into their places. He looked at Nika, then at Daanir. Then he laughed. "You're serious about this, aren't you?"

"Would you have it any other way?" Nika asked.

"Not for a second." Tarjiaan pointed. "They're closing on us. But the storm is closing faster. I'm thinking of using the storm to our advantage. Sailing into it, and letting the storm work for us."

"That's going to put all of us at risk," Daanir said softly. "Do you think we can make it through?"

"I think we can make it. And it's a better chance than going against... it looks like at least twenty ships out there." Tarjiaan folded his arms over his chest, tapping the spyglass in his hand against his bicep. "If we sail into the storm, and take the attack to them, we have a chance of sailing out the other side with little to no pursuit. Otherwise... we don't stand a chance. We don't have the speed to outrun them, or the guns to outfight them."

"Then we will trust in the Mothers to guard and guide us, as they have done already," Nika said, resting her hand on Tarjiaan's arm. "Where do you want me to be?"

Tarjiaan shifted, covering her hand with his own. "Ah... the infirmary. Wil and Chel will need the help, I think. Daan, I'll want you and the other mancers to get the force cannons working, and monitor the ship to make sure we're sound."

Daanir scoffed. "I promise you that this ship is sound."

"Humor me, Mancer." Tarjiaan softened the words with a warm smile.

"Prince-Captain!"

Nika turned, seeing a pair of men at the top of the stairs, both with blades drawn. On the stairs, one hand raised in a defensive gesture, was Antivar. A step below him, clinging to his other hand, was Navi.

"Stand down," Tarjiaan called. "Let the commander through."

"Yes, sir." The guards stepped back, allowing Antivar and Navi to approach. Antivar stopped a few paces from Tarjiaan and bowed.

"Prince-Captain," he said. "You're looking much better this morning."

"Thank you. I'm told you were looking for me. If you don't mind, can it wait? We've more pressing matters." He gestured to the horizon. "Tell me about those ships. How well would they stand a storm?"

"Like the one coming?" Antivar went to the rail and squinted, then turned his head. "May I borrow a glass?"

Tarjiaan passed him the spyglass he was holding, and the pair of them stood at the rail, talking in low voices. Navi looked around, smiling when he saw Daanir.

"Good man!" he called. "Better?"

"I... what?" Daanir looked at Nika. "I missed something."

"I called you a good man when I asked his help in saving you," Marikaar answered. "The boy is simple."

Navi made a face. "Slow," he corrected. "Not simple."

"Oh!" Marikaar turned red. "I apologize, Healer."

"Navi," Nika said. "I... no one here will hurt you. You know that?"

Navi nodded. "Safe safe here. Ivar tell."

She bit her lip, her stomach churning, wondering if she wanted the answer. Yes. She needed to know if it was true. "Is your name Ysnavin?"

"Once." Navi shuddered. "Took it," he answered. He made a gesture, grabbing and throwing something invisible into the sea. "Told no more. Only Navi." He looked at her, then reached out and tapped her shoulder. "Ysnika, no?"

"You knew?" Nika gasped. "How?"

"Felt it." Navi gestured, waving his hand between them. "Heart calls. Blood calls."

She felt tears welling up. "I don't remember you. At all. I didn't know you."

"Remember... small small. Remember... feel. Sound. Not else." He cocked his head to the side. "Know now."

"Nika?" Tarjiaan came to join them. "What's wrong? You're crying. What is it?" He looked at Navi, then Daanir. "What happened?"

"I'm going to need someone to explain it all to me," Daanir said. "Ysnavin was the name Rathsafa said, wasn't it? Nika's brother, and he never knew what happened to him?"

"Rathsafa?" Antivar put his hand on Navi's shoulder. "Who is that?"

"If he is to be believed, he is Nika's father," Tarjiaan answered. "The tale he told us was that the Emperor imprisoned his wife and daughter, and he never knew what happened to his son." Tarjiaan paused, then shook his head. "There's too much, Antivar. Once we're through this, I'll tell you everything. But to be brief, your Navi appears to be my wife's brother."

"And your wife is... Queen?" Antivar frowned. "Should I be calling you Your Majesty?"

"We'll stay with Prince-Captain for now," Tarjiaan answered. "My throne isn't mine yet, and that battle is still to come. Once we survive this one. Those ships?"

"Those are the ones that survived the last storm," Antivar said. "I can't see damage, but I'm certain it's there. Possibly half of them won't survive the next storm."

"Which leaves us the rest to deal with," Tarjiaan said. "Right. Marikaar, all hands, beat to quarters. Work with Antivar to make sure the refugees are assigned to appropriate stations. Nika, take Navi to the infirmary with you."

"What's the plan, Prince-Captain?" Marikaar asked.

"I'm taking the helm," Tarjiaan answered, taking gloves out of his coat pocket and pulling them on. "Destirian, stand down. I'm taking us into the storm. We're going to come about and sail down their throats, all guns blazing, and may they choke on it."

Chapter Twenty-Eight
Marauder

HOW LONG HAD IT BEEN since he'd last taken the helm during a storm like this? That last time on the *Sea Wolf,* right before he'd been given the *Wave Runner*. He looked up at the dark clouds, then out at the ships. The waves were wild, higher than he could remember seeing in all his time at sea. Each time they crested a wave, it sent spray washing up over the decks and made the wheel under his hands like a wild thing. It was only going to get worse — the storm was going to break at any moment. He could feel the pressure building, like the bubbles behind a cork in a bottle of that fizzy wine his father had liked. It had always exploded all over everything, and it had always made a mess, and Father's aide had always complained about it. Funny how those memories were so close to the surface today. Tarjiaan checked the horizon again, judging their speed and the winds. He could wish for more sail, but it wasn't safe. They'd do the best they could. As the moment, The *Wave Runner* was still out of range of the Imperial guns, but that wouldn't last. If the force cannons were ready....

"Comms on," he intoned, and heard an answering beep in his earpiece. "Marikaar, report!"

"*All hands ready, Captain,*" Marikaar answered. "*The mancers are working on the port side powder cannons now.*"

"And the force cannons?"

"We're down two on either side," Marikaar answered. *"The mancers found replacement power cells, but not enough of them. The rest are charged and ready, and the gunners are waiting for you to give the word."*

"We're almost in range," Tarjiaan said. "And that storm is about to break. I can feel it."

"And you say you're not a Reckoner. Marikaar out."

"Comms off." Tarjiaan chuckled, watching the ships in front of them as the *Wave Runner* closed on them. None of them had lowered sail — were they that frightened of what waited them at home that they were willing to face a horrible death at sea? He could see men running around on deck, see some of the ships on the outer edges coming about to try and intercept. He had no intention of letting them.

"On my mark!" he bellowed, and heard his voice break. He winced; he could feel the strain in his throat already. *Use the comms, Tarjiaan. That's what they're for*, he chided himself. *You promised to sing for your wife.*

A sudden realization made him laugh — he had nine months to get his voice back in shape if he was going to sing the Welcome to the baby.

Grinning, he shook his head. "First things first," he muttered. "Comms on. Gunners. Fire at will!"

The roar of the guns was almost as loud as the thunder that boomed overhead, and the rain came down in sheets a heartbeat later. The guns fell silent as their targets vanished into the wall of water. Tarjiaan was soaked to the skin in a moment. He couldn't even see the main mast, let alone the ships he was sailing toward, but he knew there were there. He could *feel* them — each ship like an individual pin in his mental map of the sea.

Maybe there was something to this whole Reckoner thing after all?

He scoffed. Then his ears popped, and he felt a... tingle spiraling all the way up his left arm. He glanced to port, but could see nothing but rain.

"Marikaar, what's on the sensors to port?"

"Hold a moment, Captain... waterspout! A waterspout just spun up. Heading away from us... toward the Imp ships!" A long pause. *"Captain, I can't see my hand at the end of my arm. I definitely can't see the spout. You can see that?"*

Tarjiaan laughed. "Let's just say that we're going to have to talk more about Reckoners. Keep me apprised."

"You'll probably tell me before the sensors do. Out."

Tarjiaan fought the wheel, turning it to guide the ship away from the waterspout, three points to starboard. The heavy rain would keep the Imps from being able to target while he showed them the Wave Runner's broadside, thank the Mothers. Then he felt movement on his mental map, and two of the Imp ships vanished as if they'd never been there. He straightened, staring out into the rain. Something was out there. Something moving faster than it should...

"Marikaar! Something coming in fast, two points aft of the port beam! I... I think it's taken out two of the Imp ships!"

For a moment, the comms crackled as lightning danced overhead. Tarjiaan almost lost Marikaar's response in the answering thunder. *"Captain, there's nothing on the sensors. Confirmed that two of the Imp ships are gone, but I don't see what... I... what... Captain, three more Imp ships just... just vanished. Four. What the fuck is out there?"*

Tarjiaan turned his head, peering into the rain and darkness. A shadow in the rain... a familiar shape that came close, then swept past the *Wave Runner* at an impossible speed.

"There's a ship out there! A Meradonese hull," he called into the comms.

"But... but there is nothing *on the sensors! Nothing!"*

Another crackle, and Daanir's voice broke through. "*I'm coming up,*" he said. "*Sensors are showing fully operational, so I want to see what it is the sensors aren't seeing.*"

The rains were starting to ease as Daanir came running up the stairs, and Tarjiaan could see the carnage out on the water — sinking, weirdly burning husks, and the surviving Imperial ships, which all seemed to have forgotten about the *Wave Runner* entirely as they fired at point blank range on a ship that moved with impossible speed, all of her sails full. She seemed to be unstoppable.

"Who is that?" Daanir breathed. "I... I can't see enough of her to tell who she is. And what in the Mother's everlasting songs is that weapon? The flames are green. Why are they green?"

"And what's she doing out here?" Tarjiaan added. "She's a long way from home." He shook his head, studying the remaining ships, and the wide gap between them. "She's cleared a path for us. I'm taking it."

"She's coming about," Daanir called. "I... Jiaan! That...."

"I see it!" The mystery ship passed them again, close enough that they could see the decks were empty... except for a figure in brilliant red armor who waved one arm as the ship sailed past. Tarjiaan held tight to the wheel as he got a good look at a figurehead he never thought he'd see again — a carved image of a woman carrying a harp. He *knew* that sculpture — it was a piece commissioned by his father to celebrate his marriage, carved in the image of his bride. It was the first thing his father had shown him when he'd come onboard the *Marauder*.

"*I know you miss her, son. I do, too. But she's the heart of this ship. She'll always be with us.*"

"Jiaan, how..."

"I..." Tarjiaan remembered Nika's story from their wedding day — *There are stories that say the Imperial waters are haunted by a ghost ship called the* Marauder. *That the ship appears in the dusk, and vanishes in the dawn. And that it is crewed by two men only, by the Demon Captain and his First Mate. That they destroy any Imperial ship that they can.*

"Comms off," he snapped. Then he repeated Nika's story to Daanir, who paled.

"It's them? It's... it's really them?"

"I don't know," Tarjiaan whispered. "I... yes. And we've got one chance to get out of here. Coming about broad on the starboard bow. Go back below."

"You think I'm leaving?" Daanir demanded. He looked back out at the fighting ships. "I just... I don't understand. How?"

Tarjiaan shook his head, pulling his attention back to the helm. To the ships that were turning toward the *Wave Runner.* He could see the flash from their guns as they fired, even though the *Wave Runner* was still well out of range. "I don't know. If you're going to stay, go down with the gunners. Looks like some of them are going to try to intercept."

"I'm staying with you." Daanir insisted. He moved to stand behind Tarjiaan. "Think they have mages?"

"I'm not going to let them last long enough to find out." Tarjiaan cleared his throat, looking down at the deck. His crew were pointing, shouting, and the guns were silent. "Comms on! All gunners, back to your stations!" he shouted into the comms. "Fire at will! Whoever that is, she's on our side! Don't waste it!"

Sailors ran, and the guns roared to life. So did the comms, and he heard Wilaanger's voice in his ear, *"What's happening up there? I've got people saying that the* Marauder *is out there, and they don't look like they're raving mad."*

"Ask Nika to tell you the story she told me."

"She just did," Wilaanger answered. *"Tarjiaan, that's impossible!"*

"And I am looking at the *Marauder* right now," Tarjiaan answered. "And I just saw Aaranji. He waved at us. He was wearing his red armor. Wil, my father and my brother..." His voice cracked, and he swallowed, feeling Daanir's hand on his back. "They are out there right now, and I don't know how. But they're cutting a path through the Imps for us, so I'm not complaining." He glanced to the side and saw another ship burst into brilliant green flames. "I'm not comfortable with it," he added. "But I'm not complaining."

"Not comfortable?" Daanir repeated. "What does that mean?"

Tarjiaan shook his head. "Comms off." He waited for the beep, then glanced at Daanir. "It means that I'm not saying I'm piss-my-breeches terrified on an open channel," he answered. "Find a place to hold on, or tether in. We're going to get rough. Comms on... brace for rough waters!"

"*Rougher than this?*"

The voice was young, female, and sounded very distressed. Tarjiaan blinked. "Kaapi? Is that Kaapi?"

"Sounds like it," Daanir answered. "I didn't know she had an earpiece. And... well, she's never been topside before. This is her first storm."

Tarjiaan grimaced. "Yes, Kaapi. Rougher than this. I'm sorry. Go to the infirmary. Let Nika take care of you." The wheel bucked under his hands, and he wrestled them back on course, trying to think of something that would make the girl feel better. "Once we're through this, you get an earring, you know."

"*I do?*"

"You and Naji both get silver, for being crew on a ship sailing through a ship-killer...." His voice died as he saw the wave building ahead of them, twice the height of the main mast. "Brace! Brace yourselves!" He felt Daanir's hand at his waist, clipping a tether to him. A quick look showed that the mancer had already clipped a similar tether to his own belt. "All hands brace!"

Then they were in the wave, climbing toward the slanted sky. Tarjiaan fought the urge to look down, focusing on the wheel, on the crest of the wave, on the angle of their ascent. Were they going fast enough to make it over? If they weren't, they were dead. He could hear Daanir's voice behind him, but it took him a moment to realize that the mancer wasn't talking to him.

He was praying.

Then they crested the wave. For one, sickening, heart-stalling moment, they were airborne. Then the nose of the *Wave Runner* crashed down into the surface, sending a wave of water to flood the deck. Tarjiaan could hear screaming. The water receded, and he saw people picking themselves up.

"Report!" he called into the comms. "All hands, report!"

The litany started, and as always, he held his breath. This was the worst part — how many of his people had gone to the Mothers because their tethers failed, or because they were in the wrong place? He listened, looking back over his shoulder.

The sea behind them was empty.

The storm raged on for hours, finally easing as the sun went down and the clouds parted, showing the slender crescent moon and the brilliant stars above. Tarjiaan blinked twice, trying to push back his fatigue. The seas were calmer now, and he could tell that they were going to stay that way. Just as he could tell that there was no pursuit. Tarjiaan firmly believed there were no ships left to pursue. That the entire Imperial fleet was gone. They were alone, except for a pod of Mothers keeping pace far below them.

They'd escaped. They'd won. But that was cold comfort when faced with the list of the injured, the missing, and the dead among his own people. Checking on the infirmary had only gotten Tarjiaan a firm response from Wilaanger — "you'll know when we have time to tell you." Daanir left him to go join the other mancers assessing the damage to the ship, promising to come back with a report once he knew the full extent, and also promising to check on Nika as he went past the infirmary.

He blinked again, then smiled as someone came up the stairs to the quarterdeck.

"Antivar," he called. "What are you doing up here?"

Antivar came over to join him, his hands clasped behind his back. "I find myself at loose ends," he said. "Navi is busy. My men are all accounted for, thank Sun and Sand. The injured are being seen to—"

"Which is why Navi is busy," Tarjiaan interjected. Antivar laughed.

"Yes. I have no duties, and Marikaar ordered me to get some rest, but I've seen things today that I... cannot explain. And I don't want to be alone at the moment. May I stay?"

Tarjiaan nodded. "Please. You can help me stay awake. You wanted to ask me something earlier. Now seems to be a good time, if you like."

Antivar coughed slightly. "I... yes. I thought I would have Navi with me to do this, but..." He coughed again, then cleared his throat. "Captain... I... Your Majesty—"

"Out with it, Antivar."

Antivar hesitated, then blurted, "May I marry your brother?"

Tarjiaan stared at him. "My... my brother? Antivar, my brother died fifteen years ago. How... wait..." He stopped. "Start over. I'm tired, and we're sailing two different currents right now."

Antivar nodded. "I... men can marry in Meradon. Correct?"

"That's right. I... wait. You're talking about Navi, aren't you?" Tarjiaan laughed. "I'm sorry. He is technically my brother now, isn't he? I hadn't made the connection. Antivar, is he... how do I ask this? Does he understand what you're asking? Can he agree to it?"

"He's competent to answer," Antivar said. "And to be honest, he's the one who asked me. He'd be asking you to grant permission, but I told him that I would do it. He understands, but it takes him time to find the words." He shifted nervously from foot to foot. "It's something I never thought I'd be able to have. Not openly. I..." He stopped and looked out over the water. "That was the *Marauder*, wasn't it? I've heard the stories."

"That was an abrupt change of course," Tarjiaan commented, making Antivar snort. "Yes, that was the *Marauder*. And... did you see the man in red armor? That was my brother. So you see why I was confused."

"I... I saw him," Antivar stammered. "And... I saw the Demon Captain. If the First Mate was your brother, who—"

"My father," Tarjiaan answered. "I told Nika that he'd have laughed his head off to be called the Demon Captain. I didn't believe the story. Then...." He looked back over his shoulder, at the water that was as calm as glass. "I wish they'd followed us. I'd have liked to see him again. To say goodbye. I never had the chance to say goodbye to either of them." He looked back at Antivar, and was surprised to see the other man nodding. Then he remembered. "You understand."

"I'd have liked to say goodbye to her," Antivar said, sounding distant and sad. "I... she knew about Navi. I told her, when I was last home. I told her that I wanted to buy him, once I had the rank and the money. I told her that I loved him." He chuckled. "She just told me that if I was going to bring a pretty boy into the house, I needed to bring a pretty girl in, too. She wanted grandchildren." He shook his head. "I miss her. What did you say? About the Mothers?"

"That the Mothers will sing her name forever." Tarjiaan gestured at the water. "There's a pod below us right now. To sing the lost ones home, I imagine."

"That's right. I remember now. She... she'd like that. She loved to sing." Antivar looked down, shaking his arms free at his side. "I... you haven't answered."

"Because I'm still working on thinking of Navi as my brother," Tarjiaan admitted. "Once he's done in the infirmary and has had a chance to rest, we'll sit down and talk. I want to be sure that he understands the choice that he's making, and I want you both to understand what marriage in Meradon means. You both should have all the information before you make your final decisions. Is that acceptable?"

Antivar smiled. "Yes. Thank you, Captain. I..." His eyes widened, and he pointed. "Captain!"

Tarjiaan turned and saw the ship on the horizon, moving toward them at unnatural speed. "Well... perhaps I should have said something about the Emperor abdicating," he said weakly.

"Say it now, say it now," Antivar blurted. Tarjiaan looked at him, and they both started laughing.

"Well, it appears we have an escort," Tarjiaan said once he'd recovered. "We'll see how long they stay with us."

"And maybe you'll get your chance?" Antivar suggested. "Captain, may I get something for you? Something to eat, or to drink?"

"You don't have to do that, Antivar," Tarjiaan said. Antivar just smiled.

"I want to. I haven't seen your aide since I came on board, so I'm assuming he's not here. And your... your friend and your wife are both busy. Let me help." He smiled. "Brother to brother."

Tarjiaan met his eyes and smiled. "Thank you. Some tea would be very welcome."

Chapter Twenty-Nine
Farewell

THE SEAS SEEMED TO be apologizing for their previous tantrum, and the ship was so steady that it would be easy to believe that they weren't moving at all. That the wind billowing the sheets above was an illusion. Antivar kept Tarjiaan's teacup filled, and they talked about what life would be like for Antivar in Meradon. How long he'd have to live in the below-ships before he could finally come back above the waves.

"Although..." Tarjiaan said as he sipped his tea. "Given how you've proven yourself already, I'm more than willing to make an exception—"

"No," Antivar interrupted, his mouth full. He swallowed and wiped crumbs from his mouth before added, "I don't want to start my new life with any sort of... preferential treatment. We'll earn our way back, the same as the rest of my men."

Tarjiaan grinned. "I want you on my ship, Antivar. I want to see the officer you become."

"And I don't want anyone thinking I'm there because I'm marrying your wife's brother," Antivar insisted. "I'll earn my way, under my own merits. When I get back above the waves — and I will — I want it to be clear I did it under my own terms." He paused. "Favors and bribes, and leaning on familial relations for advancement... that's the Imperial way. I don't want that."

"That's everywhere, to be honest," Tarjiaan said. "The girls who used to follow me around when I was below showed me that. And I was the sixth in line then!"

"Sixth?" Antivar whistled. "And now you're... well, not king yet, but soon. The war?"

"Nika said that what took the *Marauder* and my cousins was an... an Executioner?"

"Sun and Sand!" Antivar dropped the last piece of the piece of bread he was eating. "I... how did you survive?"

"Daanir saw the flaw in the design—"

"The weak plating in the back?"

Tarjiaan blinked. "I... yes. How did you know?"

"That's the reason they don't use Executioners any more. And you may be the reason why it's known. From what I remember hearing, they were put aside when someone destroyed one by punching a hole in the back plating. Word got out, and a village near the Sualimani border destroyed one with a heavy projectile. I don't think they were ever used in battle again after that."

Tarjiaan nodded, hearing the bells marking the time starting to sound. As the eighth bell chimed, he yawned. "I had no idea," he said. "It... some good came out of it, I suppose."

"Is that how...?" Antivar coughed. "I shouldn't ask this. It's rude."

"It's how I lost my legs, yes." Tarjiaan finished his tea and let Antivar take the cup. He rested his hands on the wheel and looked back to see that the dark silhouette of the *Marauder* was still following them. "On that ship."

"You served on the *Marauder*," Antivar murmured. "I... of course you did. That makes sense."

"Does it?" Tarjiaan sighed. "Sometimes it feels as if nothing makes sense. And sometimes... it's all just as it should be." He adjusted their course and closed his eyes, letting the sense of the sea wash over him.

"What is it now?"

"Tired." Tarjiaan opened his eyes. "Right now? It's tired. Go get some sleep, Antivar."

Antivar chuckled. "I think your first mate is about to tell you the same thing, Captain." He nodded toward the steps, where Marikaar and Destirian had appeared.

"Captain, it's time for you to stand down," Marikaar said. "Go get some rest. I..." His voice trailed off as he saw the ghost ship following them. "Mothers below," he breathed. "I am seeing that."

"They're escorting us home," Tarjiaan said. "And... I'm worried they might not be there when I wake up. So I'm staying."

"Captain, I have my orders." Marikaar drew himself up. "You're to go to bed."

"Orders from who?" Tarjiaan laughed. "Nika or Daanir?"

"The Captain's Lady says that if she doesn't find the Captain in bed when she gets there, she will be quite vexed." Marikaar grinned. "Go to bed."

"She did not say that!" Tarjiaan laughed. "Fine. Destirian, do you relieve me?"

"I relieve you, Captain." The young woman bowed slightly and stepped up to take his place at the helm. Tarjiaan looked up at the sky and closed his eyes again.

"Captain?" Marikaar asked.

"Tomorrow, I want to know everything you can tell me about Reckoning," Tarjiaan said softly.

"We'll talk," Marikaar agreed. "I'll tell you everything I know. Now go sleep. Antivar, I think your Navi will be heading to your bunk any minute now."

"Thank you, Marikaar."

Tarjiaan went first down the stairs to the main deck, and the sailors on watch bowed or nodded. Some on the far end of the deck waved before going back to their duties. Tarjiaan acknowledged all of them, then turned toward the door to the great cabin.

"Marikaar?" he asked. "How many did we lose?"

"Twenty-seven hurt, although none serious. A few broken bones. Twelve dead," Marikaar answered. "Ten of those were swept away in that rogue wave. Tethers snapped."

"And the other two?"

"A port side powder cannon overheated. The gunner in charge got the rest of the crew out before it exploded."

Tarjiaan winced. "How badly are we damaged?"

Marikaar just shook his head. "The Mancers are still working. Go to bed, Tarjiaan."

Tarjiaan laughed and walked into the quiet cabin. He didn't bother with a light, finding his way to the bedroom by memory. The bed was tempting, but he was too tired to think about getting out of his armor, so he sat down in his heavy chair and tipped his head back, letting the calm presence of the sea wash over him and lull him to sleep.

Warm lips on his pulled him from sleep, and he opened his eyes to see Nika standing next to his chair. He smiled and tugged her into his lap.

"That was lovely to wake up to," he murmured. His voice sounded rougher than usual, and he coughed, trying to clear his throat. "What time is it? And have you slept?"

"I slept in the infirmary," she answered. "It is almost dawn. Are you awake? There is something you need to see. Someone."

Tarjiaan blinked. "What?" He sat up, his arms around Nika growing tighter as he heard Daanir calling his name. "What is it?"

"Jiaan? Nika?" Daanir appeared in the doorway. "Good. You're awake. You need to come, right now."

"What is it?" Tarjiaan repeated, letting Nika go. She stood up, and he followed suit, groaning slightly.

"Are you hurt?" Nika asked.

"Just stiff." Tarjiaan scrubbed one hand over his face. "Daan, what is it?"

Daanir looked blank for a moment, then slowly said, "We have visitors." He looked over his shoulder. "They... Jiaan, you need to come out and see. I saw it, and I'm still not sure I believe it."

Tarjiaan blinked. "Is this about the *Marauder*? They were following us last night."

"They're alongside right now." Daanir gestured weakly. "We're not moving, and they're alongside..." Daanir shook his head, and his voice cracked as he said, "Jiaan... it's not just them."

Tarjiaan swallowed hard. "I... come with me," he said. "Both of you." He held his hands out. Nika took his right hand, and as they started toward the door, Daanir took his left. Tarjiaan couldn't tell whose hand was shaking worse — his or Daanir's.

Outside on the main deck, it seemed as if the entire crew were gathered along the port side rail. Beyond them, Tarjiaan could see tattered sails but even as tall as he was, he could see little else. Marikaar stood near the rear of the crowd, and he nodded to Tarjiaan as they approached, then raised his voice, "Make way for the Captain!"

The crowd parted, and Tarjiaan could see the rail. The ship beyond the rail. The men standing there.

The *three* men standing there.

"That's why you needed to come," Daanir murmured. "Because it's not just them."

Tarjiaan nodded, leading them toward the rail. Once he was there, he let go of their hands and rested his hand on the railing. "Father," he called. "I... thank you."

Taarik smiled. "You did well, boy. You did very well. I couldn't have taken that wave better."

"You'd have done it twice," Tarjiaan blurted, just so that he could hear his father laugh. He'd forgotten what it sounded like.

"Perhaps," Taarik called. "Perhaps. I'm proud of you, boy." He looked over his shoulder at the older man standing behind him. "We're all proud of you."

"And I am sorry, Tarjiaan," Ikaanaji added.

"Uncle, you have nothing to apologize for." He looked at Nika. "I'm sorry you didn't get to see Meradon again before you died." He looked around. "Where's Wil? Someone get Wilaanger! And Naajir!"

He heard commotion behind him, and a moment later, Marikaar came up with Naajir. "Physician Royal is on his way," he said.

Tarjiaan nodded. He put his arm around Naajir's shoulders and pointed. "Naji, that is your grandfather. And that is..."

"Uncle Ranji," Naajir finished. "I... Mother has a picture of him. It goes everywhere with us."

"Tell your mother that it's not her fault," Aaranji said. "And that I have never blamed her. And that I'm sorry I wasn't there to protect her."

"She's not going to believe me. I'll tell her, but... you know her." Naajir bit his lip and looked up at Tarjiaan. "I... I'm not sure what else to say."

"It's good to meet you," Taarik said. "A little mancer. Daan, you take care of him. And you stop blaming yourself. That's an order."

"Yes, sir," Daanir croaked. He moved behind Tarjiaan and rested his hands on Tarjiaan's waist. "I'll work on it."

"Mind that you do." He looked at Nika, and his smile warmed. "You have Nisi's compass rose."

Nika blushed and touched the pendant that she still wore. "I... the King gave it to me. He said that he saved it for Jiaan's bride."

Taarik nodded. "Nisi asked him to, with my blessing. I gave her that because she was my true north. And you're my boy's. Wear it well, daughter." He looked up at the sky. "The sun is coming up." He smiled. "Our duty is done. It's time for us to rest."

More commotion, and Tarjiaan heard Wilaanger's voice. "What is going on? What do you mean there's a ghost ship? Have you all gone...." His voice trailed off as he reached the rail, and he grabbed onto it for support. "Ika? Mothers below!"

Ikaanaji moved to the *Marauder's* rail. "Wil. I'm sorry. I'm sorry I left you. And I'm sorry I could never be what you needed. You were the one person who loved me best in the world, and I denied it. Denied you. I'm sorry." He held his hand out. "Come aboard."

Tarjiaan went cold. "What?"

"Ika?" Wilaanger looked over his shoulder at Tarjiaan. "You want me..."

"Stand at my side. Be mine again." Ikaanaji reached a little further. "Please."

Wilaanger looked down at his hands, then across the expanse of water and time. "I can't," he answered softly. "I'm needed here. My time isn't done. Not yet." He looked at Tarjiaan, then shook his head. "Someone has to take care of the children," he added, and laughed when Daanir snorted. He looked back across. "Come for me when my duty is done, Ika."

Ikaanaji nodded. "I promise."

"It's time," Taarik said. "You won't see us again."

"Father! I...." Tarjiaan felt his voice catch in his throat. Felt the tears burning. "I miss you."

Taarik smiled. "I love you, too, boy. So much. And I'm so proud of you." He glanced at Aaranji. "Sing us away?"

Tarjiaan nodded. He took a deep breath, and started singing the *Farewell*:

> *"Oh, the sun it now is setting,*

And the Mothers' sweetly singing,
And the tides are calling softly
To go and sail into the darkness..."

His voice was rough, off key at first. Then Daanir joined him, finding the harmony, supporting him as he continued. Other voices joined in, and Nika put her arm around Tarjiaan's waist, holding him as he sang. Through tears, he could see the *Marauder* fading from view, see his father raise his hand in farewell. See the three men bowing to him, their rights arms crossing their chests in the royal salute.

Then they were gone, leaving behind only the sparkle of the sunrise on the waves.

Tarjiaan didn't move. He put his arm around Nika and kissed the top of her head, then covered Daanir's hand with his own as his mancer kissed his cheek.

"Let's go home," he said softly. "Marikaar! Set course for home." He gestured. "That way."

The Farewell

(TTTO: *Wild Mountain Thyme*)
Oh, the sun it now is setting,
And the Mothers' sweetly singing,
And the tides are calling softly
To go and sail into the darkness
Will you go, my darling, go.
And we'll cast off one last voyage
For to sail for the horizon,
To join the Mother's chorus
Will you go, my darling, go.

Pronunciation Guide

IMPERIAL NAMES ARE Family name Given name. So in our world, Girantivar would be Antivar Gir.

Meranas (Mer-ah-nas) is the surname used by the Meradonese royal family and their fosterlings.

Nessunre (Ness-oon-ray) is the surname used for an unclaimed orphan.

Characters, in order of appearance/mention

Tarjiaan: Tar-zhahn (pronounced like the French name Jean. Think Jean-Luc Picard. Tar-Jean)

Ishantar: Ih-shan-tar

Meradon: Mer-ah-don

Girantivar/Antivar: Gear-ant-e-var/Ant-e-var

Marikaar: Marry-car

Logiri/Antarlogirish: Low-gear-e/Ant-ar-low-gear-ish

Ikaanaji: Ick-ah-na-zhee

Ilaris: Ill-ar-es

Daanir: Dah-near

Kaapi: Cap-ee

Riguaarin: Rig-guar-in

Quentas: Quen-tas (Quen as in quench)

Aaranji/Ranji: Ah-rhan-zhee/Rhan-zhee

Aanaji: Ah-na-zhee
Naajir/Naji: Nah-jeer/Nah-gee
Taarik: Ta-rick
Sualimani/Sualiman: Sway-lee-mon-e/Sway-lee-mon
Wilaanger: Will-anger
Rathsafa: Wrath-sa-fa
Gondarishan: Gone-dah-ri-shon
Gondanikaranthia/Nikaranthia/Nika: Gone-da-knee-kah-ran-thee-ah/Knee-kah-ran-thee-ah/Knee-kah
Lastalti/Lastalt: La-stall-tee/La-stalt
Masthaka: Mass-thack-ah
Listel: List-el
Adalia: Ah-dahlia
Falian: Fah-lee-ann
Aajinisa: Ah-jin-ee-sah
Cheladra/Chel: Chell-ad-rah/Chell
Lysson: Lyss-on
Gondanadarish/Nadarish: Gone-dah-nah-dar-ish/Nah-dar-ish
Tishaya: Ti-shy-ah
Ysnavin: Es-na-vin
Ysnika: Es-knee-kah
Ysnia: Es-knee-ah
Ilijiaan: Ill-e-zhahn
Alyaan: Ally-ann
Taliki: Tah-lee-kee
Larina: Lar-eena
Thistintal/Istin: This-in-tal/Is-tin
Ishian: Ish-ee-an
Destirian: Des-tea-rhi-an
Mentiras: Men-tir-as

The Sea Prince Soundtrack

IF YOU WANT TO LISTEN to all the music I listened to while writing this book, check out my Spotify playlist: https://open.spotify.com/playlist/ 7IpAkfv1UCtBu23PW7dDo7?si=aeef999a07284b1d

Don't miss out!

Visit the website below and you can sign up to receive emails whenever Elizabeth Schechter publishes a new book. There's no charge and no obligation.

https://books2read.com/r/B-A-KGBH-LKPFG

BOOKS 2 READ

Connecting independent readers to independent writers.

Also by Elizabeth Schechter

Heir to the Firstborn
Worlds Begin
Written in Water
Forged in Fire
Bones of Earth
Wings of Air
Visions in Smoke
Children of Dreams
Valley of Shadows

The Coral Throne
The Sea Prince

Standalone
The Rape of Persephone
Fools Rush In
Her Captive
To Market
Infernal Machine
Chains of Light

The Chronicles of John Zebedee
Snowbound

Watch for more at elizabethschechterwrites.com.

About the Author

Elizabeth Schechter has been writing award-winning Romantasy since before the word was coined. Her writing credits include the award-winning steampunk romance *House of Sable Locks*, the Celtic fantasy *Princes of Air*, and 2021 VIVIAN finalist *Written in Water*.

She was born in New York at some point in the past. She is officially old enough to know better, but refuses to grow up. She lives in Central Florida with her husband and son.

Elizabeth can be found online at http://elizabethschechterwrites.com, or on Facebook at https://www.facebook.com/Elizabeth.A.Schechter.

Subscribe to Elizabeth's newsletter at https://www.subscribepage.com/k4u7k2

Read more at elizabethschechterwrites.com.

www.ingramcontent.com/pod-product-compliance
Lightning Source LLC
Chambersburg PA
CBHW020838020726
47497CB00005B/1150